I0772384

ASKALON'S RECKONING

THE SILESIA CHRONICLES
BOOK 2

SHANNON BLAKE

For my SisterMuse, Jennifer

And for my parents

You gave me wings and let me fly.

ONE

THE SHIP SHOOK like a living thing. Sahara closed her eyes and tried to keep calm, but her breathing was ragged and her pulse galloped.

Not again. Please...not again.

The ship shuddered again, and then there was a horrible noise of rending metal. Rafe's face was creased with intense focus as he struggled to keep the ship from ripping itself apart.

"What the hell was that?" Kirin called from his seat next to Emma.

"We're coming in too steep!" Jared shouted back.

Sahara clutched her seat until her knuckles were white. The ship bounced and corrected, bounced again and corrected.

"I'm losing control," Rafe said to Jared. His voice was icy calm, but Sahara knew what he couldn't say.

He's losing control...and we're all going to die.

Jared turned around and looked straight at Sahara. "Nobody dies today."

"Easy for you to say," Kirin fired back.

Outside the window, the haze of fire licked around the glass. The ship shook like she would shatter herself.

Emma wept softly, clutching Kirin's arm as if somehow he could hold her steady in this inferno. Sahara started counting the seconds. How long would it take them to break through into K'ilenfir's atmosphere?

Ten. Eleven. Twelve.

Just a bit longer. Just a bit longer.

Thirteen. Fourteen. Fifteen.

The ship shuddered again and every alarm on the bridge went off. Rafe and Jared sang them out as they tried to clear them.

And then, almost as soon as it had begun, they were through re-entry and skimming through K'ilenfir's upper atmosphere.

But before Sahara could breathe in relief, the ship suddenly listed heavily to starboard. The alarms blared again, and then an explosion slammed them back in their seats.

"The trees!" Jared shouted. "Watch out for the—"

The ship mowed through the treetops. The glass shattered. And then, suddenly, they skidded to a stop. Rain poured down on the roof of the ship, trickling through the broken window.

For a long moment, she couldn't move. Everything hurt, and her ears were ringing so loudly that she could barely hear the drumming of the rain.

With a superhuman effort, she pushed herself upright and unbuckled her seatbelt. Then she saw Jared and Rafe, slumped over the controls. Rain pelted them through the open window, and ran red with blood onto the floor.

"No," she whispered, her voice a tiny thread. "Please...no..."

She turned. Kirin...Emma...Brytnoth...all sagging in their belts, drenched with rain.

The sudden panic of being alone almost suffocated her.

"Jared!" she screamed. "Wake up!"

She stumbled forward and then collapsed, unconscious.

TWO

A FIRM HAND on her shoulder brought Sahara back into consciousness. Vaguely, she heard a woman's voice above her head.

"Is she dead?"

"No, she's not dead," Sahara mumbled.

She opened her eyes. She was lying on a low cot in the corner of a claustrophobic room. The roof was low and bristled with thatch, and it muffled the sound of the pouring rain outside. Jared sat beside her, and as soon as their eyes met, he grinned in relief.

Emma pressed her fingers into Sahara's neck as if to verify that she still had a pulse. Sahara pushed her hand away and sat up.

The room was almost dark save for the half-hearted light of a solitary candle on the rickety table in the center of the room.

"What is this place?" she asked.

"Some kind of outpost," Jared said. "From the looks of things when we got here, it's been abandoned for a long time."

Sahara glanced around the room and scowled. "Where are the others?"

"Before the nav system went down, Rafe was able to get us

within a few clicks of the prison facility," Jared said. "We sent Kirin ahead to do some recon. Rafe and Brytnoth are outside, making sure our perimeter is secure."

"You sent Kirin on recon?"

"He volunteered."

"I'm unconscious for thirty mintues and people lose their minds," Sahara mumbled.

"He's just as capable of recon as you are," Emma said.

Sahara arched an eyebrow and glanced at Jared. He shook his head and got to his feet.

At that moment, Rafe and Brytnoth came in the door. They were soaked to the skin, but when Rafe saw that Sahara was awake, he seized her in a huge hug.

"Thought we might have lost you," he said.

"You won't get rid of me that easily," she laughed, pushing him away.

"Perimeter's clear," Brytnoth said as Sahara joined them near the windows. "Seems like maybe we managed to escape detection."

"Maybe," Sahara said.

Suddenly, she heard the erratic *slap-slap, slap* of feet plunging through the puddle-ridden mud track that snaked its way through the jungle.

She moved to the window and stared out at the thick undergrowth. It was impossible to see anything clearly, but the sound was growing louder by the second.

"Someone's coming," she said.

She slipped into position behind the door, double knives out and at the ready.

Jared, Rafe, and Brytnoth took up positions near the windows, weapons ready. Emma scrambled onto the cot, hugging her knees to her chest. Sahara glanced at the young barmaid, saw her face pale with fear. Then Rafe pinched out the candle on the table and darkness swallowed them.

In the breathless seconds that followed, they all listened to the runner, his frantic pace slowing as he approached the squat wooden structure.

Sahara slid to the window and peered out. The rain cascaded from the drooping thatch eaves and obscured the path, but she could just make out a darker figure against the hazy greens and grays of the jungle beyond. Silently, her mouth a grim line, she slipped back to her place beside the chinked plank door. Jared moved up close beside her.

"Is it him?" he whispered in her ear.

"Can't tell."

The boards of the steps outside creaked under the stranger's weight. Jared noiselessly crossed back to his position on the other side of the door and raised his crossbow.

Tap, tap-tap, tap. The stranger's knuckles rapped the warped planks of the door.

"It's him," Rafe said from the darkness behind her.

The flickering light of the candle danced out across the room as Jared handed his crossbow to Brytnoth and flung open the door.

Kirin stood there, rain running down his face, his clothes in shreds. A long, ugly gash split the length of his thigh, weeping blood down his pant leg.

"They're coming," he gasped, staggering forward. "They know."

Jared grabbed his arm and pulled Kirin inside. Sahara slammed the door shut and slid the bolt home.

"What the hell happened to you?" Rafe demanded as Kirin stumbled to a chair and collapsed into it. "You weren't supposed to make contact!"

Kirin's eyes flashed up at him. "Do I look stupid?" When Rafe's face creased in a lopsided grin, he growled, "Don't answer that."

He gingerly lifted the ripped edge of his pants away from the cut and swore.

"He's right. You weren't supposed to get caught," Jared echoed with a dark frown. "You said you could handle this. And now we're all in danger." He turned the other chair around and straddled it, his arms crossed over its back.

Kirin glanced at him, then winced as the pain in his leg flared. Blood dripped from his thigh onto the floor now, staining the rough boards. Sahara left her station at the window and crouched in front of him.

"Emma!" she snapped, more harshly than she meant. "Get the med kit."

The other girl scrambled from the cot and dug through their bags while Sahara cut a large square section out of Kirin's pants. Sheathing her knife, she examined the wound. Then she raised her eyes to Kirin's face and said, "They got you pretty good, but it's not too deep. Care to tell us what happened?"

Emma knelt beside her, clutching the bag of supplies to hide the way her hands were shaking. As Sahara began cleaning the wound, Kirin told his story.

"The prison is still heavily guarded," he gritted, teeth clenched against the pain of the astringent. "There are watch towers positioned at intervals all the way from here to the facility. You can't get into the clear without being seen. I had to crawl on my belly..." He stopped, sucking in a breath as Sahara tried to begin stitching the wound closed.

"I'll have to numb this first," she said, watching his reaction.

She reached for a small auto-injector filled with anesthetic and pressed it into his upper thigh, hearing it snap as it delivered the numbing liquid to the nerve site. She tossed the empty cartridge aside and then sat back on her heels to wait for the meds to do their work.

Kirin blew out his breath and continued. "I had to crawl on my belly through the undergrowth for five hundred meters before I could even get a look at the landing pad."

"Well?" Brytnoth pressed. "Did you see what we came here for?"

"Yes," he said. "It's there."

Jared let out a breath of relief. "Well, that's good news."

Sahara picked up the needle again, clamping down the surge of optimism that made her hands tremble. She wished that her hands were as steady as Aliya's.

Wistfully, she remembered the beautiful lady of Albadir as she moved around the healing chamber, tending to the wounds and ailments of any who came to the Great House with a tender smile and hands cool and calm. Aliya's disposition was the true healing balm, Sahara realized. Although she had made Jared teach her the basics of field dressing, she felt awkward and impatient now that she actually had to use them.

Kirin gulped and kept his eyes fixed on the wall as the needle slipped in and out of his flesh. Sahara frowned, concentrating on making the stitches as neat as possible.

"We've been holed up in this wretched hovel for a week," Brytnoth said finally, frustration edging his voice. "Our friends from Albadir might be already dead. And now this." He gestured at Kirin's wounded leg. "This is what comes of our first attempt to get any kind of hard intel on the prison facility. Not what I'd call a great start." He turned away to the window, watching the rain pour off the eaves.

They had spent their first few days on K'ilenfir finding this shelter and scouting the surrounding area. Jared had insisted on giving Kirin the mission to investigate their approach to the prison. Kirin had to prove himself capable of the kind of stealthy maneuvers and gutsy tactics that would be their bread and butter for the near future—at least, Sahara hoped that was the reason for his decision.

And he went and got caught. Sahara's scowl deepened. *He'll be useless baggage, just like the girl.*

Don't be so quick to judge, came Jared's answer in her head. Her eyes snapped up and she found him watching her with a small frown, his eyes dark but calm. *We don't have the luxury of carrying baggage. They'll both do their fair share. They must.*

She pursed her lips and turned her attention back to Kirin's leg.

Her hands were sticky with Kirin's blood, and she tried to get a more secure grip on the needle.

I'll believe it when I see it, Jared. So far, all they've done is eat through our supplies and get into trouble.

Unaware of their silent exchange, Emma sat watching Sahara work, her eyes full of quiet admiration.

"How did you learn all this?" she murmured. "I wouldn't know the first thing about stitching up a wound."

Sahara glanced at her. Unbidden, the memory of that first night in the desert, of the way Jared's healing touch had eased her fever and her wounds, flooded into her mind. The memory misted her eyes, making it hard for her to see what she was doing. She jerked her head in Jared's direction.

"From him," she said flatly, killing the opening for further conversation.

Jared ran a hand through his dark hair and rubbed it over his face. He and Rafe exchanged glances as Sahara tied off the suture thread and bit through it. Then she wound a clean bandage around Kirin's leg, securing it with a tight knot.

"Good as new," she said, getting to her feet. "I hope."

Kirin gave her a lopsided smile of thanks and leaned back in his chair.

"Glad that's over," he said. He took a few deep breaths, and then continued in a stronger voice, "So, the ship is there, just as you said it would be. But I don't know how we'll get to it."

"And now they know we're here, right?" Sahara asked, wiping her hands. And then, unable to bite back the barb completely, "How exactly did you get yourself caught, Kirin?"

"I was almost out of the danger zone," he said, glaring at her. "Almost. I was coming back through the jungle from a different direction, where I thought perhaps there was a gap in their surveillance net. There wasn't. And what's worse, they had two Guardians with them." He gestured to his shredded clothes. "That's what happened to me."

Jared and Rafe exchanged another glance. Guardians were the closest thing to a hell-hound the universe had ever seen: armor-plating instead of fur, eyes that could see in the infrared, jaws full of razor-sharp teeth and a locking grip. Rumor whispered that the Drakkin themselves had created the things, an abominable melding of dog and machine. Getting caught by one usually meant a slow and tortured death. Getting caught by two and surviving was nothing short of miraculous.

"How did you escape?" Emma breathed, gazing up at him with wide eyes.

Sahara wondered if she was the only one who noticed the self-satisfied smirk on Kirin's face. Then she looked at Jared and just caught the slight roll of his eyes and the almost imperceptible stiffening of his body.

"Well," Kirin began, "I wasn't about to let them have me without a fight. In the scuffle, I was able to take one down. A knife through that soft underbelly does wonders." What was supposed to be a cool and careless shrug actually looked more like a shudder, killing Kirin's attempt at bravado. "Anyway, once the other saw its companion go down, it seemed to lose interest in me or something. Pursued me a little ways into the jungle and then broke off. I guess it went back to its post."

"They can pick up a scent that's several days old, you know," Brytnoth remarked, turning back to the company at the table. "No doubt it will track you down eventually...and it'll probably bring its friends with it." He cursed under his breath. "That's fantastic. How are we supposed to carry out an operation like this with one of those things on our trail?"

Sahara said nothing, moving instead back to her post at the window. The rain was still driving down in sheets, and she strained to see through the gloom. Nothing caught her eye, and she turned away from the night and leaned against the casement, arms crossed.

"Maybe we can take it out first," Jared was saying. "Lure it into a trap. We've done this sort of thing before."

Sahara smiled grimly. They had taken down a Drakkin scout that way back on Silesia, and that had been the turning-point in the war against the Council. The hunted had become the hunters from that moment on.

"How do you propose we do that, exactly?" Kirin asked irritably. "You can't sneak up on them."

"No, we can't." Jared rubbed his thumb against the stubble of his jaw. "But isn't there some way we could snare it somehow?"

"We don't have rope strong enough to hold a Guardian," Rafe said. "And we don't have a net of any kind. Not to mention our lack of time to prepare. Anything more sophisticated than a snare and we're talking some serious labor."

Sahara frowned.

Had she heard something rustling in the undergrowth outside?

She turned slowly and stared out the window again, her pulse pounding louder and louder in her ears. A vague chill of dread was collecting in her gut.

There.

She hadn't imagined it. A slight movement, just the odd curl of a tree branch, but it was enough.

She waved a hand at them to be quiet, and instantly everyone's attention riveted on her.

"What...?" Rafe began, but she waved again and he fell silent.

"Do you still have those flares, Jared?" she murmured, never taking her eyes from the window. "The magnesium ones?"

"Why?" He rose, stepping carefully over the chair.

"We're going to need one." She could almost taste their growing horror as she drew her knife and tested her grip. "Now."

Jared went for his pack as Rafe darted to Sahara's side, crossbow at the ready. Emma helped Kirin to the cot. Jared tossed a crossbow onto the bed next to Kirin.

"Just in case," he said.

He pulled the magnesium flare out of his pack and joined the others at the window.

"You have a plan?" he asked.

"Blind it with the flare. And once it's blind, kill it." She looked up at him and for a moment, their eyes met and locked. Then she snapped her focus back to the window. "Thirty seconds. You ready with that flare?"

Jared held it loosely in his hand and nodded. Rafe checked his own crossbow, and Sahara glanced at it, shaking her head.

"What?" Rafe asked.

"This is knife work, my friend," she said. "If you need that, it's because I'm dead."

Rafe opened his mouth to respond, but before he could say anything, they heard the porch steps creaking beneath the weight of the Guardian.

"*Now!*" Sahara shouted.

Rafe pulled the door open. Jared popped the flare and threw it onto the porch. Rafe banged the door shut again as the white-hot light shattered the darkness outside. The air split with a howl that was almost a scream, confused and wounded.

And then, before Jared could stop her, Sahara vaulted through the open window.

———

Jared and Rafe stared at each other in stunned silence.

"Sahara!" Jared cried, every muscle in his body tensed to follow her.

A shuddering shriek from the porch answered him.

He froze, paralyzed with horror. And then, without even thinking, he lunged toward the window.

Rafe seized his arm, dragging him back.

"No! Wait! You have to wait!" Brytnoth shouted at the same moment, catching his other arm.

"Let go of me!" Jared tore himself free of their hands and stood, panting for breath, seething with helpless rage.

The downpour slowly hammered the blood-curdling scream into silence, until the shattering rain was all they could hear.

A moment later, Sahara was sitting on the window ledge, shaking the water from her hair.

As she dropped to the floor, Jared barked, "Are you completely insane? What is wrong with you?"

At the same moment, Rafe's voice echoed over Jared's. "What happened, Sahara?"

She pulled a cloth from her side pocket and began cleaning the blade of her knife.

"It's done," she said. She grinned up at Jared, ignoring his fuming. "Nice work with the flare, Jared."

She slipped the knife back into its sheath and returned to the table, apparently oblivious to the way Kirin and Emma were staring at her, dumb with shock.

Rafe broke out laughing. "Unbelievable!"

Jared frowned fiercely. "You could have warned us, at least," he muttered. "We had no idea you planned to jump out the damn window."

She dropped into the chair and crossed her boots on the table. "Well, I couldn't very well go through the front door after you threw the flare on the doorstep, could I?" Her mouth quirked and her eyes sparkled at him.

Jared glared at her a moment longer, but then his anger dissolved into a grin.

"You're a crazy woman," he said. "But nicely done."

Emma left Kirin's side and approached the table, her face ashen with horror.

"You really are what they all said, aren't you?" she said. "A...a killer."

Sahara's eyes widened in surprise. Emma's voice had no more admiration in it. It was all disgust, and even fear.

Jared frowned and watched Sahara, sensing the turmoil that

Emma's cutting words had caused within her. He waited for a moment, expecting her to respond with an equally cutting remark.

None came.

He had never known Sahara to take a punch, even a verbal one, without giving something back. He turned to meet Emma's gaze.

"No," he said. "She's not a killer. She's a soldier."

THREE

EMMA TURNED AWAY WITH A FROWN.

"I'm going to bed," she muttered.

Kirin rose, limping back to the table, and Emma curled up on the cot, facing the wall.

Sahara shook her head and sighed. It was the old struggle, still haunting her. She had been raised to kill, raised to fight. She had never had a choice. And yet, somehow, everyone expected her to be different. To be gentler, or nicer, or not such an efficient dispatcher of all things evil.

Maybe I would have been like her. She unsheathed her knife again and taking a whetstone out of her side pocket. She began smoothing the blade, the rhythm soothing her jangling nerves. *If the Drakkin had never come to Amaryl, maybe I would have been different.*

She pressed her lips tightly together and shook her red hair out of her eyes. As she watched her fingers, deft and sure, she remembered how much she had wanted to be a healer. Like Aliya.

Like her mother.

It was dangerous ground, and she set her teeth. She drowned the memory in the tears she couldn't shed.

No. Not like her. I would never have been like her.

She glanced up, breathing deeply, and started when she found Jared's gaze resting on her, a smile quirking the corner of his mouth.

"You heard all that?" she asked aloud, her cheeks flaring under a sudden wash of fear and shame.

"No, actually," he responded. "But I know you well enough now to know what you're thinking without...actually knowing what you're thinking."

She grunted and dropped the whetstone back into her pocket. She slid the knife into its sheath and then propped one boot up onto her chair, resting her chin on her knee.

"So now what?" she asked. "How do we get our ship and get off this sodden piece of space junk? I'm sick to death of this place...and the rain. It never stops. We've been here a week...it's like torture."

Rafe grinned. "We're not used to the sound of rain, coming from Silesia," he said. "Can't think of the last time I heard that sound...maybe once, when I was very small. Before the Drakkin reached their zenith. Before they desiccated the whole damn planet."

Jared nodded. "I have the same memory. But, as to our plans, we have to figure a way to get past their defenses. We can't fight a pitched battle...we can't fight any kind of battle. Not with Kirin wounded, and..." He stopped abruptly, but he couldn't keep his eyes from straying to where Emma lay, seemingly asleep.

"Right," Brytnoth said quickly. "We're down a man."

Sahara snorted quietly. "I've got a bit of an idea, if anyone's interested. Just a shred of one."

"Oh, yes?" Rafe arched an eyebrow at her. "A shred?"

"Yes. You know, I would just hate to leave all those people in prison. Seems like we should do something for them. Being freedom fighters and liberators and all that, I mean."

Jared stared at her in shock. "What?" he blurted finally. "How does that help us at all? There must be thousands of prisoners in that facility, Sahara! We can't set them all free! Where would they go? What would they do for food? There's only one ship here, and that won't carry more than a few hundred of them. And that's assuming we'd want to share a ship with a bunch of ex-cons."

Sahara speared him with a withering glance, and he immediately took her point. "One's quite enough for this crew to handle," he added. "I don't think we need any more."

"Well, maybe if you let me finish the rest of my thought," she retorted, ignoring his conciliatory tone, "you'd see what I actually had in mind."

Jared cleared his throat and subsided. "Fine. So let's have it, then."

"We need a diversion. Something that will bring everyone back to the fortress and keep them busy while we quietly relieve them of their transportation." She paused for effect and then added, "I was thinking of a prison riot."

Kirin opened his eyes and sat up in his chair, one hand clutching his bandaged thigh protectively. "Are you out of your mind?"

"How are we supposed to get inside the prison to start a riot, Sahara?" Rafe asked. His usual good humor seemed to be fading fast. "If we can't get past the guard towers to get to the ship, how are we supposed to get past the guard towers to get into the prison?"

Jared said nothing. Out of the corner of her eye, Sahara saw a faint grin flash across his face. She stifled a smile of her own.

"Well, if we can get to the prison, I know a way inside," she answered. "Didn't I tell you that I escaped from here once?"

"You did not!" Kirin retorted. "Come on, Sahara. We all know they brought you back to Silesia a prisoner...twice, in fact. So stop playing games and let's talk seriously."

"No, no," she said. "This would have been three times ago. Before I was sentenced to the labor camps. That first time, I did escape. I almost made it out this last time too, but things got...complicated. And there was no rescue team standing by to pick me up, anyway. At least, not here," she finished softly, the warmth in her voice surprising her. Her eyes flickered at Jared, and then she shrugged and added, "It all worked out."

"Yes," said Brytnoth. "We much preferred the exciting engagement with the dragon. That was a lot more fun."

Sahara measured him for a moment, and then she appealed to Rafe. "I thought you'd be all over this, Rafe! Seems like your kind of thing."

Rafe laughed and leaned back in his chair, crossing his arms over his chest. "Oh, right, because I'm the crazy one who likes impossible suicidal missions. That's me. No, wait...that's you."

Sahara frowned and turned to Jared. "What about you? You believe I can get inside there and stir things up a bit, don't you?"

Jared's eyes flicked up to rest on hers. "You might be able to get inside without a problem. It's getting out again that's the hard part."

"Well, I—" Sahara began.

"I think this whole thing is ridiculous," Kirin interrupted. "Jared, you can't seriously be considering this!"

"Tell me our other options, again?" Jared countered.

"We could limp along in our piece of crap little ship and stop at the next planet," Rafe put in. "There have to be other settlements within reach."

Jared rubbed his chin thoughtfully. "Yes. Considering that it's missing most of her landing gear and half the heat shield on her right side, I think that sounds like a great idea. If we don't burn up like a cinder on re-entry at the next planet, we can burn up like a cinder when she rips open and explodes when we land. How does that sound to everyone?"

"Been there, done that," said Sahara. "Rather not do it again, if you don't mind."

"Are you criticizing my skill as a pilot?" Rafe demanded, dark eyes cold and hard and utterly humorless. "Are you blaming me for this mess we're in?"

Feeling a shift in the conversation, Sahara sighed and stood, returning to her post at the window. Behind her, the argument carried on, growing more and more heated by the moment.

It really hadn't been Rafe's fault, she reflected. None of them were familiar with the terrain on K'ilenfir, and he'd done the best he could in setting the ship down in the middle of a jungle. It was only when they'd checked the ship over afterwards that they had discovered the extent of the damage.

He must be really sore about what happened, she thought, *if he's lashing out this way. He's not usually like this.*

A flicker of movement in the shadows outside the hut arrested her attention. Slow, this time. Slow and subtle, not like the approach of the lone Guardian before. This was the careful prowl of a thoughtful adversary, not the mindless charge of an enraged beast.

"Quiet!" she snapped.

The argument behind her died suddenly.

"Is something wrong?" Jared asked.

Sahara held up a hand to silence him and strained her eyes to see through the gloom.

Another movement, this time closer to the southeast corner of the hut. And then something else stirred the leaves on the other side of the muddy path.

"There's more than one," she muttered. And then instinct told her exactly what was happening. "We're being surrounded," she said, trying to keep her voice calm and level. "Kirin said that the Guardian would lead them to us. Looks like he was right."

Emma rolled over and sat up. "What did you say? Did you say surrounded? Surrounded by what?"

Everyone ignored her. Jared and Brytnoth dashed to their gear at the back of the hut. The ship had been stocked with weapons as well as food and supplies, and they had welcomed the upgrade from crossbows to handguns—weapons that were scarce on Silesia since the Drakkin had ascended to power. They had only a small store of ammunition, so they had kept them in reserve until they absolutely needed them.

Rafe moved to stand beside Sahara at the window, scanning the landscape for any signs of movement.

"I just had a thought," he murmured after a moment. "If this is the troop from that last guard tower and we take them all down, then we go a long way toward clearing a path to the prison facility."

Jared and Brytnoth joined them at the window and Jared handed Rafe and Sahara their night vision gear and weapons.

"We take them all down," Sahara said, strapping the holsters around her upper thighs. "All of them. Clear?"

"Clear," Jared responded. Then he turned to Kirin, who was sitting in his chair in the middle of the room, the ship's sole shotgun across his knees. "Shoot anything that makes it through this door."

Kirin nodded brusquely and blew out the candle. They pulled on their night vision gear.

Sahara vaulted herself silently through the window and landed like a cat outside, then stepped around the dead Guardian to take a position a little closer to the edge of the porch. Crouched there in the darkness, staring around at the green haze of her night-vision, she waited for a sign of movement. Out of the corner of her eye, she saw Rafe, Jared, and Brytnoth slip through the door and head around the perimeter of the shack. They would take the sides and rear of the hut, leaving her to defend the front.

A brief smile flitted across her mouth as she scanned the tree line across the path. They respected her battle skills, that much was clear. They wouldn't give her the defense of their most vulnerable side if they didn't. Earning that respect had been a long and difficult road, and she was determined not to let them down. She checked her pistols and then separated her knives, testing the grips.

A stick snapped somewhere just beyond the dense tangle of foliage that clogged the track leading to the hut.

At last.

Sahara flipped the grip on the knife in her right hand, ready to plunge it into whatever hapless creature pushed its way into the open.

A shout rang out, and they were upon her.

Not just one...ten. More than ten. Men running at her through the pouring rain. Hands gripping the railing of the porch. Feet pounding up the stairs. And then she was surrounded, knives flashing in and out of necks and guts and faces. Whirl. Strike. Duck. Whirl. Bone-crunching impact as her knives went home, slick release as they came free again. Heavy thudding of bodies on the boards.

Barely a moment to breathe.

And yet she knew she was breathing. She faded into the rhythm of the dance, macabre and gruesome, ducking and swirling, forcing her enemies to stumble over each other as they pursued her. And as they stumbled, she struck. As she struck, they fell.

Some howling horn from within the jungle echoed around her, and almost instantly, the press of bodies around her dissolved into the night. Splashing madly through the rain and mud, her enemies fled back to the cover of the trees.

She dragged a heaving breath deep into her lungs, tasted the salty, metallic stench of the blood that mingled with the rain all around her feet. All at once, her arms ached horribly. Her whole body hurt.

She wondered suddenly if she were wounded, if perhaps the adrenaline had so masked the pain that she did not even realize she had been hit. Almost in a panic, she felt herself all over. Aside from a small scratch on her upper right arm, where a glancing blow had grazed her, she was unhurt. A wave of relief washed over her.

Hearing footsteps on the porch, she whirled to face the north corner of the building, knives at the ready once again. Another surge of relief, even stronger than the first, turned her stomach to water as her friends appeared.

"They retreated," Sahara said, going to meet them. "I didn't expect so many."

Rafe leaned to look around her and whistled. "I didn't expect you to kill so many!"

Sahara glanced over her shoulder at the sizeable heap of corpses and shrugged. "It was either them or me," she said. "This time, it was them."

"My ammo is spent," Jared said. "If they come at us in those numbers again, we're going to have a hard time holding them off."

Sahara scanned the trees. There was no sign of movement, no sound suggesting their enemies were preparing another assault. But then, their first attack had come from a dead calm as well. Silence was no guarantee of safety.

"Rafe?" She glanced at him and saw his attention similarly riveted on the undergrowth. "What do you think? Should we make a break for it?"

"Kirin's wounded," he answered shortly. "And if we're surrounded, we'll have a tough time breaking through. They have the advantage out there—" he gestured toward the jungle—"because they know the terrain."

Jared swore under his breath. "They've sprung the trap on us. I wish Kirin had been more careful."

Sahara glanced at him. "It kills me to say it, but I really don't think it was totally his fault. None of us knew how heavily guarded this place was."

"This is all very well," Brytnoth remarked, "but dwelling on his clumsy woodcraft doesn't help us out of this mess."

"I'm going to reload," Jared said. He glanced at Sahara. "Seems you didn't use any of yours."

She grinned at him. "It's knives for me, you know that."

Jared disappeared once more inside the hut. Sahara could hear him giving Kirin and Emma a quiet update on their situation.

"What do you think?" she asked again, turning abruptly to Rafe and Brytnoth.

Rafe sighed heavily. "Jared's right, Sahara. If they come at us again like that, we're finished. We can't keep fighting off those kinds of numbers. Sooner or later, we'll be overrun."

"Did they come at us from the west?" Sahara asked suddenly, a thought flashing through her mind.

Rafe hesitated, thinking. "I was on the south wall. Brytnoth? You had the western side."

"There were a few, but I saw hardly any action. Nothing like the numbers I see here," he answered. "I don't think the western side was the main front of the attack...and it may not have been a front at all."

Sahara nodded brusquely. "Then that's the way we'll go. We'll head west into the trees, and if they come at the shack again, we'll blow it to hell."

FOUR

BRYTNOTH DASHED into the hut and relayed Sahara's idea to the others. She heard them start to break camp and sighed, studying the trees and praying that they wouldn't be too long about it.

"What's on your mind?" Rafe asked. He holstered his pistol and crossed his arms across his broad chest.

"I don't like it," she answered slowly. "We didn't expect this level of resistance. It's like...." She hesitated and swallowed the words.

After a moment of silence, Rafe prompted, "Yes? Like what?"

"Like they're still there. The Drakkin."

Rafe said nothing for a time. Then, "What makes you say that?"

"Why is this place still so heavily guarded? I thought their old defenses and strongholds would fall when they did. I never thought that we would meet with fortifications like these."

Rafe shrugged. "Sometimes the snake keeps twisting after it's been decapitated," he suggested. "Maybe they haven't realized they don't have a leader any more."

She frowned. "Maybe."

Rafe grinned at her. "You sound totally convinced."

"I am. Totally." She moved away from him a few paces, toward the edge of the porch, peering into the trees. "Rafe," she called softly. "Head into the trees a bit and see how far they've retreated. I want to be sure we can get out of here without running into any nasty surprises."

Without a word, he slipped away from her, melting into the night. Sahara stared after him. She knew he was skilled, but none of them were used to this terrain or these conditions. It would be so easy to make a mistake. And a mistake would be fatal.

Where are they with that gear? she fretted. *At least this cursed rain is letting up.*

Almost before she had finished the thought, Jared and Brytnoth reappeared, packs slung over their shoulders.

"Finally!" Sahara muttered. "What took you so long? We've got to get out of here." Jared jerked his head back toward the hut as he handed her a pack. "What? What's the problem?"

It's Emma, Jared's voice came calmly inside her mind. *She doesn't want to leave.*

Sahara's anger flared, electrifying her entire body, and she started for the door. Jared grasped her arm.

"Wait, Sahara..."

"Don't you dare try to stop me," she hissed, jerking her arm out of his hand. "She's going to get us all killed! If she wants to sit in this hole and rot, that's her problem. But we aren't staying another minute."

She headed for the door, but then stopped as Rafe emerged out of the trees and jogged across the path.

"They've headed back for the guard tower," he said, clattering up the steps. "If we're going to make a break for it, now's the time."

"Great," Sahara snapped, pushing her night vision goggles up onto her forehead. "If we *could* leave, that would be excellent news."

"What's up?" he asked.

"Your girlfriend, Rafe," she said. "Get her out of there or she's staying here to die. And where is Kirin?"

Jared sighed. "He said he won't leave Emma here alone. He's staying too."

Sahara pushed past them and went back inside the hut, muttering, "This is crazy. Absolutely crazy."

She felt Jared and Rafe close behind her, and she could feel Jared's mounting concern. She clenched her jaw and pushed back against his disapproval.

Emma was huddled on the cot, face buried in her arms. In the hesitating light of the candle, Sahara could see the girl's shoulders shaking with quiet sobs. Kirin sat on the floor beside her, his back against the wall, crossbow across his knees. His expression was blank, but Sahara caught the barest flicker of defiance in his eyes.

Of all the times for him to try to be a hero. It's got to be now. It's got to be her.

"Would one of you please tell me what the hell is going on here?" Sahara demanded, her voice like ice. "We need to leave. Now. Before we all die."

Emma's sobs grew more violent at this, and the last shred of Sahara's patience evaporated. She strode across the room and planted herself next to Emma.

"Look at me!" she said. "Look at me."

Emma slowly raised her face, and Sahara caught her by the chin, forcing the girl to look her in the eyes.

"Stop it right now. Right now. Get out of this bed and out that door, or I will leave you here to die, do you understand me? What do you think will happen if you stay here? Do you think anyone is coming to rescue you? There's no one else, Emma. No one will come for you. No one will save you." Her eyes flickered at Kirin. "You want to live, you come with me."

She heard Rafe choke on words behind her, but she paid him no attention. She stared into Emma's wide, frightened eyes for a moment longer, then released her grip on her chin. Emma scrambled away from her and ran to Rafe's protective embrace.

Sahara took a deep breath and turned to Kirin, who was watching her with surprisingly steady eyes.

"What do you think you're doing?" she asked. She pointed to the crossbow. "What are you planning to do with that?"

"If she was staying, I was going to..."

"What? Protect her?" Sahara laughed out loud. Seeing him open his mouth to answer, she leaned down and seized the collar of his shirt, jerking his face close to her own. "Shut up. This place is a death trap, and you know it. You want to be a hero and protect her? Then you carry her out the damn door."

She shoved him away from her and he struggled to his feet. For a moment, he stood facing her.

"I-I'm sorry," he mumbled.

Sahara said nothing, and he limped past her toward the door. She took a deep breath and closed her eyes, searching for some measure of calm. Then she turned to the others.

Rafe frowned at her and held Emma close, muffling her sobs against his shoulder. When Sahara's eyes flickered at Kirin, he ducked his head. And Jared?

He just watched her, his silent steadiness more unnerving than anything else could have been at that moment.

"You need to get something straight right now, you two," Sahara said, snapping her eyes quickly away from Jared's. "All our lives hang in the balance right now, and I will not allow you to put anyone else at risk. You will pull your weight around here and you will do as you're told. If you don't, I will leave you in this hell-hole and you can fend for yourselves. Is that clear?"

Without waiting for an answer and still muttering under her breath, she stalked out the door and led the way around the hut.

As they went, she set the charges at the base of the wall, letting the slow precision of the work calm her nerves. As she imagined the surprise that lay in store for their enemy, her anger and frustration gradually morphed into a sense of grim satisfaction.

Was all that really necessary? came Jared's reproach in her thoughts.

Sahara resisted the urge to turn and confront him. She carefully placed another charge and sighed.

I don't know, Jared. We nearly got killed out here a few minutes ago...and I'll rot before I let two deadweights endanger the rest of this crew. So you tell me. Was it necessary? I kind of think it was. She felt a string of curses bubbling up inside her, and she slammed the door on them before anything else could escape.

I know, Jared said, his calm voice soothing her raw nerves. *You were scared, too.*

She whirled to face him at that, stopping so suddenly that he nearly bowled her over.

"What did you stop for?" he asked, all innocence.

"What do you mean, what did I stop for?" she murmured. She planted her finger in his chest. "I was *not* scared, Jared. Not like that." She jabbed him again. "Not like that."

He regarded her with that same intense and unnerving stare. "Maybe not now. Maybe not tonight. But you've been there. You know what it's like. To feel helpless." His eyes bored into her, scorching her very soul. "Pillar and chains," he whispered. "Fire and stone."

"Shut up!" she snapped. "Don't you dare bring that up!"

With a savage glare at him, she turned back to her task and set another charge.

I don't want to remember, she told him.

If you let yourself remember, you'd treat Emma with more kindness, he said, inside her mind once more. *You can't escape the argument by walking away from me.* After a pause, he added, *She needs you, Sahara. She needs you to teach her how to be strong, and how to survive.*

Sahara couldn't answer him. As she placed the last charge and led the little group into the bracken west of the hut, she felt suddenly soul-weary. Would the battles never end? Would she never be allowed just to *be?*

She didn't want to look at Emma. *I don't want to teach her anything,* she realized. *And I sure as hell don't want her to become someone like me.*

The thought wrenched her so hard that she nearly stumbled, so she sped up their pace to force herself to focus.

They made their way through the dripping undergrowth as quietly as they could, crouching low and trotting single file. When they reached a point about fifty meters from the hut, Sahara signaled for them to stop.

She set down her pack and rapidly assessed their new location. A dark hollow underneath a nearby fallen tree would serve well enough for a shelter for the rest of the night. She beckoned Kirin into the damp little depression. As the others dropped their packs and readied their weapons, Sahara called softly to Emma.

Emma edged toward her, hands clenched by her sides and face set. Sahara could tell that she was trying her hardest not to cry. Sahara sniffed and jerked a thumb at the packs.

"Stow these with Kirin and then stay put," Sahara said.

Emma nodded and started ferrying their supplies to Kirin, who secured them well underneath the shelter of the log. Sahara watched her for a moment, surprising herself when she realized that she was smiling.

"Now what?" Brytnoth asked in the barest whisper.

"We wait," Sahara murmured.

She looked back the way they had come. They had left the candle burning inside the hut, hoping to draw their enemies back for another attack, and the warm yellow light looked strangely homey and welcoming now that they were out in the damp and the dark.

"Which way do we go from here?" Rafe whispered. "Are we…"

Jared suddenly held up a hand to silence him. They heard the rapid snapping and crunching of twigs and underbrush in the trees to their east.

By the sound of it, Sahara guessed that this would be an all-out assault. And then, as if to prove her right, the soldiers broke out of the trees with a roar, obviously thinking to overwhelm the little band with sheer force of numbers.

Black shapes swarmed the sagging porch of the hut. As soon as a group of them bashed through the front door, Sahara pressed the detonator.

Guttural shouts of victory warped into shrieks as the explosives blew, vomiting flames and shredded wood and bodies high into the air and down again into the trees. A hysterical outburst of clamoring voices and convulsing underbrush betrayed the frantic flight of those who hadn't been killed by the blast.

Jared nodded his approval at Sahara. "Good plan," he murmured. "Worked exactly as you said it would."

"Not exactly. Some of them still got away." She swore and blew her hair out of her eyes. "We've still got a lot of ground to cover, and that little matter of stealing the ship won't be easy. But maybe we've bought ourselves a few precious hours of rest. And now that they know what kind of bite we have, maybe they'll think twice before pursuing us any further."

They made their way back to the shelter of the fallen tree. Brytnoth offered to take first watch, and the rest crowded into the hollow, making themselves as comfortable as they could in the damp grass and moss beneath the log.

I hope there aren't any crawling things under here, Sahara thought vaguely as she closed her eyes.

She heard Jared chuckle next to her.

I thought you weren't afraid, he said, a smile in his voice at last.

His reward was a light punch in the shoulder.

———

Even though Brytnoth manned the watch, Jared couldn't force his eyes to close. The day's events mired his heart in worry and uncertainty, and he couldn't shake the dark feelings that closed in on his mind like the misty shadows around them. Beside him, he heard Sahara's breathing, deep and even, and knew she was asleep.

He frowned as he stared into the blindness above his head. She still hadn't shaken off the shackles of her past, not completely. Even now, it drove her actions. He knew she hated to remember those moments on the cliff, those horrible moments when terror, more than iron bonds, had paralyzed her, and their victory was nothing certain. She was repressing those memories just as she had repressed the memories of her family's death.

He sighed in frustration and pushed the thoughts away. He would have to figure out a way to deal with her issues later. Right now, he needed to focus on figuring out a plan for commandeering that deep space vessel. Everything else could wait until they were safely away.

Sahara's proposal of starting a prison riot made him profoundly uneasy. He was also fairly certain that, even if someone objected to it, she would do it anyway. That was her way.

Maybe, just maybe, if he came up with something genius, she would reconsider. But his mind was sluggish, and he could see nothing but the plan she had proposed. He fell asleep with visions of Sahara trapped in the midst of a violent prison riot whirling through his mind.

He woke suddenly to the touch of a cold hand on his. Sahara crouched over him, though he could barely make her out in the dense, rising mist of early dawn.

"Time to go," she murmured. "They're all ready."

"Why'd you let me sleep, then?" mumbled Jared as he crawled out from under the tree. He glanced back to see her smiling at him.

When they had all assembled in the little clearing, Kirin took over.

"Since we came west, we're a little off course if we want to reach the prison and the landing pad," he said. "But we can't cut back east too soon or we'll run into those outposts."

"Why haven't they posted guards this way?" asked Brytnoth. "There has to be a reason why they would leave the western approach to the prison open."

Rafe shifted uneasily. "Perhaps there's a beastie," he said, trying to hide the glint of genuine concern in his eyes with a cocky smile.

Sahara made a face. "Anything's possible, I suppose. I never heard anything about any...beasties guarding the way to the prison, but that doesn't mean there isn't one."

"It's because there's a river that runs north-south on this side of the prison," Kirin said. "I crossed it further to the south. We should hit it if we keep on heading northeast."

"Good to know," Jared said. "But even if there is some kind of natural fortification, let's go carefully. There may be guards patrolling the area anyway." He gestured them into a column, placing Emma in the middle. "Rafe, you and Brytnoth bring up the rear and make sure nothing follows us."

"You got it," said Rafe.

The little party set off at as brisk a pace as they could manage while still keeping hyper-aware of their surroundings. Kirin limped ahead of them with the compass, guiding them steadily northeast.

The thick mist swirled around their legs, ghosting the trees and the dense underbrush. The raw, primal smell of moist and decaying organic matter hung in the breezeless air. Occasionally, vines looped themselves across their path, forcing Kirin to pause and hack them down with his heavy knife.

It all felt so foreign to Jared, this heavy moisture and overabundance of life. He stared around at the huge moss-draped trees, awed as a child, and every now and then he inhaled the spicy sweetness of the air as if he could draw its life into himself. He could almost feel it pulsing beneath his feet, the heartbeat of this world.

He nearly ran into Sahara, who had suddenly stopped and was listening intently with her head cocked on one side.

"What's the problem?" he asked.

Kirin turned, hearing his voice, and backtracked to where they all stood now, clustered together.

"What's going on? We've got to keep moving."

"I hear something," Sahara said. "Something like…"

She fell silent as it came again, a low thrumming vibration that seemed to tremble all the air and ground around them.

"What is that?" Emma whispered, her eyes wide.

"Let's move," said Rafe. "Faster."

Kirin set off in the lead position again, and they followed him at a brisk trot. As they went on, the noise grew louder until it was a low, constant thundering.

And then, with no warning, the trees ended and Kirin was holding them back at the edge of a plunging ravine. Just up the gorge to their left, a huge waterfall cascaded into the misty depths below.

Sahara grinned at Rafe. "No beasties, I guess," she said. "And Kirin was right about the gorge."

The ravine spanned such a distance at this point that Jared could barely make out the opposite side through the mist. The sides of the gorge seemed to be composed of a slick, slate-like rock that knifed upward in places in jagged shards. Strange trees, their smooth trunks gnarled and twisted, clung precariously to the cliff sides at odd angles, their roots tangled in the bastions of rock and looking as though they would slip at any moment.

Peering down into the depths of the gorge, Jared caught sight of the violent, sinuous river below.

Even if we could get down the gorge, there's no way we could ford the river, he realized.

"Anyone see a bridge?" he asked aloud, stepping back from the edge and glancing at the others.

"There's one back south of here where I crossed," Kirin answered. "But I don't think we want to go back that way. Too many surveillance towers. Maybe there's another bridge further to the north, past the waterfall. At least that would get us beyond most of the guard outposts."

"I agree with Kirin...for once," Sahara said, flashing a grin in his direction. "We'll have to head north until we find a way to cross."

"And if there's not a way to cross?" Jared asked.

Sahara shrugged. "Then I guess we'll have to head back south. Let's go."

They trekked along the edge of the ravine for what felt like hours, and soon the thunder of the falls was just a memory. The sky above them was overcast and heavy with rain, but the slow creep of daylight gradually brightened their path. The mist lifted only a little, snagging in the treetops to their left. Shale and scree blanketed the ground beneath their feet, and it crunched horribly under their boots. Jared spared a thought in thanksgiving for the sound-muffling roar of the river and the dense underbrush on the forest side—he just hoped it was enough to conceal their passage from any listening ears.

"Look!" Brytnoth called quietly.

They slowed to a halt. A hundred meters ahead of them, the trees marched straight to the edge of the ravine and across, their roots clinging to a massive arch of solid Drakkin-green stone that brooded over the surging river far below.

"It's a natural bridge," said Rafe. "Amazing! I've never seen anything like it."

At that moment, a crunching and scrabbling echoed in the ravine from somewhere behind and below them. They looked at each other in bewilderment.

There was a pause, and then the scrabbling resumed, louder this time and more intense.

And now they knew what it was.

Something was climbing up the gorge.

FIVE

"WHY DID you have to say something about a beastie?" asked Jared in a low voice, keeping his gaze fixed on the bridge and the line of trees.

"Don't know," Rafe answered with a rueful smile. "My amazing intuition tinted by a warped sense of humor?"

They could hear a grunting breathing behind them now, as if the creature were struggling to heave its bulk up the steep slope of the canyon.

More scrabblings, like a giant rat.

"Let's run for it," Emma pleaded. "We can get to those trees before it's out of the ravine, can't we?"

Sahara glanced back in the direction of the sound. At that moment, an enormous paw, fringed with razor sharp claws and shaggy gray hair matted with blood, planted itself on the edge of the ravine. The claws shattered the rock and gripped.

"Run!" she shouted. "Run, all of you! Run for the bridge!"

The intensity of her voice had them in full career before she had even finished speaking. Even Kirin, who had been limping along all morning on his bad leg, seemed to forget the pain as he stretched to full stride. Jared held back so that he and Sahara could bring up the rear together.

What was it? he asked.

Caught a glimpse of the paw, she answered. *Large as the trunk of a small tree. Gray, and bloody. Whatever that thing is, we don't want to meet it.*

They were fast coming to the line of trees. Already, Sahara could see Kirin and Emma fading into the underbrush, angling their path toward the bridge. Rafe and Brytnoth hung close on their heels.

They heard it behind them now. Its stride shook the ground beneath their feet, nearly toppling them over. And then it let out a roar, a gurgling, savage bellow that reverberated in the canyon and seemed to bow the trees in front of them.

At the same moment, there came a screech of arrows skittering on stone and shouts of a more human sort from the tree line.

"They've seen us!" Jared shouted, ducking his head as another volley of black-shafted arrows whined over their heads.

"Are they shooting at us or that thing?" Sahara called back.

They jumped into the underbrush, yelling at their companions to keep running. Emma shot off like a bolt, but Kirin staggered, face pale as he clutched his leg. Blood seeped between his fingers in a slick stream. Before Sahara could react, Rafe and Brytnoth hoisted him between them and raced after the fleeing Emma as fast as their burden would allow.

Behind them in the trees, Sahara heard the strange baying of the Guardians, and she cursed. She felt some vague pulse of energy from Jared—a flash of irritation that mirrored her own.

Then the trees behind them shattered into bits as the ravine creature charged into the jungle after them. Men screamed in terror, and the air sang as volleys of arrows launched from their strings. The creature roared.

Sahara knew that sound. It was the cry of a beast both injured and insane with rage. She paused and looked back.

Immediately, she wished she hadn't.

The creature was as large as a house and covered with matted gray fur. Its eyes were red as blood, its gaping maw full of a double row of jagged teeth, like something out of a fable or a nightmare. She watched, horror-stricken, as its paw ripped through the tangle of foliage where their enemies were concealed. The trees splintered like matchwood and bodies tumbled to the ground. The Guardians bayed and fixated on the creature, seizing it by the hind legs and snapping at its belly, fiercely defending the men who had just been concussed into oblivion.

Without staying to watch the end, Sahara turned and fled across the bridge.

The others were already on the other side waiting for her.

"Are you crazy?" Jared cried as she skidded to a stop in front of them, breathing hard. "What did you stop for?"

"I had to see. It's not after us any longer, and neither are the Guardians. They're keeping each other busy over there. Let's put some distance between us and this river, though, shall we?" She managed a smile, but no one returned it.

"You could've been killed," Rafe said, eyes stern.

"Well, I wasn't." She glanced at Kirin, who was hanging between Brytnoth and Rafe on the verge of collapse. "We have to bind that wound. A blood trail will give them something to follow."

Jared gestured to a moss-covered boulder a few meters away, and Rafe and Brytnoth half-carried, half-dragged Kirin to it and sat him down. Emma ran forward with the med kit and knelt by Sahara in the moldering leaves.

Kirin groaned as he stretched out his bad leg. Sahara shot Jared a questioning look and he nodded at her.

"You did fine last time," he said, "so go ahead."

"I'll watch the path," Brytnoth offered, leaving Kirin's side and jogging a little way back toward the river.

Sahara quickly unpacked her supplies. The bandage roll was a bit thin, and she offered a silent prayer that there would be no further serious injuries until they found a place to restock their supplies. She never glanced at Emma, though she could feel the other woman's steady gaze on her as she worked.

Sahara stripped off the old bandage and flung it into the trees. "Maybe that will keep them busy for a while," she muttered.

The wound gaped and seeped between the rough stitches she had placed and she frowned. At least it still smelled fairly clean.

"This really needs more skilled hands than mine," she admitted. "Jared, can you do anything with this?"

He crouched beside her and inspected her handiwork.

"The stitches are a bit wobbly," he said, the glimmer of a smile in his voice. "But it's not bad work, Sahara. It's just that he needs to rest it. The exertion is straining the stitches too much, and there's nothing we can do about that until we're safely away from here." He unrolled the bandage and handed it to her. "Just wrap it well and tightly. It'll have to do for now."

Sahara obeyed, spreading a bit of topical anesthetic cream gently around the wound before she bound it, hoping it might ease the pain a bit.

"I'm sorry, Kirin," she mumbled. "I wish I could do better by you."

"It's fine," he gritted. "Let's just go."

Emma packed the supplies back into the kit and slung it over her shoulder, and Rafe helped her get to her feet. Sahara jerked her head in the direction of the bridge.

"Go tell Brytnoth we're moving," she said. Then, as Rafe headed off, she turned to Kirin. "Where do we go from here? Which way is the prison?"

"Straight northeast of us. We can follow the gorge north for a bit until we reach the prison valley. After that, you won't need me to give you directions."

Rafe and Brytnoth rejoined them and brought up the rear of the little party, supporting Kirin between them as before. As they moved off, they kept within earshot of the river but well out of sight of the edge of the gorge. Sahara and Jared walked together, blazing the trail for the others.

"What are you thinking?" Sahara asked Jared at last, after they had gone some distance in silence. She glanced sidelong at him. His mouth was set in a grim line, and she could see the muscles of his jaw working. "I know you're thinking something."

I just don't know what it is, she realized with something of a shock.

"I'm thinking that I don't like the plan," he said bluntly.

"What's wrong with the plan?"

"I don't want you going in there again, Sahara. The thought is driving me crazy."

Sahara smiled at him. "You're worried about me!" she said, a bewildered amusement in her voice. "You know I can handle myself, Jared. You don't have to worry."

"I know that. But if you start a riot, there's no predicting what will happen. No. It's just too dangerous."

Sahara felt the old stirrings of temper but just shrugged her shoulders. There were so many things she could say to that, but she just contented herself with, "Unless you've got a better idea, we'll have to go with this one."

———

Jared was silent as they made their way steadily along. Sahara had echoed his thoughts from the previous night, and he knew that she wouldn't hear his objections unless he had something to offer in exchange.

And he could think of nothing.

He heard the labored breathing of the others behind them and slowed his pace.

"Can we call a halt, Jared?" Rafe asked from underneath Kirin's muscled arm. "Or maybe trade places for a bit?"

Jared regarded him for a moment, hardly registering the question. When Rafe arched an eyebrow at him, he stirred. "Yes. A halt. And I need to talk to you. Over here."

He turned abruptly and strode a little way down the path. He stared up into the massive arched branches, woven together by curling vines to form a hopelessly enmeshed tangle of wood and greenery.

"What's the problem?" Rafe asked, coming alongside him and following his gaze upward. "What are you looking at?"

"Nothing." Jared paused for a moment, then dropped his gaze to his friend's concerned face. "Look, Rafe, I don't want Sahara going back into that prison. You have to help me think of another plan."

Rafe regarded him in some surprise. "She can handle herself, Jared," he said slowly. "Look at the way she...."

Jared ran a hand through his dark hair in frustration. "I know all that. But...." His voice trailed off and he just stood there, feeling helpless and awkward and utterly childish.

Rafe studied him in the silence that followed, and then a light of understanding suddenly dawned across his face.

"You thought she'd be done with all that now," he said slowly. "Am I right? I mean, you thought she'd be like...well, like Emma. That she wouldn't charge into danger without a backward glance... that she'd just rely on you to save her."

Jared's anger blazed, but then he checked it and frowned. "I never thought she would be like Emma," he muttered.

Rafe laughed. "Fine, but you did think she'd have changed." He shook his head. "Really, I'm not sure why you expected that. I'm sure I didn't."

"Well, I did," Jared said, frowning. "And I don't understand why she hasn't. I thought that once the Drakkin were destroyed, she'd be free. But...she's not."

Rafe turned his gaze up into the trees and sighed. "Don't make the mistake," he said slowly, "of thinking that just because she hasn't changed, she isn't free."

Jared glanced back down the path, watched Sahara as she crouched in the path, tipping her canteen and wiping her mouth with the back of her hand. Watched her as she talked with Brytnoth and Kirin, sketching something in the dirt with a bit of stick.

"You mean she will never change?" he faltered. "Is that what you're trying to tell me? That even when there's peace, she'll still...."

"Still what? Charge into a bar or a wedding wielding those double knives?"

Jared turned back to his friend, caught the glint of humor in his dark eyes. Rafe laid a hand on his shoulder and gripped it firmly. "Let her do what she needs to do, Jared," he said. "Let her do what she was trained to do."

Jared dropped his head. "You know," he said, his voice a bit strained, "it's harder than you might think, letting her go."

Rafe's hand was still strong on his shoulder. "I know it is. But you have to. We'll never get off this infernal moon if you don't. None of us have the skills to do this mission. It's got to be her, or we're stuck here for good. And our friends will surely die out there in the void."

Jared nodded and looked up into his friend's smiling face. He gripped Rafe's forearm in thanks and then they turned back to the rest of the crew.

Sahara's eyes flashed at him as she took another mouthful of water from her canteen. *Is something wrong?*

He shook his head and managed a smile. *It's nothing.*

She shrugged and screwed the cap back on the mouth of the canteen. "Are you ready to move out?" she asked. "We should be nearly there by now."

Kirin gestured vaguely toward the trees in front of them. "It should be just through that stand of trees ahead," he said. "There's an overlook where we can assess our position and decide what to do next."

"Let's get moving," Rafe said, helping Kirin to his feet once more.

They trotted along the dirt path, and soon, just as Kirin had said, the trees opened up on the edge of a steep slope covered in scree and scrub bushes. Sahara motioned for them to lower themselves into the bracken and then led them forward on hands and knees to the edge of the ravine.

Brytnoth swore softly under his breath. "How are we supposed to get past *that?*"

SIX

THE VALLEY that stretched before them was far more rugged than the terrain through which they had just traveled, pocked by deep craters and fissures and overshadowed some distance away to their east by a smoldering volcanic formation. Rock masses and boulders lay scattered about the valley floor as if they had been flung there by some monstrous hand, but no undergrowth interrupted the barren space.

Straight ahead of them, across this valley of stone and shadows, lay the hulking black walls of the Prison of K'ilenfir. Its vastness was stunning, even to Jared, who had seen it from the inside. The face of the structure erupted sheer and unforgiving from the valley floor, with the top of the wall angled out over the base to make scaling impossible. Guard turrets marked regular intervals along the battlements, and even from their distance they could see the movement of the patrols along the walls. The entire valley lay exposed in her barrenness to those watching eyes.

"Look," Sahara murmured and pointed away to their right.

"The landing platform," Rafe said. "And there's the ship."

Unlike the prison, the landing platform seemed strangely deserted.

"Why should we bother with the prison when that ship is just there for the taking?" Brytnoth whispered. "There are no guards anywhere in sight around the landing platform!"

"Don't let that fool you," Sahara warned. She pointed to the squat shelter just beneath the platform. "I sat in that hut before they brought me back to Silesia. There are guards there. *Guardians*, to be exact. They don't have to be seen to see. The silent watchers, the guards called them. Just behind that hut, they wait in open cages, scanning for infiltrators."

Rafe muttered something under his breath. "Well, how the hell…"

"That's why we need the prison riot!" Sahara pressed. "If I can get in there and get something going, then the Guardians will be brought in to restore order, leaving the platform completely exposed and unguarded."

"And you're sure about that?" Jared asked. "No chance they have other ways to deal with a riot?"

"Human guards really only work when prisoners are under control," Sahara said, voice low and cold. "And there aren't enough of them to do the job if things get messy."

They all sat in silence for a few moments, contemplating the situation.

"How do you think you're going to get in there?" rasped Kirin. He sat a little behind the others, his back against the bole of a tree. "Into the prison. I've never seen a structure like that. Ever. This is absolute suicide."

Sahara rolled onto her side and regarded him with a scowl. "Well, we're dead either way. The only way out of this hell-hole is on that ship. And the only way onto that ship is by way of a prison riot." She paused, swinging her gaze around to meet Jared's eyes. "Unless anyone has a better idea?"

Jared shook his head. "It's a go from me," he said.

Kirin cursed. "Well, let's get on with it, then."

The others crept back from the edge of the ravine and sat in a tight circle near Kirin. Sahara snapped a twig from a nearby bush and started scratching in the dirt.

"I know this prison," she assured them. "We had an escape route planned. I got out."

"Once," Emma piped from where she sat, her knees drawn up under her chin.

Sahara's eyes flickered at her. "Yes. Once." She turned back to her scratching, and soon they could make out a rough schematic of the prison. "Here at the southeastern corner there's a tunnel. It starts under a large rock formation in the valley and runs right up under the minimum security cell block. It opens into a cell on the ground floor. We used to have a man on the inside, in that cell. He was a rebel, a facilitator. He possessed certain skills—like lock-picking—that made entry into the prison quick and easy. We kept prisoners' jumpsuits stashed just inside the entrance to the tunnel. Anyone coming in could immediately blend into the general population."

"Okay, Sahara, that's fabulous," said Brytnoth suddenly. "But you can't just incite a riot overnight. How long is this going to take?"

Sahara glanced up from her drawing and studied his face for a moment, then sat back on her heels. "That's the first intelligent objection I've heard so far," she said after a moment.

"Well?" said Jared, refusing to be ruffled by her attitude.

"It's a good point," she admitted. "And it's hard to say. Maybe a week? Maybe longer."

Kirin's attempt to stifle a laugh came out as a harsh snort. "And what are the rest of us supposed to do while you prowl around inside the prison? What are we supposed to eat? Where do we shelter? We're not exactly in friendly territory here."

Sahara rose and moved away, pacing slowly along the tree line, sunk in thought. It was a difficult question, and she knew she would have to have a convincing answer if she expected the others to go along with her plan. She didn't notice how the seconds were dragging into minutes and the minutes into a quarter of an hour until the others began to grow restless. She sighed and returned to the circle.

"Here's what I'm thinking," she said, dropping cross-legged into her vacant position. "As for shelter, that's no problem. You can hide in the tunnel. What if we all went in...all except two?" She looked at Kirin and Emma. "You two would wait in the tunnel until the riot starts, and then you'd head to the ship and secure it."

"By all the holy powers," Brytnoth murmured. "You are insane."

"Well, maybe not as much as you might think," Jared said suddenly. "If we split up once we're inside the prison, we would be much more effective at inciting the prisoners. I actually think it's less crazy than Sahara going in on her own."

Sahara smiled at him wryly. "Thanks, Jared."

"But, Jared," Rafe began, "stop and think for just a minute. Extracting four people from a volatile situation is a lot more complicated than extracting just one."

Jared rubbed his chin thoughtfully. "True. But I don't see what other option we have."

"There are some provisions in the tunnel," Sahara added. "Enough to last two people for a while, with careful rationing. There certainly isn't enough for five. And depending on the situation on the inside, we might be able to smuggle more provisions out to you."

"Great," muttered Kirin. "We have to eat the food, but we don't get to have any of the fun."

Jared grinned at him and clapped him on the shoulder. "You're wounded, my friend! There's no fun in your future for quite a while, I'm afraid."

Rafe sighed. "I guess that's that, then. We'll break for the tunnel as soon as it's dark."

Sahara jerked her head at their packs, which lay in a heap next to Kirin's tree. "Eat light tonight," she said. "We need to save as much of those rations as you can."

They ate a cold meal early and then settled down to wait. As soon as it was dark enough to conceal their movements, they set out down the steep slope into the valley. At Sahara's suggestion, they had fanned out along the ridge. Brytnoth and Kirin moved together at the end of the line. Emma shadowed Sahara, partly because Sahara wanted to keep a close eye on the girl's movements. She still seemed too flighty, too unpredictable. She made Sahara nervous.

Halfway down the slope, they all paused and crouched behind large rocks in total stillness. Peering through her night-vision goggles, Sahara winced against the bright flare of torches being lit along the walls and the larger watch fires kindled in the corner towers. The guards on patrol didn't seem too interested in studying the valley, she noticed. Many were standing in little bunches, leaning on the balustrade and chatting casually. She even thought she saw one group near the northeastern tower passing around a flask.

The sight sent a warning chill up Sahara's spine. Under the Drakkin, that kind of lack of discipline would land a guard in chains in the center courtyard, where he would have been flayed and left hanging by the wrists as an example to the others.

Something's changed, she thought. *Something's not right...not the same.*

She swallowed hard, trying to choke down the doubts that came flooding into her mind. If this much had changed, then perhaps everything she was gambling on was just an illusion.

She swore to herself as she gave the signal for them to continue down the hill. She'd made these kinds of rash assumptions before without taking the time to gather enough actual intel. The last time, when Arnauld had ordered her to attack the Drakkin stronghold on Silesia, her rashness had cost countless men their lives and had landed her and Jared inside this very prison. It had very nearly cost her her own life. She shuddered at the memory.

She glanced back along the line. A surge of pride and even love for her little band welled up inside her. They trusted her...and she was leading them straight into what could so easily turn out to be a trap.

And what will it cost me this time? she wondered.

On an impulse, she started to reach out to Jared in her mind, then checked herself in confusion. She was suddenly afraid of his judgment.

A part of her chafed under the realization that his objections to her plan might not have been ridiculous after all.

Why does he always have to be right? she thought. Then she frowned, focusing on the uncertain footing and trying not to listen to that petulant, needling question. She had to tell him. She *wanted* to tell him. Even if it meant that she'd been wrong.

When we get to the tunnel, she decided. *Then I'll tell him.*

A few more cautiously sliding steps brought them to the valley floor, and Sahara breathed a bit more easily. She and Emma crouched behind a large cairn, and Sahara could hear the other girl's breathing, ragged, as if she were silently sobbing. She nudged Emma with her elbow.

"Are you alright?" she whispered. Emma nodded fiercely, and though Sahara caught the glint of tears in her eyes, she saw Emma square her chin and shoulders. "Good girl," she murmured. "Not much farther."

After waiting a few more seconds for extra security, Sahara gestured for the team to move out once more, this time angling for a large rock mass about fifty meters to the east.

So far, so good. Steady, steady.

They crept along for another five meters, and then they each found a place to hide, crouching in the shadows, counting seconds. Then up again and onward, crouch, hide, wait. It was breathless work. Sahara kept checking the guards, kept marveling at the strange laxness of their behavior. She pushed the nagging doubts and fears away, tried to focus completely on the slow fluidity of her movements.

They reached the mound of rubble near the southeastern corner of the prison without incident and collapsed within its towering shelter, groping for canteens and mopping brows. Sahara crept to Jared's side and plucked his sleeve.

What? came his voice in her mind as his eyes connected with hers.

We might have a problem, she told him.

She felt him stiffen, saw the immediate snap to full alertness in his eyes. *What problem?*

She swallowed hard and told him what she had seen of the guards. *It's strange...too strange. I don't like it.*

He frowned fiercely. *We can't do anything other than what we've planned,* he said. *But we should be careful.*

A wave of relief washed through her. She wasn't sure what she'd expected him to say—they had come too far for a total change of plans. But for whatever reason, she felt her confidence surge.

He seemed to sense something of her emotions, because he smiled quizzically at her and said nothing. She managed a smile in return, then crept away to find the entrance to the tunnel.

After a brief search, she located the heap of stones that concealed the mouth of the passage. She beckoned to the others and they began painstakingly removing the rocks, trying to be silent. Gradually, a gaping maw appeared behind the stones and a trickle of stale air wafted into their faces.

"The other end is still open," Jared murmured. "Good work, Sahara."

As soon as they had an opening large enough, they began to crawl inside. Sahara waited until last, handing stones through the hole to Jared. As soon as her pile was gone, she crawled through the gap and together she and Jared filled the rest of the opening.

As they worked, Rafe and Brytnoth scouted up the tunnel. When they returned, Jared and Sahara were just placing the last few stones in the entrance.

"There's a hollowed space a few meters down the tunnel," Rafe said quietly. "There are lockers with provisions and blankets and an extra med kit. I saw a few jumpsuits stored there as well."

"Perfect," Sahara responded, rising and brushing off her knees. "Let's go."

A short while later, they were all assembled in the small space Rafe had found. A piece of ragged fabric was hooked over a stone, and Jared pulled it loose and let it fall across the mouth of the cave. He found two small sconces set on the wall and pulled a flint from his pack.

They pulled off their night vision gear as Jared lit the candles.

"And we have light," he said as a frail brightness stuttered through the cave.

"Let's get Kirin's wound cleaned and wrapped," Rafe said. "Then we can make our plans."

As Jared tended to Kirin, Sahara and the others assembled a meager meal from the lockers at the rear of the cave. There was no fresh water—whatever had been stored in the jars had either evaporated or was brackish and foul.

"So your people built this, then?" asked Brytnoth, as they sat munching their dried meat and fruit.

Sahara shook her head. "No. These caves and tunnels are natural formations, but my people discovered them and made use of them." She added with a wry smile, "I wasn't the first prisoner we had rescued from this place."

"Who was?" Jared asked.

Sahara shrugged. "We had rescue teams who would come here every so often and break people out...mostly dissidents who had been rounded up and shipped off." She glanced around the cave. "Doesn't look like anyone's been here for a while."

"Didn't they destroy your planet?" Kirin asked. "The Drakkin?"

Sahara furrowed her brow. "They destroyed many of my people, but once I was taken prisoner..." She sighed. "I don't know what happened to Amaryl. I don't know what became of the rest of my people."

"They seemed to use a different tactic on your homeworld anyway," Jared remarked. "Killing all the men and leaving just women. Your people would die off on their own, eventually."

"Yes." She chewed thoughtfully on a piece of dried meat, then added bitterly, "I don't know why they did that to us. I don't know why they didn't just destroy everyone...like they did on Askalon, and Silesia."

"Maybe they never did that again because of you," Emma suggested, her voice uncertain as the shadows on the wall. "Because they were afraid there would be more like you."

Sahara glanced at her in surprise. "I hardly think that I would have caused enough trouble for them to change their entire intergalactic policy!" she managed at last, with something like a choking laugh. "But I thank you for the compliment nonetheless."

After their brief meal, they rolled themselves in blankets and slept. Long after she heard the steady, deep breathing of the others, Sahara kept staring at the wall, wondering about what Emma had said.

No, I didn't cause them to change their policy. Brytnoth's people were killed off long before I assassinated the Drakkin Chieftain on Amaryl. And they were destroying Silesia, too. But why Amaryl? Why did they leave the women alone?

She rolled over and stared up at the ceiling, lacing her hands behind her head. *Whatever reasons there might have been, they can't have been good.*

SEVEN

THE SOUND of voices stirred Sahara out of a deep, dreamless sleep. She opened her eyes and turned her head toward the sound. Jared and Rafe were talking in low voices near the door.

"There's something we haven't considered," Jared was saying. "Too many things could go wrong with this plan."

"What's bothering you, Jared? It's not Sahara going in there alone, is it? Because now we're all going. That should make you feel so much better."

There was another silence, one so long that Sahara thought Jared would never answer him.

"No, it's not that." Jared's voice faded almost to a whisper, as though to be sure he wasn't overheard.

"Then what is it?"

"It's just…" A pause. "If we all go in there, Rafe…all of us except Kirin and Emma…" Jared's voice trailed off again.

"I get it," Rafe said. "You think they're going to screw this up." Sahara heard him chuckle. "I don't know why you should worry. A wounded man and a girl with zero combat skills will be entrusted with the mission to secure our only ticket out of here. What could possibly go wrong with that?"

The dripping sarcasm in his voice wrenched Sahara's lips into a grin in spite of herself.

"It's a stupid gamble," Jared said. "And we both know it. If they fail, we're as good as dead...and so are our friends."

Rafe sighed in frustration. "So what's the solution? Sahara has to go in there to start that riot. There aren't enough provisions in this hole to keep all the rest of us alive if this operation takes as long as it could."

"And I really don't think she could start a riot on her own...not in a place this size. We need a coordinated insurgence—that was the reason for the rest of us to infiltrate this cursed facility."

"But that doesn't answer my question, Jared. I get that part of the plan. But someone else has to stay behind to make sure we take the ship. And it's got to be someone..." His voice suddenly trailed off and his head drooped. "Damn. It's got to be me. It's got to be the one person in this mad bunch who knows how to fly."

Jared clapped him on the shoulder. "Thanks for solving the mystery for us, my friend," he said. "And there's no one I'd rather leave behind than you."

Sahara rolled off her mat and joined them.

"He's not being left behind," Sahara said quietly. "He's heading up the other half of this crazy mission." She smiled at Rafe, hoping he understood how much his skills were valued.

"Thanks, Sahara," he said, managing a smile in return. Then he whispered, gesturing toward the far side of the cave, "But I have to stay with those two! Seriously, Jared. You owe me. You owe me big time for this one."

"Put it on my tab," Jared answered with a grin.

"And I didn't think you'd mind staying with Emma," Sahara said, frowning.

Rafe shot her a quick glance. "I...don't. It's not her so much, but..." He fumbled for words, then just shrugged.

Jared, watching his friend with keen interest, said softly, "Oh, let him be, Sahara. He's got to look out for them and make sure we take the ship. I don't envy him the task!"

Even if you got to stay with me? wondered Sahara. *If it was me, not Emma, staying behind?*

Jared's eyes flickered at her, and Sahara knew he had heard her thought. But he made no answer, and that unsettled her even more than her growing suspicion that Rafe's feelings for Emma might not be as strong as she had supposed.

"Brytnoth should stay with you, then," she suggested, trying to disguise her hurt confusion beneath the tinge of venom in her voice. "Jared and I can manage the prison. The real mission here is securing the ship, and we can't afford to jeopardize it by putting all our resources into creating a diversion. Brytnoth can protect the others, and Rafe can focus his attention on the ship."

"I agree with her, Jared," Rafe admitted. "I could use the help. Kirin's mobility is compromised, and Emma doesn't know what to do in these kinds of situations. Not yet, anyway."

Jared thought for a while, rubbing his thumb and forefinger along his jaw. "All right," he said finally. "You and Brytnoth will take the others and secure the ship. Sahara and I will infiltrate the prison."

They set about making their preparations and consolidating their gear, deciding to let the others sleep for a while longer. As they worked, Sahara kept silent, mulling over the conversation.

Why can't things ever be simple? she wondered, absently loading bullets into the magazine of her pistol. *Why does love have to be so complicated? This business with Rafe and Emma now...and...*

She eyed Jared from under her lashes, watching as he expertly rolled and packed his essential gear in Brytnoth's pack. He seemed to be completely unperturbed. And silent.

Silent *inside.*

She turned back to loading weapons and frowned fiercely. He must have figured out a way to block her from seeing his thoughts.

What does that mean? she wondered. And the sudden wave of

fear that washed over her, making her hands shaky and damp, only compounded her confusion.

Her eyes flashed at Jared again and two bullets slipped out of her hand, clinking softly on the stone floor. Jared glanced up at the sound and met her startled gaze. His expression turned quizzical, questioning.

And then the question itself, there in her mind.

What's wrong, Sahara? You look like you've seen....

She rose slowly and backed away from him toward the cave entrance, shaking her head. She couldn't block him. She'd tried.

The pistol in her hand trembled and she slipped it into its holster before she dropped it.

Jared took a pace toward her, his eyes now full of concern.

What is it?

She clapped her hands to her head, and then rushed from the cave, ghosting down the passage. When she reached the end of the tunnel, she sank to the ground, her head buried in her arms.

She would *not* be an open book if he had decided to shut her out. She had to figure out a way to block him, too.

If he doesn't trust me, then I'm not going to trust him either.

Angry tears burned her cheeks, and she let them flow, silent in the dark.

———

Jared stared at the black mouth leading to the tunnel, completely bewildered. Rafe approached and stood beside him, the rag he'd been using to clean his weapon dangling from his hand.

"What's wrong with Sahara?" he asked. "What did you say to her?"

Jared spun to face him. "What did I say? I didn't say anything! Not a thing! Why do you just assume I said something?"

Rafe shrugged. "Well, I never can tell what you say to each other, since you use that weird mind-channel thing. And if she's upset, it must be your fault."

Jared gaped at him. "That's...that's not..." He stopped and frowned.

Is it my fault? he wondered.

"Well, go after her!" Rafe clapped him on the back and propelled him toward the door. "We can't have you two at odds when you're supposed to be infiltrating an enemy prison and starting a riot together."

Jared didn't answer, but allowed himself to be shoved gently out into the tunnel. He paused for a moment in the darkness, listening to the bustle of preparations behind him and the silence ahead of him.

What did I say? He shook his head and ran a hand through his hair. *I didn't say anything!*

But then it dawned on him.

Maybe it's not what I said. Maybe it's the way I said it? Or maybe...maybe it's what I didn't say?

Almost as if on cue, flashes from the morning's conversation flared within his mind. It had never occurred to him that, by learning to control the power of mind-speech on his own, he had left her completely vulnerable. He could block her out, but she couldn't do the same.

He frowned and strode down the passage toward the exit. His paces slowed when he saw a huddled form at the base of the rough rock wall.

"Sahara," he said, resisting the urge to speak directly into her mind. That was something he should no longer take for granted, he realized. He might not be welcome.

She stirred, but didn't look up. "What do you want?" she muttered, her voice dull and resentful.

"I wanted to...to say I'm sorry. For what happened back there."

Her eyes glinted at him in the gloom. "That's nice."

He stood there for a moment, not sure what to say. It was as though they had been transported back in time, back to the moment when he'd first found her, lying in a crumpled heap in the desert sand.

"Well," he mumbled, "I just wanted to say...if you like, I can teach you what I've learned. About the mind-speech thing, I mean. If you like." Inside, he cursed his fumbling awkwardness. He sounded like a schoolboy. And the way she was staring at him—as though her eyes could bore holes straight through him—didn't help his feeling at all.

"Really."

"Why are you talking to me like that?" he finally snapped. "I came down here to apologize and to offer to help you, and you're treating me like...like...well, I don't know what exactly. And I don't understand it at all."

She got slowly to her feet, crossing her arms tightly across her chest. "Stay out of my head, Jared," she said, her voice like ice.

She pushed past him and was soon swallowed by the gloom. Jared stood there, staring after her.

Was that what I think it was? he wondered, stunned. *Did she just say...*

He couldn't even bring himself to finish the thought. Things were spiraling out of control faster than he had imagined possible. She must have jumped to some kind of conclusion about their relationship that had never even occurred to him.

It was so horrible and so unexpected that he had to laugh.

It took so long, he thought. *So long for her to trust me. So long for that spark to become a little fire. And now, for some reason, she's figured she'd better throw water on it and cut her losses. She still doesn't really trust me, even after everything we've been through. If she really trusted me, she'd know that I'd rather cut off my own leg than hurt her.*

He squared his shoulders and followed her up the path.

Well, I'm not going to let her leave without a fight.

When he came back into the cave, he found Brytnoth up and

Sahara, already in a prisoner's jumpsuit, was giving him and Rafe their final instructions.

"...and if you have to get out of here, do it. You can come back for us, if you make it."

"But, Sahara," argued Rafe, "you can't really mean for us to leave you and Jared here! Not really."

She stared at him in stony silence. "I'm sorry," she said, "didn't you hear what I said?"

"She's right, Rafe," Jared said, joining them. "If we fall behind, or if it's a choice between waiting for us and getting the ship, take the ship and go."

"How are we going to communicate with you two?" Brytnoth asked. "How are we supposed to know what to do or what's happening to you?"

"Once the riot starts, you should be able to tell—if all goes according to plan, it should shake everything up," Sahara answered. "Head for the landing platform, secure the ship, and wait for us. Give us until nightfall. If we don't show, then leave without us."

Rafe shook his head in protest, but Sahara squared her shoulders and stared him down.

"I'm heading up the tunnel," Sahara said, turning to Jared. "Follow me tonight. I'll scout things out and meet you in the cell."

Before he could say anything to her, she was gone.

As soon as the swinging curtain was still once more, he swore viciously and ran a hand through his hair.

"What's going on?" Kirin asked from his makeshift cot in the back of the cave. "Is there something that I don't know?"

"We've had a slight change in plans," answered Brytnoth.

Emma stirred and propped herself on an elbow. "What change? What's happening?" She peered around the cave, sleep still clinging to her lashes. "Where's Sahara?"

"She's gone," Jared said flatly.

"Gone!" For not liking Sahara much, the panic in Emma's voice was nearly palpable.

"Gone to the prison, like we agreed," Rafe explained. "Brytnoth and I are staying behind with you and Kirin. We're going to secure the ship as soon as the riot starts."

"So that's the change in plans?" Kirin asked. "We need some babysitters?"

Jared turned on him so fiercely that Rafe and Brytnoth recoiled a few paces. "Damn your idiocy, Kirin! If you hadn't gotten yourself caught and half-killed back there, all four of us would be going into the prison! And if Emma was capable of more than just cooking dinner, we wouldn't need the extra hands to make sure the mission succeeds! So shut your mouth and be thankful we didn't leave the pair of you back at the hut!"

Jared turned on his heel and left the cave, trekking a little way up the tunnel. After a few hundred paces, he stopped and leaned against the wall, rubbing his hands over his face and through his hair. A few moments of silence passed, and then he heard footsteps coming up the tunnel toward him.

"Well, that was something," Rafe remarked, leaning against the wall next to him. "Is there any more of that in there, or can we talk some sense for a minute?"

"I'm fine," Jared growled.

Rafe took a breath. "Look, I know Kirin is annoying as hell sometimes and Emma..." His voice trailed off into an awkward silence. "But we have to work together, Jared. They're survivors...just like everyone we're hoping to rescue." He glanced sidelong at Jared. "They haven't done much to earn our confidence, but try to give them a chance."

Jared sighed. "Sorry, Rafe." He hesitated, wondering if he should explain. If he *could* explain.

"I know," Rafe assured him. "You don't have to say anything. And I can explain it to the crew...as much as they need to know. This is a difficult and dangerous business we're about to undertake, especially for you and Sahara. We all get that. Just keep it together."

Jared gripped his shoulder and flashed him a smile. "You always did know how to reel me back in. Thanks."

"Well, I can string you out too," Rafe said with an answering smile. "But I'll save that for another time. Now let's get you suited up."

EIGHT

IT WAS WORSE than he remembered.

But then, the one and only time he'd been in the prison of K'ilen-fir, he hadn't really been treated like an ordinary prisoner. Now, huddled in the corner of the dank cell that served as their entry point, keen eyes watching the movement of guards patrolling the corridor, he wondered how Sahara had survived.

And where could she possibly have gone? he wondered.

There was no trace of her in the cell. For all he could tell, there was no way out except back the way he had come. He had no sense of time, no sense of direction or location. For a moment, he raged against Sahara for abandoning him in this place, for leaving him without any inkling of where or how to find her again.

She may know this place backwards and forwards, but I sure as hell don't, he thought, the flame of his anger fueled by his uneasiness. *She could've given me some idea of what to do once I got in here if she was planning on just running off.*

He half-expected to hear her answer him. She used to pick up on his thoughts, especially when they were directed toward her. Lately, he'd become guarded about that, and he'd taught himself how to shield his thoughts from her.

He frowned suddenly, remembering how upset she'd been when she'd figured out that he could conceal his thoughts from her.

I shouldn't be surprised that she's not answering me, he told himself. *She probably can't hear me anyway. That, or she's just ignoring me.*

He sighed and waited for a few minutes, hoping that she would reach out to him. But nothing happened. The silence settled around him like a heavy cloak, and his frustration at last hardened into resolve.

Fine. Guess I'll do this my own way, then.

Settling his back more comfortably against the rough stone of the wall, he focused new attention on taking stock again of his surroundings.

The guards.

Sahara had said something about the guards before they'd entered the tunnel. He watched them carefully now, marking the lazy swing of the arms, the slouching gait. His brow knotted as he tried to place the strangeness of the scene unfolding in front of him. And then, as another guard moved past his cell, it swept over him like a Silesian sandstorm.

Human.

They were all human...*too* human. Rogues and ruffians, undisciplined rabble, the lot of them.

His eyes narrowed to slits. *What's happened to...*

So you noticed that, did you?

Sahara's voice, jagged and almost cruel, cut through his own thoughts. The swift blossoming of his relief and joy at hearing her voice withered at her tone.

What the hell is your problem? he demanded. *Where are you? And what happened to this place?*

Whatever my problem is, it's mine, not yours, so don't concern yourself about that. As for me, I managed to infiltrate the women's sector. That's where I am now.

Women's sector? Jared's bewilderment spiked. *They never used to segregate...*

Well, they do now. The lot of fools running the place doesn't seem to know much, but they do seem to have a keen interest in keeping the populations separated. Not sure why yet. Working on it.

But the guards! he said. *What...?*

The place has obviously changed management since you dispatched the Drakkin. I haven't been able to gather much yet...this is a closed-mouth lot. But from what I can tell just by listening to the guards themselves, they've turned this place into a base for some kind of interplanetary slave trade. Slaves sold for profit, I mean...not shipped to labor camps for punishment.

Jared ran a hand through his hair and sighed. She'd been right to notice that something was different, back there before they made their final approach to the prison. He wondered now if they'd made a fatal mistake in coming here at all.

So how does this change things? he asked.

Not sure about that yet, either. See what you can gather from your end. Maybe we'll see each other soon.

I hope so, he said, wondering if she could tell just how much he meant it.

She was striving against him, he could feel it. He felt as distant from her as that very first night they met. But after everything they had been through together, to feel this distance now was so much more painful. It was just one more riddle in the web of riddles that now threatened to entangle him, and unfortunately, it was the riddle that had to wait.

He got to his feet and approached the gridwork of iron bars that separated him from the passageway beyond. He was eyeing the substantial padlock on the door and wondering how he would ever get out when a raucous clanging made him jump back into the dense shadows of the cell.

After a moment, he saw a disheveled and mostly toothless guard approach the door to his cell. The horrible clanging continued, now muffled by the sound of hundreds of feet shuffling down the corridor.

"You want food or don't you?" the guard snarled. Keys rattled in the lock and the door swung open. "Meal time, dog's spawn. 'Less you want me to lock you in again, get out!"

Jared hurried past him and merged with the sea of bodies flowing past his cell. A sense of triumph surged inside him— he was loose, and now he could do what he came here to do.

After what felt like an eternity, the crushing mass around him suddenly slackened and flowed away from him. They had reached a vaulted room of huge proportions. Letting his gaze drift upward as he entered the chamber, Jared could see twisted skeletons of metal jutting from the wall near the ceiling.

They must have blasted this place, he realized. *They blew up part of the prison to make this...* His thoughts trailed off as he sized up the room.

Crude tables were scattered haphazardly around the room. Some had benches. A jostling at one side of the room drew his attention, and he saw what might almost have been a line beginning to form. A moment later, he noticed that those at the head of the line were leaving a ragged hole in the wall with metal trays of food.

"Are you just going to stand there and gawk, or aren't you hungry?"

The voice was light, full of good humor. Jarringly so. Jared turned to face the man standing just behind his right shoulder, everything inside him tensed for a fight.

"Well?"

The speaker was young, maybe in his late teens. Dark, reddish hair fell to his shoulders, and his eyes....

Jared couldn't keep back a small gasp. The young man standing in front of him could have been Sahara's double.

Seeing the change that must have come over Jared's face, the young man frowned. "What? Why are you staring at me like that?"

Jared managed to say, "Do you have a name? And a homeworld?"

The young man shrugged. "Deor, some call me. And when I had a different homeworld than this, it was Amaryl."

Jared's mind raced frantically. *It's her brother. The brother she thought she lost...*

For a split second, he stood, stunned, mind racing, unsure what to do next. Then he made a decision. He took the young man by the elbow and propelled him toward the food line.

"Look, Deor. I'm kind of...new here. You seem to know the ropes. Mind showing me around? Give me the lay of the place?"

"Happy to oblige," Deor said with an easy smile. "But new here? There hasn't been a ship in since a week ago. It's still here, in fact. I saw the crew—"

"That's right. I came in on that ship."

Deor's friendly eyes suddenly narrowed a bit. "I haven't seen you here at the mess before this. I would have noticed."

Jared sighed inwardly.

Pulling one over on this kid just might not be an option...he's too savvy for that. But then, he is her brother. And there's no way that I'll leave him in this place. He might as well know the truth.

"I've got a story," Jared told him, his voice low. "I'd like to tell you...you seem like the sort that would understand. But not here, if you know what I mean."

Deor's expression relaxed a bit and his smile returned. "Of course. No need to explain now."

They reached the window where the food was distributed, and Jared looked with disgust at the nondescript and completely untextured mush the server slapped on his tray. A stale stick of bread clattered down next to it. He must have hesitated too long, because angry murmurs rose behind him and the surly server glowered at him, his battered metal ladle poised threateningly over Jared's left hand.

"Move it along with ye!" he shouted.

Deor, balancing his own tray in one hand, now took the lead, guiding Jared toward a corner of the hall that seemed more thinly populated than the rest of the room.

"Join me at my favorite table, won't you?" he said over his shoulder.

"It has a bench!" Jared exclaimed.

Deor laughed. "Yes, my bench. My table."

Jared looked around and noticed that the other inmates were giving them a wide berth. The table was long—at least ten feet—and not a single soul set his tray on the board.

"You must have had one hell of a turf war to stake this out," Jared said, studying the youth with new appreciation.

Deor shrugged modestly. "Busting a few heads together does wonders. I like my space. And I've made it so they're all happy to let me have it."

He chose a spot midway along the bench and set down his tray. With a sigh, he began propelling the mush into his mouth with the stick of bread. Jared sank down next to him, wondering how he would ever choke the stuff down. He picked up the bread and could get no further.

"It's surprisingly tasty," Deor noted, observing Jared's hesitation. "And anyway, there's no other food. At all. Never changes. Breakfast, lunch, dinner...same mush, same bread."

Jared smiled wanly at him, but still his bread hung poised above the tray. Deor scanned the room and then added, "If you need another reason to force it down, realize that not eating it makes you the object of very unwelcome and unfriendly attention."

That did motivate him. He plowed through the plate, never stopping until it was done. By the end of it, the taste, which hovered just above rancid, was no longer prompting his gag reflex.

"So now you can tell me your story," said Deor. "I know you didn't come off that ship. You look nothing like their kind. Something about the eyes...you're not from their world. So where are you from, then?"

Jared pushed the now-empty tray a few inches further from him. "You don't miss much, do you?"

"No."

Jared sighed. "I'm from Silesia."

"Silesia! Why didn't you say that at the start?"

Jared's gaze snapped to his face. "What difference does it make? What's your interest in my homeworld?"

Deor stared at the table in silence. "I've been here a long time," he confessed at last. "Since the Drakkin ran the place."

"And...?"

"And I've been around long enough to know a lot. Probably more than is good for me."

Jared watched him and waited. Deor didn't fidget like most young men who are forced to talk about something they'd rather keep hidden. Clearly, he had incredible self-control.

He reminds me so much of Sahara.

"They went to Silesia, this last time," Deor said finally, his voice so low it was nearly a whisper. "They all went, and they never came back."

"I know," Jared said, deciding it was time to level. "I'm the one who destroyed them."

NINE

DEOR STARED AT HIM. There was no shock or surprise in the young man's eyes, only a steely keenness. Jared realized that he was being measured, so he met Deor's gaze without flinching away, hoping this simple steadfastness would show Deor that he was telling the truth.

Finally, Deor seemed to return to an awareness of the rest of their surroundings, and he glanced around with a mild curse.

"So if you're the one who dispatched that lot, then what in hell are you doing back here?" he asked.

"They got to my people before I got to them," Jared replied. "Shipped them out on some deep space vessel bound for nowhere. We're going after them, and we needed a ship. So we're here to commandeer one. The one you mentioned before."

"We? Who's *we?*" Deor looked around. "I see only your new face here."

"One of my companions is with the women." He hesitated, and then decided that her identity could wait a bit. "The others are waiting outside the prison."

"Waiting? For what? To get caught?"

Jared managed a smile. "For my signal."

"And that would be...?"

Jared shook his head. He'd already told this kid more than perhaps he should have, and for no other reason than that he was Sahara's brother. But then, perhaps it was worth the risk. He studied Deor for another minute or two and then made the gamble.

"We're going to start a riot." He grinned as Deor's mouth dropped open. *Finally found a way to shock the kid*, he thought and added, "You could help me. And then you could come with me."

"I think you're crazy," Deor said, keeping his voice low. "But then again, if you really did what you claim you did, then I kind of like your breed of crazy." A bright, warm smile suddenly lit up his whole face. "And wouldn't I just love to get out of this hell-hole!"

"We're keeping a low profile for now, trying to get a sense of the place. Who's the new crew in charge of things?"

Deor glanced in the direction of the food line and then at the door, where a few guards slouched about, keeping less than half an eye on the prisoners.

"What a sorry bunch," he muttered. Then he turned back to Jared. "They're slavers," he said simply. "They swooped in here like a bunch of vultures right after the Drakkin fell from power. I think they must have had their eye on this place for a long time. They rearranged things. Remodeled the joint." His eyes skimmed over the eviscerated roof above them. "Anyway, ships have been coming in and out ever since. Some come full and leave empty. Some come empty and leave full." He shrugged. "Sooner or later, everyone gets shipped out. It's just a matter of time."

"Shipped out? Where?"

"Wherever the price has been paid. We're slave labor, remember?"

Jared frowned and rubbed his chin. "So who runs things?" He jerked his head toward the slovenly guards. "Not these idiots."

"No. But I've heard a lot of talk about some group called the Triumvirate. And usually it's interchangeable with the word *boss*."

Jared had just opened his mouth to ask another question when that horrible clanging noise began once again. Obediently, all the prisoners began to shuffle toward the door, choking in a bottleneck as they tried to get through it all at once. As he and Deor moved to join the throng of bodies, Jared managed to get his question out.

"Where are they based?"

Deor glanced at him. "From what I can tell? Askalon."

Later, as Jared sat once more in his cell, his mind whirled from the day's events. It was a day of ghosts, that much was sure. First, to meet Sahara's brother—the brother she thought had been murdered—in this place, at this time…it was incredible. And then to learn that Brytnoth's homeworld of Askalon was the home base for the Triumvirate, a ruthless gang of killers and slave dealers.

But why Askalon?

These kinds of gangs were never random in their choice of base, he knew. They had picked Askalon for a reason.

Something clicked in his mind.

Askalon was a mining world. Its mines were the source of exotic precious metals, like those forged into the blessed weapons they had used to bring down the Drakkin. But something tugged at his mind. It wasn't just rare metals they produced there, though that alone might be enough to tempt gang leaders.

And then, suddenly, the pieces all fell into place.

Askalon's mining trade centered mainly around fuel sources. It was a nexus of the interplanetary energy market. Controlling Askalon meant controlling that market. And that control in turn would go a long way to ensuring the emergence of a new tyranny, one that exerted its power by holding fuel—not water resources—hostage.

He rubbed his hands over his face.

That's not what we came here for, he told himself. *We're not out here to stop some gang takeover of the energy market. We're just here to rescue our people.*

He knew he was trying to convince himself. The truth was, he wanted to take them on…to travel to Askalon and liberate Brytnoth's homeworld and ensure security and freedom for the rest of the planets in their system.

He sighed and lay back in his bunk. *Focus,* he told himself. *Just stay focused.*

———

Sahara frowned so fiercely that the pale, slim figure in front of her seemed to wilt.

"You have no idea?" she demanded. "Are you sure about that?"

"Look, I don't know who you are…" the girl began, blinking her crystal blue eyes rapidly.

"I'm about to be your worst nightmare if you don't start answering my questions."

The girl chewed her lip. "Why are you asking me? Why not one of the others?"

Sahara sighed. She was losing patience, and she was running out of time.

"I know you were on that ship," she said, trying to keep her voice level. "I don't know about the others. So I'm asking you. Where did you come from and why did they bring you here?"

The girl fidgeted and plucked at a loose thread in the thigh of her jumpsuit. "I'm from Aegis. My name's Althea. And I don't know why they brought us here. We knew they were coming. But we didn't have time to prepare. We're a peaceful planet…we have no soldiers, no weapons. Farmers, mostly. You know."

Sahara crossed her arms and paced the floor. Althea had been transferred into her cell just this morning. Sahara hadn't wanted any company and the girl's fragile presence annoyed her.

"Aegis," Sahara repeated. "Who were the men who captured you?"

Althea shrugged again. "Slavers. From Askalon."

Sahara pulled up short and spun to face her. "What did you say?"

She started like a frightened animal. "I said they were slavers from Askalon."

"What's happened on Askalon?" The question came out before she could find a better way to phrase it.

"My father said that things were unstable there," Althea answered. "I heard him tell my mother so. We received a conscription notice from some group called the Triumvirate. They demanded more than half our goods in exchange for peace. We raise wheat and oats, cattle, sheep, horses even...and fruits and vegetables of every kind. Everyone grows enough for himself and to trade. No one is ever lacking. But sending away half of all we produced...we would all starve. So we refused. And then they came."

"They didn't take your whole planet?"

Althea shook her head sadly. "They killed our High King and all his court...the local barons and their wives and children. All gone. They put their own men in charge. They took many of us captive and brought us here. We were made an example for the rest, I guess."

"It's almost worse than the Drakkin," muttered Sahara. "So Aegis is basically now just a fief of these slavers from Askalon."

"They're scouring the system and taking whatever they need or want. They're especially after slave labor, it seems, and food. I heard some of the men talking. It sounded like some other ship had been intercepted a few days before we got here. Men, women, children...all bound now for the mines on Askalon."

Sahara jumped forward and seized the girl by the shoulders. "Did they say anything about that ship? Anything else? Where it was from, perhaps? Anything at all?"

Althea twisted in Sahara's grip. "No! They didn't say! They didn't say! They just said they were happy to pick up the crumbs from the Drakkin' table!"

Sahara let her go and staggered back against the far wall. *It has to be them. Has to be.*

She slid down the wall and pulled her knees up under her chin.

Bowing her forehead, she closed her eyes and took a deep breath. She hated it, but she had to do it.

Jared.

Sahara! There was unmistakable joy in his voice, and she was smiling at him before she could stop herself. *I have a lot to tell you.*

Likewise.

These thugs...they're based out of...

Askalon, she interrupted. *I know. But there's more.*

They're after the system's energy reserves, Jared said. *The Triumvirate.*

Is that what they call themselves? she asked. *Whatever their name is, it seems they also deal heavily in slave labor.*

Yes, exactly, Jared said, his voice urgent. *This is an outpost for them now—a way station and a slave market. There's an auction three days from now, so whatever we're going to do, we'd better do it soon. They're planning to clear us all out...one way or another.*

And once we're clear of this place, I know where we need to go. After we get that ship.

Where?

Arnauld's ship was intercepted by the Triumvirate a little over a week ago. They've been taken to Askalon.

There was a long silence, and then Jared said, *I was hoping to pay Askalon a visit anyway.*

She grinned suddenly, unable to help herself. *You're a man after my own heart. I think we've got the same idea.*

It's got to happen tomorrow, Sahara, Jared said. *We're out of time. And I'm bringing someone else with me.*

Like I said before. A man after my own heart.

She raised her head and looked at the bunk across from her. Althea was perched there, still watching her with those frightened but curious blue eyes.

I'm bringing someone too.

TEN

THE TENSION in the mess hall was almost palpable.

Jared hesitated in the doorway, jostled from behind by several fellow prisoners until they figured out to go around him. He scanned the room, trying to figure out the source of the changed atmosphere. Faces swirling past him were grim. The clatter of trays on stone seemed obnoxiously loud, undulled by gruff conversation.

And then, in a flash, he had it.

The women were in the room.

Almost fifty of them stood at the back of the hall, watching the men cycle through the food line with ill-concealed uneasiness.

What are they doing here? he wondered. *What kind of a game are the guards playing?*

But almost before his mind had framed the question, he knew the answer. She was striding toward him, shouldering through the crowd and oblivious to the angry glares of the men she displaced.

"So there you are. Finally." Her words, blunt like a cudgel, almost seemed to echo in the strangely silent room.

"What are you doing here?" Jared hissed, moving out of the doorway and pulling her aside, gesturing for her to lower her voice.

"This is crazy! Those women will get hurt or killed... This is *not* a good plan! Not a good plan, Sahara."

"We were brought here," Sahara retorted. "What, you thought this was my idea of fun?" She gave a snorting little laugh. "Hardly. But, I think it could prove useful. We needed a spark...this could be it."

Jared's eyes slid away from her face toward the women huddled at the back of the room. "Maybe so." His gaze snapped back to her face. "Why did they bring you here?"

"Boredom, maybe?" She shrugged. "They don't tell us that, Jared. They just order us around."

Jared sighed in frustration. "I know." He hesitated, searching her eyes. "Sahara..."

A sudden commotion from the back of the room drew their attention. A big man, obviously more brawn than brain, was hauling one of the women out of the little cluster. Some of the women were weeping silently. The girl from Sahara's cell was clinging to the woman's hand, trying to hold her back. But the big man jerked her out of the girl's grip and dragged her roughly toward a larger group of men.

The girl fell to her knees, sobbing, holding out her hands, pleading wordlessly.

Jared felt something like an electric charge shiver through Sahara. Her eyes flashed at him, burning with cold fire.

"It starts now."

Before he could open his mouth, she was through the crowd, sliding over a table and sending trays crashing to the floor. She landed just in front of the big man, and he recoiled in surprise as she straightened and folded her arms across her chest.

"You really don't want to mess with her," Sahara said, her voice like ice.

Jared shoved his way through the mass of bodies, trying to keep her in sight. By now, a ring was forming around the knot of players, and Jared knew they hoped there would be sport or blood...or both.

"Who the hell are you?" growled the man, tightening his grip on the girl's wrist.

Sahara shrugged, then planted her right foot squarely in the center of his chest. With an explosion of air and a gasping croak, he flailed wildly, losing his hold of the girl. He staggered backward, falling over a bench with a crash.

"Get out of here!" Sahara shouted at the dazed girl. She gave her a shove in the direction of the knot of women, and then turned again to face her opponent.

He had managed to extricate himself from the toppled bench, and he clenched his hands into fists, cracking the knuckles.

"You've got yourself into a mess, little girl," he growled. "And now you're going to pay."

Jared, pushing through to the front of the ring, saw her toss her head and grin.

"Let's see you try and make me," she retorted.

Her eyes, flitting around the circle of men around them, suddenly lighted on Jared's face. As soon as her gaze locked with his, sadness welled up in their depths.

See? her voice murmured inside his head. *You don't want me. I'm dangerous. You should just stay away.*

He could find no words to say. So many images and moments flooded his mind that he knew he could never express them in words. He watched her helplessly, hoping that she could sense the outpouring of feeling, that it would strengthen her somehow.

The man lumbered toward her. Watching the man's clumsy movements, Jared knew that the fight was over before it had even begun, but the certainty did little to allay his fears.

Sahara sidestepped the man's first attempt to pound her sense-less, her cold gaze following him as his momentum carried him a few stumbling steps past her. Then, almost casually, she buried her elbow in his kidneys and swiped his legs out from under him. He sprawled on the floor, smashing his nose into the stone. Blood gushed from the split skin of his nose and lower lip, and the crowd around them began to chant.

"Blood...blood...blood...blood..."

Jared's whole body tensed. It wouldn't take much to push this crowd over the edge.

I know that's the point, but she could get herself killed, he thought. The idea made his hands slick with sweat.

He met Sahara's gaze again, saw no traces of sadness left, just a quiet intensity that chilled him to the core. Then her attention was back on her work.

"Get up." Her well-aimed kick into his ribs made him grunt. "Get. Up. Or don't you want to fight anymore, little girl?"

The man groaned as he pushed himself to his knees. His face was a mess of blood, and a couple of his front teeth hung by scant threads.

"Bors has had enough," another man said. He stepped forward from the knot of men. "I'll take his place. And I'll make you regret it, too."

Jared swallowed. *This one is different.*

The man's movements were lithe, betraying an agile strength that had none of Bors's oafishness. His eyes were cold and calculating. Sahara swept a quick, critical gaze over him.

"You got a name?" she said.

"Eorlan."

Jared never saw clearly what he did. But he watched, horrified, as Sahara staggered and fell. A roar went up from the crowd around him and he felt them press forward. The chanting grew louder as Eorlan moved to stand over Sahara's prostrate form. He kicked her over onto her back and then clucked his tongue.

"A pity," he murmured. "Such a pretty face."

Eorlan knelt beside her and raised his clenched fist. But before he delivered the final blow, he glanced up, a self-satisfied smirk on his face, to drink in the adulation of the blood-hungry mob.

The frenzied chanting grew louder still, until the stone chamber echoed with it.

Eorlan turned back to his victim, and started with surprise. Sahara was watching him calmly, with something like a smile tugging at her lips.

"What...?" he started, his fist dropping just a fraction.

Her leg slammed into the side of his head, sending him flailing into the overturned bench. The edge of the bench caught him under the arm, popping the shoulder out of joint. He howled with pain, and a string of curses dribbled from his mouth with a ribbon of saliva.

Sahara got to her feet, facing the remaining men in Bors's gang.

"Anybody else want to dance?" she asked.

With a roar, they all rushed at her. But the larger crowd that had gathered was on Sahara's side, wanting to see her fight another bout. Jared was nearly lifted off his feet as the press of bodies around him surged forward, breaking through the knot of men attempting to encircle Sahara. As soon as they broke through the ring, Jared leaped forward and seized Sahara's arm. Fists began flying all around them, and they vaulted over a table and ran to the far side of the room.

"Wait!" Sahara shouted.

Before Jared could respond, she darted back to the group of women, snatched one of the girls by the hand, and dragged her back to where he was waiting. Without questioning her, he turned and led the way toward the entrance.

They had almost reached the passage back to the prison wing when someone stepped from the shadows to block their path.

"Planning on going somewhere?"

It was Deor.

Jared grabbed his arm and propelled him through the exit. Sahara and the girl followed on their heels. They sprinted down the passage toward Jared's cell and the tunnel back to the outside world.

The raucous clanging of alarm bells erupted all around them. Guards careered past them, everyone shouting orders and no one stopping to listen. Prisoners banged on the iron grates that held them, alternately shouting curses and pleas for freedom. Somewhere behind them, one of the gates, a rusted and twisted shadow of its former self, burst free of its hinges with a deafening clang, and the roar of angry voices swelled in sudden triumph.

"Keep running!" Sahara shouted. "This is about to get really ugly!"

Taking the twists and turns of the corridor at full tilt, they soon distanced themselves from the mob, which was surging toward the mess hall to join in the chaos there. Before long, they were standing, panting and sweating, in front of Jared's cell.

"Keys!" he shouted, kicking the bars. "We don't have the damn keys!"

Without a word, Sahara sprinted back down the corridor.

"Where does she think she's going?" Deor asked. "She's going to get herself killed!"

"She's going to get the keys off one of those guards back there," Jared answered.

Deor snorted. "You can't be serious."

Jared's eyes flickered up to meet Deor's, and he smiled mirthlessly. "You don't know her."

Within a few minutes, Sahara was back, holding a ring of keys in her hand.

"It's perfect," she told Jared, unable to hide her grin of pleasure. "The whole place is in total uproar. I just hope the others figured out what's happening and have headed for the platform."

Jared cycled through the keys until he found one with a death's head embellishing the bow. He shoved it into the lock and forced it open. Stepping quickly into the cell, he jerked his head toward the back corner.

"Let's go. Exit's that way."

As soon as they had all filtered into the cell, he slammed the gate shut behind them and reached through the bars to relock it. Then, tossing the keys into the corner of the cell, he followed Deor and the others through the escape shaft.

ELEVEN

THEY COULD HEAR the commotion before they had even reached the entrance of the tunnel.

Sahara held up a hand as they neared the open mouth in the rock, peering out to see if they had a clear path toward the landing platform. The alarms that were going off inside the prison were reverberating through the valley, and she could see men sliding down the rocky hillside that separated them from the river. The pouring rain was pooling at the tunnel entrance.

"There's enough chaos that we shouldn't be noticed...much," she said, pulling her head back inside the tunnel. "Stay alert and watch for my signals. Ready?"

She slipped outside and beckoned for them to follow her. They moved at a rapid pace, keeping behind cover as much as possible without appearing to seek concealment. The last thing Sahara wanted was to attract unwanted attention by looking like they were sneaking around.

All of a sudden, she jerked to a halt, heart hammering.

She threw up her hand, fist closed, and dropped back behind a large stone outcropping. The others crouched beside her, rain streaming down their faces.

What is it? came Jared's voice inside her head, while the others watched her with the same question in their eyes.

With a flare of annoyance, she remembered that she still hadn't figured out how to block him.

Guardians.

In a moment, they all saw what she had seen. A dozen Guardians rushed past their position. Their handlers, jerking and hauling on the chains that encircled their throats, skidded and slipped behind them in a jumbled mass.

Jared and Sahara exchanged glances.

That's one way to end a riot, Jared said.

At least they're single-minded, Sahara replied. *Or we'd be suffering the same fate.*

Her mouth flattened into a tight line. Death at the jaws of the Guardians would be painful and gruesome. With a shake of her head, she dismissed the images that were quickly forming inside her mind, images that made her hands cold with sweat and her heart pound.

As soon as the Guardians were well past their position, she led them on again. As they came within a few hundred yards of the platform, she launched into a full run.

I just hope Rafe and the others can cover our approach, she thought.

Just ahead of her, the hut squatted in the mud, exactly as she remembered it. She glanced toward it, saw the door ajar and the caged yards empty beyond. The plan had done its job. Their way was clear

With a clatter, they swarmed up the rusted-out stairs and out onto the platform. In a blur, she saw Kirin's face crease with relief as they appeared. He lowered his weapon and beckoned them toward the open door of the ship.

"Go, go, go!" he yelled.

The ship's engines flared and roared, setting the platform humming beneath her feet.

Kirin followed the others inside, but Sahara hesitated, covering her ears and glancing back for one moment toward the prison. Part of her wished they had been able to save more of them. Faces of the women she had met there flashed through her mind, and she shook her head.

It's a damn shame. May they be at peace.

"Sahara!" Jared shouted. "Let's get out of here!"

She jerked her head inside the ship and Kirin closed the door.

"All here?" she asked.

"All here," he answered.

Rafe's voice came over the com as Kirin led them down the corridor toward the bridge.

"Take your seats and hold on to something. And Jared, get up here and tell me where I'm going!"

They stumbled into the crew seats in the cockpit as the ship lifted off, hurtling toward the void of space. Jared planted himself in the co-pilot's seat.

"Set the coordinates for Askalon," he told Rafe.

Rafe started. "Askalon?"

"Who said anything about Askalon?" Brytnoth asked, entering the crew bay.

"Where've you been?" Sahara asked. "I thought we'd left you back there!"

"Gun turret. Just making sure no one thought to hinder our progress." He strapped in next to Sahara. "All clear, Rafe. Nothing's after us."

"So why are we going to Askalon?" Rafe persisted.

"That's where they are," Jared said. "Our people. They were taken by the Triumvirate and shipped to Askalon."

Brytnoth stared at him, bewildered. "The who? There's no such thing as the Triumvirate on Askalon."

"There is now."

A few minutes of silence passed as the sky darkened rapidly ahead of them, heading into the black beyond. Once they'd broken clear of K'ilenfir's atmosphere, Rafe punched in the coordinates for Askalon, set the autopilot controls, and unbuckled his harness.

"Let's head to the mess," he said. "There's food and drink and a table. Seems you all have a lot to share."

———

Kirin led the way through the ship to the kitchen and mess hall. While the others settled themselves around the large, round table in the center of the room, Emma and Brytnoth headed into the kitchen to prepare a meal.

"Well, I just hope that's the last time I ever have to set foot on that cursed moon!" Sahara said, heaving a sigh and running a hand through her hair. "I'm tired of that place!"

"You and me both."

Sahara's attention snapped to her right, where Deor sat, arms folded across his chest.

"Who the hell are you?" she snapped.

"I might ask you the same thing."

Deor seemed totally unphased by her tone, but Jared saw Sahara's brow darken and knew that she was taking his flip attitude as a challenge. Before she could open her mouth and escalate the situation, Jared decided it was time to intervene.

"Who's your friend, Sahara?" he asked. He gestured toward the girl who sat huddled and trembling in the seat to Sahara's left.

Sahara glanced at her and shrugged. "She's from Aegis. Came in on that slave ship that just arrived..." She suddenly paused, glancing at the girl. "This ship, in fact."

That explains the shivering, Jared thought, feeling a surge of sympathy for the girl. "What's your name?" he asked her.

"Althea," she answered, her voice barely more than a whisper.

She turned bright blue eyes from Jared to Sahara and back again. "Who *are* you people? Where did you come from?"

"We're from Silesia," Sahara answered.

"So you're the one, then," the young man interrupted. "The one he told me about."

"What did he tell you about me?"

The youth shrugged. "He just said you were the other one…the one who would help him start that prison riot. And that's exactly what you did. A piece of work, that. You must be proud."

Sahara grinned. "Well, it wasn't as elegant a plan as I originally had in mind, but it worked. And that's all that matters."

At that moment, Brytnoth and Emma entered, carrying loaded trays. Emma handed around mugs of some strong-smelling brew while Brytnoth set plates of bread, dried meat and fruit, and hunks of buttery cheese on the board.

"These slavers don't deprive themselves much, do they?" Kirin asked, smelling some of the cheese and then tasting it. "Where did they get all this?"

"They raid every planet, not just for slaves," Althea told him, her voice a little stronger. "When they came to Aegis, they took most of our harvest—grain, malted ales, dense fruited breads. My people were left desolate."

"So who are these slavers?" Brytnoth asked. "And why are they on my homeworld?"

"Before we get to that," Sahara interrupted, "I want to know who *he* is." She pointed at Deor, then turned to Jared. "You brought him. Care to introduce him?"

Jared thoughtfully rotated his mug on the table, considering.

"He doesn't need to introduce me," the young man said. "People call me Deor."

Jared's eyes snapped to Sahara's face, saw the color drain from her cheeks. At the same moment, with his hyper-awareness of her internal state, he felt the shiver of recognition run through her.

"And...your homeworld?" Sahara asked, her voice brittle and hoarse.

Deor shrugged. "The Drakkin took me when I was a baby. I've had many homeworlds...but I've been on K'ilenfir for the last two years."

Jared watched Sahara process the information. "How old...?"

Deor shrugged again. "Near as I can guess? Eighteen."

"That must've been a brutal life, friend," Brytnoth said.

Deor smiled, a sharp, desolate smile. "You can't possibly imagine."

Without another word, Sahara pushed her chair away from the table and left the room.

"What's...?" Rafe began, looking at Jared.

Jared shook his head briefly and rose to follow her.

He found her back in the crew seats, staring out the cockpit window at the star-strewn blackness.

"Why didn't you tell me it was him?" she murmured without turning around. "Why didn't you tell me you had found him?"

Jared sank down in the seat beside her. "I was trying to wait for the right moment," he answered awkwardly.

She studied him then, tears in her eyes. "The right moment? What would have been the right moment to tell me that the brother I thought I had lost was alive?"

"I just thought...once we were away from the prison...once the plan had succeeded...."

Sahara watched him, shaking her head until he finally stopped, feeling like a hopeless and total failure.

"No, Jared."

"I didn't know how it would affect...." He knew as soon as the words slipped out of his mouth that he had made a mistake.

"What's that supposed to mean?" The tears in her eyes were gone, and they were hard as steel now. "You think I would have compromised the mission? You think I'm that foolish? Really?"

"No, that's not what I meant! I—"

She stared him down. "You *did* mean it," she insisted. "That's exactly what you thought. I thought you trusted me...and I thought you knew me better than that."

Jared sat there, feeling more and more wretched, fighting back the words he wanted to say. *I'm the one who isn't trusting? It's all right for you not to trust me, but it doesn't go both ways?*

In the end, all he said was, "I'm sorry, Sahara."

"Yeah."

She turned away from him again, and he felt, though she didn't say so, that he was no longer welcome.

"I'm sorry," he repeated softly, then rose. As he ducked under the bulwark and left the cockpit, he thought he heard her sobbing.

TWELVE

WHEN SHE REJOINED the group half an hour later, they were discussing the prison riot.

"...she just laid the big guy out flat," Deor was saying, a huge smile on his face. "Couldn't have done it better myself."

They all fell silent as she resumed her seat.

"Everything okay?" Brytnoth asked.

"Fine," she said tautly.

Her face felt hot and swollen, and she hoped it wasn't totally obvious that she'd been crying. She hazarded a glance at Brytnoth. Their eyes met, and she knew he wasn't convinced. But he was silent, and she realized with profound gratitude that he had enough sense—or kindness—not to pursue the subject.

"I was just telling your crew about your legendary brawl back at the prison," Deor said.

Sahara shot him a sharp glance, and she could see out of the corner of her eye that Jared had reacted in exactly the same way. "*My* crew?" she asked.

"Yeah, your crew. From what they tell me, I gather it's not the first time you've pulled a stunt like that."

Sahara dropped her eyes, but couldn't help peeking at Jared from under her lashes. His expression was blank, but with just a little reach of her consciousness, she could feel the roiling conflict within him.

She understood how he must be feeling. To her, this had always been Jared's crew. He was in charge of operations, not her.

So why did Deor assume that I'm in command here? she wondered. And she knew that Jared must be wondering the same thing.

"You wanted to know about Askalon," Sahara said, turning to Rafe and deciding it was best to steer the conversation in a new direction. "Now's as good a time as any to let you all in on what we know."

"Askalon's been overrun by some kind of gang," Jared said, rousing himself with a sigh. "They're the new crew in charge of the prison, and they seem to be masters of the slave trade. But I have a suspicion that they're into something else as well, and I think the slave trade is their means of finding labor as well as funding their other operations."

"They seem to be just as brutal as the Drakkin ever were, if that's possible," Sahara added. "And, from what Althea's told us, they're just as hell-bent on terrorizing every planet in the system and abusing resources for their own ends."

"The Drakkin were focused on domination," Jared said. "They wanted us all wiped out, except those they could easily enslave and use for their own ends. They worked toward that goal systematically. But the situation with this gang is different. We're dealing with a human element—a scurrilous element, to be sure, but a very, very human one nonetheless. They aren't dedicated to a program of extermination."

"What drives them, then?" asked Brytnoth. "And what does Askalon have to do with all this?"

"They want money, power, control. And that's why they need Askalon." Jared turned to Brytnoth. "You said yourself that it was a mining world, rich in natural resources. Am I remembering this right?"

Brytnoth nodded. "Our planet holds the largest reserves of fuel in the system. Before our world was broken, the Lords of Askalon mined the fuel strategically, providing plenty for all while still preserving the other resources of our planet. We had priceless stones in abundance, precious metals, and marbles for carving. Artisans came from all over the system to study under our masters." He shook his head sadly. "The Drakkin destroyed all of that. They killed our Lords and countless others...and you know where the remnant of us ended up. I thought I was the only survivor."

"But where did this gang come from?" Kirin asked. "And how did they get so powerful?"

"The Drakkin set up the Triumvirate to manage things after they had destroyed Brytnoth's people," Deor answered, and the certainty in his voice made them all turn to look at him. "The Drakkin needed the resources to fuel their armies and maintain their control, but they couldn't be bothered to oversee things themselves. Once the Drakkin were destroyed, it would have been an easy thing for the Triumvirate simply to step into the void."

"So what's their plan, do you think?" Rafe asked.

"Think about it," Jared replied. "If they control the fuel reserves —if they dominate the market—then they can dictate interplanetary trade."

Everyone was silent for a few minutes, considering what such control would mean, both for those doing the controlling and for those being controlled.

"But Jared," Sahara protested, "there are fuel reserves on other planets. They can't have completely cornered the market...at least, not yet."

"I suspect that's why they need so many slaves," he said. "I'm sure that they're building alliances and making arrangements—peaceful or otherwise—with any other planet that might threaten their monopoly. And if they can't get the resources by stealing, then they'll buy them out. They'll provide the labor force and mine them dry."

"Extraordinary," murmured Kirin.

"What is?" asked Jared.

"Well, first of all, that you've thought all this out. But secondly, I'm just still marveling that they could have established this amount of control in such a short amount of time."

Jared rubbed his chin thoughtfully.

"It really does push the limits of the believable, Jared," Rafe said. "I mean, to assume that they've gotten all this off the ground so quickly."

"But they were already off the ground," Sahara said. "Deor just said that they were set up to do exactly this sort of work by the Drakkin. Who's to say they weren't cutting deals and making plans of their own even while the Drakkin were still in power? We conveniently eliminated the only thing that was standing in their way. I'd be willing to bet that the Triumvirate had a plan for overthrowing the Drakkin' regime themselves...we just beat them to it."

Rafe shook his head and laughed grimly. "Ironic, isn't it?"

"What is?" Brytnoth asked.

"We worked so hard to destroy the Drakkin to free our people...and now our people have been enslaved by the very bunch we propelled to power when we killed the Dragon. Turns out that we really didn't free them at all...we just changed their masters."

No one had much to say after that, and one by one, they filtered away from the table. After a few minutes, only Sahara and Deor were left, measuring each other.

"Why did you leave before?" Deor asked finally. "And why are you looking at me like that?"

"I'm just..." She hesitated, not even sure how to begin this conversation. "It's hard to believe, that's all."

"What is?"

Sahara shook her head. "I'm really not even sure how to break this to you," she confessed.

Deor's eyes narrowed slightly, and Sahara noticed that his hand, resting on the table, suddenly clenched into a fist. "Break what to me?"

She studied him, her eyes fixed on his—so much like her own, so familiar and yet so strange. "I'm...you're...you're my brother, Deor," she said.

He sat motionless. So motionless that she wasn't sure he had heard her.

"Did you..." she began.

He cut her off. "I heard you well enough. I just don't exactly believe you."

She couldn't fault him for that. He'd been just a baby when the Drakkin had taken him away. They had assumed that he'd been killed, like so many of the others. Her mother had died believing it.

She swallowed hard against the tension in her throat.

"I know you don't believe me," she said. "But it's true anyway. We all thought you were dead. They took so many, killed so many. We never knew. Father would have...I would have...we would have found you, Deor. If we had known you were alive." She met his steady gaze again, tears filling her own in spite of her efforts. "I hope you know that."

He arched an eyebrow. "I don't know anything," he said matter-of-factly. "Family's never even been on my radar. I don't even know what that would be like."

Sahara studied the table, not daring to meet his gaze. "Maybe it's better that way," she mumbled. "Lot of good it did me."

"You have no idea what you're talking about." His voice was level, but full of so much power that she felt crushed by it. "None."

Her fingers stirred on the table, a helpless little gesture. She had never felt so out of control in a situation. She wanted him to believe in the love their family had shared before everything had fallen apart. She wanted to believe in it herself.

"Maybe...and maybe not," she managed. "All I know is that..."

"You want to know what my childhood was like?" Deor cut her off. "I was raised to be a house slave—a servant to the Drakkin chieftains on some backwater planet halfway across the system. I was raised with a dozen other wretches. I guess they must have picked them up here and there. We were beaten a lot, fed just enough to keep us alive. I never saw another human being smile at me until I was eight."

The flood-tide of his story came to a sudden halt, and Sahara lifted her eyes to his face. His jaw was set in a line, his eyes fixed on some point behind her. She waited, breathless, for him to continue.

"I'll never forget her face. They killed her, eventually. She was too high-spirited for them. They couldn't break her down...so they cut her down." Realizing that she was watching him, he focused on her face once more. "After that...well, let's just say that I made up my mind to make them pay."

"What did you do, Deor?" Sahara murmured. "What did you do?"

"By the time I was eleven, I had earned my way to the position of page. By sixteen, I was the Chieftain's personal runner. And one night, I ran him through with his own sword."

Sahara swallowed, hard. "And that's what got you sent to K'ilenfir, isn't it?"

He nodded. "That's right." A pause. "How did you know?"

"Because I got sent there for the same reason."

He stared at her for a few seconds, and then broke out laughing. "No kidding?"

She smiled then. "No kidding. But I'd been trained for it. Father trained me...before he was killed by the Drakkin. Then we trained ourselves. There were no men left on our homeworld, Deor. We had to do something to save ourselves."

"What happened to Mother?"

Sahara steeled herself, tightening her grip on her quavering feelings. "She died, Deor. Just after they took you away. It killed her."

He said nothing for a long time, but stared at the table as though his gaze could burn a hole through it. "It's a lucky thing for them that you destroyed them already," he said finally. "Because I wouldn't have done it so quickly."

He rose suddenly and left the room, leaving her alone with her thoughts and memories.

A horrible burning seared her gut, like her heart was crying and she couldn't do anything to stop it. She didn't know why she had expected him to be different. But remembering him as a baby—his sweet disposition, his smile—and seeing him now, a ruthless killer... It broke her heart all over again.

"It's exactly what they did to you," said Jared, coming into the room and sitting down in the seat Deor had vacated.

Her head snapped up and she glared at him. "How did you know what I was thinking?"

Jared shrugged. "I didn't read your mind, if that's what you're asking. It doesn't take mind-reading to figure out how you must feel right now."

"How do you know so much about him? How do you know what they did to him?"

"He told us his story while you were gone."

She pursed her lips, fighting tears and grief with anger. "It's like he's died all over again," she said. "Like they just...just killed him right in front of my eyes."

"I know."

"No, you don't know!" she snapped. "How could you possibly know? How could you possibly understand?"

"They killed my family too, remember?" His voice was so steady, so calm. It infuriated her.

"Not like this, they didn't," she retorted. "They didn't take your family from you and make them into monsters." Her breathing came ragged and shallow, her breast heaving.

Jared studied her and sighed. "They made us all monsters, Sahara. We all had to become something else in order to survive."

"You didn't!" she protested fiercely. "You're no monster! But Deor...and I..." She couldn't bear to look within herself, so she looked into Jared's eyes instead. "You have to stay away from me...from us," she whispered. "We're dangerous."

"Sahara..." he began, but she waved a hand and cut him off.

"Stay away. Just stay away."

THIRTEEN

JARED SAT for a long time with his head in his hands. He had sensed that a rift was growing between him and Sahara, and now it seemed an impassable chasm. He had a vague feeling that it was fed by some kind of profound misunderstanding, but he didn't even know how to begin analyzing her motives. He didn't know if he wanted to try anymore.

A light touch on his shoulder made him start, and he wondered for a moment if he'd fallen asleep. He looked up and saw Althea standing beside him.

"You seem troubled," she said. He stared at her blankly, and she gestured to the chair beside him. "May I join you?"

He shrugged and sighed, rubbing his hands over his face and through his dark hair. "Suit yourself."

She sank into the chair, her eyes never leaving his face. She was so silent, and for so long, that finally Jared said irritably, "What do you want?"

"Oh." The shadow of a frown crossed her brow and then was gone again. "I was just wondering...I mean...I'm not really sure what I'm doing here."

Jared shrugged again. "You should ask Sahara that question, not me. She's the one who brought you along."

Althea's smooth brow creased again. "That wasn't very nice, Jared."

"What?" The word came out like a bark of amazed laughter. "Not very nice?"

"No, not nice." She looked all the world like a mother scolding a child, and Jared found himself staring at her in disbelief, a feeling that grew as she continued speaking. "You took me away from my people..."

"I'm sorry, those scurrilous slave traders did that, not us," Jared interrupted.

She shook her head, her blue eyes sharp with reproof. "There were plenty of us there in the prison," she said. "And now I'm going...I don't even know where I'm going. Or why."

His short laugh was incredulous, and he shook his head. "Well, I beg your pardon for saving your ungrateful self from a slave auction," he said, a harshness that he couldn't check coloring his words. "And you do know where we're going. We're headed for Askalon. But I'll be happy to leave you at the next refueling stop. Just let me know."

"It's not that I'm not grateful!" Althea protested. "But you have to understand..."

"I don't understand. Not even the slightest little bit. Now, if you'll excuse me." He stood abruptly and headed for the door.

"I'm not a warrior, Jared," she said from behind him. "So what use am I to you?"

The irony of it all.

"I'll figure something out," he answered, never turning around.

Unbelievable, he thought as he made his way toward the bridge. *What the hell am I supposed to do with all these confused and maladjusted people?*

He pushed open the door to the bridge and found Rafe alone, leaning back in the captain's chair with his boots crossed and his hands laced behind his head.

"What the hell, Rafe," he muttered, dropping into the co-pilot's seat.

Rafe sat up, a grin creasing his face. "Trouble with the ladies, Jared?" he asked.

"That really isn't funny right now," Jared growled, but he couldn't keep himself from grinning back at his friend. "How'd you guess?"

Rafe laughed. "Well, let's see. Sahara's been in some kind of funk for days, and it gets worse whenever you're around. And the new girl is enough to drive anyone mad."

"Did she bother you, too?" Jared asked. "Did she honor you with her whole '*Why did you take me away from all my friends before I could be auctioned off as a slave?*' speech?"

"Yes. I told her to talk to you. Because you're in charge."

"Well, I sent her to talk to Sahara." The thought made him laugh. "Oh, how I would love to eavesdrop on that conversation!"

Rafe laughed with him for a moment, but then his face grew serious. "It is odd, though, you have to admit."

"What is?"

"That Sahara rescued her in the first place. It's the same with Emma. Sahara doesn't seem to like her much, but she doesn't let anything happen to her, either. She could have left her back there on K'ilenfir, you know? When Emma broke down and wouldn't leave the hut. I thought she was just going to walk away."

Jared shook his head, feeling the sorrow creep back into his heart. "Then you don't really know her, Rafe."

"Well, that's probably true."

Jared sat for a long time without saying anything, staring out the window into the void. "She thinks she's some kind of monster," he said finally.

Rafe glanced at him in surprise. "Really?"

"You remember how she never quite fit in at home. It got to her. Everything that's happened to her...everything she's done...it's gotten into her soul somehow, and I don't think she can forgive herself."

"What's to forgive? She's strong—she's a fighter. A survivor. That deserves respect, Jared."

"I know that, but she doesn't see it that way. She thinks she should be shunned. I don't know what to do, Rafe. I've tried to love her. You know how hard I've tried. I thought it would make a difference. But now that Deor is here..."

"That does seem to have made things worse," Rafe agreed. "Why is that, exactly?"

"I forgot that you didn't know." Jared hesitated for a moment, then said, "He's her brother."

"Her *what?*"

"Her brother. She thought he'd been killed by the Drakkin when he was just a baby. All these years, she thought he was dead. And now she finds out his story...all the things he's had to do to survive. You heard what he said. But now she's taken that on herself as well— like it's some kind of family badge of shame or something. Like they're monsters together, and if we know what's good for us, we'll shun them before we become corrupted."

"Because we're such angels," Rafe quipped, and then he added with a frown, "Jared, that's crazy talk. Doesn't she realize how crazy that is?"

"No, I don't think so. I'm just not sure how much more I can take, Rafe. She won't let me love her. She won't believe she deserves to be loved at all. What will it take for her to realize she's worth it?"

Rafe rubbed his stubbled jaw. "I don't know what it'll take. Maybe it's just time for you to let her go." A pause. Don't look at me like I've just punched the wind out of your lungs."

"But..."

"But nothing. She has to find her own way out of this, Jared. You can't make that journey for her. We destroyed the Drakkin, but that wasn't enough. She has to accept who she is and realize that, as she is, she deserves to be loved and respected."

Jared swore softly. "I know you're right. But still."

Rafe laid a hand on his shoulder. "You'll see. She'll figure it out someday. And when she does, you'll be right there on the other side waiting for her. She's got to walk through that fire herself. Just step back and let her do it."

———

Two days later, they landed on the tiny planet of Gladius, the final refueling station before their deep space run to Askalon. They stepped out onto the space dock and stood there for a moment, looking out over the vast city-world sprawling beneath them.

"This place looks rough," Brytnoth remarked.

Crowds of dirty, ragged people thronged through the narrow sandstone streets. Scrawny stray dogs and cats scurried underfoot, scrounging for bits of food that fell from vendors' tables. Bread-sellers balanced long stakes speared through dozens of flat loaves, and Sahara could see them bobbing high above the heads of the crowd. Intermixed with the din of fruit merchants and bead peddlers came a steady noise, a rhythmic thudding that seemed to come from somewhere beneath their feet.

"What is that horrible noise?" Rafe asked. "It's like being inside a drum."

"The wells," Deor answered.

"What?" Rafe cupped a hand around his ear. "Not sure I caught that."

"It's the fuel wells," Deor repeated, the glint of a smile in his eyes. "Down there, about a mile beneath our feet, is a second city...it's where all the fuel mining takes place. The pumps work constantly. And that's the noise you're hearing."

"How do you know this?" Althea asked.

Deor glanced at her and then shrugged. "I spent some time here a few years ago. Got to know some people." He moved out ahead of them and beckoned them forward. "Follow me. And stay close. Brytnoth's right...this place is rough."

Sahara watched Deor stride away, totally in his element. Her baby brother wasn't a baby any longer, and, with a sick feeling in her stomach, she realized that the people he had gotten to know were probably the roughest of this rough lot.

She heaved a sigh and then flushed as she realized that Jared was watching her, sadness and pity mingled in his eyes. He held her gaze for a moment and then turned away, following Deor into the stone jungle of the city.

Sahara stared after them, the two men that meant more to her than her own life's blood. She knew that Jared had sensed her troubled feelings.

And he just walked away.

He had never walked away from her before. He had always reached out to her, offering words of encouragement that only she could hear. His silence was as deafening as the wells under their feet.

"Let's go," Rafe said from beside her.

She managed to smile at him, then trailed after the group as they clattered down the steps to the street below.

Deor seemed utterly sure of his direction, in spite of the complete labyrinthine layout of the city. The sandstone walls of the buildings rose two and three stories high, sometimes higher, on both sides of the street. Small windows cut narrow chinks in the stone, and the doorways were little more than larger holes in the rock. Everything about the place felt oppressive. Even the light seemed to have the same dirty hue as the stone, thanks to the cloak of fine dust and smoke that shrouded the sky and the sun.

"What a wretched place," Sahara muttered to herself.

After the better part of an hour, the steady thrum of the wells had faded into the background, no longer setting her teeth and nerves on edge. Althea stumbled behind her, and she turned just in time to see Emma catch the girl's hand and speak softly to her. A tide of bitterness suddenly swelled into her throat and she opened her mouth to snap at them. But then she snapped her mouth shut, swallowed the hurtful words, and hurried to catch up with Jared and Deor.

As soon as she came level with them, Deor stopped abruptly and turned to the left.

"Here we are," he said.

The group clustered around him and stared up at the doorway, indistinguishable from the others but for a series of strange carvings set in the stone lintel.

"What does it say?" Kirin asked. "Where have you brought us?"

"It's the closest thing that passes for a tavern on this world," he said and led the way inside.

If the air had been stuffy and thick outside, it was nothing compared to the stifling and oppressive half-darkness inside the tavern. It stopped Sahara in her tracks, and she had to pause for a few moments to catch her breath and let her eyes adjust to the gloom.

The tavern was mostly empty, save for a few ragged men hunched over tankards along the far wall. No one looked at them, and silence, thick as the stale air, hung about them.

"Deor!" she heard someone shout. "I never thought I'd see you again, my boy!"

She hurried forward to rejoin the group at the bar. Deor and the wiry barkeep seized each other by the wrist, and then the barkeep pulled Deor into a rough embrace.

"It's good to see you, Deor! And you've brought friends! Good for business, eh?"

"We're here to refuel our ship," Deor told him, sitting down on a stool. The others fanned out along the bar, following his example.

Sahara managed to claim a spot on Deor's left, and she noticed Jared sitting on his right. She tried to catch his eye, but it seemed that he was deliberately avoiding her gaze. She frowned and turned her attention back to the barkeep.

"Haska," Deor was saying, keeping his voice low. "We need some information."

Haska was rapidly filling mugs with some kind of dark ale. As he moved, the tattoos twined around his corded arms and neck rippled. *This isn't a man to be trifled with*, Sahara realized.

"Information?" he said. "What can I tell you, Deor?"

"What do you know of the Triumvirate?"

Haska, who was handing the mugs around, suddenly jerked his arm back, sloshing Sahara's drink onto the counter.

"Why do you come in here and speak of them?" he murmured, his eyes flashing at Deor. "Do you want to bring trouble down on my head, boy?"

Deor shook his head. "Never. You know that."

"Then don't speak openly of them here, if you know what's best for you," Haska cautioned, his voice barely more than a whisper. "They have ears everywhere, and they don't take kindly to talk."

"So I've noticed," Sahara said, glancing over her shoulder at the silent figures behind them.

Haska nodded grimly. "It's been that way since they came to power," he murmured. "No one talks. No one gathers together. It's best not to be seen in a group. People who meet in groups seem to end up dead."

He snapped his mouth shut and returned his attention to distributing their drinks. "And I've already said too much," he muttered.

"What about Tripp and Steele?" Deor asked. "Are they still around somewhere?"

Haska paused again. "They were taken. Devil only knows where. It's just me now."

Deor frowned fiercely. "That's unhappy news."

"Look," Jared interrupted. "We certainly don't want to get you into trouble, but we need to know more. We're headed for Askalon, and it would be helpful to know what we're up against."

"You're suicidal, then," he muttered, setting Jared's mug down with a trembling hand. "No one goes there by choice. And no one who goes there ever comes back. Worse than hell, the rumors say."

"That's not good enough," Jared pressed. "If you know something, tell us."

"Please, Haska," Deor said. "For Tripp and Steele. Help us."

Haska's eyes flickered over the rest of the tavern, and he

mumbled something to himself. Then he turned back to Deor. "Fine. The three of you to the back," he said finally. "You and her and him." He nodded to Sahara and Jared. "Come with me and I'll tell you what you want to know."

FOURTEEN

HASKA LED them into a dim room behind the bar, the curtain of swirled glass beads tinkling softly as they passed through it. A dusty oil lamp in one corner threw hesitating shadows on the stone walls and made the thick air seem somehow thicker. A small table stacked with parchments squatted against the far wall.

Haska settled himself into the rickety chair before it with a heavy sigh and rubbed his chin.

"So, you want to know, eh? You want to know what I know about the Triumvirate?"

Sahara, watching him from her post just inside the bead curtain, noticed his shoulders slump as Deor and Jared both nodded.

"We're not here to threaten you," she said, when he didn't say anything for several minutes. "What do you have to fear?""

"I told you before. *Them*. Tripp and Steele...they were taken. Plucked right out of the streets. They knew what we were planning somehow, even though we were so careful. They left me here. I still don't know why."

"How long ago?" Deor asked.

"Six months, maybe?"

"Before the Drakkin fell?" Jared asked.

Haska barked a laugh. "You must be joking. The Drakkin were already dead to the Triumvirate. They didn't realize it, maybe, but it was over. The Drakkin set up the Triumvirate to run the commerce and the fuel trade and everything else. We never bowed to the Drakkin here on Gladius. Only to the Triumvirate. Only ever to the Triumvirate."

"It doesn't matter to us when they came to power," she said, her voice harsher than she intended. "They're in power now and they've taken our friends. So tell us what we're up against and we'll leave you alone."

Haska studied her for a moment and she crossed her arms over her chest. When she didn't drop her gaze, he sighed and turned back to Jared and Deor.

"They're brutal," Haska said. "They have spies everywhere. Tripp and Steele were working underground, trying to build a revolution. But when they disappeared, it all fell apart. No one had courage to keep things going, not when you couldn't tell who you could trust. They were betrayed, I think. Ratted out."

Deor frown deepened as Haska talked, finally turning fierce and ruthless.

"Betrayed, were they? Really?" he asked, his voice like ice.

"Yes, I-I think so." The barkeep's eyes slid away from Deor's, and he seemed very interested all of a sudden in a chink in the stone floor.

Deor measured the man for a long time through narrowed eyes, and Haska began to fidget, beads of sweat standing out on his pale brow.

"It was you, wasn't it, Haska?" Deor said finally. "You ratted them out, didn't you, you sniveling cur?"

Haska started violently in his chair, and Sahara knew Deor had hit a nerve. His hand scrabbled on the tabletop, groping through the parchments, his eyes riveted on Deor's face.

"No, it wasn't! It wasn't me!" he protested. "They were like my brothers! You know that, Deor!"

Deor's hands hardened into fists. "That's why they left you here, isn't it? And that's why no one in your bar says a damn thing. Because you're a filthy rat!"

Haska jumped to his feet, holding out the object he had been searching for under his papers. It was a penknife, not much longer than Sahara's forefinger.

Deor snorted. "What's that for? Do I look like a wax seal to you, you fool?"

"You came back just in time," Haska sneered. "You were so high and mighty before, servant of the servants of the Drakkin. And now you're going to be just like Steele and Tripp...sent to the mines of Askalon to waste whatever's left of your miserable life rutting in the rock for that ore they're so keen on finding!"

Sahara's eyes snapped from her brother's tense shoulders to Haska's face. *What ore? What's he talking about?*

Deor laughed. "So you'd like to think, I'm sure. But when I walk out of here, it will be on my terms. I can't say as much for you."

Haska waved the penknife in front of Deor's chest. "They're already coming," he hissed. "They'll be here any minute."

Without any warning, and so quickly that it took Sahara's breath away, Deor slapped the knife out of Haska's hand and then drove his other elbow into the man's nose, sending him crashing back onto the table. Haska slipped unconscious to the floor, his nose askew and gushing blood.

Deor crouched and moved him so that he could see the back of his neck. He pointed to a strange tattoo—three interlocked circles with a triangle at the intersection.

"Triumvirate scum," he said. "Guess it's time we were leaving, then."

He shook out his arm and shouldered his way through the beads and back into the taproom. Rafe and the others were already on their feet, weapons at the ready.

"Did he give you trouble?" Rafe asked Jared.

"Not much," Jared answered. "But we need to move."

They scrambled to follow Deor, who was already out the front door. As soon as they caught up with him, Deor led them quickly around the corner into a side street. They flattened themselves against the wall and he motioned for them to be silent. Not thirty seconds later, they heard the heavy tramp of boots, and then the troop itself came into view.

They were roughnecks, all ten of them, dressed in black and carrying long, viciously curved knives. Their belts hung heavy with ammunition, and they had some kind of double-barreled weapon slung by a strap over their shoulders. As they passed, Sahara could make out that same tattoo on the back of their necks.

Triumvirate thugs, she thought.

As soon as the troops entered into the bar, Deor led them at a run back down the street. He took so many twists and turns that Sahara quickly lost all sense of direction. She noticed, though, that they seemed to be climbing steadily uphill. Once, she glanced back, hearing the labored breathing of the girls behind her. She couldn't see any sign that her brother was slowing down, so she sprinted a little to catch up to him.

"Where are we going, Deor?"

"Here."

He stopped and faced a gated doorway on their left. A dull metal panel stood a few inches out from the wall beside the door.

"It's locked, Deor," Sahara said, glancing back down the street to see if they had been followed. "How does this help us?"

"It won't be locked for long," he answered, flipping open the panel and punching in a code. The lock slid back and the gate swung open.

"Go," Deor commanded. "Up the stairs, all of you. Go!"

Rafe led the way this time, and Jared brought up the rear. Sahara hesitated, waiting for Deor at the foot of the steps. She watched her brother pull the door shut and then take up a position in the dark shadows just inside.

"You're not coming?" she asked.

"Didn't I tell you to go?" he barked. "Get up those steps before they get here, Sahara!"

"There's no way they possibly…"

Before she could finish, she heard them coming up the street.

"Go!" Deor hissed.

Still she hesitated, desperate to join him. But when he turned on her, eyes blazing, she ducked her head and scurried up the steps after the others.

"Where's Deor?" Jared asked as soon as she appeared.

"Down there. They found us."

"How is that even possible?" Rafe asked, alarmed. "And how did you leave him down there by himself?"

She grinned crookedly at him. "No choice of mine. My little brother is very…persuasive when he wants to be."

Jared moved across the long, low room to a set of windows set in the street-side wall. He crouched to one side and peered out, trying to get an angle on the street below. Seeing what he was doing, Sahara joined him, craning to see over his shoulder.

They were all there, clustered in the middle of the street.

The door below them clanged against its lock.

Twice more.

"Locked," one of the soldiers grunted. "They're gone, captain."

The captain, who looked like he might have been carved out of steel rather than flesh, glared at him. "Maybe and maybe not."

"Haska was dead?" another soldier asked.

"Who pays you to ask questions?" the captain snapped, and the man fell back.

"So what do we do now, boss?" the first soldier asked. "Wait for them to come? And what if they don't?"

The captain rubbed his chin and shifted his gun. He tried the gate once more and then grunted. "They'll come…if they're not here already. Zoza and Mede will stay and wait. I've got a bad feeling about this place. You know what used to be here?" He looked up the façade, and Jared and Sahara flattened themselves against the wall just in time.

"No, captain," said the first soldier. "What used..."

"Shut up. Something's not right. I don't like this place, and we have another call anyway. So we're leaving."

"What do we do if they come?" one of the men asked, taking his position on one side of the door.

"Call it in, Mede, and then get the hell out of here. Don't mess with this bunch. There's only one reason to know about this safe house. Either he's one of us, or he was one of them." The captain sniffed and turned away, beckoning for the rest of the troop to follow him. "We've got the ship in lockdown, so if they try to cut back to the landing platform, we'll catch them."

Without another word, he turned and led the troop at a double-time trot down the street and around the far corner. Zoza crossed to the other side of the doorway. They didn't say another word.

Sahara and Jared moved away from the window and returned to the middle of the room. Althea huddled against Emma along the far wall, haggard and pale in the safety of Emma's quiet hold.

"What's the situation?" asked Brytnoth in a low voice.

At that moment, Deor came up the steps. "They've got the ship."

"After all the trouble we went through to get the damn thing!" Kirin muttered. "Now it's under someone else's thumb!"

"I have an idea," Deor said.

"Too risky," Sahara interrupted, glancing at him. When he turned questioning eyes on her, she shrugged. "It's what I was thinking too."

"Would you care to elaborate at all for those of us who don't read minds?" Brytnoth asked with a grin.

"He wants to take down that troop so we can steal their uniforms and weapons. Then we'll have free access to the ship...and anywhere else we might need to go."

"How is that a bad idea?" Jared asked. "Sounds like our kind of crazy." He winked at Deor, but Sahara frowned.

"We're outgunned and outmanned. Not sure how you propose to take all of those guys down."

"We're not outmanned at the moment. There's just two of them down there. And once we have their weapons, we'll be much less outgunned than we are now."

"That would still leave the rest of that troop, and only two of us to have the equipment to infiltrate," Sahara said. "It's too risky...too dangerous. Even for us. And for what? A disguise? It's not worth it."

Deor grinned at her, completely unfazed. "That may all be true, but it doesn't mean we can't nab the guns off those two downstairs. And anyway, they're blocking our way out." He clasped his hands behind his back and watched Sahara expectantly. "Sis? What do you say? We could take them, no problem."

Sahara started at the endearment. Encouraging her brother to further violence went against every instinct she had, and yet she couldn't just ask him to stand aside.

Or can I?

"Jared and I will handle this one," she said. "You took out Haska, after all."

Jared glanced at her swiftly, and she half hoped that he would sense what she was trying so desperately to conceal from Deor. She saw his jaw tighten, but he said nothing.

Deor measured Sahara for a moment and then shrugged. "Fine with me. I'll back you up, just in case there's trouble."

Without another word, Sahara turned and led the way back down the stairs.

The base of the steps was shrouded in shadows, and she slowed to a creeping pace as the guards came into view. They leaned lazily against the gate, leaving Sahara to marvel once again at the Triumvirate's obvious lack of military discipline.

Stupid and careless, Sahara thought grimly, slipping her dagger from its sheath and separating the blades. She tested the grips. *Just like the idiots on K'ilenfir. These aren't soldiers. They're just bullies who decided to get all dressed up today.*

She glanced behind her when she reached the ground floor. Jared and Deor crouched on the steps just above her.

I got this, she told Jared, speaking directly into his mind. He nodded curtly.

We're here if you need us.

Taking a breath, she faced the gate, coiled her muscles. Then she sprang forward and buried the daggers up to their hilts in the soft, exposed flesh where the neck met the shoulder. As she pulled the knives free, the guards fell sideways without a sound.

For a long moment, she stood, head bowed, staring at her hands and the bloodied knives. She heard Emma's voice, judging, despising.

You really are what they say you are...a killer. A killer.

The word enveloped her, penetrated her, seemed to fill every crevice of her soul.

Killer.

Startled by the sudden sense that someone was beside her, she glanced up and met the admiring gaze of her little brother.

"You have to teach me that trick," he said, grinning widely at her. "Comes in handy in a tight spot, that."

Sahara's eyes dropped again to the red-slick knives in her hands.

"Yeah," she mumbled. "Real handy."

FIFTEEN

THEIR WAY CLEAR ONCE MORE, Deor led them swiftly through
the serpentine twistings of streets and alleyways. Dusk was all
around them, and the slanting rays of the sun made the haze in the air
almost blinding. The dust seemed thicker with the approach of
evening, too. It stuck in Jared's throat and choked his lungs, like a
Silesian sandstorm.

"What a foul place!" Kirin muttered. "Never mind the Triumvirate. Just staying here too much longer would kill us!"

Jared glanced back at him. Kirin was managing much better now
that the wound in his leg was almost healed. Jared hardly noticed the
limp in his gait any more, and he thought with some satisfaction that
he could soon put Kirin back to work.

Though I'm not sure what I'll have him do, he thought. He
couldn't help remembering Sahara's comment about baggage back on
K'ilenfir and he sighed. He'd find something for the man to do, even if
it was just cleaning weapons every night.

They worked their way steadily downhill, and as the stench of
fuel became more and more powerful in the stagnant air, Jared saw
the landing platforms rising in front of them. Like a long row of

mushrooms crouched over rotting matter, they squatted just above the tops of the machine shops and sheds that surrounded them. A wide avenue ran between the decks, and there was a steady bustle of activity as crews loaded and unloaded cargo, and fueled and repaired their ships. Most of the people hurrying past them toward the city proper were a rough-looking sort.

Definitely not tourists, Jared thought.

Deor motioned for the party to stop in the shelter of a narrow alley just off the main boulevard.

"They're smugglers, mostly," Deor murmured to Jared and Sahara, jerking his head toward a surly-faced and well-armed knot of men that tramped past. "A lot of black-market dealings go on here."

"What's the plan for getting our ship back?" Rafe asked.

They had all seen it before ducking into the alley—the platform ringed by Triumvirate thugs, with more streaming in and out of the ship like a parade of busy insects, carrying whatever they could toward a warehouse at the end of the street.

"We're not going to have much left by way of provisions," Brytnoth observed. "They're stealing us blind!"

"Weapons are probably gone too," Rafe said. "They don't seem to be leaving much of anything."

"You know this area," Jared said to Deor. "What are our options?"

"I've got one," Deor said. "And it's a long shot. But it might be worth a try."

"This isn't another one of your so-called friends who's actually a traitor, is it?" Kirin asked. "Because that last little reunion really didn't turn out so well."

Deor frowned at him. "It is another friend, and I highly doubt that he's betrayed anyone. Least of all to the Triumvirate."

"How can you be sure, Deor?" Sahara asked. "They do seem to have a lot of pull around here."

Deor shook his head. "Not with Jaffa. You'll see."

Without waiting for any further objections, Deor led them down the alley and then on into the warehouse district.

The sandstone buildings here hunkered long and low and squalid, their walls more grey than white. Trash was piled in heaps behind the buildings, and the constant scurrying from the shadows betrayed the presence of a hardy and bold rodent population.

Deor led them around the side of one of the furthest buildings and stopped in front of a steel door. He rapped several times in a distinct pattern. When no one answered, he repeated the pattern more forcefully. Before he could finish, the door opened under his fist.

"Whaddya want?" the man behind the door snarled. He leveled a heavy gun at Deor's chest, his scarred face taut and uncompromising.

"I'm here to see Jaffa," Deor said.

Jared couldn't help marveling once more at the boy's unflappable nerves. *Not many grown men could stand in the face of a gun like that without showing fear.*

"Who's askin'?" the man barked.

"Deor."

The man's expression changed suddenly. The hostile light in his eyes suddenly shifted into cringing fear, and his surly face dissolved in a stupid servile grin. The gun, so menacing a moment before, fell by its strap to the man's side.

"Of course, of course! Come inside, come inside, all of you!" The man beckoned them through the dark doorway. "Just wait here while I fetch the master." He scampered away to find Jaffa.

"What did you do to him?" Rafe muttered, looking with new respect at Deor. "He seemed absolutely afraid of you, kid!"

Deor made a dismissive gesture and grinned. "We've met before, that's all. I told you...this lot won't double-cross us."

A moment later, a red-faced man rolled toward them, followed by the now-cringing doorman. An immaculate robe of flowing silver spilled over his many folds of flesh, and a large garnet ring glowed on his pudgy pinky finger. Jeweled sandals flapped the dusty floor beneath the wide cuffs of his pants.

"Deor!" the man shouted with a loud laugh. "Come back to me at last, eh, my boy? Reconsidered my offer, have you?"

Deor shook his head. "No, Jaffa. I'm no drug-runner. I told you that before."

"Well, a man can't help but try. Talents like yours, my boy, are hard to come by. Hard to come by. We mostly get idiots." He aimed a good-natured smack at the back of the doorman's head, sending him stumbling forward. "Ain't that so, Jeremiah?"

"Yes, boss. That's so."

"I need a favor, Jaffa," Deor said, ignoring the exchange with Jeremiah. "Something that's probably as much in your interest as it is in ours."

Jaffa let out another roaring laugh. "I'm interested already. But let's not talk thirsty, eh?"

He turned and led the way toward the rear of the building, where a set of metal stairs ran up two stories. They followed Jaffa up and into a large room rimmed with windows, obviously the overseer's post and the warehouse's main offices. A wide oval table sat in the center of the room surrounded by plush, richly-upholstered chairs. As they seated themselves around it, Jaffa sent Jeremiah off to fetch drinks.

"So, my boy," Jaffa said, puffing to catch his breath as he sank into a huge armchair at the table's head. He swiveled experimentally and sighed with satisfaction. "Tell me your proposition."

Jeremiah returned with a cut-glass decanter on a tray and enough squat glasses to go around. The liquid in the decanter gleamed a claret-red, and when he unstoppered the bottle a thick, fruity aroma drifted onto the air. Once drinks were in hand, Jeremiah retreated to the doorway and waited.

"Always the best," Deor said, sipping appreciatively and appraising his glass.

"Always! Everything of mine is of the highest quality, as you well know." Jaffa swirled his own drink, sipped, and then turned suddenly to Emma and Althea, who sat quietly together beside Kirin. "Such fine flowers," he murmured. "Where'd you pick these, Deor? Into a new line of trade, are you?"

Deor followed his gaze and then laughed shortly. "No, not at all."

"It's quite a profitable line to be in just now," Jaffa continued, his eyes never leaving the two women's faces. "Quite profitable. The Triumvirate is working very hard to corner that market for themselves…just like everything else. And I do so hate a monopoly."

"I didn't come here to discuss the workings of the slave trade with you," Deor said smoothly. "Though I don't doubt that what you say is true. About the Triumvirate, that is."

"Did you know, my boy, that they've made some planets quite into regular suppliers? Those early planets, you know, where the Drakkin thought they could get away with killing just the men, not exterminating everyone? Well, the Triumvirate has figured out how to profit from worlds full of women. Quite ingenious of them. Waste not, as they say.""

Jared saw Sahara's hand tighten convulsively around her glass.

"You mean planets like Amaryl?" she gritted.

Jaffa turned to her in some surprise. "Why, and here's another one!" He chuckled and looked Sahara up and down. Then he frowned and glanced at Deor. "But this one's different, Deor. She won't do, I'm afraid. Not at all."

Jared couldn't help chuckling to himself as he saw Sahara's cheeks flare.

"I told you, Jaffa—" began Deor, but Sahara cut him off.

"You mean planets like Amaryl, don't you?"

"Oh, I suppose Amaryl might be an example." Jaffa waved a hand in the air. "What does it matter, girl?"

Sahara said nothing, but Jared saw the smoldering in her eyes. Jared knew that it burned her soul to know that her own homeworld was now a center for the trafficking in female slaves.

I wonder if Deor feels the same way, he thought. He glanced in the young man's direction, but Deor's face was an absolute mask.

"Enough," Deor said. "I already told you that we're not here to discuss the slave trade, Jaffa."

"Fine, fine," Jaffa muttered, conceding the discussion with another careless wave of his hand. "So what are you here to discuss, then?"

"The fact that a bunch of Triumvirate thugs are squatting practically on your doorstep."

"Yes, I know that. They're raiding some ship...or, excuse me, they're guarding some ship."

"No, raiding really does sum things up quite nicely," Deor corrected him. "And it's our ship."

Jaffa laughed quietly. "Ah, I see. I begin to see the workings of your mind, my boy," he said. "You hope that I'll have an interest in getting rid of nosy Triumvirate troopers before they stumble into my own operations, eh? If I intervene, I save you the inconvenience of fighting it out with them...and save myself the inconvenience of explaining my business. Is that what you're thinking?"

Deor shrugged. "Well, it did seem to me that we might have a mutual interest along those lines, yes."

"Perhaps we would, but they're already under strict orders to leave me alone, you see."

Deor's eyes flashed at him. "Is the Triumvirate into the drug trade now, too?"

"That all depends on what you mean. Not officially, no. Not yet. But wheels are turning, my boy. Wheels are turning. My sources tell me that there's been a lot of communication lately between Triumvirate headquarters and Halcyon."

Deor leaned back in his chair and measured Jaffa for a few moments in silence. "So was I mistaken about our mutual interests, then?"

"Now, hold on a moment. I don't work for the Triumvirate directly," Jaffa said. "But you must understand the—how shall we say?—the delicacy of my situation. I don't want to disrupt relations between my suppliers in Halcyon and the Triumvirate. I run the largest smuggling ring on this side of the system, so...I've become rather an important person of late." He curled his fingers and studied his ring, smiling to himself.

Deor still said nothing, and Jaffa finally glanced up to meet his steady, unflinching eyes. After a moment, Jaffa smiled easily and folded his hands together.

"That's not to say that I might not be able to see my way clear to help you out of your present difficulties. I could. I really could. On a certain condition."

"Condition."

"Of course, Deor!" Jaffa laughed. "I'm a businessman, after all." He drained off the last of his drink and then sat back. "You know, one of my products has become quite indispensable to the Triumvirate recently. It's a potent drug, with many unusual properties—chiefly, loss of willpower and total amnesia while under the influence. I'm not exactly sure what they use it for, but they are demanding it in quantity these days."

"That should be good for you."

Jared had to marvel once again at Deor's incredible self-mastery. *The kid's a natural*, he thought.

Jaffa's frown was almost a pout. "They're trying to hedge my profits, my boy, and that is something I won't tolerate! I told you before that I appreciate your talents. I especially value your talent for persuasion, and your exceptional negotiating prowess. You're just exactly the person I need to represent my interests." He produced a folded and sealed document out of the silver folds of his tunic and laid it crisply on the table. "My new contract with the Triumvirate."

Deor considered the parchment for a moment, then his eyes snapped back to Jaffa's flaccid face. "Let me understand you," he said. "In exchange for handling this little problem with our ship, you want me to negotiate your new drug contract with the Triumvirate. You want me to be sure they agree to your new price and accept these conditions. Is that right?"

"That's right."

"And how do I know that's what this is?"

Jaffa laughed and slapped his knee. "What interest would I have in double-crossing you, Deor?" he asked, wiping a tear from the corner of his eye. "After all we've done together, you still suspect me! No. It's not to be thought of, my boy. So do me this one service, and I'll get rid of those maggots infesting your ship."

"And just where am I supposed to take this?" Deor asked.

"The Triumvirate has made Askalon their chief base of operations. That's where you'll go."

Deor never blinked.

"I think we can come to an arrangement."

SIXTEEN

THEY WATCHED from the shadows of the alley as Jaffa, with Jeremiah two paces behind him, trundled toward the Triumvirate captain standing at the base of the landing platform.

"This is a stroke of incredible good fortune!" Brytnoth said quietly, unable to wipe the smile off his face. "He's sending us to Askalon, and he basically just gave us open access to the Triumvirate's headquarters with that piece of paper!"

Deor glanced at him, obviously not sharing in Brytnoth's good humor. "It gets us past the guards at the door," he said. "But little more than that, I'm afraid."

"Maybe that's all we'll need," Jared said quietly.

"We don't know anything about their operations," Deor reminded him, "and we don't know what's happened to your people yet. This contract won't buy their lives. That will have to come through some other means."

They fell silent again and watched Jaffa's gestures, trying to guess at the flow of the conversation. Whatever he said, it was effective—a moment later, the captain shouted to his men and they began to disembark. Jaffa turned away as the men formed up into a line and set off at a trot down the street. By the time he reached their position, the men had disappeared around the far corner of the avenue.

"So there you are," Jaffa said with a wide grin. "Now that you're on official business for me, you shouldn't have any more trouble with meddlesome fools like those."

"We'll need to inventory our supplies," Kirin said. "They've raided our stores, and we'll need plenty for the run to Askalon."

"What's mine is yours," Jaffa replied, bowing slightly. "Anything you need, tell Jeremiah here and he'll see to it."

Deor nodded brusquely and clasped Jaffa's hand. "I'll send word when we've finalized the agreement with the Triumvirate."

"Yes. You be sure to do that."

Deor smiled easily at him, unruffled. "It's me, remember? No worries."

He turned and led them up the ramp to the ship.

They spent the rest of the next day getting the ship outfitted for travel once again, and, with Jaffa's generosity, they were soon well-supplied with provisions, weapons, and goods for barter. By dusk, they had left Gladius behind them.

"I can't say I'm sorry to leave that hideous planet," Emma said to Althea as they strapped in for the deep-space run.

"Me, either. It's been nothing but haze and death."

Jared, who was inspecting guns and stashing them in the weapons case, noticed that both girls glanced at Sahara as Althea spoke. Sahara, occupied with the same task across the passenger bay, had her back turned and had either not heard or had chosen to ignore Althea's words.

A sick feeling clutched at Jared's gut. With supreme effort, he fought down the urge to reach out and sense her mood, to say something reassuring to her. This letting her alone was slowly killing him.

He stared wordlessly at her back until she finally straightened and glanced in his direction. By the light in her eyes, he knew that she had heard them. And she knew that they were talking about her.

And, though he heard no words in his head to confirm it, he read something else there too.

A silent plea, asking him to speak, begging him to say something. Anything.

He turned away from her, swallowing hard.

"Get those weapons loaded and stored," she snapped. "And hurry up about it."

Jared cursed himself inwardly, cursed Rafe for his advice. *How can this possibly help anything?* he wondered.

"She scares me," Althea confessed in a whisper, and Jared knew that Sahara must have left the bay.

"She's always been like that," Emma said. "Ever since she came to Silesia. But it's worse now. Worse since the Drakkin were destroyed… since they took our friends."

"Worse how?"

Emma was silent for a long time, and Jared made himself busy as slowly as he could, loading guns meticulously, feeling only the tiniest twinge of guilt about eavesdropping on their conversation.

"I don't know, really. But she's…harder, somehow. For a while, we all thought…" She stopped abruptly, and Jared knew that she was going to say something about him. After a pause, she continued briskly, "But that didn't happen, so here we are."

Jared placed the last of the weapons in the case and closed it with a sigh. Then he turned to face the two women.

"You're wrong about her, both of you," he said quietly.

"Come on, Jared," Emma retorted. "You don't really expect us to believe you about that, do you? You know it's true as well as I do! Maybe you don't say anything, but it's obvious."

"There's so much that you don't understand about her, Emma. And you're passing judgment on what you don't understand. It's not right. You should give her a chance."

"A chance for what?"

Jared shrugged. "Just give her a chance. She may surprise you, in the end."

He left the passenger bay and joined Rafe on the bridge, his heart heavy.

"What's wrong?" Rafe asked as he flung himself into the co-pilot's seat.

Jared shook his head irritably. "Nothing. Doesn't matter."

Rafe adjusted the controls and pursed his lips. "I've been your friend since we were kids tearing up Albadir with our pranks," he said. "Don't tell me I don't know when you're upset about something."

Jared sighed. "You gave me bad advice, Rafe."

"Me? Bad advice? When was that?"

"When you told me to let Sahara be."

"Ah. I see."

"It's killing me. I can't keep this up. She needs me, Rafe."

"Maybe."

Jared stared at him for a few minutes, and then a horrible suspicion stretched its cold fingers into his consciousness. His eyes narrowed. "Really."

"Maybe she needs you. Maybe she doesn't. But if you haven't been able to figure her out by now, well..." He let the sentence dangle unfinished.

Jared stood abruptly. "Don't give me any more advice," he said. "Understood?"

Rafe shrugged, then smiled easily at Jared. "Have it your way. But I'm a problem-solver, my friend. I may not be able to help myself."

"You need to try," Jared said.

He retreated to his own bunk with his miserable thoughts. All those horrible suspicions about Rafe and Sahara that he thought he had left buried with the dragon on Silesia were resurfacing now.

I knew deep-space travel could mess with your mind, he thought. *But this is crazy!*

———

Three days later, Rafe announced to the crew that they would have to stop again to recharge the fuel cells before they reached Askalon.

"I thought we had enough to get there without another stop," Jared said. "Didn't they finish the process back on Gladius?"

"It's looking less and less likely," Rafe said. "When those Triumvirate troops showed up, they probably ordered everyone away from the ship. And she seems to be struggling with the deep space warp, too...like speed bumps or hiccups or something. We're not keeping a steady pace, and she's eating the fuel much more quickly than she should."

Jared frowned. "What are our options?"

"There's one other refueling outpost before we reach Askalon. It's a little bit out of our way, but not much. It's a trading world, not a smugglers' den like Gladius. Agora is home to the largest market on this side of the system. All that traffic means higher fuel cost...but we don't really have a choice at this point. We'll never make it to Askalon without filling the fuel cells."

"Make it so, then," Jared said. "And get us there as fast as you can. We're wasting precious time."

They landed on Agora two days later. The port bustled with people and the streets buzzed with the noise of shuttlecraft ferrying people to the market city of Lagon. It reminded Jared of a beehive, except that there was no order to anything.

They stood on the platform, waiting for Rafe to return from the foreman's shed. A gray dawn was pouring a sickly light across their faces, casting long shadows onto the street below.

Everything about this place is gray, Jared realized. *The paving stones, the buildings, the light, the sky....*

Only the swirling crowds of people, with their strange motley of foreign garb, provided any color to this drab world. Deep purples, glaring reds, muted golds, all changing faster than he could capture it. It was what the dawn should have been.

"This place makes Gladius look like a graveyard," Sahara

murmured, and she glanced at Deor. "You've been here before, too? You know where to go?"

Deor shook his head. "I've never set foot on this planet before. My duties with the Drakkin kept me mostly on worlds like Gladius. They were concerned about keeping a choke-hold on fuel supplies...that, and exterminating planets. If Agora was under the rule of the Drakkin, though, it may have been a graveyard not so long ago too."

"What's the plan, Jared? Are we just going to stand around here while they fix the ship, or are we going to see what all the bustle is about?" Brytnoth asked. He pointed to the crowd below them, jostling for places on three shuttles that had just arrived. "We could hitch a ride to the city. This close to Askalon, there's a good chance of getting some information."

"We've got nothing better to do," Jared agreed. "And I like the idea of trying to gather some more intel on the Triumvirate before we get to Askalon."

Just as he finished speaking, Rafe returned. "Done," he said. "But we'll be here for at least a week. We're last on the work list because we don't have the coin to persuade them to hustle it up. So we might as well head into the city and find some accommodations."

"Did you tell them we were on an errand for Jaffa?" Jared asked. "Would that name be coin enough?"

"Everybody's on an errand for somebody," Rafe answered with a short laugh. "I tried that. They laughed in my face. I took my leave before things got any uglier than that."

"There's nothing for it, Jared," Sahara said, laying a hand on his arm. He glanced down at her swiftly, ready to smile at her, but the emptiness in her eyes killed it before it reached his lips.

"Let's go, then," he said with a little sigh.

They descended the flight of wide stone steps, and as they neared the street, the crowd around them thickened until it threatened to separate them. With a good deal of shoving, they managed to stay together and found seats on the next shuttlecraft that approached.

The trip into Lagon proved longer and more unpleasant than anyone wished. The smooth metal walls cinched suffocatingly close around them, compressing too many passengers into the narrow space. Jared could barely find room to draw a breath. And even when he did, the noisome smell of bodies around them made his stomach churn.

Sahara grabbed Jared's arm as the shuttle hurtled around a corner in the road, throwing bodies together.

"This is going to be the death of me," she muttered. "Why don't they come up with some better way to get around this place?"

At last, the shuttle scraped to a halt and the doors slid back. People poured out into the gray haze of Lagon, and Jared's crew jostled their way out. Althea stumbled to the short stone wall that separated the loading zone from the street beyond.

"I can't breathe," she choked. "Can't breathe."

Deor followed close behind her, and Jared watched with some surprise as he deftly pulled Althea's long hair back from her face and off her neck. The furtive breeze, though still heavy with shuttlecraft fumes and the sweat of an unwashed crowd, was cool, and Althea took several heaving breaths.

"That's it," Deor murmured to her. "Just like that."

Jared glanced at Sahara. She was watching Deor with a mix of surprise and envy in her eyes.

After a few more deep breaths, Althea straightened and Deor let her hair fall. She smiled at him, her eyes warm and bright. "Thank you, Deor. I feel much better now."

"Where do we go now?" Emma asked.

"Let's follow the crowd—none too closely, mind you—and see where it takes us," Brytnoth suggested. "These people all seem to know where they're going."

They trailed some hundred paces behind the last stragglers of the crowd and made their way up the path. It zigzagged its way into the maze of gray stone buildings, gradually narrowing until there was room for just three of them to walk comfortably side-by-side. At the summit of the path stood a massive gate, arching some fifty feet over their heads. Gazing up as they passed underneath it, Jared saw a steel gate suspended by chains as thick as his waist. Guards stood motionless on both sides of the arch, six within and six without. They held long pikes in their hands and Jared could see the muzzle of some kind of rifle over their left shoulders.

Something was different about these guards, though.

"Triumvirate troops?" he murmured to Rafe as they emerged on the other side of the gate.

Rafe shook his head. "I don't think so. No tattoo or insignia of any kind."

"Interesting."

"Very," agreed Sahara from his other side. "So whose guards are they, then? And where are all the Triumvirate troops?"

Once in the city proper, the thoroughfare widened again and brightly-blazoned wooden signs swung idly in the breeze. A glass-blower's shop here to their left, an armory just ahead on the right. Further down the street, on the far corner, stood a sprawling stone ale-house and inn.

"That's more like it!" Kirin exclaimed. "Hopefully they have decent food. I feel like I haven't eaten in days."

SEVENTEEN

THE INFLUX of traffic for market day meant that the inn was crowded and boisterous. Sahara sighed inwardly and realized just how much she missed the calm and quiet of those hot, sun-soaked, lazy days in Albadir—before the Drakkin ruined her life for the second time.

She hung back near the doorway as Jared and Deor pushed through the crowd toward the bar, hailing the barkeep with upraised hands and voices.

Staring at Jared's back, at the muscular shoulders and dark hair that she knew and loved so well, she felt suddenly and completely alone.

This is all my fault, she realized. *I pushed him away...again. But I never thought he would just...just let me go. He fought for me so many times. How can he just walk away?*

For a moment, she ached to call out to him, to reach her mind out to his and call him back to her. It was almost overpowering, and she had to struggle hard against it, wondering all the while why she didn't just let her anger and all her fears go.

What if he turns me away? What if he blocks me? she fretted. And then the core of her fear revealed itself. *What if I've destroyed the only thing in my life that ever really mattered?*

A single hot tear slid down her cheek.

I will not do this, she told herself. *I won't. Not here. Not now.*

And with an almost superhuman effort, she slammed the door on her emotions and followed the others into the bar.

More people were returning to their errands in the city than were coming in at this hour, so they were able to find a large table in a dark corner of the room. Sahara found herself sitting between Kirin and Rafe, facing Jared across the rough expanse of wood. Deor, she noticed, had taken the seat next to Althea.

So strange, she thought. *I chose her out of all those women...and Jared chose Deor. And now...*

She stared down at her hands, resting on the lip of the table. She could hardly blame him. Every man wanted a girl like that.

"Look at these people," Kirin said suddenly, gesturing around them. "Do they look like people living in fear of some gang lords to you?"

"No," Jared answered. "I was just thinking the same thing."

Raucous laughter chased the sounds of clattering plates and forks and mugs through the exposed rafters of the high ceiling. There was no silent huddling here as there had been in the inn on Gladius, or even at the inn back on Silesia.

"But this close to Askalon, why aren't people afraid?" Emma asked.

At that moment, a plump woman swept up to their table, quieting their conversation. Her dark curly hair was streaked with silver, and her apron, which had once been white, was stained with long wear.

"You're not one of our usual groups," she said, her accent strangely foreign and lilting. "Where are you from, then?"

"Far away," Althea said wistfully. "So very far away."

The woman smiled at her as she handed tankards around. "Our famous mead, my loves," she said. "Drink up, for there's plenty."

"You don't fear the Triumvirate here?" Sahara asked, overcome by the woman's easy manners.

A shadow flickered across the woman's face and she frowned at her. "Why do you speak of such things?" she asked in a low voice. "None speak of them here."

"But...why not?" Sahara persisted, genuinely confused now. "We've seen worlds where...."

"That's not our way here," the woman interrupted. "They do not come here."

Sahara and Jared exchanged glances across the table.

"Why not?" Jared asked.

The woman, finished with her work, rubbed her hands on her apron. "Must see to the other guests," she mumbled, and whisked the tray over Deor's head and melted away into the crowd.

They watched her go in silence. Sahara tasted the mead and found it slightly sweet, slightly effervescent, not unlike the *estevalia* they made back home on Silesia. The taste of it plunged her into the memory of the night of the summer festival...the night she had danced with Jared. All of the sights and sounds and feelings of that night returned, coursing through her like molten silver.

It wasn't until Jared lifted his eyes to meet her own that she realized she was staring at him. Her breath caught in her throat and the tears blurred her sight. Jared's dark eyes held hers, and she thought she saw that familiar fire in their depths, mirroring the light of the three candles between them.

Sahara.... came his voice inside her head.

Before he could say more, she saw a heavy hand descend on his shoulder and she jumped.

"I hear you're asking difficult questions of the good innwife," said the man from behind Jared.

He stepped forward, moving into the flickering circle of candlelight. His features had a hard and chiseled edge, as if he had been etched out of marble. Unlike so many of the people they had seen, his dress was muted—a white, open-necked shirt under a leather jerkin, studded leather wrist-cuffs. The man's golden beard and mustache, tinged with silver, were trimmed close and neat, but his gray eyes reminded Sahara of the stone outside—hard and cold.

Jared shrugged his shoulder from beneath the man's hand. "Who are you?"

The man didn't answer immediately, but instead slid into the empty chair between Emma and Jared.

"I hear you ask after the Triumvirate's health," he said in a low voice. His eyes roved over them, bright and earnest.

"And if we do?" Deor retorted. "What's that to you? And who invited you to join us?"

The man studied Deor for a long moment, and then his eyes suddenly narrowed to thin slits. "Don't I know you from some-where?" he said at last, his voice edged. "You seem familiar to me."

Deor regarded him. "You're not familiar to me at all," he said. "And why should you be? I've never been here before."

"Did we cross paths on another world?" the man persisted, his voice growing sharp as he added, "On Askalon, perhaps?"

Deor leaned forward across the table. "I said I don't know you."

The man leaned back in his chair, rubbing his beard thoughtfully. "Oh, but I know you. It seems to me you were with a different crew last time I saw you. Traipsing into my palace on Askalon with a troop of Drakkin soldiers, I think you were."

"That's impossible," gasped Brytnoth.

"How is it impossible?" the man asked. "I was there...I should know."

"Because there were none left alive on Askalon...not after..."

The man looked at Brytnoth with a sudden flare of interest, and his voice lost some of its edge. "You are from Askalon?"

"I was. The Drakkin shipped us out. All of us. I'm all that's left."

The man studied him for a long time, and then he began to laugh, a low, bitter laugh.

"So, the lion sups with the lamb, is that it?" he asked, his hard gaze riveted once more on Deor.

"You don't know me," Deor said coldly. "Not even remotely. Yes, I worked for the Drakkin, but don't assume that I did their bidding of my own will. And I never led anyone against you on Askalon."

"All I know," the man said, "is that you helped them. They sent my people into exile...they established the Triumvirate to rule in our stead. And now..." His voice trailed off, and his eyes darkened. "Now that the Drakkin are gone, they are destroying my world."

"Who *are* you?" Brytnoth asked quietly.

"My name is Aelred, and once, long ago, I was one of the Lords of Askalon."

There was a stunned silence, and Aelred seemed to enjoy the impression he had made.

"How is that possible?" Brytnoth asked, finally finding his voice. "We were all that was left!"

Aelred's eyes flickered toward him again, a tinge of sorrow in his eyes. "No, not quite all. They saved us for last. They let us rule over a shadow world for years. While we sat in our silent hall and grew old, the Drakkin massed their forces and brokered a deal with the Triumvirate. When the pieces were set, they came for us. That was three years ago." His eyes flickered at Deor. "And that's where you come into the story, isn't it, my friend?"

"That's my brother," Sahara said, her voice very quiet. "So be very careful what you say."

Aelred glanced at her. "Why?" he scoffed. "Should I fear you, maiden?"

"You would if you knew what was good for you," Rafe said with a short laugh.

"I told you before, stranger," Deor said, "that I didn't serve the Drakkin of my own free will. I was taken from my own homeworld as an infant. I was their slave before I ever knew what freedom meant...but not forever. Two years ago, the Drakkin sent me to the prison on K'ilenfir."

"Why? You were the new warden, I suppose?"

"No. Because I had killed the Chieftain with his own blade."

Now it was Aelred's turn to look stunned. "You did *what?*"

"You heard me well enough. I've been in prison ever since. These, my new friends and my long-lost sister, rescued me from that hell-hole. So you see? I don't know you."

Aelred stared at them all, trying to fit the pieces together. "So you assassinated a Drakkin Chieftain. This one"—he indicated Brytnoth—"is one of my own people, back from the silent tomb of space. What about the rest of you?"

"They rescued me from K'ilenfir as well," Althea answered. "My homeworld of Aegis was overrun by Triumvirate slavers not many weeks ago."

Aelred nodded. "I had heard of the raid on Aegis. They grow more ruthless by the day. I'm sorry."

Althea made a small gesture with her right hand, and Sahara saw Deor reach out to cover her left hand with his own.

How does he know how to love like this? Sahara wondered. *How can he be so much like me and yet...so very different at the same time?* A lump rose in her throat and she quickly looked away.

"And what about you?" Aelred asked, turning to Sahara.

"I have a long and...complicated history," she answered haltingly. "But I was never a friend of the Drakkin, and since the time that fate set me free from their chains, I have been from Silesia."

"The rest of us are all from Silesia," Jared added. "We're looking for our people. The Drakkin shipped them out, just like they did to Brytnoth and the rest of your own people."

"They did not survive Silesia, it's said," the man said.

"I should think not," Rafe snorted. "I watched the dragon fall into the abyss with his sword through its heart."

"That was *you? You* destroyed them?" Aelred stared around at the Silesians, an awed respect finally replacing his ire.

"Yes. To save her." His eyes flickered at Sahara for a moment, then he turned back to Aelred. "As I said, we're looking for what's left of our people. From what we learned on K'ilenfir, their ship was raided by the Triumvirate and they were taken to Askalon."

Aelred shook his head grimly, a dark frown on his face. "You should fear the worst, I'm afraid. Those who are taken to Askalon are slaved out in one way or another. Some work the mines, some are traded to other worlds. And some..." His eyes flickered at Althea and Emma, but he left his thought unsaid. "The world of kings has become a den of serpents."

"One question," Rafe said. "Whose troops guard the streets here? They aren't Triumvirate."

"No, they aren't. They are more like...a private security force. The Triumvirate rules here with a very light hand. They need Agora to flourish for many reasons."

"You seem to be very well informed," Kirin said.

Aelred laughed sadly. "Yes. I'm very well informed."

"Will you help us?"

Aelred raised his head, his gray eyes flashing. "I think the better question might be, will you help me?"

EIGHTEEN

AELRED WOULD EXPLAIN NOTHING FURTHER. Instead, when the plump hostess returned with steaming plates of food, he rose and said that he would meet them again later that night.

"We have much in common and much to discuss," he said. Then he added, "While you're here in Agora, you should go to the market. It's quite something."

They decided to follow his advice. Soon after breakfast, and after procuring rooms for the next three nights at the inn, they set out on the main road for the city center. The frantic bustling of the early morning had diminished, but a steady stream of people still meandered its way into the heart of the city, swelling each time the main road crossed a side street.

After walking steadily uphill for the better part of half an hour, they reached another massive stone arch. This one spanned three times wider than the city's lower gate and twice as high, soaring into the gray sky. Once through the gate, a huge square, so wide that Sahara couldn't make out the other side, spread out before them. Tents of every size and color lined the walls, giving the whole square a patchwork feel. A raised platform sprawled in the center of the square, looking like a comfortable spot for a dance...or a hanging.

Crowds of people flowed around the space, many carrying packages or parcels, some leading slaves by ropes tied to steel collars around their necks. And the noise. Laughter, chatter, shouting, bartering, arguing, greeting, cursing. It roiled in a deafening chaos, like a flock of maddened birds.

"Look!" Althea cried, pointing down the square to their left. "How lovely!"

A jeweler's tent had caught her eye, and she seized Emma's arm and headed toward it. Not having a better object in sight, the others trailed after her.

"All our money is spoken for," Rafe cautioned. "We'd do better to avoid such places."

But no one listened to him, and soon they stood at the entrance of the tent. Althea and Emma wandered within, exclaiming over the delicate workmanship and seductive glitter of the precious stones.

"From Askalon these be," the merchant said, thumbs jammed into the folds of his dingy purple robes. A lopsided cap with a tarnished silver tassel covered his grimy mop of black hair. "No finer in all the system."

The mention of his homeworld drew Brytnoth forward to look. Gingerly, he touched the links of a bracelet made of a metal that had just the faintest rose tint.

"Fairer than gold, that is," the merchant said with a wide grin, revealing blackened gaps between his teeth. "Rarer by far. Came from the wrist of a fine lady, I'm told."

Brytnoth's head snapped up and his fingers hovered above the bracelet. "What did you say?"

"Came from a fine lady's wrist," the man repeated, obviously not taking the hint.

A chill prickled down Sahara's arms. She and Jared both stepped forward as Brytnoth seized the man by the collar, scaring a squawk of fear and surprise from his white lips.

"How did *you* come by it, then, scavenger?" Brytnoth said, his voice low and dangerous. "Where do you get your wares?"

"I'm an honest man, your honor! I get my wares honest-like, not stealing like some do!"

"Where do you get these things?"

The man cowered as far away from Brytnoth as the young man's grip on his shirt would allow, his eyes darting here and there, searching the crowds milling outside as if he were looking for something. Or someone.

"Who will come to your aid?" Jared said quietly. "Answer his question. Or I cannot guarantee your safety."

"I buy them from a merchant on Askalon," the man whimpered. "No idea of his proper name...he just sells me what I ask for, that's all."

"Does he work for the Triumvirate?"

As Jared spoke the name, the blood suddenly drained from the man's flabby face and he goggled at them. "Why should you ask me that? Why should I know that?"

"Why, indeed. Is this trade in stolen artifacts run by the Triumvirate, or is it just some underworld traffic that flourishes in its shadow?"

The man spluttered and his mouth flapped. Brytnoth gave an exasperated sigh and suddenly drew his knife, laying its cold edge against the man's throat.

"Perhaps this will help jog your memory," he said. "It's a foolish merchant who doesn't know his source."

"Kalkas knows," the man croaked. "Kalkas! Over there...in the white tent. The one in the northwest corner of the square. I didn't send you...don't tell him it was me what sent you to him!"

Brytnoth sheathed the knife and shoved the man roughly away from him.

"Let's go and see what this Kalkas fellow knows," he said, then speared a warning glare at the merchant. "If he doesn't give us the information we're after, we'll be back."

The man cringed back against the side of the tent, feeling his throat all over with trembling fingers.

They made their way across the square, pausing just momentarily to note the long line of steel-collared slaves assembling near the platform.

"Looks like a slave auction is about to begin," Rafe said.

"Not just any slave auction," Deor corrected. "Those are all women, or didn't you notice?"

This observation brought the party to a halt. Every woman in the lineup was clad in a thin, sleeveless white shift. Those that wept were beaten by the traders who paced back and forth in front of and behind the line.

"As if that would stop their tears," Sahara muttered, a well of sorrow opening within her gut.

Then, like glimpsing the bright petals of a flower against a sea of grass, she caught sight of a familiar face. She gasped and gripped Jared's arm so hard that he winced in pain.

"What's the matter with you?" he cried. "You're hurting my...."

She pointed, unable to form the words.

"Aliya!" Rafe cried. "Jared, that's Aliya!"

Sahara was already running.

"Sahara, wait!" Jared shouted after her, but she ignored him.

The slaver had made his way to the far end of the line. As she closed the distance to the line of women, Sahara scanned the square. There were no guards within easy range. This was her chance.

She pulled up short in front of Aliya. The woman's graceful neck was bowed, weighed down by the steel collar that bit cruelly into her skin.

"Aliya!" Sahara whispered, laying a hand on the woman's arm.

Aliya's head snapped up, and Sahara's eyes suddenly blurred with burning grief. This woman had loved her when she was despicable, when she was a *xenali*, an unknown. And now...

"Sahara!" Tears spilled from Aliya's own dark eyes now. "How did you find me? How did you ever...?"

"There's no time!" Sahara interrupted, squeezing her hand. "I have to get you out of here."

Aliya shook her head sadly. "That's impossible. Unless you come to buy my freedom and my life."

"*You!*"

The shout rang out from the end of the line, where the slaver had finally registered Sahara's presence.

"Get away from here, you!" He scuttled down the line, his whip raised menacingly.

You've got to be kidding me, Sahara thought.

As the man approached, she saw the line of women with their tear-stained faces and downcast eyes sway away from him to avoid being clipped by the leather thong. He stopped in front of her, breathing hard, and raised the whip to strike at her.

She favored him with a mirthless smile. "You really don't want to do that."

"Don't I just, though?" the man growled. "I'll beat you silly! And then you'll join my ladies here. I'm sure no one will miss you." His eyes darted over the square as if to double-check his words. He hesitated for a second when he saw Jared and his friends, who were obviously watching Sahara and were obviously more than capable of dispatching him and the rest of his gang without too much trouble. He swallowed nervously.

"Get going, you, before I flay you." Looking a little pale, he brandished the whip feebly in her direction.

Sahara dodged the tongue of the whip, caught his arm, twisted it, and then dropped her elbow. Something cracked, and the man howled with rage and pain. The whip fell to the ground.

"You let this one go," Sahara said, bending forward to speak into the man's ear, "and I'll let you go, understand? Otherwise I'll be happy to take care of the other arm too."

"Let go, let go...please let me go!" the man whimpered. "Who...what....?"

"Pay very close attention, friend," Sahara said. "I won't say this again. Let this one go. Right now. She comes with me. No questions asked, and no payment required."

The man craned his neck and saw Aliya watching the scene with wide but unsurprised eyes.

"But she's the best of the lot!" he wailed. "No way do I let her go to you for nothing! She's worth twenty of the rest of these wenches!"

Sahara applied a little extra pressure on the man's arm and said, her voice dangerously low, "I really hate repeating myself."

"All right, all right!" A string of curses dropped from the man's pale lips. "Just let me go, you hell-fiend!"

Sahara released the man's arm and it fell limp at his side. He stumbled toward Aliya and slowly and awkwardly unhooked the collar with his one good arm.

"Get out of my sight, the two of you! And don't you ever come back here, or I'll have you executed!"

Sahara smiled coldly at him. "I'm sure you'd try. Don't forget to wrap that arm, now. It'll help with the swelling...some."

Without another word, she caught Aliya's hand and led her back to Jared and the others.

Rafe swore admiringly as she rejoined them. "You have got some nerve, Sahara!"

Jared took Aliya's other arm and they made their way to a small pavilion across the square, where benches and tables had been set up for those purchasing from the various food vendors. Jared helped Aliya to sit, and the others took places at the table.

"My lady," Jared said, pressing her hand to his lips. "I'm so glad that we found you...but I wish it had been under different circum-stances."

Aliya smiled sadly at him and placed a hand on his bowed head. "To be found at all is a miracle beyond miracles," she said softly. "Arnauld would thank you, if he were here."

Jared raised his head. "Do you know where he is, my lady? Or any of the others?"

Aliya was silent for so long that they thought she would never answer. Finally, in a choking voice, she said, "He and some of the others are still on Askalon, I think. We were separated almost immediately. They took the men—the young and the strong were assigned to kill squads. The older men were farmed out to some kind of exploration crews. They sold us women to slavers like him." She nodded her head in the direction of the platform.

"So they use the slave trade to fund...what exactly?" Sahara mused. "And exploration crews? Exploring for what?"

Aliya shook her head. "I don't know. We were never told anything that could jeopardize their operations. They didn't trust us."

She fell silent again, rubbing her long fingers over the red marks on her neck where the collar had been. After a few minutes, she took a deep breath and roused herself.

"Some of you are familiar to me," she said, smiling at Rafe, Emma, Brytnoth, and Kirin. Then she turned to Althea and Deor. "But I do not know your faces."

"I'm Sahara's brother," Deor said.

Aliya glanced at Sahara in surprise. "I didn't know you had a brother!"

"I didn't think I did any longer," Sahara admitted with a small smile. "For all we knew, he had been slain by the Drakkin as an infant. But they only took him...made him a slave."

"They found me on K'ilenfir," Deor said. "As you said, a miracle of miracles."

"So it would seem!" Aliya exclaimed. "And you?" she asked Althea.

"I'm no one at all," the girl said. "I was taken from my homeworld of Aegis and would have been sold, like you. But Sahara found me on K'ilenfir and saved my life."

Sahara cleared her throat and looked at the table, feeling a strange warmth flooding her face. She could feel Aliya's gaze fixed on her, but she didn't dare meet it.

"I think," Jared said, "that a few of us should go after this Kalkas fellow and see what he has to say. Sahara, Deor, Brytnoth, you come with me. The rest of you can wait here. Find some food for Lady Aliya, but don't wander far. We can't afford to be separated in this place."

The four of them rose and made their way down the line of tents to where a black-and-white striped pavilion crouched, a crimson flag marked with an apothecary's sign hanging limply from its apex. The front flap of the tent was barely tied back, indicating that the shop was open while still concealing everything inside from the eyes of passersby.

Once inside, Sahara caught the mixed fragrances of herbs—pungent, sweet, fresh, grassy. As her eyes adjusted to the gloom, she glimpsed a small censer in the corner, its spicy smoke threading into the air and mingling with the delicate odors of the dried herbs laid out on the shelves. In the center of the pavilion stood a low table covered with dark amber bottles of varying sizes, some empty and some containing liquids.

"Can I help you?" asked a deep, reedy voice behind them.

They turned as the speaker came forward, his hands tucked inside the wide sleeves of his black tunic. Sahara frowned as she studied him. The silver embroidery that webbed over his robe caught the scant light inside the tent so that he seemed to shimmer. His silver beard was cropped close to his chin, but his hair hung down to his shoulders and was held back from his sharp face by a black leather band around his forehead.

"You are Kalkas?" Deor asked. "Apothecary, are you?"

"Yes on both counts, young man. Can I help you to something? Perhaps a salve for wounds or a tincture to make you more alert in battle?" He gestured toward the low table. "Does it please you to look?"

"No," Brytnoth said coldly. "We didn't come here for that."

Kalkas' dark eyes flickered at him, and then he turned to Jared and Sahara. "Perhaps something for those special evenings, then? Incense for the chamber?"

Sahara recoiled, and she could almost hear Jared's laughter inside her head. "No!" she said, a bit too quickly. Jared never looked at her, she noticed, but he too shook his head.

"We're here for information," Deor told him.

Kalkas moved to the tent flap and released the heavy fabric, shutting out the day and enclosing them in a world of shadow and smoke.

"What kind of information would that be?" he asked, returning to stand in front of Deor. "And who sent you to me?"

"We need to know about the Triumvirate," Jared said.

"I see."

"It seems they have quite a trade network set up...whores, slaves, stolen goods...and we need to know how they come by these things and where all the money goes."

"I see. And you think I know such things?"

"We were told to speak to you," Sahara said.

"By whom?"

Sahara hesitated. It suddenly occurred to her that they might be approaching this the wrong way. Dangerously wrong. It was impossible to guess where this mysterious man's loyalties lay, and it was very possible that this interview might be setting them up for another encounter with the gang's thug squad.

"Let's go," Deor said suddenly. "It appears we were mistaken. But we can let our affiliates on Halcyon know that this man is no longer a reliable asset."

He turned to leave, but as his hand touched the tent flap, Kalkas said, "Wait! Stop!"

Deor glanced over his shoulder. "Why? You plainly have nothing of value to us here."

Kalkas stepped forward and said, his voice soothing, "But you didn't let me answer! Please, come back."

"Give me a reason right now why we shouldn't just walk out of here."

"I know why they need more of the Demon's Breath. I know what they are planning to use it for. It may help you to negotiate a better price if you understand their...needs." A strange pleading lit his eyes, and Sahara sensed that a genuine fear lay behind his sudden eagerness to help them.

But fear of whom? she wondered. It was plain that the man was far more afraid of their supposed connection to Halcyon than he was of the Triumvirate.

Deor stepped back from the tent flap.

"Talk fast," he said, "and tell us what you know."

NINETEEN

TRUE TO HIS WORD, Aelred met them at their table at the inn that night. They had waited until late in the evening to take their meal, and the large taproom was nearly empty. Aelred slid into the empty seat next to Jared, and accepted a tankard of ale from the innkeeper's wife.

"So, Jared," said Rafe, "can you finally tell us what happened this afternoon?"

"I think we should begin by hearing what account Aelred has to give of himself." Jared turned to him. "You said this morning that we had much in common. Would you care to elaborate?"

"It's plain to me that you have no love for the Triumvirate," Aelred answered, "and your errand to Askalon may well be more complicated than you imagine. Let me be quite blunt so that there can be no mistaking my meaning." He paused and drew a breath. "There's no way to free your friends without overthrowing the Triumvirate."

Rafe laughed quietly. "I just *knew* that he was going to say something like that!"

"You have got to be kidding," Kirin said. "We aren't here to fight another war of independence. We're just here on a simple, straight-forward search and rescue mission."

"I really don't care what you think you were here to do," Aelred retorted. "Your crew has a rather unique skillset. One that I would be very, very interested in employing."

"Employing?" Sahara asked quickly. "You intend to hire us?"

"Not...exactly. I was more hoping that you would see our mutual interests in this situation. That our paths would cross in such a way that your pursuit of your own purpose would help my cause."

"Why don't you just tell us what you have in mind?" Deor suggested.

Aelred leaned back in his chair and stroked his beard. "Ever since I left Askalon, I've been gathering my fellow exiles together here. As I traveled to other planets in search of my people, I found many who had been oppressed and abused by the Triumvirate. Slowly but surely, more and more people joined my little band. We chose Agora for our base of operations because the Triumvirate has, for the most part, left the planet alone. It needs trading operations here to flourish so that they can fence their stolen goods. My guards are the ones you saw posted at the gates—my people rule here."

"And you let them continue to operate here?" Sahara snapped. "You let them bring their slaves here to market? You permit all this?"

Aelred's eyes flashed at her for a moment. "I understand your feelings," he said. "But to do otherwise would be to make our presence known to the Triumvirate, and I was not yet ready for that."

"It's hard for me to accept the argument when I see what I saw today," Sahara said. "Those women...Aelred, if you have the power to stop this and you don't..." Her voice trailed off.

"Not so fast," Aelred cautioned. "I didn't say I just let it run here. We have a ransom system in place. My people are at every slave auction, either buying the slaves themselves and setting them free, or ransoming them from their new masters."

"That must cost you a fortune," Brytnoth remarked quietly, regarding Aelred with new respect.

"Yes," said Aelred. "But we have generous supporters, and I've managed to usurp a little corner of the stolen goods market for myself. We have men on Askalon who smuggle things out and we have a front operation that sells them here. The money goes to free those who are brought here to the slave auction."

"It's quite an operation you have running here," said Jared, his tone betraying his admiration.

"You haven't heard the half of it yet," responded Aelred, a smile flashing across his face. "We've begun striking back at the Triumvirate."

"Where?" Brytnoth asked.

"We've been quite successful at destabilizing Triumvirate control of some of the outer planets. And with every victory of ours, the Triumvirate becomes more desperate. They've started concentrating their forces on the planets closer to Askalon, especially those where they have a strategic interest."

"Like Gladius," Emma piped.

"Yes, exactly. They can't afford to maintain the border planets—they lose too many men. So, even as they scrabble for control, their territory is collapsing upon itself."

"So you're ready to meet them on their own turf now," Sahara said. "You've got them right where you want them and now is the time to strike, is that it?"

"That's right." Aelred leaned forward again. "I hope you begin to see where our interests might be mutually served by our alliance. I have an army, and you have, as I said, a unique skillset."

"You mean we're damn good assassins, and you hope we can eliminate them before it comes to pitched battle, is that right?"

Aelred laughed a little at her brazenness. "Well, I wouldn't have put it that way, but that's about the gist of it, I guess."

"Overthrowing the Triumvirate won't be a simple operation, and simply assassinating the leadership won't necessarily solve the problem," Jared said with a bitter laugh. "Trust us on this—we've already learned that lesson. And there's another piece of this puzzle that we need to consider. That's where the information we obtained from Kalkas comes into play."

"It turns out that the Triumvirate is now indebted to the drug lords on Halcyon," Brytnoth said. "Crushingly, impossibly indebted. They've been using a mind-control amnesiac drug called Demon's Breath to keep the slave population on Askalon subdued. And they've expanded its use now to a select group of armed squadrons— the kill squads—who are tasked with hunting down anyone who gets even remotely out of line."

There was a strangled sob from Aliya, who had been listening silently to their talk from her place next to Emma. "Arnauld!" she murmured through her tears. "What have they done to you...to our people?"

Emma took Aliya's hands in her own and tried to comfort her, and Aelred cast a pitying glance in her direction.

"Unfortunately, that's not all," Brytnoth continued. "It's to the point now that they don't know how to run their operations without it. And the drug lords, good businessmen as they are, have increased the price for the stuff. And they are demanding payment of the debt in full under the threat of cutting off the supply."

Aelred took a deep breath. "And the Triumvirate doesn't have the money, do they?"

"No, they don't. That's the reason for the trafficking in slaves and stolen goods. They're trying to make enough money to afford the drug and pay their debt to Halcyon. But it's still not enough."

"So what are you saying, then?" Aelred asked. "How does their problem with the drug lords impact my plans?"

"Just this," answered Jared. "If you overthrow the Triumvirate, you won't be starting with a blank slate. You have to consider how you're going to solve the Halcyon equation."

"I see your point." Aelred sat silent for a few moments. "Will you help me, or is this where we part ways?"

"Oh, I think we're in," Rafe answered, glancing for confirmation in Jared's direction. "But we just need to wait around for a week for our ship to be fixed."

Aelred smiled at him. "No need for that, my friend. Our ships are already fueled and on standby."

"You have weapons?" Sahara asked. "Enough weapons?"

"More than enough weapons."

"There's just one more thing to consider," Deor said suddenly. "Kalkas told us that the Triumvirate has created an entire class of addicts to this Demon's Breath drug. We can't just cut off their supply...we'd probably end up massacred. We need a way to wean them off the drug."

"Kalkas would know how to do that," Sahara said. "He'd know if we have to taper off their supply or if we can just wean them off onto some kind of surrogate instead."

"You think he's still around?" Deor asked. "I'd have fled the city if I'd been questioned like that."

Sahara shrugged. "We'll just have to see."

Just after dawn the next morning, she, Jared, Deor and Rafe left for Kalkas's tent in the market square, hoping to persuade Kalkas to help them. The streets were as busy as they had been the previous day and they made painfully slow progress.

"Doesn't the sun ever shine here?" Rafe said, shoving his hands into the pockets of his black combat pants. "It's all just shades of gray."

Sahara glanced up at the sky, still blanketed by the dense clouds that kept the light muted. "It doesn't seem like this cloud cover ever breaks," she said. "And have you noticed? There's not a plant to be seen anywhere."

"How miserable," Jared said. "To be locked always in a world of stone and steel."

They entered the square in silence and made at once for the striped tent in the far corner. To their relief, the flap was slightly open, just as it had been the day before. And when they entered, they found Kalkas.

Sahara blew out her breath in a sigh of relief. "We were afraid you had gone!"

"Gone where, my dear?" the healer asked. "Agora is my home. And I do not flee my home because of some uncomfortable questions."

"We need your help," Jared said.

Kalkas cocked an eyebrow at him. "Again?"

"Yes, again. But in a different way this time."

At that moment, several customers pushed their way inside the tent, chattering noisily about their morning's shopping successes. Jared and his group scattered around the tent, pretending to look over the healer's wares and trying to remain inconspicuous.

Sahara found herself at the incense table, and she inhaled the fragrant blend of scents deeply. She examined the different sticks arranged on the table, smelling some that looked intriguing. She especially liked one, a sweet, spicy wood that made her think of warmth and stirred vague memories of her childhood. The scent seemed full of promise and left happiness in her soul. She clutched the little bundle in her hand.

"An excellent choice," said Kalkas quietly from over her shoulder. "It suits you."

Sahara turned and held out the bundle guiltily, not daring to ask what he meant. When she met his gentle gaze, he smiled at her.

"Keep them," he said, closing her fingers around the bundle once again. "As a gift."

"Thank you," she murmured, feeling that the words were somehow inadequate.

Why should he show me such kindness? she wondered, her hand tightening around the little bundle of sticks. *He certainly hasn't known any from me.*

As soon as the other customers paid for their purchases and left, Jared and the others gathered around Kalkas once more.

"So," the healer said, "you need my help. And what is it this time?"

"You told us yesterday that the Triumvirate has basically created an entire population of addicts to Demon's Breath," Jared said.

"This is true."

"If the supply was cut off suddenly, that would create an ugly situation, wouldn't it?"

"Of course. It must be done slowly, gradually, or you'll have madness and hysteria, and very likely violence. Understand that the drug alters consciousness. These people, if they have been subjected to the drug for a long period of time, no longer recognize reality in the same way. They don't want to. They want to remain in that suspended state where nothing is painful. And if they have been forced to commit crimes and atrocities under the influence of the drug...." His voice trailed off.

"They wouldn't remember those things, would they?" Sahara asked quickly. "I thought you said it erased their memory."

"It does. But those acts still change something inside, whether the memory of them is there or not."

That's far truer than you know, thought Sahara, a weight of sadness settling within her.

"Tell us how to help these people," Jared said. "How can we rid them of the addiction? Do we have to keep supplying them with this particular drug, or is there a substitute?"

Kalkas nodded slowly. "Yes, there is a surrogate. It is non-addictive, and it is highly potent. It takes only a few doses to release the addiction from Demon's Breath."

"And do you have access to it?" Jared pressed. "We're going to need a lot of it."

Kalkas looked down at his hands. "Unfortunately, I cannot just give you a packet of some herb. The surrogate must be manufactured, and then you need someone who knows the process and the dosages to dispense it."

"You're right," Deor said. "We need you."

Kalkas raised his eyes to Deor's face.

"When do you leave?"

TWENTY

AELRED'S FORCES were ready to leave for Askalon in a fortnight. He had six transport ships in all, each with a 100-man crew and more weapons than Sahara had ever expected to see gathered in one place. Each ship was outfitted with a set of Triumvirate uniforms so that they would appear to be slave transports, thereby avoiding any uncomfortable questions at the port. Aelred explained that the ships would leave Agora by twos over the course of the next three weeks, allowing them to infiltrate Askalon without drawing too much attention to themselves.

"We're going in first," he told them. "We'll be able to get a feel for things and make arrangements for the rest of the troops. And Kalkas can start working on that surrogate."

"That will take me some time," the healer sighed. "Tinctures like these need time to achieve maximum potency. I wish we had more than just three weeks—six would be ideal. But we do what we can."

At first, the others in the group had received Kalkas with suspicion. His eagerness to help their cause seemed strange, given his high position within the Triumvirate-Halcyon drug axis.

"It's not a position I chose for myself," he had told them. "Like so many who fall under the shadow of the Triumvirate, I was impressed into their service. I never dealt in hard drugs before they came to Agora, and I would never deal in them again if I could avoid it. But they have threatened to kill my family unless I do as I'm told."

Aelred had immediately issued orders to find Kalkas's family and move them to a secure location, and, with that, Kalkas had become one of them.

———

The trip to Askalon took the better part of two days. As they began their descent into the port of the capital city of Pentapolis, Brytnoth stood at the gallery window in the crew's quarters with Sahara, watching his homeworld slowly materialize through the thick bank of clouds. Sahara could read the raw emotion written all over his face—the tight line of his jaw, the white knuckles of his balled fists, the flush in his cheeks. She wondered if this was how she would feel if she ever got the chance to return to Amaryl—this gut-wrenching mix of wild hope and terrified anticipation.

They broke through the last of the cloud cover, and the hectic color drained from Brytnoth's face. Everywhere they looked, the charred ruins of once-magnificent buildings clawed their way into the sky like skeletons tumbled in a mass grave. Enormous channels pitted and gouged the land, obviously man-made and gaping like hell-mouths. Hulking derricks squatted over the ravaged landscape as far as they could see, and an endless array of pumpjacks churned in constant motion, like cogs in a single huge wheel of machinery.

The city of Pentapolis proper sprawled out to the west of the port. Closest to the landing platforms, dingy cubes of buildings crowded one on top of the other, with no clear design or attempt at order. Beyond these lay a range of hills that had once cradled the valley land like a mother's arm. On the slopes of the nearest hill, Sahara could see the remnants of the gorgeous villa homes that had been the glory of this wealthy metropolis. At the peak of the hill, overlooking the now-wasted vista beyond the city, stood what had to be the Great House, still intact. Its graceful lines and elegant proportions, which had once made it a queen among courtiers, now looked as ostentatious as a harlot on a street corner.

"What have they done?" Brytnoth gasped at last. He dropped to his knees, his hand sliding down the glass. "What have they done?"

He bowed his head, and Sahara, feeling awkward and strangely numb, slipped silently away.

Even as the ship descended, Sahara's anxiety grew. They looked official enough in their stolen Triumvirate uniforms, but Sahara knew there was more to a disguise than a costume. Sahara's group knew nothing of Triumvirate protocol. When the ship touched down on the landing pad with a gentle bump a few minutes later, she took a deep breath, brushed off her black jacket, and hoped that Aelred's men had enough experience to keep them all out of trouble.

They filtered down the ramp and onto the platform. There was no bustle of activity here as there had been on Agora or Gladius. A trio of empty shuttles waited on the platform, and one of Aelred's men ran toward them. A moment later, he was backing one of the shuttles up to the cargo door.

"Where is everyone?" muttered Deor.

Jared gestured to the guard house, which squatted on the far side of the platform.

"Playing cards?" he suggested.

They all turned in that direction, and Sahara saw that Jared wasn't joking. The lurid glow of powered lighting illuminated the inside of the station, revealing ten men in various stages of disarray sitting around a large round table, passing around cards and a bottle of something. A chill, not unlike the one she had felt back on K'ilenfir, shivered through Sahara.

Something's not right here, she thought. She caught the flash of Jared's eyes and knew that he had heard her.

A tall man with shoulder-length black hair stumbled out the door of the station, tugging a stained black jacket over his half-untucked shirt. The action seemed to unbalance him, and he clung to the door-jamb like a crutch to keep from falling over.

Sahara glanced over her shoulder at the ship, where their crew, dressed in slaves' garb, was unloading their cargo onto the shuttle at the direction of three other men dressed like Triumvirate troops. Her breath caught in her throat. This was the moment. Those crates were full of weapons and supplies, and if the guard decided he wanted to inspect things, they could have trouble. Her attention snapped back to the guard station.

"Supplies go to th' warehouses," the man bawled at them, his voice slurred. "Slaves to th' check-in...down there. In the Village." He waved a hand vaguely in the direction of the blockish buildings at the edge of the city.

"Thanks, captain," Jared called.

The captain staggered back inside after watching them for a moment, and Sahara saw him fall into his chair and receive the hand of cards that one of the other soldiers dealt to him.

"We need to move these goods fast, before they decide to take more interest in us," Sahara murmured.

"It doesn't look like they care what we're bringing in here," Jared replied. "But the less loitering we do, the better. Drunkards are unpredictable."

"It's a shocking lack of discipline," Rafe commented, joining them and jerking a thumb toward the station. "I mean, I expected to run the gauntlet here. There was more security on Agora!"

Guess I didn't need to worry about protocol, Sahara thought.

"Let's just move out. I'll take the supplies to the warehouse with Deor and thirty of the others. Hopefully we'll be able to find a secure place to stash everything until it's needed. Sahara, head to the city with Aelred and the others." He glanced at her, looking oddly unsure of himself. "Can I contact you when we're done here? You can let me know where to find you."

"You're *asking* me?" Sahara blurted.

Jared shrugged awkwardly. "It's fine, then?"

She nodded, frowning, and Jared returned to the shuttle. She saw him pause briefly to explain things to Deor, and then he headed off to give his orders to the men.

"What was that about?" Rafe wondered aloud. "He's never asked you that before, has he?"

Sahara shook her head, still staring after Jared.

"Well, he has been acting a bit strange lately," Rafe said with a sigh and a shrug of his powerful shoulders. "Don't ask me what's in the guy's head."

After a moment, he left her side to collect the rest of the men for the trek into the city. Sahara lingered where she was, watching the supply shuttle disappear from view, her mind tumbling with questions that she dared not frame into words. When she finally turned to join her own party, the tail end of the column was just stepping off the platform onto the road. Jogging to catch up with Aelred and Rafe, she flashed them a smile of apology and fell in.

Their path was sparsely illuminated by the same ghastly lights that she had seen inside the guard barracks. These were mounted on tall poles that leaned at crazy angles to the ground. As the street leveled out, the lighting became sparser still, leaving deep pools of gathering dusk between flickering islands. They were heading into the outskirts of the Village, that borough of squat buildings that Sahara had seen on their descent into Pentapolis. A cold, crawling uneasiness stirred in her stomach as they continued down the street, and Aelred, seeming to feel the same way, quickened their pace.

Some of the buildings were clearly occupied, with yellow light seeping through dingy windows. Others stood completely dark and seemingly vacant, though Sahara was sure at one point that she saw a blur of movement in one of the casements.

As they passed the second block, Sahara suddenly checked her pace.

"Look," she said, laying one hand on Aelred's arm and pointing with the other.

An armed patrol was heading straight for them.

Aelred held up a hand and they stopped, waiting in breathless silence as the troop moved toward them at a brisk trot.

"Where are you taking this lot?" the commander bawled as his troop approached.

"These are new arrivals," Aelred answered.

The patrol halted in front of them, and the commander peered over Aelred's shoulder at the men gathered behind him. Then his unfriendly eyes flashed back to Aelred. "Didn't they tell you to take them to the check-in station?"

Sahara's breathing changed instinctively as she slipped her hand behind her back to grasp the hilt of her double-bladed dagger. Slow, steady, rhythmic.

If they want trouble, they'll get it, she thought.

And yet, glancing sidelong at Aelred, she felt a sudden surge of admiration for him. The man was obviously a natural leader, and if the commander's hostile manner intimidated him at all, he didn't show it. He was in total control of the situation, and that meant that she could just watch and wait. For now.

Aelred snorted in disgust. "What? You mean those drunken sots up the hill?" The commander's expression soured, but Aelred didn't give him the chance to speak. "No. They didn't tell us a damn thing."

"Crank's always drunk on duty," the commander mumbled, almost to himself. "Don't know why he always gets that assignment while the rest of us have to run the city like rats in a cage."

"If you were Azel's brother, you'd probably get that assignment too," said the man standing at the commander's right hand.

Sahara's gaze snapped to his face. His features were chiseled and hard, and a jagged scar ran down his right cheek. His corded arms were crossed over his chest, and he stood at least half a head taller than his commanding officer. He didn't look like the sort of man to take kindly either to drunkenness on duty or to favoritism.

He might be useful, Sahara thought. *And if that idiot commander up the hill is the brother of one of the Triumvirate leaders, that could prove very useful indeed. We may have to pay him a visit later.*

"Shut your mouth, Derrek!" the commander snarled, cursing furiously under his breath.

Derrek shrugged his shoulders, his bored gaze shifting over the road.

"Are you finished?" Aelred asked, interrupting the commander's subaudible rant. The commander scowled at him, but Aelred continued in a more soothing tone, "Look, I'll take them to the check-in station in the morning. Isn't there an empty barracks we can use to put them up for tonight?"

The commander hesitated for a moment, and then jerked his thumb over his shoulder. "After the next intersection, the barracks on this side of the street are vacant. The kill squads got shipped out yesterday and won't be back for two weeks."

He turned to go, but then paused and glanced back over his shoulder. "I don't usually tell this to crews I don't know, but I like you." He grinned wolfishly at Aelred. "Once you get these drudges doped up and settled for the night, bring your crew over to the Aymatis."

Aelred gave him a blank look. "We're off-worlders, commander."

"Oh. Right. Forgot that part. Head to the end of the boulevard and take a left. You can't miss it." With another grin, he added, "You won't be disappointed."

Aelred nodded. "Thanks for the invitation."

"Don't mention it."

The commander ordered his troop to move out, and as the troop disappeared down the darkening street, Sahara released the hilt of her knife. Rafe saw the motion and laughed softly.

"You were ready for a fight."

"Always," Sahara said with a faint smile.

"Let's go, before we run into anyone else," Aelred said, waving them forward.

The next set of buildings offered no more welcome than the block they had just left behind, but here all the windows were dark. Somehow, that seemed reassuring to Sahara. Aelred continued along the row, finally stopping in front of a structure near the center. He gestured for the men to stay outside as he, Sahara, and Rafe went in to inspect the quarters.

Rafe flipped a switch near the door, and a light in the center of the room slowly flickered into life. The shadows sprang up and away, crouching against the walls and under the beds. There was room enough inside for fifty men, but the small quarters would be packed to capacity. Aelred frowned and rubbed his chin.

"All of these buildings are empty," Sahara said, sensing his thoughts. "Do we need to lodge everyone together?"

"No," he replied. "We'll use this as our command quarters. Rafe, let's distribute the men among the other buildings. And make sure Kalkas gets room to work."

They returned to the street to make the arrangements, Sahara stood where she was, shivering a little. A chill hung in the room, and she hated the look of the ugly light swinging from the ceiling by a twisted cord. It seemed cold and sterile, and it made the patches of grease on the huge central table gleam. Sahara wrinkled her nose in disgust.

The fireplace that dominated the far wall promised warmth, but there was no supply of wood anywhere in sight. Rows of narrow bunks lined the walls, and a set of metal steps ran up to a second floor, where Sahara could just make out the dim shapes of more beds.

It's as ugly as the rest of this planet, she thought.

She shifted from her thoughts as the others entered the room. Brytnoth busied himself with lighting a fire, which, Sahara now saw, ran on gas power instead of wood. Kirin and Rafe opened packs and set to preparing a meager meal. Sahara slipped past them and climbed the stairs to the loft. She glanced to her right as she reached the top of the steps and spied a small table with four chairs in the corner just above the fireplace. With a sigh, she collapsed into one of the chairs, which creaked ominously under her weight.

It was time.

We're here, she said, reaching out to Jared with her mind and hoping he was listening for her.

His face and warm, smiling eyes filled her consciousness. Her breath caught in her throat. For a moment, she forgot the greasy barracks and everything else and thought that they were back on Silesia, before any of this had ever happened, before she had chosen to push him away.

We've finished unloading the gear, Jared said, bringing her back to the present with an unpleasant rush. *We found a vacant warehouse. Tell Aelred that I'm going to leave a troop here to make sure no one else tries to use the place. And we're bringing all of Kalkas's gear down with us.*

Sahara nodded. *I'll tell them. Watch out for patrol groups on your way here. We had a bit of trouble with them, but Aelred impressed the commander and we ended up with an invitation to the Aymatis.*

The what? Jared frowned.

I don't know what it is. We're planning to head over there once you get here. She hesitated, and then decided to level. *I don't like it, Jared. I have a bad feeling about it.*

Jared's frown deepened. *We'll be there soon.* He looked for a moment as though he wanted to say something else, but he never let the words go.

Then something beyond her sight called his attention away and the thread was broken. He was gone.

Sahara buried her face in her hands, feeling the hot tears slip into her palms.

A short time later, Jared and Deor arrived at the barracks. Sahara watched silently from her perch above the fireplace as Aelred gave him directions regarding the rest of the men, and Jared went out again into the night. Then he returned again, and Aelred beckoned for him to join the small command group at the long table.

"Where's Sahara?" she heard him ask, and Aelred shrugged.

With a sigh, she made her way downstairs once again.

"There you are!" Jared exclaimed as she approached the table. "I was just telling Aelred that we've met with strange good fortune so far. An empty warehouse...and now an entire block of empty barracks. It's almost too good to be true."

"I don't like it," Aelred said, scowling fiercely. "It's all too easy. We need to be on our guard."

Sahara slipped into the chair beside Jared and nodded her thanks to Althea, who handed her a trencher of dried meat and fruit.

"Sahara mentioned something about an invitation to the Aymatis," Jared said. "Any idea what it is?"

"No idea whatsoever," Rafe said. "Just the promise that we won't be disappointed."

Jared snorted. "Right. It could be a lousy alehouse where old men sit and throw dice all day."

"Perhaps I can help," Kalkas offered, leaning forward to look down the length of the table at them. "I know something of this planet, and I have heard of the Aymatis."

They turned to him with interest, and Jared gestured for him to continue. Kalkas sighed deeply, his eyes flickering as he glanced at Emma, Althea, and Aliya, sitting quietly across from him.

"The Aymatis is the...tavern district of Pentapolis."

"Pentapolis has no tavern district!" Aelred protested, his mouth twisting in distaste.

"It had no such district when you ruled it, lord," he said. "But all that is changed now."

"Taverns?" Jared echoed, looking nonplussed. "It's just what I said. Stale ale and bad company, that's what it amounts to."

Kalkas hesitated, head bowed. "Not only that, Jared. I wish that were all. But there are the dancers."

"Dancers?" Kirin echoed.

"They train them here, and then ship them to the slave market on Agora," Kalkas said, his eyes once more flickering in Aliya's direction.

Aliya stared straight ahead, but Sahara could see the tears that glittered on her lower lashes. "It's true," she said in a choked voice.

"Not all the girls are sent to the Aymatis. But some are. I was not so unfortunate...but many of our women were."

Black anger darkened Jared's face, and Sahara could see the familiar tightness in his jaw. "I see."

"So, if you plan to go there, I'm sure you'll understand if we stay here," Aliya continued, clasping Emma's and Althea's hands. "There is nothing for us there."

Sahara sighed. Even in a Triumvirate uniform, Aliya looked completely the lady, and the graceful lift of her chin and the flash in her eyes reminded Sahara of their days on Silesia. Even as the lump of tears knotted itself in her throat, her stomach burned with fury.

Vengeance.

She wanted vengeance.

And then, with a start, she realized that everyone was looking at her.

"No way in hell am I staying here," she declared. Then, sharply, as no one moved a muscle, she added, "What are you all staring at?"

At that, there was a general awkward clearing of throats, and everyone seemed to take a sudden keen interest in the food on their trenchers. Only Jared continued to watch her, eyes dark and steady and inscrutable. She met his gaze and shrugged.

What? You can't tell me you're surprised, she challenged, speaking directly into his mind. *You think I want to sit around here with them and do nothing?*

The faintest ghost of a smile passed across Jared's lips, but he didn't answer.

TWENTY-ONE

"WELL, he said we'd know it when we got here," Kirin said. "I guess he was right."

They stood in the middle of the narrow boulevard, staring down the hill at the riot of light and color and noise below them. Jared glanced back the way they had come, toward the dark and silent streets that wound their way around the landing platform to the east.

"It's uncanny," he muttered. "What is this place?"

"There's only one way to find out," Sahara said, moving off down the hill.

A few minutes' walk brought them to the edge of the Aymatis, and once more, they found themselves hovering there, staring. It was as though they stood in the no-man's-land between two worlds - the one behind them, dark as death, and the other before them, crazed as hell.

"Damn," Rafe breathed. "I've never seen anything like this...ever. *Ever.*"

Just ahead of them, a group of tumblers in white-face somersaulted and vaulted over one another to the roaring approval of a drunken crowd in Triumvirate uniforms. To the left of the tumblers, a sprawling white stone manor house had been converted into some kind of tavern, with strings of ghastly red and white lights winding around what used to be simple and stately turrets and delicately arched doorways. Every window glared with the light of those lurid powered bulbs. Just above the massive front gate of the manor hung a sign that alternately flashed pictures of ale tankards and dancing girls.

A small group of girls, many of them only fifteen or sixteen years old, huddled together in the pool of light beneath the sign. They all wore flimsy knee-length white tunics, gathered over the left shoulder with the right shoulder left bare. Gaudy wide sashes wrapped around their waists, and simple gold or silver sandals protected their feet from the cobbles of the street.

Jared felt Sahara's body stiffen at the sight and before he could catch her arm, she had moved toward them.

"Damn," he said under his breath.

Sahara skirted the tumblers and planted herself in front of the girls at the gate. Jared and the others reached her just as she began to speak to them.

"What is this place?" she asked, pointing to the building behind them.

One of the younger girls shook her head mutely, her dark eyes wide. She frantically gestured for them to move on, but Sahara crossed her arms and Jared could see by the determined lift of her chin that she wasn't planning on leaving without answers.

Tell me what this place is," Sahara repeated, her voice a bit more firm this time.

One of the older girls stepped forward and wrapped her arms protectively around the younger girl, whose eyes were rapidly filling with tears. She glared at them as she gently stroked the girl's hair.

"Get away from here before you get us all killed," she hissed, pressing the girl's head into the crook of her shoulder.

Jared looked at her with new appreciation. With her ruddy curls piled on top of her head, she had a queenly look about her, and her gray-green eyes were bright and fearless. He sensed an intense strength there, and when he heard Rafe's sharp intake of breath, he knew he wasn't the only one who had noticed it.

"This isn't a place for the likes of you," the girl continued in the same harsh whisper. "Now go!"

Jared glanced from the girl to Sahara, and his breath caught in his throat. There was a strange resemblance between the two of them, something in the shape of the eyes, maybe, or the curve of the chin. Or perhaps that air of strength.

Before Sahara could speak, Jared intervened. "We'll go," he said gently. "We don't want to bring you any trouble. But can't you answer her question first?"

The girl's eyes narrowed as she regarded him. "Spare me your pleasantries, soldier," she snapped. "I've no use for sweet talk."

"What's your name?" Sahara asked.

The girl laughed, a sharp, clear sound with no joy in it. "What does my name matter to you?" She looked Sahara up and down like a piece of rotting meat. "How can you wear that uniform? How can you serve them? How can you do that to our people?"

The minute the words left her mouth, her eyes widened and she snapped her mouth shut. Sahara reeled back a pace as if the girl had struck her, and Jared suddenly understood.

That was the resemblance.

This girl was from Amaryl.

"Trouble's coming," Rafe warned.

Jared turned and saw a group of Triumvirate officers making their unsteady way toward the tavern gate.

"They look more than totally drunk and unusually prone to acts of violence," Rafe said. "Unless we want a fight, we should be on our way."

Jared hesitated. "We can't do that, Rafe," he murmured. "Look at these girls. We can't just leave them here."

"I don't want to leave them here," Rafe said, scowling. "But if we get tossed into some prison or other for starting a brawl—"

"Or finishing one," Brytnoth put in, catching the drift of the conversation.

"—or finishing one," Rafe continued, "then our entire mission is compromised."

The stumbling bunch of officers was barely a hundred feet from them now, their whistling and catcalls cutting over the general din of the street.

"We're not leaving," Sahara said staunchly, her eyes never leaving the girl's face. "And I'm not one of them."

The green-eyed girl gently pushed her younger companion back toward their group at the gate. "Leave us alone," she said to Sahara. "I can take care of my girls...and I certainly don't need help from some traitor like you!"

"Ho, girlies!" hollered an officer as the group finally pushed its way past the tumblers and entered the circle of light at the gate. "Here we are! Lord Baltek will have no reason to beat you tomorrow!"

Sahara stepped between the men and the group of girls. Her right hand was already behind her back, grasping the hilt of her dagger.

"Get going, scum," she said, her voice clear and calm, "before I beat your sorry hide all the way into whatever hell waits for you."

The man started and blinked rapidly, trying to focus his drink-bleared eyes. Then he thrust his finger in her face.

"What's this girl doing in a uniform?" he slurred, his voice too loud. "Whose idea was this?"

"Jared," murmured Rafe in his ear. "Do something, or this is curtains. She'll kill him."

Jared sprang forward and grabbed Sahara's arm before she could draw the dagger.

"Cute, ain't she?" he asked, laughing like a drunken idiot. "We thought she looked cute all dressed up, didn't we, boys?"

"Let me go!" Sahara hissed, trying to jerk her arm out of his grip. "What is *wrong* with you?"

He tightened his hold on her arm and shot a pointed glance over his shoulder at Rafe and Brytnoth, cuing them to play along.

What the hell are you doing? Let me go! Sahara's voice cut through his consciousness, dragging his attention inward.

Shut up! Do you want to get us all arrested and those girls killed? he fired back. *Just play along!*

Rafe reeled forward and slapped the man's hand out of Sahara's face. "And you're too late anyway," he said, seeming to struggle to keep his words coherent. "We've already engaged these ladies for the evening...so get on home before you get into trouble."

"Why are they still standing out here, then?" the officer snapped, his face flaming with more than just drink. "We'll just take one of them inside to serve us some ale."

He grinned wolfishly at Rafe and made to move past them. But the stultifying effects of liquor had muddied his reflexes. He didn't even flinch before Sahara's right fist caught him squarely on the bridge of his nose. He stumbled backwards, his eyes streaming tears and his nose gushing blood.

Jared guffawed and slapped his thigh. "She got you good!"

The others joined in, laughing uproariously and hoping that this would send the crew packing. But the soldiers rallied around their leader, murder in their eyes.

"What gives?" one of them said, balling up his huge fists. "She needs a bit of manners, don't you think, boys?"

Grunts of assent from the rest of the gang faded into the whisper of steel on leather as several daggers were drawn.

"Get out of the way," he growled to Jared and Rafe.

He planted a hand in the center of each of their chests and gave them a shove. Jared lost his hold on Sahara as he reeled backward into Brytnoth, who stood just behind him. Kirin caught Rafe before he fell to the ground.

Jared fought his way upright, his eyes riveted on Sahara's back. He saw her slip the dagger from its sheath and felt, even though he wasn't touching her, the supple tension of her muscles as she readied herself for the attack.

"Damn," he mumbled again under his breath.

"Captain Teon!"

The shout came from within the tavern gate and shattered the killing moment. The hulking man's attention snapped to something behind them, and Jared and his friends turned to follow his gaze. The crowd of girls scattered into the shadows hedging the entrance as a huge man rolled his bulk into the street.

"Captain!" he shouted again, shoving his way through Jared's group. "You disorderly lout! You're not welcome here, you cursed drunken fool! Get you gone!"

Teon, who had finally managed to staunch the flow of blood from his nose, pointed accusingly at Jared and his friends. "They're the ones causing the trouble, Brogan," he countered sourly. "We just came for some drinks and a bit of fun."

"I've told you before that I don't want your sort here! My girls don't like you, and neither do I!" Brogan shouted. "Now get out of here before I take the matter up with Lord Baltek!"

With some sullen murmurs and malevolent looks in Jared's direction, Teon's party slunk away, back across the street and then north along the thoroughfare. Jared watched them until the shadows swallowed them.

"Good-for-nothing trash," muttered Brogan beside him. "Useless idiots."

Jared turned to the tavern keeper with some interest. "You saved them a savage beating," he said, and out of the corner of his eye he saw Sahara slip her dagger back into its sheath.

"Eh?"

"I said that you just saved them a savage beating."

Brogan snorted. "Don't like them bothering my girls," he said. "I didn't even see your lot out here...just them." He shook out his richly embroidered tunic with fat fingers that glowed with rings. Then he cocked an inquisitive eye at Jared. "I haven't seen you here before."

"We're from off-world. Just came in today with a new shipment."

Brogan's eyes flicked to Sahara, who was watching them with her arms crossed and her head thrown back. "She's a feisty one," he remarked. "Where'd you find her?"

"She found me, actually," Jared answered with a wry smile. "She's one of my crew."

Brogan studied him thoughtfully. "It seems I owe you a drink," he said. There was a strange light in his eyes now, and Jared felt suddenly wary of him. "Bring your crew inside...second floor," the tavern-keeper continued. "The girls can show you the way. Just ask for the Lion's Den."

He turned and headed back to the tavern, clapping his hands at the girls near the gate as he passed them.

"The Lion's Den?" Kirin muttered. "Sounds like not such a good plan, Jared."

Jared rubbed his chin thoughtfully. "I'm not so sure," he said. "Aelred, do you know anything about this character?"

"Nothing at all."

"Look, Jared," Deor said suddenly, "we shouldn't all head in there. If this fat barkeep turns out to be a Triumvirate darling, then we'll have just committed operational suicide."

"Exactly," Kirin agreed.

"But," Deor continued, glancing in Kirin's direction, "I think that some of us should see what he has to say. Maybe he'll turn out to be an ally instead of an enemy. You saw how he handled that drunken lot just now."

"It's sound reasoning," Jared mused, then thought for a moment. "Aelred, take Kirin and Brytnoth and head back to the barracks."

"Why us?" Aelred asked.

"Because you're supposed to lead your men, and you can't do that if you're dead or in some Triumvirate prison."

"And you're taking these girls with you," Sahara added, gesturing to the group once more huddled under the gate.

"We can't do that!" Brytnoth protested. "What are you going to tell Brogan? And how are we supposed to get ten girls back to the barracks without getting seen or stopped?"

Sahara flashed him a bright smile. "We'll think of something, and I'm sure you will too."

"I'm not going," said the girl from Amaryl, who had been edging her way closer to the group while they discussed matters. Now, looking for all the world like Sahara, she pushed her way forward. "I'm not leaving the rest of my girls."

"The rest?" Jared asked. "How many more of you are there?"

"There are twenty more girls inside," she said. "They need me. You don't understand..." Her voice trailed off.

"What if we promise to get your girls out?" Sahara asked. "Would you go then?"

The girl laughed brusquely. "Don't make promises you can't keep," she scoffed.

"I don't."

The girl fell silent and regarded Sahara curiously for a moment. "Who *are* you?" she asked finally. "If you're not one of them, then who are you?"

Sahara put out her hand. "I'm Sahara," she said. "Daughter of Lord Anwar Acwellan, prince of Amaryl."

She paused and then added with a slow smile, "Welcome to the revolution."

TWENTY-TWO

THE GIRL STARED AT SAHARA, her mouth dropping open, and Sahara could feel the eyes of the others riveted on her as well.

"You!" the girl gasped finally. "But we all thought...we all thought you were dead!"

Sahara shook her head, her hand falling back to her side. "No." A brief smile flickered and was gone. "Not yet."

"But the Drakkin...I remember when they took you away! They all said you were dead!"

"They took me away, but they couldn't hold me. Fate set me free, and he found me." She nodded in Jared's direction. "And he destroyed them all."

The girl's eyes widened as she turned to look at Jared. "I can't...this is all just too much." She took a deep breath, then reached out and seized Sahara's hand in both of her own. "I'm Liana," she said. "And I'm sorry...I'm sorry I didn't believe you before. Your father was a legend..." Her voice trailed off as she met Sahara's steady gaze, and then she added, "You were a legend."

"Let my crew take these girls back with them," Sahara offered.

"They'll be looked after, and no one will hurt them again. And I promise you, we won't leave the rest here to suffer."

Liana glanced from her to Jared and then she nodded. "Let it be as you say."

Jared and Sahara stood just outside the circle of light before the tavern gate, watching Aelred lead the small group away. Liana kept turning back, but finally the night swallowed them and Sahara sighed.

"So. Your father was a prince," Jared said matter-of-factly. "Why didn't you ever tell me?"

Sahara studied him sadly for a moment, shook her head, and then turned toward the tavern. "Let's go," she said.

"If it's any comfort to you," Deor said, touching Jared's elbow as they moved to follow her, "I didn't know that, either."

The tavern yard was more like a cobbled drive, and it swept around a central space dominated by a silent stone fountain. Only dirt remained around its massive base, but Jared could imagine the flowering plants and grasses that might have once grown there, misted by the splashing water in the huge oval basins.

"This must have been a beautiful place once," Sahara said softly as they cut across the yard, their boots scuffing up a small cloud of dust.

Another few steps brought them inside the tavern. In contrast to the relative silence of the yard, where only the faintest noise from the streets breached the walls, the atmosphere inside throbbed with voices and grating music. Darkness as deep as the night smothered the taproom, every now and then pierced by pulsing flares of white light. As the lights flared, they saw the dense crowd that packed the room.

Rafe's usually strong voice barely audible. "This is hell."

The lights flashed again, and they saw, as if frozen for a moment, the raised arms, the flying hair, the stomping feet. Then the shadows drowned them again, and their half-blinded eyes could barely adjust before the lights flared once more.

"Let's just go," Sahara gritted, her voice taut. "Forget this. I hate this place."

"We have to see this through," Jared said. "I saw the stairs over there."

The lights pulsed again, and in that instant they all saw what he had seen—a wide, curving staircase that arched away from them into the darkness. Pushing through the crowd, they made their way toward it and then up. At the end of the stairs, a wide balcony opened out, giving them a bird's-eye view of the taproom below.

From that vantage point, they could see crystal chandeliers suspended from the high, vaulted ceiling three stories above them, relics of an era that had passed into dust. Jared noticed now that the white, smooth stone of the balustrade was carved into elegant and intricate designs, a testament to the skill of Askalon's craft-masters.

"Look," Jared said, pointing.

Straight in front of them stood a heavy wooden door marked with the head of a lion wrought in gold.

"The Lion's Den," Deor said, raising his voice above the din.

They crossed to the door and Deor pounded on it twice. Almost immediately, it swung open, and a silent, grim-faced hulk of a man beckoned them inside.

The door clicked shut behind them, and the noise of the taproom ceased as suddenly as if it had been switched off. By contrast, this room seemed ponderous in its silence, as if the air itself were made of velvet. Dim, reddish lights glowed in bronze sconces set at regular intervals along the walls, and a heavy, rich carpet lined the floor.

"Come," the man said. "Brogan is waiting."

They followed him down the length of the room, and then through another door. This opened into a smaller space dominated by a huge round table. Brogan slouched in a massive wooden chair at the far side, and two other men, sitting on his left and right, turned as they entered the room.

"Ah, here you are!" Brogan called. He waved a hand, dismissing the servant. As soon as the door closed behind him, Brogan gestured for them to sit at the table. "These are friends of mine," he said, indicating the men seated with him.

Jared considered them for a moment, but none of them moved. "What's this about?"

"It's just this," Brogan answered, clasping his hands together and leaning forward. "You don't seem like Triumvirate to me. And I want to know why."

This was dangerous ground. Jared fought the temptation to glance around at his companions, and kept his gaze fixed on Brogan. "I'm not responsible for what you think," he said, shrugging his shoulders. "What's that to do with us?"

Brogan frowned and rubbed his fat chin. "You don't look like one of us," he said, trying another tack. "You're not from Askalon."

"Of course not," Jared affirmed, trying to keep his voice from sounding harsh. "We're off-worlders. Just here to drop off slaves and cargo."

"You're not all from the same world, either," Brogan said, his eyes flitting from Jared to the others.

"No."

"And what about her?" Brogan gestured toward Sahara, who stood just behind Jared.

Jared glanced at her, then turned back to Brogan with another shrug of his shoulders. "What about her? She's one of my best men."

Brogan's eyebrow went up, and one of his companions made a small sound like a snorting cough.

"I wouldn't have thought...that's a surprising way to put things, friend," Brogan said.

"It's the truth. She's the best fighter in my crew. I never go on a run without her."

Brogan's eyes slid from one of his companions to the other, and then he fixed Jared with a slow smile. "But that's just the problem. Last I heard, women weren't allowed to wear the Triumvirate uniform."

Jared swallowed hard, and he felt Sahara stiffen next to him. It was a fatal mistake.

"That's why we called you here," Brogan continued. "Because if you're not Triumvirate scum, then I want to know you better."

"I'm sorry," said Rafe, stepping forward. "What did you say?"

Brogan laughed and gestured once more for them to take seats at the table. "Please, won't you sit and allow me to explain things? It's so uncongenial to talk to statues!"

After a moment's hesitation, Jared pulled out a chair and sat. The others followed suit, though Jared could see that they were perched on the edge of their chairs, ready to make a move if the situation deteriorated.

"That's better," Brogan said. "You are safe here, friends," he added with another of his broad smiles. "There is no Triumvirate spy here...no one to betray you."

"So you say," Jared responded. "But you are not known to us except as the master of this Triumvirate hell-house." He speared a pointed glance at the two men sitting next to Brogan. "So if anyone has any explaining to do, it's you."

"And if we don't like your explanation," Sahara added, "you'll be very sorry indeed that you invited us here."

Brogan started to laugh, but then he saw the expression on Sahara's face. And when she drove her unsheathed dagger into the wood of the table, he jumped.

"Now, now," cried the man sitting on Brogan's left, raising his hands as though surrendering, "we don't need any violence here! Why don't you put that away?"

Sahara shook her head. "I like it where it is."

"Start explaining," Jared said, folding his arms across his chest.

Brogan sighed heavily. "Not how I expected this interview to go," he muttered. "But," he continued hurriedly as he saw Sahara's hand slide closer to the dagger hilt, "so be it. Yes, I am the master of this Triumvirate hell-house, as you so eloquently put it. But I wasn't always. Before the Triumvirate came to power, I owned the three largest taverns in Pentapolis. I was a wealthy man, well-respected. Dristan—" he nodded toward the man on his left—"managed my business affairs. And Gervais here ran my household. I brewed my own ales."

"We don't give a damn about your ales," Deor said flatly.

Brogan seemed not to have heard him. "Then the Drakkin came, and they swept the Lords of Askalon out of their high seats and established the Triumvirate to govern us. They laid waste to our world. They exterminated our people. So few of us were left that the Triumvirate had to raid other worlds for slave labor. For a while they did the bidding of the Drakkin, but we are far from K'ilenfir, and soon the Triumvirate ruled in their own name here and in the surrounding worlds. Their reach has been growing ever since. And always they bring in more slaves...some they work to death in the mines, some do their killing work, and some they slave out to other planets."

"You mean the women," Sahara interrupted. "You mean they bring the women here, and then they slave them out."

Brogan nodded. "Yes, I mean the women. They bring some of them here first for training." He fell silent, staring down at his hands.

"We aren't stupid or blind," Rafe spat. "We know what this place is. Get to the point, Brogan."

"We want out," Dristan said. "There are rumors—"

"Are you the ones we've been expecting, or should we look for someone else?" Brogan interrupted, his voice tense with hope and fear.

Jared regarded him for a moment, then turned to Dristan. "Rumors of what, exactly?"

"Rebellion," answered Gervais. "Rebellion against the Triumvirate."

"I see. And what have these rumors led you to believe?"

"They say that there are others. That some of our people have survived, and even that Lord Aelred himself survived. People claim to have seen him, and they say he is raising an army. They say that he will return and take back his own." Dristan's voice rose with his growing excitement.

"I'm not Aelred," Jared said, "if that's what you're asking."

"We know that," Brogan retorted. "Do we look blind to you? As I said before, it's plain that none of you are from Askalon. But we had hoped that this was the beginning...that he would follow you here."

Jared glanced at the others, and for a long time he said nothing.

Should I tell them? he asked, reaching out to Sahara. *What do you think? Are they to be trusted?*

Don't tell them that Aelred is already here, she answered. *But they could be useful...they're well-positioned to gather information.*

"We're here to gather information for Lord Aelred," Jared said aloud. "The pieces are moving."

Brogan rubbed his hands together, his knuckles cracking. "Then it seems we can talk business after all," he said. "We can tell you what you need to know." A wide, genuine smile lit up his face.

"We're here to find our people," Rafe said. "We're from Silesia, and we had word that a ship full of refugees from our planet was taken by the Triumvirate and brought here."

The smile fell from Brogan's face as quickly as it had appeared. "That's...unfortunate."

"Why?" asked Sahara.

Brogan swallowed noisily. "You will have a hard time, I think, finding many who are left."

"And why is that, exactly?"

"Most of the women have been taken off-world...sold, or sent as payment to Halcyon."

Rafe swore under his breath, and Jared saw Sahara's face pale with horror. A cold, sick knot was growing in his own gut.

Dristan nodded. "It's true, I'm afraid. We had some of them here for a short time, but Lord Baltek wanted them shipped out."

"What about the men?" Sahara asked, her voice taut.

"Some have been farmed out to the kill squads," Brogan answered. "Some are working the mines." He shrugged apologetically. "But look, there's something else in motion now. They've been sending teams off-world, but no one has been able to find out for sure what they're doing. The crews are doped up so heavily that they don't remember anything...and the commanders aren't talking, either."

"Do commanders usually talk?" Jared asked.

"Some do. They'll come in here and have a drink or two and they'll let things slip, but not these. Whatever the Triumvirate is up to, they don't want word getting out."

"Does it have something to do with Halcyon?" Jared asked.

"Everything has to do with Halcyon now," Gervais replied, his eyes glittering. "They sold their soul to the devil, and now they're trying to keep him from collecting." He snorted. "And they are ripping Askalon to shreds in the process."

"Find out what you can about those off-world squads," Jared said, standing suddenly. Deor and Rafe rose from their seats and moved to stand behind him. "How many others like you are there? How many here on Askalon are ready to rebel against the Triumvirate?"

"Hard to say accurately," Brogan answered, rubbing his chin thoughtfully. "Many of the merchants are vestiges of the old Askalon, and if the Triumvirate didn't keep the slave population drugged on that damned Demon's Breath, they'd have no control at all."

Jared nodded. "Good. Get in touch with those you know to be friends of Askalon, and tell them to be ready. In the meantime, keep a low profile and follow the Triumvirate's orders. We'll contact you soon."

Jared reached the door with Deor and Rafe on his heels, but stopped and turned when he realized that Sahara was still sitting at the table.

"Something else on your mind?" Brogan asked, the slightest tremble in his voice in spite of himself.

"Get all the rest of the women out of this place by tomorrow night," she said, her voice low. "Or I'll be back to get them, and that won't go so well for you."

She rose slowly from her seat and jerked the dagger free of the wood of the table, spearing a pointed glance at Brogan as she slipped it into its sheath. Then she stalked out the door, leaving Jared and the others to scramble after her.

TWENTY-THREE

THE NEXT MORNING, Sahara stood in the street, leaning against the frame of the door and sharpening the blade of her knife on a whetstone. A strange chill hung in the air, and the sun never quite seemed to be able to break through the endless, scudding banks of gray clouds. Over the steady *hsk, hsk, hsk* of steel on stone came the equally steady noise of machines, a metallic grinding, whining, and thumping that filled her ears and set her nerves on edge.

She paused as a squad of men shuffled past her at a steady jog, their eyes blank and staring. Two guards set the pace at the front of the column and one brought up the rear. They glanced in her direction, but if they had a mind to ask her any questions, the knife in her hand persuaded them to leave her alone. The guard at the end of the column nodded curtly at her but said nothing.

Interesting, Sahara thought, *watching the troop round the far corner and disappear. They have a lot of confidence in that drug. That might prove useful when the time comes.*

She returned to honing the edge of her knife, allowing her gaze to wander over the buildings and then up, following the steady slope of the hill beyond the Village. The remains of what must once have been a magnificent, tree-lined avenue wound its ruined way up to the summit, ending at the high-columned gate of the Great House. It held its glory tightly veiled now, but Sahara could just imagine it soaked in sunlight, glistening like a milky gem in an emerald field of tall, straight trees.

They're not so different from the Drakkin, she thought. *Destroying everything good and beautiful...and for what?* The hideous cranking of the machines ground its way again into her brain. *For profit? For power?*

Anger surged up inside her, just as it had when she had seen Aliya in slave's rags, ready to be sold at market. The Triumvirate had ravaged Brytnoth's Askalon, and they would pay dearly for it. She would make sure of that.

A small noise behind her made her start and she glanced over her shoulder.

"It's a nice morning," Jared remarked, joining her in the doorway.

Sahara said nothing and returned her attention to her knife, feeling her pulse accelerate as he settled himself against the other side of the door. She kept her eyes fixed on her task now, afraid to meet those intense dark eyes.

"That looks sharp enough," Jared attempted after seconds of silence dragged out into nearly a minute.

Sahara nodded mutely, testing the edge with her thumb. She wanted to say something to him, but she couldn't frame the words and her voice seemed to stick in her throat.

She stood there, thumbing the edge of her knife, feeling more and more awkward as the uncomfortable silence mounted between them. Finally, she heard Jared sigh, frustrated, unhappy. She knew how he felt, but nothing could make it past the tightness in her throat.

"Look, Sahara."

The tone was business-like, but she felt the emotion that quivered underneath the words. It forced her gaze up to meet his at last, but she still couldn't speak.

"Things have been rough between us lately," he continued. "I really don't understand why, but I'm happy to let you be, if that's what you want. But this mission this morning...well, I'm not letting you leave without clearing the air." He hesitated for a moment, then added quietly, "If this is the last time I ever see you, I don't want it to end this way."

Now tears threatened to overwhelm her, and she wondered for the hundredth time how she had let things go so awry. Her feelings made no sense, even to her, and she didn't have the faintest idea how to begin explaining them to Jared.

"I can't make you understand," she finally choked. "I just...I can't. I'm sorry."

"Why do I need to understand?" An intense pleading filled his voice, his eyes. "I'm not asking to understand, Sahara."

She stared at him, feeling almost as if she had never seen him before.

"I don't pretend to know all that you are, but I know what you've been. I *know*, Sahara. I'm not a child needing protection, least of all from you. I don't fear you, and I'm not afraid of your past. I love you. I love *you*. You."

The raw honesty, the soul-baring earnestness in his voice, took her breath away. And, even as his strength warmed through her, the cold fingers of her fear of her own unworthiness stretched out to choke its life out of her.

"I know that...I mean, thank you...but I'm no good for you, Jared! What does a killer have to do with a just man?"

Jared laughed quietly. "I don't know what I've done to earn that description, or why it is that you seem to think I'm so much better than you are. We're both children of war, Sahara. We've both done things we regret...things we had to do to survive." He regarded her for a moment as a new thought seemed to strike him. "You know, perhaps it's you who doesn't really know me."

The possibility that he wasn't what he seemed to be—that he wasn't the man she had come to love—staggered her so completely that she could only manage to gasp, "Not true! That's not true!"

"Why not?"

"Because...because you haven't let it change you! For me...it's like...." She fumbled for words for a moment. "Back in Albadir, I found a tree once. Part of it was green and healthy, but there was a gaping hole in the trunk where the wood was rotting. Some of the branches were already dying, and I knew that it would soon have to be cut down. It just couldn't survive. The rot had penetrated to the core...and even though it looked alive, it was already dead inside." She searched his eyes, desperate to make him understand. "I—I'm like that tree, Jared."

She took a breath, and, seeing him open his mouth to speak, she blurted, "I want to love you, to just live and love and be! Like Aliya and Arnauld did, before all this. But part of me...I can't. And I'm afraid...so afraid that it will consume me in the end, because, really, it's consumed me already."

He stared down at her, his dark eyes shining with a depth of sorrow that she had never seen before. Wordlessly, he laid his hand over hers, and she realized just how hard she was clutching the hilt of her knife.

"You don't know how much all this has changed me, Sahara," he said, his voice little more than a whisper. "After my sister was killed, after that first revolution that took my family from me, there was a time when I lost myself. When I felt exactly like you describe."

"You did?"

"Love freed me from those chains," he continued. "Rafe...and Aliya, and Arnauld. My friends. They brought me back to myself, restored me to life. But I let them do it, Sahara. I let them save me."

Sahara's eyes blurred with tears, and when she blinked, they spilled over her lashes onto her cheeks. She squeezed her eyes shut, dragging a ragged breath into her chest. The pressure of his hand on hers increased suddenly, and she opened her eyes.

"No one can save you, Sahara," he said, his voice low and trembling. "*No one.* Not Deor, not anyone. Not me. Not if you won't let me."

He pressed her hand again and smiled at her sadly. As he turned to leave, she felt just how hard it was for him to let her go.

Sahara slid her knife into its sheath and wiped her face with her palms. She heaved a shuddering sigh and swung her gaze back to the Great House. She took another breath, clamping down on the tears that were threatening to brim over again.

Can't do that right now, she told herself, clenching her hands into fists. *I can't. I won't. I have to focus.*

She cleared her throat and crossed her arms over her chest, forcing herself to study the structure on the summit of the hill. That was her objective this morning. Jared had his mission; she had hers.

She would find her own path.

A short time later, Sahara, Deor, and Rafe traded in their Triumvirate uniforms for the flowing merchants' robes that Aelred had brought from Agora. Up in the loft of the barracks, Aliya twisted Sahara's red hair into a coil around her head, threading the thinnest ribbon of silver through it. Sahara's simple white robe was girdled with silver, and a gossamer-thin green wrap covered her bare shoulders.

"This reminds me of good times," Aliya said softly, arranging the wrap over Sahara's shoulders and brushing a stray curl out of Sahara's eyes. "Of the day Jared first brought you to us." She smiled at the memory, and the warmth in her eyes made a lump of tears rise in Sahara's throat.

Sahara frowned fiercely, trying to bury her emotions. "That was a dark day for Albadir," she muttered. "I've done nothing but bring ruin on you all."

Aliya smiled and shook her head. "No, my dear, that's not true! Through you, we won our freedom from the Drakkin!"

"Only to be enslaved by a far worse enemy," protested Sahara. "And you have lost Arnauld, and I've lost...." She turned away from Aliya's ministrations. "I don't know how you can even speak to me, my lady."

"Sahara," Aliya said gently. "You are brave, and you have so much more strength within you than you realize." She took Sahara's shoulders and turned her around again, looking intently into her eyes. "So don't let them win."

Sahara left her standing on the landing and joined Deor and Rafe downstairs.

"Sis," Deor exclaimed with a fond laugh, "you actually look like a girl!"

Sahara's face flamed, and Rafe joined in Deor's laughter.

"Well, the pair of you remind me of a pair of *gemmala* birds," she retorted.

She had seen flocks of these jewel-colored birds on Silesia, roosting in the trees near the river. The male's plumage was a riot of color, red and gold and blue, but the female's dun-colored feathers gave her excellent camouflage in the branches of the trees.

"I don't even know what that means," Deor said, still grinning at her.

"Just take my word for it," she said. She gestured at his claret-hued tunic and intricately worked silver scabbard, which held a curved scimitar. "Does that even work?"

Deor jerked the scabbard, popping the cruelly-edged blade several inches out of the sheath. "Of course it works."

"Halcyon's traders carry ceremonial swords," Aelred told her. "But the scabbard conceals a sharpened blade just as easily."

"Good," Sahara said.

"You do credit to my home," Brytnoth said to them. "And don't pay any attention to your fool brother, Sahara. I had no idea you could look so very lovely," he added, bowing slightly and smiling.

Sahara felt the heat rise to her cheeks again and she shrugged. "I'd rather have the battle uniform any day," she muttered. "I'm a bit lost in all this."

Her eyes flickered in Jared's direction, but he said nothing, and very obviously avoided looking at her. Disappointed but not surprised, she turned back to Deor.

"You've got the letter?"

Deor patted his chest, where he had tucked Jaffa's letter into a fold of his tunic. "Right here."

"Don't expect us back here anytime soon," Rafe said. "My guess is that the Triumvirate will have us stay at the palace, and that's just as well."

"Sahara and I will be able to communicate," Jared said, glancing in her direction with the barest flicker in his eyes. "Let us know what you find out."

"Likewise," Rafe said.

They slipped from the barracks and wound their way through the Village. Several times they had to dodge troops like the one Sahara had seen that morning, secreting themselves in side alleys and door-ways until the streets were empty once more. Finally, they emerged onto the wide boulevard at the base of the hill. Its leisurely way was flanked by crumbling stone walls that had once stood as high as Rafe's shoulders.

The slope seemed gentle enough, but they soon discovered that it was anything but easy. The path was often blocked by the blasted and twisted trunks of trees or the ruins of a wall, forcing them either to pick their way over or to squeeze around—a delicate business for Sahara in her long skirts. And the road itself, which had once been paved with huge, smooth stones, was now pocked with ragged pits, as if it had been bombed and never repaired.

"I'm never going to make it up there in one piece," Sahara grum-bled as she edged her way around a tumble of rocks that obstructed their way. She felt something snag and froze, fumbling with the deli-cate fabric. "Or, at least, my dress won't."

Deor backtracked to help her, freeing her robe and then giving her a hand over the last of the rubble. They hurried to join Rafe, who was standing a hundred paces away.

"Look," said Rafe as they came level with him. He pointed through a gap in the wall to their right.

Crouched behind a row of shrub-like trees lay the remains of a sprawling villa. Ornate columns still flanked its wide portico, but half of them were broken and the roof sagged crazily to one side. The furtive breeze, finding its way through the chinks and crevices of tumbled walls, fluttered silken curtains that hung half inside, half outside the gaping holes of windows.

"What this place must have been!" breathed Sahara. "It's heart-breakingly sad."

"Wait!" cried Deor, grabbing her arm as she started to walk away. "Rafe, wait!"

As Rafe turned back, Deor was already clambering over the fallen stones. He dropped silently down into the yard below.

"Deor!" Sahara hissed, leaning over the wall and watching as he crept across the open space to the collapsed portico. "What are you doing? *Deor!*"

He waved at her to be quiet, and then he vanished into the ruined house. Sahara glanced helplessly at Rafe, who had joined her at the wall.

"Where's he going?" Rafe asked.

"How should I know?" she snapped. She moved to run a hand through her hair in frustration, then checked herself, remembering its careful styling only just in time.

A moment later, they heard a strangled cry from inside the house.

Rafe vaulted over the wall in an instant and ran toward the building. Sahara, struggling with her long skirts, was left cursing in the street.

"Deor!" she cried hoarsely. "Rafe! Damn these stupid clothes!"

Finally, she saw them emerge from under the collapsed roof carrying someone between them. They stopped just below her and dumped the body. As it hit the ground, it rolled once and then came to a stop, arms spread-eagled on the ground and face tilted upward.

It was Gervais.

"What do you think you're doing?" Sahara gritted, glaring at her brother. "What did you bash him for? And how did you even know he was in there?" She yanked at her skirts in frustration. "I can't get down there!"

"No need, sis," Deor said, holding up a hand as she hiked her skirts up to her knees and moved toward the wall. "Don't even try it. Not a good idea."

Sahara dropped her skirts and crossed her arms over her chest. "How did you know he was in there?" she repeated.

"I saw him in the window there. But I didn't know it was Gervais when I went after him."

"Didn't you recognize him before you knocked him out?"

"Not really." He grinned up at her. "But I didn't want to find out too late, either. I figured it was better to bash him first and ask forgiveness afterward."

"Is it really a good idea to wait around for him to wake up?" Rafe asked. "Do we really want him to know that much about our business? It seems to me that there's only one good reason to be on this road, and that's if you're heading up there." He gestured toward the Great House, still some distance above their current position. "And the only reason you'd be heading there," he continued, "is if you have business with the Triumvirate."

"You think he's a spy?" Sahara asked quickly.

Rafe shrugged, his dark eyes troubled. "Why else would he be prowling around some ruined house along the road to their headquarters? I'm not sure I want to stand around and wait to ask him questions."

"But we can't just leave him here!" Sahara protested.

"If he is a Triumvirate spy, he'll just run straight up the hill and blow our cover as soon as he wakes up!"

"Why don't you contact Jared and have him send someone to collect him?" Deor suggested. "They can keep him in custody and question him...and keep him from compromising our mission."

"It's a good idea," Rafe agreed.

Sahara frowned at them. "It's our only idea," she said, moving a short distance away from them.

Jared.

For a moment, she was afraid that he had blocked her out, but then her vision blurred and he was there.

What's the problem? he asked, his face a mask.

It's Gervais.

What? His blank expression faded into confusion. *Gervais? From the Lion's Den?*

The same. We just found him poking around in the ruins along the road to the Great House. Deor bashed him over the head and we don't want to leave him here. If he's up to no good, he'll betray us to the Triumvirate.

Jared nodded. *I'll send a team up there to collect him.*

Sahara explained their location, and then hesitated. *Jared?*

What?

She paused again. *Nothing. Just...stay safe.*

He nodded at her, and then he was gone. With a deep sigh, she returned to the wall and reported the news to Deor and Rafe.

"Good," Deor said.

Gervais groaned and his eyelids fluttered. Deor dropped to one knee next to him, studied him for a moment, and then sent him back to oblivion with a solid punch to the face.

"He reminds me of someone, you know," Rafe said, grinning up at Sahara.

She couldn't keep herself from smiling back. "It runs in the family, I guess."

TWENTY-FOUR

IT DIDN'T TAKE LONG for Jared's men to arrive. Dressed in Triumvirate uniforms, they had cut straight through the Village, not fearing any interference from the other patrols. As soon as they had Gervais safely gagged, with his hands bound behind his back, Deor and Rafe clambered back up onto the road.

"Take him back to headquarters," Rafe told the soldiers. "I'm sure Jared will want to ask him plenty of questions."

They continued their trek up the boulevard. Sahara glanced back over her shoulder once and saw Jared's men half-carrying, half-dragging Gervais back down the road into the city. She shivered a little.

"I'm glad you caught sight of him," she said to Deor. "That could have been the end of us, no question."

Deor shrugged and grinned at her. "I'm just glad I got the jump on him. Did you see the size of the man?"

The gray sky overhead had reached its lightest when they finally gained the summit of the hill. The road ended abruptly at the massive arched entrance to the Great House and transitioned to a drive of finely crushed white rock. Even in the dull light, Sahara could still see the slight shimmer of the stones.

"I bet this was something to see in the sunshine," Rafe said, gesturing to the drive.

"Where are the guards?" Deor asked, his eyes searching to the left and right of their position.

It was all eerily still and silent within the curving walls. They stepped inside the arch and stopped again, scanning the area for any sign of movement. Huge skeletons of trees marched in even lines down the sides of the drive, the gray remains of a greener world, but nothing stirred.

"Let's move," murmured Deor, beckoning them forward.

They moved quickly, following the lane until the trees halted at the edge of a drive that looped around what must once have been an exquisite garden of flowers and stone. Only the stones remained. A rectangular pool, which had once reflected the sun-soaked sky in its still waters and was now parched and cracked, occupied the central space.

Sahara shook her head, feeling her throat tighten as she drank in the barrenness around them.

"What?" Deor asked, seeing the motion.

"It's just so sad," she said softly. "Isn't it? I mean, you can see what it used to be...it's like a ruined icon. Maybe one day it will all be restored."

"Men who are consumed by greed and hate have no time for love or beauty," observed Rafe. "All this...it's like looking into their souls."

Sahara regarded him in surprise. "How philosophical of you!"

"I have my moments," Rafe grinned.

"At last. Someone's finally come to greet us."

They turned to see Deor pointing toward the manor house. Two soldiers, dressed in the black Triumvirate uniforms and carrying heavy pikes, were headed across the courtyard.

"Here we go," Deor murmured, taking a deep breath. "Let's give them a show."

He strode forward to meet them, and Rafe and Sahara fell in

behind him. "You there!" Deor shouted, waving at the soldiers. "Is there no ceremony left in Askalon?"

They met beside the pool, and the taller of the two guards shook his head. "Ceremony?" he snorted. "You must not have been here lately. Who are you, and what's your business here?"

"We represent certain...strategic interests. The Triumvirate would do well not to leave us standing out here in the cold," Rafe snapped. "Show us to your betters."

"Ain't nothing better about them," growled the other guard, but they turned and led the way back to the manor house.

Sahara's jaw dropped as the guards shouldered open the massive wooden doors and then stood aside for them to enter. The entry gleamed in white marble, with soaring arches and a rib-vaulted ceiling that had once been painted in gorgeous deep reds and golds. The plaster of the ceiling was faded and crumbling now, but just enough of it remained intact to give Sahara an idea of what it once must have been.

The taller guard returned to his post outside the door, leaving his companion to escort them to the audience chamber.

"Follow me," the guard barked, startling Sahara out of her imaginings.

As Sahara and Rafe followed the guard and Deor down the corridor, she whispered, "This makes the Great House in Albadir look like a country farmhouse!"

Rafe nodded and was about to answer when Deor glanced at them over his shoulder, shaking his head and glaring them into silence.

The passage took several turns, and Sahara saw a number of side halls leading off into various other parts of the manor. Finally, they stopped in front of a set of wooden double doors, and the guard pounded twice.

"Wait here," he commanded and then entered, leaving them standing in the passage.

He was gone for several minutes, but when he returned, he held the door open for them to enter.

The audience hall stood several stories high, with the same gilded rib-vaulted ceiling as they had seen in the entryway. Clerestory windows down both sides of the hall filtered in the gray light and Sahara could see three massive chandeliers, which would supply light to the hall when darkness fell, suspended from the ceiling by thick cables. Three massive wooden chairs dominated the dais at the end of the hall, but only one was occupied.

"My Lord Ergeron will see you now," the guard told them as he left, slamming the door on his way out.

"Let's do this," murmured Rafe.

As they paced down the length of the hall, Sahara studied the man slouched carelessly in his seat on the dais. He would have been tall, even regal looking, if he had taken the care. He wore all black, from his shirt and doublet to his tall, cuffed boots, matching the dark, untidy curls that skimmed his shoulders. His mustache and goatee had been carefully trimmed, and seemed to be the only part of his appearance that he cared about. He regarded them lazily, as if they bored him to death, but when they reached the dais and Deor stepped aside to let her and Rafe come level with him, Ergeron suddenly sat up in his chair. His eyes, a deep and piercing blue, fixed on Sahara's face.

"Who the devil are you?" he asked, his voice much deeper than Sahara expected.

Deor folded his hands behind his back and measured the man for a few moments. "Lord Ergeron, I expect?" he said finally.

"Who else?" Ergeron asked, his sudden, easy smile once again taking Sahara by surprise.

Deor looked pointedly at the two empty chairs on Ergeron's right and left. Ergeron laughed.

"Oh, you expected to see my brothers, did you?"

"I told the guard we had something of importance to discuss,"

Deor replied, his voice sharp. "I expected him to relay that information."

"Well, he did relay it...to me. Because I am, as you see, the only one here." Ergeron's good humor seemed to be eroding quickly, and the last two words were bitingly sharp. "You must know, we get all manner of twaddle-peddlers who come in here thinking they have important business...and, really, it's just twaddle."

Deor arched an eyebrow. "Twaddle?"

"Twaddle. All of it. So boring. So infinitely boring."

Sahara wondered if her companions were as mystified by this strange man as she was. He didn't seem evil, and she'd been expecting evil.

"Is your contract with Jaffa and Halcyon twaddle, then?" Deor asked.

Now Ergeron really did sit up in his chair. "Halcyon? What contract?"

"Don't play stupid with me," Deor advised, "or I'll return to Jaffa and tell him the deal's off."

Ergeron laughed again. "Don't be so hasty, friend!" he said, his voice placating. "I didn't say anything! But come, introduce yourselves properly and then let's sit and have a bite to eat, shall we? Business is always better when hunger isn't growling at the door!" He rose and stepped down from the dais, holding out a hand to Sahara. "You first, my lovely lady!" he said lightly, smiling at her. "What shall I call you?"

Sahara could feel the blood rising to her cheeks. She was so distracted trying to choke down her anger at her own confusion that, for a moment, she couldn't remember the name she had chosen to use.

"Calypso," she managed. And then, remembering her court manners, she inclined her head slightly and added, "My lord."

He smiled at her again, his eyes bright. "I like that," he murmured. "Calypso."

Sahara swallowed and pulled her hand free. After gazing at her for a few more seconds, he turned to Rafe and Deor. "And gentle-men? You are...?"

"Alec," answered Deor. "And this is Jason."

"See how much better that is, Alec?" Ergeron said smoothly. "Now that we're all on friendly terms?" He clapped his hands, and a servant appeared at the small door left of the dais. "Food and wine for my guests!" he ordered, and the man bowed and vanished.

A few moments later, three other servants entered and moved a small wooden table from the side wall into the center of the hall. With smooth efficiency they placed chairs and finely worked goblets and plates at each place, then disappeared through the door once more. Ergeron beckoned for Sahara and her companions to sit. He held the chair for her and then claimed the place at her right hand. Deor sat on Sahara's left, and Rafe took the seat facing her. As they settled into their seats, the servants returned with a large bowl of fragrant fruits, some kind of roasted meat with a delicate sauce, and a decanter of ruby red wine. A basket of small buns completed the meal.

"I have all of this brought in," Ergeron said, waving the servants away. He poured the wine himself and then served them food as well. "We are a mining world, as I'm sure you have seen, and we do no farming here. No domestic arts for Askalon, I'm afraid."

Sahara carefully cut her meat and tasted a small piece, all warm juices and surprisingly delicate flavor. She tried a piece of bread next, still warm and soft, and couldn't help a smile of pleasure.

"Now, tell me what your business is with us," Ergeron said after they had satisfied their immediate hunger.

Deor pulled the parchment from the folds of his robe and dropped it into the center of the table. "Jaffa sent us to discuss the terms of your contract," he said. "It seems we need to come to a more mutually beneficial arrangement."

Ergeron studied the parchment for a long moment without touching it. "Is that so?"

Deor leaned back in his chair and studied Ergeron. "Yes. That is, unless you don't care to continue your relationship."

Sahara glanced at her brother, then met Rafe's gaze over the table. He winked at her, his mouth twisting in his usual quirky smile as he lowered his head and continued his dinner. Sahara stared at him a moment, her stomach knotting strangely, but she pushed her confusion aside and turned to Ergeron.

"My lord," she said, putting on her best imitation of Aliya's soft, supplicating tone, "won't you at least look at what Jaffa has proposed?"

Ergeron's eyes flickered at her, his expression softening. "If you ask it of me, I will." Again, that easy smile, and now something else too behind his eyes.

Sahara twisted her hands in her lap, tensing her muscles against the shudder she felt run through her. This man was odious—evil in a different way than she had expected. Prepared to meet a dragon, she had overlooked the serpent in the grass.

Ergeron lifted the parchment and broke the seal. His fingers were long and strong, Sahara noticed, and an immense ruby set in an etched silver band encircled his right index finger.

"How lovely!" she exclaimed before she could stop herself. When he glanced at her, she gestured to his hand. "The ring, I mean."

"Ah, yes. It is lovely, isn't it?" He turned his hand so that the ruby caught the light, seeming to glow from its very heart with its own radiance. Then he pulled it off. "Hold out your hand."

Sahara obeyed and he dropped it, heavy and warm, into her palm. Then, with another of those unnerving smiles, he returned his attention to the parchment.

Like a father giving his child a bauble to amuse her, she thought.

And suddenly, holding that ring, still warm from the heat of his hand, she felt like she couldn't breathe.

She dropped it onto the table as if it had been a live coal and reached for her goblet, taking several draughts of wine before setting it down again with a shaking hand. It wasn't like her to feel this unnerved, this overwhelmed. A chill of panic wormed through her. All her muscles were tensed now, and only a supreme effort of will kept her from fleeing the room. She forced her expression to remain blank, but she stared earnestly at the top of Rafe's head, begging him to look up. He continued placidly eating his dinner, completely oblivious, and Sahara realized once again what an incredible gift it was to be able to speak directly into Jared's head.

Jared. She could....

No.

She was being weak and stupid. The last thing she wanted was for Jared to know it.

She swallowed hard. She had to do this, and she had to do it alone.

Raising her goblet once more to her lips, she caught Deor watching her, concern plain in his eyes.

"Are you all right?" he mouthed silently.

Sahara hesitated. She started to nod her head, but then stopped. She gave the tiniest shake of her head and then glanced pointedly at Ergeron, who was still absorbed in reading the contract.

Deor smiled at her reassuringly, and she felt a little warmth creep back into her chilled hands.

At least he knows, she thought. *I'm not alone, after all.*

"I'll have to discuss these terms with my brothers," Ergeron said suddenly, setting the parchment aside. "I invite you to stay here until we've reached a decision. I have no doubt that we will have a counter offer to discuss. You are empowered to negotiate for Jaffa, Alec?"

"Yes," answered Deor. "And we'd be pleased to take your offer of hospitality. We saw nothing much appealing on our way here."

Ergeron laughed. "No, I imagine not. We are a utilitarian city without much in the way of comforts for travelers."

Sahara desperately wanted to say something biting about this, more from a fighting impulse to reassert her control over the situation than from anything else, but she had sense enough to realize how counterproductive this would be. She stared at her plate and held her tongue.

"I expect you must be weary from your travels," Ergeron continued, pushing back from the table and standing. "I beg you to excuse me, but there are some matters I must attend to. If you're finished, my servants will conduct you to your apartments. We'll summon you when we're ready to begin negotiations."

He picked up the parchment, folded it, and placed it inside his jerkin. He caught sight of his ring, sitting on the table where Sahara had dropped it. With a glance at her, he slipped it back on his finger. Then, bowing slightly to them, he turned on his heel and left the hall. As if on cue, the servants reappeared and cleared away the dishes.

"I wasn't done with that!" muttered Rafe as they carted away the dinner things. "Can't a man finish his dinner in this place?"

"I'm sure they do three squares here, Rafe," Deor laughed.

"I think they'll haul us out next if we don't get up," Rafe said, eyeing the servants warily. "They seem pretty efficient...and in an awful hurry to put things away."

As the servants came for the table and chairs, they rose and moved to the far end of the hall. One of the men pattered after them.

"Come with me, if you please," he said, waving them out the door.

He led them through several twisting passages and up a wide flight of stairs. Turning left, he continued a little ways down another wide hallway, then stopped and unlocked a door.

"My lord requests you stay here," he said, pushing the door open for them to enter. "Ring the bell if you require anything." He gestured to a silken pull-cord hanging just inside the doorway. "You will be summoned when my lords are ready to receive you."

Without waiting for them to speak, he shut the door again, and they heard the key turning in the lock.

Rafe jumped at the door, fighting with the handle. After a few moments' struggle, he gave it up.

They were trapped.

TWENTY-FIVE

SAHARA, Rafe, and Deor stared at the door for a long time without speaking. Then Sahara wandered into the small sitting room and dropped into an overstuffed chair. Rafe and Deor trailed after her, and Rafe sprawled at one end of a long settee. Deor paced the room like a caged animal, his eyes fixed on the door.

"What are we supposed to do now?" Sahara asked finally. "Deor, sit down. They're not going to let us out just because you wear a hole in the floor."

Deor complied, perching on the edge of the settee, and Sahara laughed quietly. "Yes, that's *so* much better," she scoffed.

"We knew this would happen," Rafe reminded her. "This is the game. We just have to play it now."

"We thought we'd be staying here, Rafe, not be trapped here." She swore softly and rubbed her hands over her face, a sudden weariness washing over her.

"What happened in there, sis?" Deor asked suddenly.

"Something happened?" Rafe sat up and frowned at her. "What? What happened, Sahara? Did I miss it?"

Sahara shuddered and tucked her feet up further underneath her. "I hate him," she said. "I hate him, Deor!"

He nodded appreciatively. "So you should. He's evil. What did you expect?"

"I didn't expect...I didn't expect *that*. I didn't expect the serpent."

"Excuse me," Rafe leaned between them. "Can you start at the beginning and tell me what's going on?"

"There's something wrong about him," Sahara said. "He has some kind of...some kind of power over me or something."

Rafe arched an eyebrow in surprise. "Over *you*?" He shook his head, an incredulous frown on his face. "That's not possible. The man was interested in you, no doubt about that. But I can't believe his oily charm was actually working..." His voice trailed off as she sat there, staring at him in stricken silence. "It can't have been working!" he tried again weakly.

"Rafe, it's awful!" Sahara said. "It's like a magnet...I've never felt power like that. I never want to see him again!"

"That's impossible, you know that. You have to see him again or this whole act falls apart." Rafe's brow furrowed and his frown deepened. "I just can't believe...you really...I mean, he was getting to you with all that? All that smiling and nonsense?"

Sahara glowered at him, miserable and huddled in her chair.

"Smiling with a knife under his cloak," Deor said. "She's right, Rafe. The man's a serpent. You can't blame her for never wanting to lay eyes on him again."

Rafe's gaze never wavered from Sahara's face. "Incredible," he murmured. "All the horrors you've faced, all the battles fought and won...and it's the enemy that smiles that's got you spooked."

Sahara dropped her eyes, thoroughly humiliated. She wished she'd never said anything at all, that she'd been stronger and not revealed her struggle to Deor. She glared at Deor from under her lashes, wishing he'd just kept his mouth shut.

"You know, this could all work to our advantage," Deor said

thoughtfully. "He's obviously interested in you, Sahara. We could exploit that."

Forgetting her humiliation in an uprush of horror, Sahara stared at her brother. "I'd have to see him again for that to work, Deor. And I just told you..."

Deor waved her protests aside. "Nobody blames you for feeling that way, Sahara, but you know that it's impossible. So if you do have to see the fiendish creature again, why not make him grovel?" He regarded her quizzically for a moment, a half-smile crooking his mouth. "You don't seem to understand how this sort of thing works."

"Jared could have told you that," put in Rafe suddenly.

Sahara felt as though he had just punched her in the stomach. "What did you just say?"

"Nothing."

Deor studied them both for a moment. "There's clearly backstory here that I'm missing."

"Yeah," Rafe answered. "There is, and you are."

Deor waited for another moment, but neither Rafe nor Sahara offered anything further. "So I'm guessing no one's going to fill me in on that, then."

Rafe shook his head. "Just explain what you're getting at, Deor. Forget what I said."

"Fine." Deor turned back to Sahara. "He's attracted to you, sis. So lead him along a bit. His affection for you will make him weak and vulnerable...and that's good for us. He might drop some valuable information in his attempt to impress you, and that's good for us, too."

"I get that," she said. "But I don't play those games. That's not who I am, and that's not what I do." Her eyes flickered at Rafe. "You know that."

Rafe said nothing, and she felt suddenly unsure of how to read his silence.

"Anyway," she continued, "I don't know if I can pull that off. Like I already told you, he has some kind of power over me. I don't know who would be in control of that situation, and I don't have a way to get out if it goes bad."

"Yes, you do," Deor argued. "I'll put a dagger in his guts. That's your way out."

"No. I'm not doing it, Deor. I don't think it's a good plan. At all. I don't even know how..." She stopped suddenly and fumbled with the hem of her skirt, her emotions tumbling like mad.

Give me a knife and a straightforward fight, she thought. And then, with a rush of bitterness, *I'm obviously a wretched failure in the romance department. If they wanted someone to play these games, they should have brought Emma along instead.*

When she finally risked a look at her brother, Deor was frowning at her. "Sis," he said sternly. "This is war. We have to take the Triumvirate down, and I know you're skilled enough to recognize a tactical advantage when you see one. Frankly, I'm shocked that you didn't come up with this idea yourself."

Sahara snorted. "Maybe because I don't think like a man, Deor."

"You don't?" Rafe piped from his corner.

"Shut up, Rafe!" she snapped, glaring at him again.

"No, Sahara, I won't." Rafe suddenly abandoned his bantering tone for a deadly earnest one. "He needs to understand. If we're talking about making this a mission priority, then he needs to under-stand. My dear, you are brutal with the double knives, but the deadly art of flirtation obviously wasn't taught in assassin school."

"I can't believe we're having this conversation," Sahara muttered. "I'm going to bed." She stood abruptly and stumbled over her long skirts, and she swore, jerking them up into a bundle. "I hate this stupid dress!"

She retreated with all that was left of her pride into the bedroom and shoved the door closed with her elbow. Then she dropped her skirts and considered the massive four-poster bed, carved out of a rich, dark wood. Its creamy white coverlet and generous heap of pillows in varying hues of green and gray begged her to bury her cares in their softness. Ignoring the temptation, she slipped down to sit on the floor, leaning her head back against the door and drawing her knees up to her chest.

"What's her problem?" she heard Deor ask after a moment.

"She's in love with Jared," Rafe answered. "And she doesn't know how to show it."

Sahara bowed her head onto her knees as a long silence dragged by on the other side of the door. She wasn't sure she really wanted to hear what her brother thought about Rafe's statement. She heard the murmur of voices begin again, and she crept to the bed, curling up on the smooth coverlet and hugging a pillow to her chest. She closed her eyes, trying not to strain to hear the conversation in the other room.

It's true, she thought. *I don't know anything about love. Not really.*

As she always did in these moments, she remembered her father. She had loved him so fiercely, and he had been taken from her. Deor had been taken. Her mother had been taken. Everything she had ever loved in her young life had been taken away. She would have died to save them, but she was never given the chance.

Maybe that's why I fight so hard.

A sharp rapping startled her, and she realized that she had fallen asleep.

"Sahara!" It was Rafe's voice, muffled by the closed door.

It cracked open, and then Rafe's face appeared, peering around the door at her. She blinked at him, trying to force her muzzy thoughts to focus. He slipped into the room and stood at the foot of the bed.

"I'm sorry," he said. "I didn't want to wake you...but we have a situation."

She sat bolt upright at that. "What situation? What's happened?"

"You've been invited to dinner," Rafe answered, his face grave. "Alone."

Sahara frowned at him. "But I'm not the one Jaffa appointed to negotiate the—"

"You've mistaken my meaning," Rafe interrupted, shaking his

head, fighting—and failing—to keep a straight face. "Lord Ergeron wants you to have dinner with him. Just you."

She scowled at him. "I'm not going. I told you. I hate him."

"Look, sweetheart," Rafe said. "You've got to go."

Sahara's scowl deepened. "Don't you dare call me that again. And I'm not going. He's a snake. I'd rather have dinner with an insect." A wicked grin flashed suddenly across her face. "Like you."

Rafe laughed then. "There! You see? You do know a thing or two." Before she had the chance to reply, he swept on, "The dress is all right...maybe a bit wrinkled, but passable. But we're going to have to do something about that hair."

An hour later, she sat stiffly at the wooden table in the hall, facing a hideously charming Lord Ergeron.

"You know," he said, filling her goblet with wine. "I was so happy to hear that you had accepted my invitation. It isn't often that we receive guests here at the Great House, but it's a pleasure to do so. Especially when they are as lovely as you."

Sahara's stomach tightened into a cold knot. Her hands, clenched together in her lap, were slick with sweat. When he picked up his fork with his perfectly manicured fingers, she felt a shudder of revulsion, and then the sudden flare of hatred banished her fear like a shadow.

If he wants to play this game, she thought, *then that's fine. But I'll win.*

She took a deep breath, unclenched her hands, and forced herself to relax. *Here goes nothing.*

"Why, Lord Ergeron, you're all politeness," she said with a sweet smile. "We weren't sure what to expect, you know."

"What? From me? From Askalon?"

"Yes. From it all." She glanced around, slowly, until finally she let her gaze rest on him. "This is lovely, and you are truly charming."

He smiled at her and waved his hand dismissively. "My dear, we are a rustic lot compared to what you must be used to."

Truer than you know, you forked-tongued devil.

"I was so honored when Alec asked me to accompany them on this trip," she said. "I love to travel, you must know, but this is the farthest I've ever been." She took a sip of her wine, and then continued, "So, tell me! You said before something about Askalon being utilitarian? And you said it's a mining world?"

"We are the energy center of the system, my dear! And we're finally tapping Askalon's true potential. The Drakkin didn't understand anything about such matters...that's why they appointed us to oversee things here. We have had a devil of a time trying to repopulate the planet. Their damned destructive methods left us with nothing! But we've managed."

"How fascinating!"

It sounded idiotic to her, but it seemed like the right thing to say. And he seemed not to really hear her anyway.

"We've just begun drilling operations in the last mines in the southern quadrant of the planet," he continued. "Our production should easily double, and, of course, now that the Drakkin are out of the way, demand has skyrocketed. Trade is opening up once again between the planets, and fueling stations are cropping up all over the system."

"And you supply them all?"

"Oh, yes! And even as we increase our production here on Askalon, we're acquiring other energy assets around the system as well. I'm in charge of exploration and trade, so I've been managing our expansion."

"I can't imagine how busy you must be! And your brothers? They have specific duties as well?"

"Of course." He waved a hand as if to sweep them aside. "But they're dull and boring, the two of them."

Sahara laughed, and he laughed along with her. "Brothers often are," she said.

"Indeed."

At that moment, the servants brought their dinner on covered plates. When the silver covers were removed, fragrant steam escaped, and Sahara couldn't help exclaiming in surprise and pleasure. A gorgeous, deep red fruit sauce smothered several slices of meat, and delicate golden rounds of some kind of root vegetable sat beside them. She cut into the meat and tasted it, then tried the root. It really was delicious, and she spared a thought of sympathy for Deor and Rafe, who she imagined must be eating some kind of cold meat and bread in their rooms.

"This is exquisite," she said aloud. "Your chef is to be commended, Lord Ergeron."

He inclined his dark head. "He has served here at the Great House since before my time," he said. "We kept him on because he really was just too excellent to let go."

Let go. You mean murder or exile.

"Well, it was a wise decision."

They ate in silence for a few minutes, and Sahara studied Ergeron from beneath her lashes. Impeccably dressed once again, she noted, though he had changed his black shirt for a white one. Its wide sleeves showed beneath the slashed folds of his black doublet. The ruby ring was back on his finger, and she caught herself staring fixedly at it.

"I meant to ask you before," she said, "about your ring."

"What about it?"

"Is the stone something they mine here as well? I've never seen such claret red in a gem before."

He turned the ring and examined the stone. "Yes, they once mined such treasures here," he answered. "But this is a more ancient artifact, given to me by the lord of this house before he departed."

Given. You mean you stole it. And that means it's probably Aelred's ring.

"I consider it a reminder," he continued, "and keep it as the principal treasure of my house."

"Reminder, my lord? Of what?"

He smiled at her again. "The turning of fortune's wheel, one might say."

She regarded him in surprise. He was such a confusing person, a maddening person.

Is he really that evil? she wondered. *His brothers are probably the evil ones...they're the brutal and cruel tyrants. Not Ergeron.*

He turned the ring so that the stone caught the glow of the dozens of candles in the chandelier that swayed gently over their heads. She stared at it, mesmerized.

She was slipping. She was drowning, and soon she wouldn't remember who she was or why she was here.

I have to fight it...fight him.

"You said you were in charge of exploration," she managed. "What do you look for?"

She forced her breathing to deepen, desperately struggling against that terrifying suffocation. *How does he do it? What's happening to me?*

"New resources," he answered vaguely. He chewed thoughtfully on a piece of bread, and it seemed to Sahara that he had almost forgotten that she was there.

As his thoughts took him away from her, Sahara felt as though someone had suddenly opened a window for her own mind, letting in the fresh air and easing that oppressive heaviness. Mentally, she shook herself and set about reinforcing herself for the next onslaught.

"I should like to think that I can trust you," he murmured, his distant gaze snapping suddenly to her face. He turned the ring slowly on his finger in what appeared to be an unconscious gesture. "I feel that we have a special bond, you and I. Like destiny, perhaps."

Sahara barely suppressed a shudder. The waves were over her head again, the current threatening to pull her under. He smiled at her, raising his goblet to toast her.

"To destiny," he said.

Mechanically, she raised her own glass, and she felt herself smiling back at him.

"Destiny," she echoed.

"Now," said Ergeron, his voice soft and soothing, "I think you were about to tell me why Halcyon really sent you here."

Sahara.

In an instant, Ergeron's hold over her shattered like glass, and she came back to herself in a dizzying rush. At the same moment, she saw Jared's face in her mind's eye, but before she could connect with him, Ergeron's voice overpowered the vision.

"Calypso, tell me," he said. "Why are you really here?"

She could feel Jared's presence just outside her mind's reach, and she clung to that shadow. It was all that kept her from sinking under the flood of Ergeron's influence. A strange dizziness came over her, and she could barely focus on what was in front of her.

"We're here for the contract. Jaffa's contract. Halcyon's contract." She forced the words out of her mouth, her voice sounding strangely breathless.

Sahara!

Jared was pushing harder, and the harder he pushed, the clearer her thoughts became. She lifted her eyes to Ergeron's face, saw the black scowl of frustration that he instantly smoothed away when he realized that she was watching him.

"Your glass is empty," he said, his easy smile drawing her in once more. "Can I refill it for you?"

He poured before she could answer, and as the rich red wine filled her goblet, her throat burned with an overpowering thirst. She started to reach for the goblet.

Don't! Sahara, don't!

She frowned. Why was Jared telling her not to take a drink when she was so unbelievably thirsty? Didn't he know how charming Ergeron was?

"Is there something wrong?" came that soothing voice. "You look unhappy."

"No, no," she murmured.

"Good."

His stunning blue eyes caught and held hers, paralyzing her gaze.

Her hand moved for the goblet again, and his gentle smile encouraged her.

"You're not here," he began again, his voice thrilling and low, "to confiscate our supply of *zanthos*, are you?"

Zanthos? The one corner of her mind that was still free registered the word and wondered, but she couldn't hold the thought.

The liquid slid down her throat.

As darkness swallowed Jared's face, as she felt the last of her control slipping away with it, she heard Ergeron murmur, "Because we haven't found it yet."

No!

Jared flung the word at her with such force that she dropped the goblet, spilling the wine on the table and all over the front of her gown.

She gasped and recoiled. Air flooded into her lungs, and the darkness in her mind cleared away.

"I'm so sorry!" she gasped.

"No matter!" he said, waving a hand to dismiss her concern.

But she had caught the scowl on his face again, and she knew that he knew she was free of him.

She had to get out...had to get away before he got hold of her again. Her head throbbed so badly that she could barely hold her eyes open.

If this battle for control of my mind continues much longer, she thought, *I'm lost.*

"I'm so sorry," she repeated, "but I have to go. My dress..." Her voice trailed off as she stared down at the front of her gown.

"Of course! I'll have something sent to your rooms." He stood, reaching out to help her to her feet.

She grasped his hand.

It was like taking hold of lightning.

The warmth of his touch flooded through her. She felt suddenly like she had so many months ago, when she had drunk too many glasses of *estevalia* at the Summer Festival. She found herself smiling up at him.

"I hope you have a restful night," he said with a slight bow. "Someone will come for you in the morning so that we can discuss our business matters."

A servant appeared beside her and gestured for her to follow him. She felt herself stumbling after him through the passageways, her mind and body reeling. She saw the door to their quarters, saw Rafe's face as he opened the door, and then darkness overwhelmed her and she collapsed.

TWENTY-SIX

HER EYES FLUTTERED OPEN. At first, all she could make out was a blur of light and shadow. She heard a door open and two sets of footsteps approaching, and then then the concerned faces of Rafe and Deor materialized from the haze

"You're awake at last!" Rafe said. "What happened to you?"

Sahara blinked. Her tongue felt like lead in her mouth and her limbs were still heavy. She felt something soft cushioning her, and then, as her range of vision improved, she saw the turned posts of the bed in their suite of rooms.

"Sahara, what happened?" Rafe repeated, his dark eyes earnest.

"Water," she croaked.

Deor held a cup to her lips, and cold, clear water slid into her dry mouth and down her throat. After a few swallows, she moved her head and he took the cup away again. She struggled to sit up, and Rafe grasped her arm to help her.

"I told you," she managed. "I told you that I didn't ever want to see that devil again!"

"But what happened to you?" Deor pressed, sitting beside her on the bed. "Did Ergeron do this to you?"

She rubbed her hands over her face, trying to force her mind to function properly. "I don't know. I think...maybe the wine? Or that ring? I don't know."

Deor's face twisted into a dark, murderous scowl. "I'll kill him," he gritted. "Did he drug you?"

Sahara glanced at him, hesitated, and then answered carefully, "It feels like he did. But then...I'm not sure."

"Well, that's the last time we let you see him alone," Rafe said. "I'm sorry we didn't trust your instincts."

"Don't be too quick to say that," she said. Her mind was clearing rapidly now. "I was able to find out some things, just like you suggested I might. He thought I was totally under his thrall, I imagine. He was trying to get information out of me. He wanted to know why Halcyon had really sent us here."

"So he didn't fall for the contract? He suspected something?" Rafe asked quickly.

"No, not like that. He's convinced that we're from Halcyon. But he thought they might have sent us here for another reason—that the contract was just a sham. They're looking for something here, and apparently Halcyon is after it."

"Did he tell you what it was?" Deor asked.

Sahara frowned. She knew he had named it. The name was there, nagging her just outside her conscious memory. "I don't...remember," she said. She closed her eyes, forcing herself not to chase it away.

And there it was.

"*Zanthos,*" she said, opening her eyes with a smile.

"*Zanthos?* What's that?" Deor's brow furrowed. "I've never heard of it. Rafe, you?"

"No. But I bet I know someone who has."

"Who?"

"Aelred." Rafe turned to Sahara. "You should contact Jared. Have him relay the information to Aelred and see what he knows about it. Because whatever this stuff is, I'll wager it's the center of their whole operation and the key to their power."

"Well, whatever it is, they haven't found it yet," she said. "They're looking for it, and Ergeron thinks Halcyon sent us here to take it from them." She closed her eyes again and sighed heavily. "How long was I out?" she asked after a moment.

"All night," Deor answered. "And that dress is ruined. Ergeron sent some other clothes for you." He gestured to the large armoire that stood against the far wall. "In there. Why don't you change and then we'll figure out our next move."

He stood and left the room, and Rafe moved to the door to follow him. Then he hesitated and turned back for a moment.

"I think you're very brave," he said softly. "For what it's worth."

Then he was gone, leaving Sahara staring after him and wondering.

With a sigh, she swung her legs over the side of the bed and then eased herself upright. She was relieved to find her legs steady underneath her, and she quickly crossed to the armoire and jerked the doors open. She couldn't help the grin that spread across her face.

"Now, that's more like it!" she exclaimed.

When she entered the sitting room a short time later, Rafe and Deor seemed to be deep in a very serious conversation, heads together, poring over something that Deor held in his hands. As she approached the settee, they both glanced up, and she heard Rafe catch his breath.

"That seems more your style," Deor remarked, smiling at her.

"I suppose women's clothes must be in short supply here," she said.

The black breeches, ruffled white shirt, and soft, wide-cuffed black boots were slightly too big, but she had taken the green wrap from her dress and used it as a wide sash to cinch the waist. It fell in soft folds now to her knee. She had smoothed her hair back into the twist around the crown of her head.

"And look!" she added, turning so they could see her back. "A handy place for my dagger, finally!" She had fixed the sheath inside the sash, within easy reach but well out of sight.

"And that's the Sahara I know so well," Rafe laughed. "Now come and tell us what you think."

She sat down beside him on the settee and gestured to the paper in Deor's hand. "What's that?"

"Aelred gave me this before we left," he responded. "It's a map of the city of Pentapolis and the surrounding areas. We decided that, as long as we're trapped here, we might as well consider how best to—"

He was interrupted by a sharp knock on the door. They heard the key rattling in the lock, and then one of Ergeron's many servants pushed the door open.

"My lord Ergeron requests you to accompany him today," he said flatly. "You will follow me to the Great Hall." When no one moved, he added, "Now."

Ergeron was seated in his chair on the dais, drumming his fingers on the carved arm. As they entered, Sahara noticed the dark scowl on his face, which disappeared as soon as he saw them coming.

"There you are, my honored guests!" he called as they entered. Sahara cringed as he smiled at her approvingly. "I am touring our weapons facility today," he continued, "and I want you to join me."

"What of our contract?" Deor demanded. "Have you discussed it?"

Ergeron waved a hand. "That can wait until dinner. My brothers will join us then, and we'll go over it in full. Don't worry, my friend!" he added, seeing Deor's face. "You'll be satisfied with the result, I don't doubt! But for today, I want you to see the crown jewel of our industry."

"How are we going to get there?" Rafe asked. "Walk?"

Ergeron's ringing laugh echoed off the vaulted ceiling. "Are you mad?" he asked. "Of course we're not going to walk! My ship waits for us. We can breakfast on board."

The ship was a small commuter affair, not intended to travel beyond the planet's atmosphere. Its two-deck design was trim and functional—a lower deck that housed the crew's quarters, galley, and storage, and a luxuriously appointed upper cabin, divided from the bridge by a set of metal double doors

Ergeron had ushered Sahara into a roomy window seat in the main cabin when they boarded, and now she sat with her face pressed against the glass, trying to fix landmarks so that they could find their way back to the facility later.

"Have you tried these honey cakes, Calypso?" Ergeron asked.

Sahara sighed in annoyance. He kept bothering her with his silly questions, and she wished he would just leave her in peace. Reconnaissance work was hard enough, but her head still felt fuzzy from whatever he had given her the night before. She needed to apply all her attention to the task at hand.

"Yes, yes," she said curtly, waving a hand at her tray, where a half-eaten cake sat on a plate.

She heard Deor and Rafe murmuring quietly in the row behind her, but they kept their voices so low that she couldn't make out the words. Ergeron, who sat facing her, stared out the window for a moment or two, and then took a breath to speak again.

"What's that?" Sahara asked suddenly, pointing out the window.

Ergeron leaned forward just in time to catch a glimpse of what she had seen. "That's the entrance to Gil-Gareth, our largest mine complex," he answered.

Sahara stared wordlessly at the landscape slipping below them. They had left Pentapolis behind them some minutes before, and there had been no sign of human habitation for miles—just row upon row of cranking pumpjacks. But here, a shanty town huddled around the gaping chasm that Ergeron had identified as a mine. She could make out scores of people scuttling like insects in and out of the rift. Just ahead of them was a small landing pad, and she saw dozens of people loading five small cargo ships that sat on the platform.

"What do they mine here?" she asked.

"They used to mine gems," Ergeron answered. "And we do some of that still. But we've sunk new shafts far deeper into the planet's crust, where the fuel deposits are most plentiful. That's our main focus now, you know."

"And did you dig that hole like that?" she pressed. "That huge gash in the land?"

Ergeron frowned slightly, obviously sensing the criticism in her words. "We enlarged it, yes. We had to get our equipment in there and run the piping out again."

Sahara said nothing.

"Our weapons facility isn't far now," Ergeron added, raising his voice so that Deor and Rafe could hear him over the hum of the engines. "It's just about twenty miles to the north of the Gil-Gareth mines."

They spent the last few minutes of the trip in silence. The landscape was depopulated once more, dominated by huge derricks. Sahara could see that this part of the country used to be a forest—the felled trunks of massive trees littered the ground as if they had been flung there by some kind of massive explosion.

"Did you blast all those trees?" she asked, gesturing out the window. She thought of Brytnoth, and tears stung the back of her eyes. She clenched her jaw and swallowed hard.

Ergeron laughed and regarded her quizzically. "We didn't blast anything! But they were in the way of our heavy equipment. Small price to pay for progress and industry."

He was hideous.

She took a deep breath, clenching her fists. A question had been needling her all morning, and it was time to ask Ergeron for an answer. She turned away from the window and fixed his eyes with hers.

"Why does Askalon need a weapons facility, my lord?"

He favored her with that languid, easy smile that she was coming to hate so much.

"Ah," he said. "What an excellent question. And here we are."

It wasn't until they disembarked that she realized he hadn't answered her question at all. But she had no chance to press him—he was far ahead of them, talking with the foreman at the gate to the facility.

"What is the Triumvirate up to?" Deor muttered. "This place is enormous!"

Sahara nodded. Their angle of approach had prevented her from getting a good look at the facility from the air, but as the immense gates rolled back for them to enter, the sheer expanse of the place took her breath away.

"Look," Rafe said, indicating the roof with a subtle nod of his head.

Guards stood all along the roof, stark against the banks of clouds that roiled overhead. Sahara counted five on this side, each patrolling a set distance. She glanced back over her shoulder at the guardhouse at the gate. Four more there, all heavily armed.

"Infiltration might be difficult," Deor murmured, guessing the track that her thought was taking.

"Maybe." She quickened her pace. "Let's move."

Ergeron was waiting for them at the facility's entrance. He punched in a code on a small keypad next to the door and then pulled it open, standing aside for them to enter first. As the metal door clanged shut behind them, Ergeron resumed the lead.

"This is both a manufacturing and storage facility," he said as they turned right and headed down a wide hallway. "Manufacturing happens in this western wing, and we use the less expansive east wing for storing the finished materiel."

They stopped at the double doors at the end of the hallway as Ergeron once more punched in a code on the keypad. He held the door for them and they stepped out onto a wide metal walkway.

"Welcome to Taur Isis, the crown jewel of Askalon's industry," he said, sweeping his hand majestically to encompass the space before them.

They stood a hundred feet above the floor of the manufacturing wing, overlooking a maze of massive machinery. Another fifty feet above their heads spanned a second walkway, and Sahara caught sight of guards pacing off regular intervals. She frowned and turned her attention back to the assembly line, leaning over the railing to get a better look. Everything was automated, and the few men she saw working were there to ensure that the machines functioned properly. The sheer speed and volume of production was like nothing she had ever seen before.

She glanced up to say something to Ergeron, but realized that they had already moved on. She ran to catch up with them.

"We opened this facility three years ago," Ergeron was saying. "At the time, we still served under the aegis of the Drakkin. We were going to use these weapons to free ourselves from their rule. But then the Drakkin fell, and we were masters of ourselves once more."

He was leading them all the way around the walkway, and Sahara watched the cycling machines through the railing, mesmerized. She nearly stumbled into Rafe, who had paused to get a better look.

"You're still running the production line," she said, not realizing she had spoken aloud until Ergeron replied.

"Yes. And it's this fact that I hope will influence our discussion later. But come! Wait until you see what I have in store for you, my friends!"

As he turned and led the way toward the exit, Deor grasped Sahara's arm and slowed her pace. Once Ergeron was twenty paces ahead of them and well out of earshot, he bent to whisper in her ear.

"I hope you're taking notes, sis," he said. "Because Jared and Aelred have to know about this place."

"Yes, I am, and yes, they do." She flashed a smile at him. "This is getting more interesting by the minute."

Ergeron reached the door and waited for them to catch up to him once again, his hand ready over the code panel. They passed through the door and out onto another metal walkway. This time, however, they were only twenty feet up, and Ergeron led them immediately down two flights of stairs onto the floor below.

"It's much better to walk through," he said, smiling his odious smile.

This entire third of the complex was filled with rows of weapons of all different types. They passed through racks of assault rifles, pistols, shotguns, larger machine guns, and rocket launchers, all cast of the same dull silver metal. It was an arsenal to equip an army, Sahara realized. And then, as they emerged from the racks, they were confronted by a huge tank.

But something was missing.

"Where's all the ammunition?" Rafe asked as they stood, staring up at the tank.

Ergeron chuckled. "Why, my dear fellow, that's the beauty of it all. We don't need ammunition. All we need is *zanthos*."

TWENTY-SEVEN

JARED SIGHED.

He never enjoyed interrogations, but this one was frustrating in the extreme.

Gervais sat sullenly in his chair, his hands bound behind his back and his legs secured around the ankles. His head was bowed, and he had refused to speak in the two hours that Jared had been asking him questions.

Now, pacing up and down in front of the fireplace, he caught Gervais's eyes flickering at him from under their lids. They were at an impasse, and Jared knew that Gervais sensed that he had the advantage. He would have to change the variables if they were going to get anywhere.

"Let's try this again, shall we?" Jared said, dragging his chair in front of Gervais. He leaned forward, resting his forearms on his thighs. "My men caught you prowling around where you had no reason to be. I want to know what you were doing there."

Gervais shrugged.

"You will tell me," Jared continued, his voice even.

Gervais shrugged again.

"No, you *will* talk to me, or I'll make sure you don't talk to anyone ever again."

Gervais shrugged a third time, a smile on his face. "If I die, you don't find out what you want to know," he said.

"I didn't say I was going to kill you," Jared said, his voice still level. "I'll just cut out your tongue."

Gervais swallowed hard, his eyes betraying a sudden burst of fear. The man had probably steeled himself to die valiantly and triumphantly in silence, and that glint of terror told Jared that he'd found the right pressure point.

"You wouldn't do that to me," Gervais croaked.

Now it was Jared's turn to shrug. He pulled out his boot knife and whetstone and started sharpening the blade. Gervais's eyes were riveted on the deliberate, rhythmic action.

"You...you wouldn't..." Gervais mumbled.

"Why were you in that house?" Jared asked, his voice mellow.

Gervais swallowed again, watching as Jared tested the edge of the blade against the pad of his thumb. Not satisfied, he continued sharpening it.

"Why were you in that house?" Jared asked again, speaking slowly, but with a growing threat in his voice.

"I was sent there," Gervais blurted, seeing Jared move to rise out of his chair. "Please don't...I was sent there!"

"By whom?"

Gervais hesitated for the briefest moment. Jared stood and flipped the knife into a more comfortable grip.

"I don't work for Brogan," he squeaked.

Jared snorted. "You think that's a revelation to me? Why don't you try telling me something I don't know?"

"I work for Lord Baltek."

"Baltek? The Triumvirate lord?"

Gervais nodded frantically. "He oversees the slave trade. Brogan is supposed to report to him, but he doesn't do what he's told. He's too easy on the girls…and sometimes they go missing. I think he sneaks them out to get them out of the trade, and I told Lord Baltek so. He was very appreciative…he told me I was essential to the regime." A note of pride crept into Gervais's voice. "He told me to keep an eye on things, and to report to him directly if anything looked suspicious."

"So you're a pathetic little snitch," Jared said scornfully. "A Triumvirate tattle-tale."

Gervais shook his head. "I'm a trusted associate of Lord Baltek's," he said. "I'm an important—"

"Shut up," Jared told him, and Gervais ducked his head as if Jared had thrown something at him. "You're a rat. You ratted out your friend, and for what? Because Lord Baltek batted his eyes at you and told you that you were valuable to the regime?"

Gervais squirmed in his chair. "Yes."

Jared snorted again. "That's pathetic." He let the words sink in for a moment, then continued, "So what, then? You were sent to spy on Brogan and what? Find out where he's hiding the girls?"

"No, not exactly." Gervais's eyes flickered at him for a moment, and he clapped his mouth shut.

Jared sighed and moved closer to Gervais. He tried to scoot his chair backwards and out of Jared's immediate reach, but with his hands and feet bound, he only succeeded in tipping himself over. He cried out in pain as his full weight and the wood of the chair crushed his hands and wrenched his shoulders. Jared reached down and grabbed him by the front of his shirt, heaving him upright again.

"Then what were you there to do?" Jared pressed. He jerked him forward so that his face was only inches from Jared's own. "Tell me."

Gervais tried to pull away from Jared, but Jared's iron grip on his collar held him firm. When he discovered that he couldn't budge, his words came flooding out. "Lord Baltek, he…he also runs the kill squads. We've orders to find revolutionaries…to make sure they don't spread…"

"I see."

Jared flung the man away from him, sending him toppling over again. Gervais, groaning with pain, managed to roll himself onto his side, taking the pressure off his injured hands. Jared moved around the prostrate figure, planting his heavy boots just in front of Gervais's face.

"So you weren't there as a trade enforcer," Jared continued. "You were there as a political spy."

"I followed you here last night," Gervais continued, his voice squeaking. He made a few feeble attempts to scoot himself away from Jared's boots, then gave up. "After you left the tavern, I mean. And then I saw the girl leave with your friends this morning. When I saw them heading in the direction of the Great House, I took a shortcut and waited for them."

"Too bad for you," Jared said.

He kicked Gervais in the gut, then turned and walked out of the room, leaving the man spluttering and gasping for breath.

Outside, Aelred crouched in the street, his back against the wall of the barracks. "How's it going?" he asked, glancing up as Jared emerged.

"He works for Baltek," Jared answered. "He's a snitch."

"Why should we care about Baltek?" Aelred asked. "He just runs the slave trade."

"That's what I thought, too. But it turns out that Baltek also commands the kill squads. They've been spying on the people, taking out anyone that they suspect of revolutionary tendencies. Gervais trailed us home last night, and then he tried to follow Sahara and the others to the Great House this morning. He was going to report us all to Baltek."

"It's a lucky thing we caught him, then," Aelred muttered. "He might well have blown our entire mission. Do you think he knows anything else that might be useful?"

Jared shrugged. "Hard to say. Depends on how high up in the ranks he was, I suppose. He thinks he was practically Baltek's right-hand man, but I have my doubts. Still, Brogan's operation is a critical one for the Triumvirate, which means that Gervais is pretty highly placed. It's possible that he knows something of the Triumvirate's larger plans."

Aelred studied the street. "Worth asking," he said matter-of-factly.

Jared turned on his heel and re-entered the house.

Gervais was still lying where Jared had left him. Without a word, Jared crossed to him and heaved him upright again. Then he sat back down in his own chair.

"We're off to such a great start," Jared said, favoring Gervais with a mirthless grin. "Let's see if we can't get better acquainted."

"Go to hell!" Gervais growled, his voice hoarse.

"That's not a nice way to talk. I'd like to know more about Lord Baltek. What can you tell me about him?"

Gervais glowered at him. "Why should I tell you anything more? You already know why I was trailing your friends. Isn't that enough?"

"Not quite. You see, I've got a feeling that you know a lot more than you're letting on."

"I don't see why I should tell you anything," Gervais said and spit on the floor in front of Jared's right boot.

Jared rubbed his chin and then ran a hand through his hair. "How many kill squads are there, Gervais?" he asked. "And how do they operate?"

"You expect me to tell you that?" When Jared nodded slowly, he barked a laugh. "Not likely."

Jared drew his boot knife again and studied the edge for a few seconds. "You sure about that?" he asked.

"What are you going to do with that?" Gervais' mirth seemed to die suddenly, and though he still had a grin pasted on his face, his voice quavered.

"I can think of all sorts of things," Jared said evenly, his eyes burning into Gervais's own. "I'm creative like that."

Gervais sniffed and dropped his gaze. "Well, I'm not talking," he said. "So you can—"

The rest of his words were swallowed by a howl of pain as Jared planted the dagger firmly in the fleshy part of his thigh. Gervais tried to shove his chair out of Jared's reach, but with his right leg now weakened by the wound, he couldn't get enough traction. A stream of curses flooded out of his mouth.

"Now," said Jared, yanking the blade free, "would you care to be civil, or shall I do the other side as well?"

"I'm bleeding!" Gervais bellowed, gaping as the bright red blood seeped through the leg of his pants, onto the wood of the chair, and finally onto the floor. "I'm bleeding! What's *wrong* with you? Are you crazy?"

"Tell me what I want to know."

Gervais stared at him for a few moments, panting. Jared wiped the blade of the dagger on a rag, which he tossed onto the table behind him. When Gervais still said nothing, Jared raised the dagger and made a move for his left thigh.

"Wait!" Gervais screamed. "No, wait! Wait! I'll tell you! Stop!" He wriggled frantically in his bonds, thumping the front legs of the chair on the floor as he tried unsuccessfully to move.

Jared sank back into his chair, eyebrows raised expectantly. "Talk fast."

"Lord Baltek has been deploying more squads lately, and he's catching a lot of flak from his brothers for it. He's paranoid, you know, and he ends up murdering groups of miners and taking out commanding officers...sometimes he doesn't have much evidence to support his suspicions."

"He goes after his own troops?"

"Of course. If an officer doesn't show the proper respect, Baltek gets suspicious. And once he's suspicious, it doesn't take long for him to find a reason to send in a killing squad. Take Yelsin, now. He used to be in charge of the guard station at the port...but he crossed words with Baltek once, and Baltek had him assassinated. Lord Azel, who's in charge of the military, almost murdered Baltek when he found out. But they agreed to appoint Crank, their idiot half-brother, to the post instead."

"How many kill squads does he have?"

"Maybe ten...maybe fifteen? There are four men to a squad. And these men are hard to come by. He doesn't just take anyone, you know. He pulls the best from the slave lots—anyone with military experience or skills. And getting selected for a kill squad means you don't get sent to the mines. It means you have a chance to live."

"Going to the mines is a death-sentence?"

"Pretty much." Baltek sniffed again and shrugged. "If the toxic gases down there don't kill you, then they'll work you to death. Or you die from the drug. Mine slaves last three months—six months tops."

"No wonder Baltek's worried about revolution," he muttered.

"That's just it, captain," Gervais said, leaning as far forward as his bonds would allow. "If those slaves ever got off those drugs, there'd be no stopping them. Every once in a while, you know, we get one that's resistant to the drug. He pretends to be doped for a while so he doesn't get noticed, but sooner or later he snaps. He tries to rally supporters. Might even try to jump the guards at the mine and lead the slaves to freedom. Trouble is, the other slugs are drugged out of their minds." He broke into a snorting laugh. "Nobody follows him. He's all alone, standing there like a fool. And then the kill squad's there to take care of him. No more problem."

Jared regarded him in silence for a few minutes. "That drug," he said finally. "That's Demon's Breath, right? From Halcyon?"

"That's right. It's powerful stuff. Like I said, if they survive the mines long enough, it'll kill them. There have been a few that survived long enough..." His voice trailed off and he shuddered. "Awful," he muttered.

"What happened to them?" Jared asked, a horrible sinking feeling in the pit of his stomach.

"It drove them completely mad," Gervais said, his voice low.

"Absolutely crazy. Like they weren't even human anymore." He shuddered again, and then added, "Those were mercy killings."

"How long?" Jared asked. "How long before that happens to them?"

"They're a time bomb after two months. But if they live more than three months, that's when we start to see strange things happening. They hear voices, they act like they're two totally different people...they're insane."

"So the kill squads serve two purposes, then," Jared mused. "To take out anyone who might threaten the regime and to take the crazies out of the slave population before it self-destructs."

"That's right." Gervais was nodding. "This whole thing, this was all Baltek's idea. The slave trade and the trafficking in stolen goods, that's all to buy this damned drug. Halcyon promised it would keep the slaves from rebelling. They didn't tell us that it would make people into monsters. And now they're all addicts, so it's not like we could just cut off the drug, even if we wanted to. They'd tear us to shreds."

Jared measured him for a moment. "It baffles me," he said finally, "why you would ever choose to serve someone like Baltek. How did he buy your allegiance? What was your price to turn traitor?"

Gervais's face flushed and he dropped his eyes from Jared's face. "They're working on something new," he said softly. "And they promised me a cut. I can leave this hell-hole and start over..."

"What are they working on?" Jared asked, leaning forward. Gervais clenched his jaw and sat in dogged silence. Jared seized the hair on top of his head and jerked his head up so that he could look into his eyes. "What are they working on?" he repeated, every word sharp as the knife in his hand.

"I can't tell you," Gervais said, his earnest expression telling Jared that he was speaking the truth. "Because they wouldn't tell me much. All they said is that it will make their energy monopoly look like child's play. It'll make them a fortune, they said. And powerful, too—establishing the Triumvirate's primacy in this system and beyond."

"So," Jared murmured, "They're planning an assault on Halcyon."

Gervais nodded. "This thing, whatever it is? It will make them unstoppable."

TWENTY-EIGHT

"WHAT DO you want to do with him?" Jared asked Aelred, jerking his thumb toward the figure slumped in the chair in front of the fireplace.

They stood together near the open door of the barracks. Jared watched the lowering clouds fade to a charcoal gray as the banished sun began to set. Aelred was studying the figure over Jared's left shoulder, and now he rubbed his hand thoughtfully through his silvering hair.

"Killing a man in cold blood sits ill with me," he answered quietly.

"The man's a spy and a traitor," Jared said. "What are we going to do with him? We can't set him free. He'll betray us to the Triumvirate."

"I know that, Jared."

They stood a few moments in silence, and Jared could see the heaviness of the decision descending in a dark frown on Aelred's brow.

"Look," Jared said. "We could lock him up somewhere, but we can't spare the men to guard him. And we'd have to feed him."

"I know that as well."

Jared sighed. "Tell me what you would have me do," he said finally. "He's your subject, after all."

Aelred's eyes snapped to his face and a slow smile eased the tense lines on his forehead. "So he is." Aelred's shoulders straightened and he heaved a deep sigh. "Take him to the warehouse where our gear is stowed. It's guarded already, so we won't have to assign anyone special to watch him, and we can send some provisions with him so that our men don't go hungry on his account. We'll decide what to do with him later...but he may be useful again before the end. I'll get an escort ready for him."

Jared nodded and returned to Gervais's side, while Aelred went out again to gather the escort troop.

"Am I going to die today?" Gervais asked Jared, lifting his head.

"Your lord has willed it otherwise," Jared answered. "And you should be grateful. I wouldn't have spared your life." He drew his knife. "Relax," he said, seeing Gervais flinch away from him. "It's to free you from the chair."

Jared quickly cut the ties and then rebound Gervais's hands in front of him. Then he signaled to the four heavily armed men in Triumvirate uniforms that waited by the door.

"Take him away," he ordered as they came forward.

They shoved Gervais roughly out the door. Jared watched them go and then crossed to the fireplace, leaning on the rough mantle and staring into the flames.

His vision swam a bit and he blinked rapidly, then moved to step back a bit from the heat. Suddenly, his eyes darkened and, instead of the fire, he saw Sahara.

She was sitting at a table set for a feast, the elegant china dishes catching the flickering candlelight in creamy pools. He caught his breath, shifting his mind's gaze to her companion. Dark curls fell to the man's shoulders, a ruby ring shone on his finger, and a smile played on his lips. It was all malice, and he knew that Sahara was in danger. The man didn't seem threatening, but something was wrong...like a note out of tune.

He turned back to Sahara and caught his breath. She was deathly pale save for two hectic splotches of red on her cheeks. Her eyes were incredibly and unnaturally brilliant.

Sahara.

He called out to her, felt her reaching out for him with her own mind. But the connection came crashing down, almost as if it had been severed by something...or someone. He felt her struggling with whatever it was that had divided them.

Sahara!

The connection pulsed again, stronger this time. Whatever he was pushing against crumbled slightly. And then he saw the stranger pouring something into her glass. He watched her reach for it.

Don't! Sahara, don't!

She drank it.

He reeled back. The connection to her mind slammed closed.

"No!" he shouted.

The room around him rushed back into focus, and he fell to his knees in front of the fire, burying his face in his hands.

He heard hurried footsteps behind him and then felt a strong hand on his shoulder.

"Jared! What's happened? Are you hurt?"

It was Brytnoth.

Jared reached up and grasped his friend's hand. "It's Sahara," he said hoarsely, slowly getting to his feet. "Something's happened... something's wrong."

"What? What happened?"

Brytnoth's hand fell from his shoulder as Jared turned to face him. "I don't know. She was drugged...or something just as bad. I couldn't get through to her...couldn't stop it...." He felt his voice catch in his throat as he gripped his friend's arm. "I couldn't save her, Brytnoth."

Brytnoth frowned. "Drugged? By whom?"

"I never saw the devil before in my life. But it must have been one of the Triumvirate. I don't know where Deor and Rafe were. I couldn't see them at all."

"They weren't with her? Did something happen to them?"

The pain surged through Jared's pounding head and he tightened his grip on Brytnoth's arm to keep himself from falling. "I don't know."

Brytnoth's frown dissolved into hard resolve. "Let's go. You need a drink."

He slipped Jared's arm over his shoulders and half-led, half-carried him out of the vacant barracks and back to their command post. As they staggered in the door, Aelred and the others jumped to their feet.

"What happened to you?" Aelred asked, his eyes snapping to Brytnoth's face. "What happened to him?"

Jared collapsed into a chair in front of the fire. Emma brought him a tumbler of wine, and he downed it in a single draught. He thrust the cup back into Emma's hand.

"More," he said. As Emma scurried away to fetch it, Jared caught sight of Aliya's worried face. "I'm all right," he mumbled. "Just a horrible headache."

"He had a vision. Something's happened to Sahara," Brytnoth explained.

"What?" Aelred's gaze swung back to Jared. "What happened?"

"All I know," Jared answered, "is that the Triumvirate is a new breed of evil. The Drakkin were one thing. Predictable. Straightforward. But this is something else entirely. Paranoia, murder, drugs, deception..." His voice trailed off. "As for Sahara, I really don't know what happened. But she's in danger...and somehow, they have a way to cut off our ability to communicate. I'll just have to wait and see if she is able to contact me again."

No one spoke, and he closed his eyes. *Maybe she shut the connection*, he thought. But he knew what it felt like when she shut him out. This wasn't like that. It was almost like...

Like someone else was there too.

The thought filled him with such horror that his arms prickled into gooseflesh. Emma set the tumbler on the table beside him, and he gulped it down.

"I need to talk to Kalkas," he said, getting to his feet. "And then we're going to see Brogan."

"Who's *we?*" Brytnoth asked.

"You and Kirin. And me. Be ready to go in twenty minutes."

Deep dusk shadows were seeping out of their hiding holes as Jared left the barracks and headed up the street. They had stowed Kalkas and his gear in a building of his own, just a few doors down from the command post. The healer had been closeted in there since their arrival, working on the Demon's Breath surrogate.

Jared paused at the door and rapped twice, then pushed into the room.

He couldn't help but gape at the sight that met his eyes. The entire long table in the center of the room was covered with an elaborate network of tubes, burners, and beakers. Something was bubbling in each one. A collection jar sat on the floor at one end, and a tube dripped slowly into it.

Kalkas himself was barely visible behind all of his paraphernalia, but when Jared ducked to look through the apparatus, he saw the healer sitting in front of the fire, his feet propped up on a chair. Jared closed the door behind him and carefully skirted the table. He stopped in front of Kalkas and hesitated. The healer appeared to be dozing, his chin on his chest and his eyes closed.

"Well?" Kalkas said, raising his head suddenly and fixing Jared with a bright eye. "Are you going to say hello, or are you just going to gawk at me?"

"I didn't think you were...awake," Jared said haltingly.

The healer smiled. "Just dozing. But I heard the door open, and I recognized your step."

"Quite a setup you have here." Jared waved at the table.

"Yes. But it's taking longer than I hoped to distill the essence for the surrogate. This process is faster and will result in a more potent product than creating a tincture, but it still takes time." Kalkas frowned, and then held up a hand as Jared opened his mouth to speak. "It's a delicate process. I'm going as fast as I can."

"The last transport of men should be arriving in four days' time. And I know that Aelred will be ready to make his move soon after they arrive. Will you be ready? We're going to need a lot more than that." He gestured to the collection jar, which was only a third full.

"Well, that is my fifteenth jar," Kalkas said modestly, pointing up to the loft.

Jared turned and saw a line of large jars in front of the second floor railing. "Still," Jared said, turning back to the healer. "We're talking about a lot of people."

"I know." Kalkas sighed, and then slipped his feet off the chair in front of him. "Please sit down," he said with a small smile. "I don't think you came here just to discuss my progress on the surrogate."

Jared sank down across from him and leaned forward, his elbows on his knees. "I have a...a problem," he began. "Have you ever heard of the ability to communicate mind-to-mind?"

He glanced up at the healer's face and saw the quick interest in his dark eyes. Jared sighed, his mind flooding suddenly with the memory of this same conversation with another healer so many months ago—and he had been a traitor.

I hope things work out differently this time, he thought grimly, pushing the memory aside.

"I have heard of it," Kalkas answered. "But I have never known anyone who could actually practice it." When Jared said nothing, he ventured, "I take it that you can?"

"Yes. Sahara and I can use it. We've always been able to do so, even before I actually met her."

"How fascinating!"

Jared grinned wryly at him. "Fascinating, maybe. Frustrating, definitely." He fell silent again.

"So what's the problem?" Kalkas prodded gently.

"Tonight, I was shut out...cut off. But not by her. She was with someone, and it seemed like he was asking questions, but I couldn't hear them. I think he was the one who interfered." He met the healer's gaze again. "Can this Demon's Breath drug have that effect? Could he have been controlling her mind? Could he have been reading her mind? Does it work that way?"

Kalkas leaned back in his chair and stroked his silver beard thoughtfully. "It's hard to say," he said finally. "It's a mind-control and amnesiac drug, as I told you before. And because I've never known anyone who could communicate that way, I don't know what effect it might have on that ability."

Seeing the lines of worry that creased Jared's forehead, he smiled gently and continued, "Take comfort in one thing, Jared. It's not a drug that facilitates mind-reading. It only allows the administrator to dictate action. And it's clumsy as a truth serum, though it can have applications in that respect as well."

Jared breathed a little easier. "Would she be addicted to it after the first exposure?"

Kalkas shrugged. "It depends on what dose she was given. But my guess would be that, if he used Demon's Breath, he probably didn't give her much. The dosage for a truth serum is pretty minuscule, and it wouldn't be enough to cause her to become addicted after just one exposure."

Jared dropped his head in his hands for a moment, then took a deep breath and got to his feet. "Thank you. That's a relief."

"I'm sure it is," the healer replied.

Jared edged past the table again and headed for the door. "Keep up the good work!" he called over his shoulder. "And be ready with that stuff...we're going to need it. Soon."

He found Kirin and Brytnoth waiting for him in the deserted street.

"Now, let's go have a chat with our friend Brogan," he said, clapping them each on the shoulder as he stepped between them. "Ready for a night on the town?"

As they approached the Aymatis, Jared held up a hand to slow their progress. Something was different. No sound from the streets ahead wafted toward them on the stale breeze, and even the hectic glare of lights seemed subdued. He beckoned them forward, but they moved cautiously, eyes darting into the shadows.

"Where is everyone?" Kirin murmured.

They skirted across the street to the tavern. No girls loitered outside the gate tonight, no tumblers, no rowdy crowds of half-drunken soldiers. Once inside the tavern's courtyard, they increased their pace and crossed the deserted space at a trot.

They had almost reached the inner doorway when a soldier, obviously on sentry duty, stepped out of the deep shadows of the awning.

"What're you doing here?" he barked. "You'll be executed for disobeying orders!"

Jared swallowed, debating for a few minutes how to play this situation. He decided to try to diffuse things with a bit of humor. "Come on, soldier!" he said. "I promised my girl I'd meet her here tonight! Orders or no orders, I made a promise!"

"Disobedience is death," he said. "You're a fool." His hard gaze traveled past Jared to Kirin and Brytnoth. "So're you. Fools."

"Brogan's not in trouble, is he?" Jared pressed, still wearing an easy smile and keeping his tone light. "That would be a shame!"

The soldier regarded him icily. "What do you think I'm standing here for, you idiot? Of course he's in trouble. In fact, he should be dead by now."

"Dead!"

"Kill squad should be finishing him off right about now. That's what happens when you cross Lord Baltek. And they'll be after you next for disobeying orders. No one was supposed to be in the Aymatis tonight. Who's your commanding officer?"

"Oh, you know him, I'm sure. He's—" Jared finished the statement by planting his elbow in the man's face, knocking him senseless to the ground.

"Let's go!" he said, shoving the man aside with his foot. "Weapons ready, boys!"

Jared eased the door open and they slipped into the shadows of the eerily vacant taproom. As they advanced toward the stairs, they could hear muffled shouts from the second floor. They ghosted up the steps and down the hall to the door with the lion's head boss. It was ajar.

Jared listened for a moment, and then he beckoned for them to follow him inside. They moved more quickly now, their footsteps muffled by the heavy rug. The inner door was partially open as well, and Jared waved them to the wall, where they would be out of view from anyone inside. Jared peered through the crack. Four men in black Triumvirate uniforms were closing in on a wildly gesticulating Brogan.

"What did I do?" Brogan squealed, his face bathed in sweat. "Tell me my crime! What did I do?"

Jared glanced back to his companions and held up four fingers to indicate the number of enemy troops. Then he kicked open the door.

TWENTY-NINE

ALL FOUR TRIUMVIRATE soldiers lay dead at Brogan's feet. Three had been gunned down. The last had fallen with Jared's knife planted in his neck.

Brogan dropped to his knees, tears of fright and relief streaming down his flaccid face. Jared, Kirin and Brytnoth stepped fully into the room, slinging their rifles back over their shoulders. Jared retrieved his knife and cleaned the blade on his thigh.

"It's lucky for you that we decided to pay you a visit this evening," Jared remarked, slipping the knife back into its sheath.

Brogan got heavily to his feet and wiped his face with shaking hands. "What brings you back here? You're the reason Baltek came after me in the first place!" His fear twisted into sudden anger, and he turned all his impotent fury on Jared and his friends.

"That's hardly fair." Jared folded his arms. "Gervais was a Triumvirate snitch. He ratted you out to Baltek a long time ago. Our interview yesterday was probably just the tipping point, taking you from person of interest to outright threat."

"How dare you come in here and accuse Gervais!" Brogan demanded. "He was my most trusted—"

"Trusting that rat was your first mistake," Jared interrupted. "We caught him this morning trailing our friends. He's confessed every-thing. He won't be talking to anyone else for a long time."

"You killed him!" Brogan staggered forward a few paces and stumbled over one of the bodies. "You killed him!"

"No, we didn't, though we would've been well within our rights to do so. No. He'll be cooling his heels in solitary confinement for a while."

Brogan stared for a moment at the three men in front of him, then began to shake his head, his anger dissolving now into grief. "What have I done to deserve all this?" he moaned.

"You're a good man," Kirin said. "You've been doing the right thing for these girls here, as much as you can. And that put you on Baltek's hit list."

Brogan looked up. "They'll come for me again. Word will get back to Baltek...he'll find out."

"That's almost guaranteed," Jared assured him. "I don't think the disappearance of a kill squad would go unnoticed for long, and if you stay here, he'll know they missed their target. But if you help us—"

"There's nothing I can do for you now," Brogan said, waving a hand wearily at Jared. "I've got to go into hiding. My tavern will close...my connections will all disappear. It's over...all over for me."

"No!" Brytnoth protested. "That's where you're wrong. Let your tavern close if you must, but when you disappear, activate your contacts in the underground. The revolution is here, Brogan. You can still help us, and soon you won't have to hide any longer."

Brogan measured them for a moment, then stepped over the bodies and beckoned for them to follow him. "I need a drink," he said. "What about you three?" He grinned ruefully and added, "It's on the house."

"Then how could we refuse?" Brytnoth asked, grinning in return.

Back downstairs in the taproom, Brogan disappeared behind the massive bar and set about filling voluminous tankards with foaming ale. Jared and the others settled in the stools at the bar and sipped appreciatively at the brew. Brogan pulled up a seat on the barkeep's side and took up his own tankard. After several deep draughts, he wiped his face on his sleeve.

"So what is it you want from me, exactly?" he said.

"Two things," Jared answered. "First, do exactly what Brytnoth said upstairs. Go to ground and contact everyone you know who wants to be rid of the Triumvirate. You are better positioned than anyone to help us coordinate our efforts here. And we have a week—ten days at most—before Aelred leads his people to freedom."

Brogan's eyes popped. "That's all? Seven days?"

"So, now you know," Jared said. "Are you with us? If not, we'll finish the job the Triumvirate started upstairs."

"Save your threats," Brogan said. "Of course I'm in. I've waited for this day for too long."

"Good. Now, I said there were two things we needed from you. I need you to set us up with guides who can take us to the mines. We're not here just for some revolution. We're here to find our people. Do you know of anyone who has access and can get us in?"

"You're dressed like Triumvirate troops," Brogan protested. "Why not just take a map and go yourselves?"

"Too risky," Jared answered. "We don't know the protocols. These outfits work well enough when all we need to do is play the drunk or stand around looking tough. But if we actually have to speak to anyone, we'll be arrested or shot on the spot. When we infiltrate the mines, we'll have to go as slaves. We need someone who has access or knows how to get it."

Brogan twirled his mug thoughtfully on the bar for a few moments. "I know two men who might be able to help," he said softly. "Jack and Thane. They used to be supervisors, so they know all the routines."

"Yes, but can we trust them?" Kirin asked sharply. "You're not always very careful in your choice of friends."

"I suppose my track record isn't so good as you see it," Brogan replied. "But any man can be betrayed, even by those he loves the most. I trust these two. I can't say more than that."

"How soon can we meet?" Jared asked.

"Come here tomorrow morning before dawn. They'll be waiting for you."

When Jared, Kirin and Brytnoth entered the tavern courtyard the next morning, a damp fog was nosing its way through the deserted streets and the tavern yard, obscuring the door from their sight. They had donned slaves' garb for the trip to the mines, and Jared shivered as the surprising chill in the air bit through the thin garments.

"You always have such fantastic ideas, Jared," Kirin grumbled, hugging his arms against his chest and blowing into his hands to warm them. "Why didn't you just leave me out of this?"

Jared slapped him on the shoulder. "You looked like you needed some exercise, and the weather this morning is so...bracing. Anyway, where's your sense of adventure?"

"What in our history together would possibly make you think that I'm the adventuring type?"

"Yes," said Jared, mock seriousness in his voice. "Kirin Hearth-Stalker, I think we named you."

"Shut up, you two!" Brytnoth hissed.

He pointed toward the door, which was just materializing through the mist. Jared screwed up his eyes and could just barely make out the figures of two men standing on either side of the entrance.

"All right, Brytnoth," he murmured. "I see them."

He loosened his knife, and he saw Kirin stoop to draw his pistol from his ankle holster. A few more paces brought them to the foot of the short flight of stairs leading up to the tavern door. The two men stared down at them, their faces impassive.

"Brogan said you'd come," one said, his voice gravelly, one eye squinting through the cruel scar running down the right side of his face.

"Jack and Thane?" Jared asked.

The man nodded gruffly. "Let's get where we're going before someone takes an interest in our little party."

"A party, a party!" the other man cried, winking at Jared. His wide grin revealed pockets where teeth were missing. "Don't want no trouble this early in the morning! We'll dance with 'ee later, oh later, my Nell!"

Jared stared at him for a moment, trying to hide the sudden horror that flooded through him. *The man's cracked*, he realized.

"You have a way to get us to the mines?" he asked the first man.

"*The* mine, you mean," he answered. "Brogan says you're looking for your friends. They would've been on a recent shipment, and so there's just one place to start. Fresh ones go to the big mine. To Gil-Gareth."

"Jack! Gil-Gareth, Gil-Gareth!" echoed the other man, spluttering a laugh. Then he began to warble, "To Gil-Gareth, Gil-Gareth! Deep and dark, foul it smelleth! Breathe it in, aches forgetteth...death is a friend, soul it taketh...the mine of Gil-Gareth!"

"Shut up, Thane!" growled Jack. Then he turned to Jared, an apologetic look on his face. "He lost his mind somewhat down there, I'm afraid. But he's my brother, and if I ever came to the mine without him, we'd never get through. He knows all the passcodes. Something to do with his rhyming and such. Don't understand it myself." He shook his head. "A sad business. A damn shame."

Without another word, he pushed between Jared and Brytnoth, Thane scampering after him. Jared and the others followed them as they headed around the side of the tavern toward what used to be a carriage-house.

"He's more cracked than a roasted nut," Kirin murmured as they went.

"No, I don't think he's crazy," Jared said, keeping his voice low. "But something happened to him...he's like a child. Look at him."

They focused their attention again on the figures ahead of them, watching as Thane clapped his hands at something Jack was saying to him. Jack put his arm around Thane's shoulders and they could see the smile that creased his face as he looked at his brother.

"Well," Brytnoth choked, "I don't trust Brogan farther than I could toss him. But that right there...I trust love."

Jack and Thane stopped in front of the huge doors of the carriage-house and Jack punched a button on the wall. The doors creaked open, revealing a small passenger shuttle inside.

Ten minutes later, Jack had them in the air. As they watched the mutilated landscape scud by beneath them, a sick feeling wormed its way through Jared's gut.

"They've destroyed your planet," he said to Brytnoth, unable to tear his eyes from the window. "Can you recover from something like this?"

Brytnoth was silent for a long time, and when Jared finally glanced at him, he saw the tears in his friend's eyes.

"She's still beautiful," Brytnoth said, his voice thick. "She's been roughed up, but she's still beautiful. And with love, all things are possible, I think. She'll probably always bear the scars, but she'll heal."

"You think so? Really?"

Brytnoth smiled at him. "Yes, really. It's not always what we imagine, you know. Love heals, but it doesn't always transform. Just remember that."

Jared nodded. He turned back to the window, but the mangled landscape slipped past unnoticed now. He was thinking about Sahara, remembering the scars of the lash strokes on her back, the scars of grief and anger on her soul.

She's still beautiful, he thought. *She's been roughed up, but she's still beautiful.*

"We're here," came Jack's voice over the com.

Jared shook himself out of his thoughts, his attention once more on the land below them.

"Would you look at that?" Deor breathed.

They stared out the windows at the huge fissure in the earth and the shambles of a town that hugged its rim. Droves of people scuttled in and out of the mine, and Jared saw more making their way down from the village.

As the ship settled onto the landing platform, they made their way forward to the ramp. Jack and Thane were already there, waiting for them.

"Let Thane handle this," Jack told them as he punched the switch for the ramp.

"If you say so," Kirin muttered, with a shrug that plainly voiced his doubt. "Let's hope they like his brand of crazy here."

Almost before the words were out of Kirin's mouth, Jack pinned him against the bulkhead.

"He's not crazy!" Jack gritted, slamming Kirin against the wall. "You hear me?"

Jared jumped toward them, grabbing for Jack's arm. Jack shook him off and bashed Kirin against the wall again. Then he pulled Kirin's face close to his own and murmured, "If you ever say something like that again, I'll kill you."

At that moment, the ramp touched down, revealing two Triumvirate soldiers standing on the platform.

"Hey!" yelled one, starting up the ramp. "What the hell you beating that slave for?"

Jack dropped Kirin like a dead fish, and he slumped to the floor with a groan.

"Just making sure he knows who's boss, that's all," Jack answered.

"You all right?" Brytnoth whispered, reaching down to help Kirin to his feet.

Kirin rubbed the back of his head. "I think so." He swore softly when he felt the beginnings of a large bump under his probing fingertips.

"You're just in time," the soldier told Jack. "We needed three more for this exploration squad. Lord Ergeron's ordered ten more squads to be shipped off-world today. They're upping the time-table on us, boys. We need more men."

"You seem cheerful enough about it," Jack remarked.

"Don't pay to get hot about it," the soldier answered with a shrug. "Get your drudges off there and load 'em up. Pad three." He turned to go, and then seemed to remember something. "Almost forgot your challenge question," he chuckled. "Code in 'dagger'."

"Journey," piped Thane from behind Jack. "Dagger hilt and boss, journey roads will cross." He laughed and clapped his hands together.

"Yeah, that's the one." The soldier edged away from Thane and then added, "I've heard of you." He eyed him with something between horror and curiosity for a moment, then turned back to Jack. "All right, get your men to the transport. Pad three, remember. You've got ten minutes before launch."

He waved to his companion and they headed off across the platform. As soon as they were out of earshot, Kirin turned to Jared.

"Now what, Jared? We were supposed to go looking for our people in this hell-hole of a mine, and now we're getting shipped off-world. I didn't sign up for this, Jared!" Rubbing his head again, he glared at Jack and added, "And I didn't ask to get beaten up, either! What's your problem, anyway?"

Jack balled his fists and started for Kirin again, but Jared stepped between them. "Excuse my friend," he said to Jack. "He's an idiot." Then he turned back to Kirin and hissed, "Do you want to get us all killed? Shut up and let's go. This is our chance to find out what they're looking for!"

"I thought we were here for Arnauld and our people," Kirin snapped. "Not some damned Triumvirate treasure-hunt."

Brytnoth touched Jared's arm. "He's right, Jared. We came here today for our people, not to investigate the Triumvirate."

"And just how exactly do you propose we get out of this off-world mission now?" Jared asked, feeling a flare of impatience. "From where I'm standing, it looks like we've got no choice but to see this through first."

"You better move," Jack growled at them. "Five minutes. And then they'll have our heads."

"Just trust me on this," Jared pleaded. "Have I ever let you down before?"

Kirin snorted, but they followed him down the ramp without another word. They trotted briskly across the platform, with Jack and Thane bringing up the rear. Jack directed their way with hoarse shouts. Pad three sat at the far end of the landing platform, and by the time they reached it they were damp with sweat. Kirin and Brytnoth boarded the ship, but Jack caught Jared's arm before he could start up the ramp.

"We'll stay here," he murmured in Jared's ear. "We'll look for any sign of your friends. If we find them, we know what to do."

Jared squeezed his hand in thanks and followed Brytnoth.

As he shouldered his way into the crew cabin, he suddenly stopped short. Brytnoth and Kirin had taken two seats in the first row, leaving a space for him to join them, but Jared's eyes slid past them to someone sitting three rows back.

A ragged beard and dark eyes glazed and half-shut should have made the man a stranger, but Jared would have known him anywhere.

"What is it?" Brytnoth whispered, seeing Jared's face.

"It's Arnauld." Jared's eyes flickered to the faces of his companions, and a sudden smile quirked the corner of his mouth.

"Change of plans," he said. "We're going to get him out of here. Now."

THIRTY

"AND JUST HOW the hell are we supposed to do that?" Kirin demanded, his voice barely above a whisper.

"On my signal, you're going to break for our ship. Catch Thane and Jack and tell them to fire it up. Brytnoth and I are going to do a little smash and grab." Jared's eyes flitted over the inside of the cabin, fixing briefly on the two Triumvirate soldiers just making their way up the galley stairs at the back of the cabin. "Now! Get up. Go! Go! Go!"

Kirin darted out of his seat and pushed past Jared. Jared heard the surprised shouts of the crew as Kirin pelted down the ramp and across the platform.

"You ready?" Jared murmured to Brytnoth. He glanced at his friend, who nodded shortly. "He's two rows behind you. Middle seat. Right side. You grab, I'll smash." He hesitated for a moment. "Wait. I've got a better idea. Let's try a little diversion first."

He nodded to Brytnoth, then staggered forward and started shrieking at the top of his lungs.

The two Triumvirate guards started violently and backed a few paces away as Jared continued to play up his act.

"Hey!" one yelled. "What's wrong with that slave?"

Jared stumbled forward until he was just past Arnauld's row, and then he let out another blood-curdling scream. He heard Brytnoth in the aisle behind him, and he redoubled his efforts, adding in some strange jerking movements to enhance the spectacle.

"Now!" Brytnoth hissed from just behind him.

The soldiers had regained their nerve and were slowly edging toward Jared. When they were just two rows away, Jared saw their hands move for their holsters. He wobbled toward them, changing his screams to a pitiful, crooning wail. The soldiers stopped in confusion.

"What the...?" one began.

Before he had time to react, Jared sprang on them, dagger flashing in hand. As he knocked the guard senseless with a blow from his left elbow, he glanced back to see Brytnoth dragging Arnauld out of his chair, hauling him back down the aisle toward the ramp.

He grinned with pleasure, but as he turned back to finish off the other guard, his momentary lapse in concentration was rewarded with a stunning right hook in the jaw. He staggered back against the seats. The guard pushed at him, trying to pin him while he raised his gun for a kill shot. Jared knocked the weapon aside and planted both his boots in the man's chest. With a grunt, the man toppled backward over his fallen comrade, his head knocking against the metal frame of the seats. He tried feebly to move, then lay still. Dead or unconscious, Jared didn't wait to find out. He ran for the ramp as the engines began to hum beneath him.

Two more Triumvirate troops were making their way up the ramp when Jared barreled through them. Before they could recover their balance or their wits, he vaulted over the crates of cargo stacked next to the landing pad.

As he sprinted across the platform, he heard the commotion behind him degenerate into chaos. Some kind of alarm horn started blaring, and he knew that at any moment more troops would flood the platform. He pumped his legs harder, gasping against the burn in his lungs, until finally Jack's ship loomed just in front of him. The ramp was down, the engines purring. Brytnoth was perched at the top of the ramp.

"Behind you!" he yelled suddenly, waving his arms frantically. "Jared! Look out behind…"

Jared ducked instinctively as the shots rang out. He ran, stooping low, as bullets peppered the ground around him. He saw several bury themselves in a fuel drum just as he passed it. He flung himself forward, trying to propel himself out of range in time.

Even as he heard the massive blast, the world tumbled beneath him in a sick surge of fire and choking smoke. For a moment he hung suspended in freefall, and then he slammed into a bed of metal with a sickening crack.

Through the ringing in his ears he thought he heard Brytnoth shouting, "Get up! Jared! Get up! Jack, get us the hell out of here!"

Jared pushed himself to his feet, his vision blurred so that he could barely make out the ramp beneath his feet. It shifted suddenly, and he scrabbled for balance. Brytnoth's hand shot out and grabbed his arm, hauling him up and into the mouth of the shuttle. Jared landed in a panting heap at his friend's feet.

"Go!" Brytnoth shouted to Jack. "Go, go, go!"

Jared felt the ship lift off the ground. Laughing and choking all at the same time, he crawled to the wall and leaned his back against it. He groaned and shook his head to clear it. Something was tickling his chin, and he realized that blood was trickling from his split lip.

"Well, I thought you were going to cash it in," Brytnoth said, squatting beside him and handing him a rag. He laughed and shook his head, swearing softly.

"Not this time," Jared croaked, wheezing a laugh. Then he winced and hugged his ribs. "You know, that hurt."

"I'll bet it did."

Jared daubed his now swollen mouth with the cloth. "Damn, Brytnoth," he said, glancing at his friend. "That was close."

"Too close." Brytnoth rose and helped Jared to his feet. "Let's go."

Kirin was slumped in a chair near the door of the crew cabin when Jared and Brytnoth entered. Jared slapped him on the shoulder.

"Well done!" he said. "Not bad, Hearth-Seeker! Not bad at all."

But Kirin's face was solemn as he glanced up at Jared. "What's happened to him?" he asked, jerking his head toward the silent figure sitting by the window.

Jared's smile dissolved as he turned to Arnauld. His eyes were staring straight ahead, and he looked as if he hadn't moved a muscle since Brytnoth had dumped him there.

"It's like he doesn't even know where he is," Kirin continued. "Like he can't even register that we just pulled him off one ship and put him on another."

Jared gripped Kirin's shoulder. "I know," he said. "When I took out those troops on the transport, all those men...they just sat there. Like statues. Like nothing was happening. It's that damned drug. The sooner we're back to Pentapolis, the better. Kalkas will heal him."

A muted rattling suddenly echoed around them and the ship veered sharply to starboard. Jared, still unstable, stumbled into Brytnoth, and both of them fell awkwardly into the seats across the main aisle.

"What was that?" Brytnoth cried.

"We took some fire from the platform," Jack's voice came over the com. "One of the engines is out. But I think we've got enough to get us to Pentapolis. We're out of range of the guns now."

"Great," Kirin muttered. "I just hope we don't run into any more trouble."

In spite of Kirin's misgivings, the rest of the journey back to the city passed without incident. Jack set the shuttle down in the tavern courtyard and shut off the one remaining engine. As they disembarked, they had to cover their mouths and noses against the steady stream of black smoke that poured from the port engine.

"That's going to take some fixing," Jack remarked.

"You can't just leave this thing here!" Kirin said, coughing. "That smoke's going to draw very unwelcome attention from the Triumvirate...and there goes our hope of secrecy."

"Don't fret, young master," Jack said amiably. "As soon as you get yourselves gone, we'll take the ship to the rebel outpost just northeast of the city. She'll be fixed up. That's where we're holed up. If you need us again, send word to Brogan. He knows how to contact us."

"Thank you," Jared said, shaking his hand. "For everything."

Jack grinned at him. "Anytime." Then he turned to Kirin and held out his hand. "No hard feelings, I hope?"

Kirin hesitated for a moment, then clasped his hand firmly. "No hard feelings." He glanced at Thane, then smiled at Jack. "I understand."

With a final shake, Jack released Kirin, saluted to Jared and Brytnoth, who supported Arnauld between them, and headed back to the ship.

"Let's get back to base and get him some help," Jared said.

———

Three hours later, Kalkas entered the barracks where they sat around the table, plates of food untouched before them.

"How is he?" Jared asked, starting up out of his chair as the healer approached.

Kalkas smiled reassuringly, waving Jared back into his seat. "No worries. He'll be fine. He's sleeping now. By tomorrow morning he should be recovered, though I should warn you that he likely won't remember much, if anything, of his drugged life. If you're hoping that he'll be able to tell you anything about Triumvirate operations, you'll probably be disappointed."

"We'll just have to wait and see, I suppose," Jared said. "Please, join us for supper, won't you?"

As the healer took a seat and helped himself to some food, Jared blinked rapidly. His vision was beginning to blur.

Jared.

And then Sahara's face sharpened into focus, swallowing everything else around him. The surge of joy and relief that washed over him at the sound of her voice and the sight of her face nearly took his breath away.

Sahara! You're all right.

Her sudden smile took him by surprise. *Thanks to you, yes, she said. If you hadn't intervened when you did last night, I don't know what would have happened.*

I didn't know if you could hear me, he replied. Who was that man?

Lord Ergeron. He controls the exploration and trade branches of the Triumvirate's operations.

Did he drug you? And how did he shut me out?

I think he did, and I don't know, she answered. But that can wait. Listen, something's happening. Something huge. He took us on a tour of the Triumvirate's massive weapons facility north of the city.

Weapons facility? Jared frowned. *I thought they dealt in fuel.*

They're looking for some kind of energy source—it's called zanthos. And it powers these weapons. They don't need ammo, just energy. I think this all has something to do with Halcyon. He thinks we represent the drug lords, and he's trying to tip his hand to influence the contract negotiation later.

Of course it has to do with Halcyon, Jared said suddenly. *Gervais told me that the Triumvirate is planning to extend its influence beyond this system. They must be planning for war.*

Or they're planning to sell the weapons to Halcyon in payment of their debt, Sahara suggested. But either way, we have a problem. If the Triumvirate gets hold of that energy source before we do, Aelred's troops don't stand a chance.

How does he know the weapons will work? Jared asked.

They found a tiny amount of this zanthos here. Not enough to satisfy them, but enough to conduct research and development trials.

He demonstrated the tank for us while we were there. Her eyes widened in horror. *It...melts rock, Jared. And anything softer than rock is basically...vaporized.*

Jared swore softly. *So what do we do now?*

You have to talk to Aelred. Find out if he knows about this stuff. They can't find it. They keep sending exploration squads off-world to search, but they don't even know where to look.

I know that much, Jared told her. *We nearly got ourselves commissioned.*

Sahara stared at him. *How did that happen?*

It's a long story, Jared grinned. *But we found Arnauld.*

Arnauld! Where? How?

Jared paused for a moment as he saw tears in Sahara's eyes. He swallowed hard and forced himself to focus. *That's a long story, too. But he was about to be shipped off-world with one of those squads. He's here with us now. Kalkas has already administered the surrogate, and he's recovering.*

Something seemed to distract Sahara's attention for a moment, and the connection between them wavered.

I have to go, she said hurriedly. *Talk to Aelred. And find a Triumvirate soldier named Derrek. He may be able to help us...and we're going to need all we can get.*

She was gone.

Jared heaved a shaking sigh and rubbed his hands over his face. When he looked up, he realized that his friends were watching him in silent concern.

"Was that Sahara?" Brytnoth asked.

Jared nodded and turned immediately to Aelred, who was discussing something in a low voice with Kalkas. "Aelred, do you know anything about an energy source called *zanthos?*"

Aelred started violently. "Zanthos? Who's talking about *zanthos?*"

"The Triumvirate. That's what they're hunting for. And Sahara says that they have a huge facility full of weapons just waiting for it to be found."

Aelred's face drained of color and he sat very still, his hands clenched on the table. "I had hoped," he murmured finally, "that they would never find that. But I should've guessed that they had from the way they're tearing up my planet."

"What is it?"

"Our craftsmen sought it for centuries," Aelred answered, speaking slowly at first. "It was the stuff of legend. Ancient texts spoke of an ore that produced its own energy. Totally stable, totally self-sustaining, and incredibly powerful. It promised to transform the world, to put an end to the need for other fuels, to bring harmony and peace. Dreamers and philosophers fell in love with it, and our rulers were swayed to fritter away the wealth of the kingdoms in search of it. And instead of harmony and peace, we had civil war, and strife, and death, and destruction.

"Then people rose up against the kings and the philosophers and appointed a new government, the council of Lords. We vowed to leave off the search for *zanthos* and instead devoted our many resources to creating things both beautiful and useful. We shepherded our resources so that there was balance. And when one of our mining crews found a pocket of *zanthos* at Gil-Gareth, we concealed it from everyone, locking it in the treasure-room underneath the Great House and setting a great seal upon the door."

"It sounds like the Triumvirate must have found it," Brytnoth said. "And that explains what they've done at Gil-Gareth."

Aelred slowly turned to stare at him, his face pale with dread. "What have they done at Gil-Gareth?"

"It's a huge chasm now. And I'm sure that it's worse underground than it looks from above. They're tearing Askalon apart."

Aelred buried his face in his hands. "I wish they had never found it at all. And the worst of it is that, aside from that tiny amount, its source isn't even on Askalon. We were able to determine that the rock containing the *zanthos* had come from our farthest moon, Perseon. It was a fragment of the meteoroid that had created the original crater of Gil-Gareth."

"So," Jared said, leaning forward across the table, "this stuff is on Perseon?"

"Yes." Aelred and Jared measured each other for a long moment, and then Aelred added, his voice rising, "You're not thinking of going there to get it, are you?"

Jared grinned at him. "Why do you say it like that? Of course we're going to get it. And we're going to do it before the Triumvirate finds it. And then—" He paused for a moment.

"Wait for it," Brytnoth warned the others, a smile spreading across his face. "There's more."

"—then we're going to take over their weapons facility, and we're going to use them to free this land once and for all."

Aelred stared at him, then swiveled his gaze to Brytnoth. "Is he serious? Or is he out of his mind?"

"Do those have to be mutually exclusive?" Brytnoth asked, still grinning.

"What other option do we have?" asked Jared, sitting back in his chair. "If we sit here and they find this stuff, they'll power up those weapons and we might as well pack up and head back to Agora."

"No, we can't let them find it," Aelred agreed softly.

"And the situation with Halcyon is even worse than we had originally thought," Jared continued. "The Triumvirate has promised to deliver this *zanthos* to Halcyon in payment of their debts...but with the firepower they're putting together, it looks more like they're planning to start a fight. So we can go get the stuff and use it to restore Askalon's freedom, or we can wait for the Triumvirate to find it—in which case, we'll be annihilated and Askalon and Halcyon will destroy each other."

"My lord, I agree with Jared on this," Brytnoth said. "I would rather have the *zanthos* in your hands than in theirs. And Jared's right. If they start a war with Halcyon, then Askalon won't be the only casualty."

Aelred sighed heavily and sat, deep in thought, for a long while. Finally, he roused himself and said, "So be it, then."

"In that case," Jared said, pushing back from the table and standing. "I need Brytnoth to come with me. We've got a call to make."

"What about me?" Kirin said.

Jared grinned down at him. "I thought you might've had enough adventure for one day. But if you want to come, then get ready. We leave in half an hour."

THIRTY-ONE

DUSK WAS SETTLING ONCE MORE over Pentapolis. Jared sat in the doorway, dressed in his Triumvirate battle gear, waiting for Kirin and Brytnoth to join him. As the darkness around him deepened, he felt a heaviness settle on his soul.

We found Arnauld, but what of the rest of our people?

And how could he dare to think that they would be able to accomplish what they had set for themselves?

The slave population in Pentapolis alone probably numbers in the tens of thousands, he told himself. *All drugged, all addicts. All needing Kalkas's surrogate.*

And then a new and staggering thought occurred to him.

What if the Triumvirate has programmed them to fight on command? What if there is some code word that will turn them into a lethal, if mindless, killing force?

He gripped his head in his hands. The more he contemplated the idea, the more likely it seemed, and the more it propelled their plans to the verge of the impossible.

We have to take out the Triumvirate first, he realized. *Cut the head off the snake. If we move too soon and they get wind of it, they'll have time to activate the slaves, and we'll have no choice but to destroy everything Aelred is fighting to save.*

He sighed and rubbed his hands through his hair. *The final group of Aelred's troops is slated to arrive in two days' time. The pieces have to be set. We have to be ready.*

"Are you ready?" asked Brytnoth, appearing behind him in the doorway.

Jared glanced up at him and smiled. "Let's do this."

"Kirin didn't want to come," Brytnoth said as they jogged up the street in the direction of the landing platform. "Hearth-Seeker really is a fitting name for him, I think."

Jared said nothing. He was still mulling over the problem of the Triumvirate and the slaves. They had to have the timetable set perfectly, and that meant that they would need a highly coordinated attack.

And narrowly targeted, he realized.

There was no way for them to conquer the planet by sheer force of numbers. They would have to maximize the pockets of resistance and focus on the power centers, crippling the Triumvirate's ability to respond.

"Taking that weapons depot has to be our top priority," he mumbled.

"What?" Brytnoth asked, peering at him in the growing darkness.

"Sorry. Just talking to myself," Jared answered, flashing him a grin. "I think we've overlooked something. I'm thinking that the Triumvirate may have some kind of code word or mechanism that will turn the slave population into a mindless but lethal fighting force."

Brytnoth swore softly. "I never thought of that."

"I didn't either until tonight," Jared confessed. "But think about it. Think about how numb the slaves were during the fight on the transport ship. But maybe there's a trigger word, something that would make them rise up and fight."

"It makes sense," Brytnoth said. "If the Triumvirate is planning to take the fight to Halcyon, they'll need a massive army, but from what we've seen, there's just a skeletal force of Triumvirate soldiers based here. That army would have to come from somewhere."

Jared chewed his lip thoughtfully. "That's why I said that taking that weapons facility has to be our top priority." He glanced at Brytnoth. "What do you know about a Triumvirate soldier named Derrek?"

Brytnoth frowned. "Derrek? I don't know anyone…wait." He snapped his fingers. "Derrek. I remember now. He was part of the troop that intercepted us that first night. He seemed to have attitude." He glanced quizzically at Jared. "You were at the warehouse! How did you find out about him?"

"Sahara told me to find him. She thinks he might be useful."

"So that's what we're doing?"

"That's what we're doing."

They continued along in silence as they reached the base of the hill leading up to the landing platform. A troop of soldiers was just cresting the hill, and Jared and Brytnoth started up the road to meet them.

"State your business!" the troop commander called out as they approached.

"We're looking for Derrek," Jared answered.

A tall man with a jagged scar running down his right cheek stepped out of the ranks and looked Jared up and down, his eyes bright in the light of the crazily canted street lamp. He dominated the troop's commander both in stature and in his attitude of complete authority.

"Who's asking?" he said.

Brytnoth turned as if to look back down the way they had come. "That's him," he murmured.

"Lord Azel wants to see you," Jared snapped. "Now."

Derrek swore, and the commander slapped him on the shoulder.

"Well, you've had it coming!" he laughed. "Hope you don't get sent to the mines like that last insubordinate fool Azel called up!"

Derrek glared at him and stepped forward to join Jared and Brytnoth. "Let's go."

Even when he's not in charge, he's still giving orders, Jared marveled, grinning to himself. *I like this guy.*

They turned and headed back into the city, quickly outpacing Derrek's troop. Once they were well within the web of streets and houses of the Village, Jared and Brytnoth each took hold of one of Derrek's arms and pulled him into an alleyway.

"What's going on?" Derrek demanded, his voice loud in the stillness. He jerked his arms free and faced them, his whole body at the ready.

"Shut up and listen very carefully," Jared said. "A friend of mine thinks you might be the right man for a certain job. I don't know about that, but I'm willing to entertain the notion. It seems you're on someone's black list, is that right? A bit too much criticism of the Triumvirate, perhaps? Unwelcome attention usually follows that, you know."

"And? I couldn't care less. I'll say what I think, and I'll say it to whomever I like." He crossed his arms over his chest. "Is that what this is about? Azel sent you to take me into some alley and rough me up a bit?" Jared saw the flash of the man's teeth as he grinned. "Because that's not really going to be good for your health."

"No. We're not from the Triumvirate at all."

It caught Derrek off-guard. He had already gathered breath to say something, and now it all came out in a single syllable. "What?"

"To hell with them," Jared said. Then, with a grin, he added, "And we'd like your help escorting them there."

"Wait. What?" Derrek's confusion was written all over his face, and he dropped his arms to his sides. "What?"

"So did I get the wrong man?" Jared pressed. "Or are you up for the job?"

Derrek looked at Brytnoth. "Is he for real?"

"Absolutely and completely," Brytnoth replied. "So, are you in or not?"

Derrek's face suddenly broke into a huge grin, and he extended his hand to Jared. "What do I call you?"

"Jared Alareth. And this is Brytnoth." Jared clasped Derrek's hand and smiled. "Glad to have you with us."

———

Back at the barracks, they introduced Derrek to the rest of the crew. As they sat nursing mugs of ale and discussing their next move, Derrek studied Aelred.

"You know, I thought there was something funny about you when you showed up here," he said. "Our commanders are getting sloppy, and they don't pay attention like they should." He shook his head. "The Triumvirate used to run things with an iron fist. They were suspicious of everyone and everything. They brutalized the neighboring planets—worse than the Drakkin ever did, in some cases. But when they got away with everything without resistance, things started to unravel a bit. Baltek is a paranoid freak—his kill squads are no joke, and he doesn't need much excuse to send one after you. We don't see much of Azel anymore. But Ergeron's something else again. He loves his fine clothes and delicacies—imports them from off-world and doesn't care about the cost. And he's got big plans. He's the visionary of the bunch."

"And that's exactly where we need your help," Aelred said. "We know the Triumvirate is looking for *zanthos* to power that stockpile of weapons they're hoarding north of here."

Derrek started in surprise. "How did you know about that?"

"We have a team that infiltrated the Triumvirate headquarters, and Ergeron took them on a tour of the facility."

"Why would he do that?" Derrek frowned. "That facility is top secret...only a select number of officers even know it exists! Why is he parading people through there?"

"Because he thinks our team is from Halcyon, there to negotiate a new drug contract," Jared answered.

Derrek swore under his breath. "I knew it," he said aloud. "So he really has gone insane."

"We have to get hold of the *zanthos* before they do," Aelred continued, "and we have to seize that weapons facility. Our men are ready to move against the Triumvirate, but we can't until those two things are secure."

"How can I help?" Derrek asked.

"We know where the *zanthos* is," Aelred said. "We need a ship and clearance to head to Perseon. And we need you to help us coordinate a raid on the weapons facility."

Derrek grinned at him. "Oh, is that all?" And then, when Aelred stared at him blankly, obviously not certain how to respond, Derrek laughed aloud. "Teasing. Consider it done."

They worked long into the night planning the details. Derrek assured them that the easiest part of the plan was getting the ship. Exploration squads were leaving all the time, and he could easily disguise them as one. They agreed that Aelred and Derrek would have to stay on Askalon in order to coordinate the more complicated task of taking over the weapons facility. Kirin insisted on staying as well, so Jared and Brytnoth would lead the team headed to Perseon.

Long after everyone else had retired for the night, Jared stayed up, sitting alone in front of the fire. This new business of the weapons facility and the mission to Perseon was fraught with unanswered questions and variables that made their plans seem even more unstable.

Infiltrating the facility might be easy enough, he thought, *but what about the zanthos? How are we supposed to accomplish that task with just ten men?*

He sighed.

Everything would have to be placed on hold. And that meant that Rafe, Deor, and Sahara couldn't remain in position at the Great House as he had hoped. They would have to finish their sham mission and leave, and Jared knew from experience that the second infiltration was always harder than the first.

He rubbed his hands over his face and leaned back in his chair, crossing his boots on the fender. It was late, and he was tired. So tired.

A hand on his shoulder made him jump.

"You're still up?" said Aliya as she crossed in front of him and sank into the chair facing him.

She looks haggard, he thought. *Haggard, but still beautiful.*

"I haven't seen much of you," he said, smiling at her.

"You've given me a full-time job, overseeing all these girls," she said, returning the smile. "And now..." She leaned forward and took both of his hands in hers. "You've given me back my husband." Her eyes were shining with tears. "And I don't know how I can ever thank you for that."

Jared squeezed her hands gently. "You needn't thank me at all, my lady," he said. "I'm just happy that we found him alive. Had we gotten there even five minutes later, he would've been gone."

"I know." Her voice was a whisper, and a tear slipped down her pale cheek. "How well I know."

Jared stared at her mutely for a moment, not sure what to say. He had the sense that these were tears that had to be shed, and so he dropped his eyes and held her hands as quiet sobs shook her.

Finally, she pulled one of her hands free and laid it against his cheek, rough with the stubble of a beard. He lifted his eyes to hers.

"You're like a son to me," she said, her voice now hoarse from crying. "I love you like my own son. And no son ever did better by his father than you have done by Arnauld."

Jared felt his throat tighten. "Any one of us would have done the same, my lady," he protested, but she shook her head.

"I know what I know," she insisted. Then, making sure that she held his gaze, she said, "Don't give up on her, Jared."

He furrowed his brow, though he knew very well whom she meant. "My lady?"

Aliya leaned forward, her hands gripping his shoulders now, her dark eyes intense as they stared into his own.

"Love is strong as death, Jared. Don't you let her go. Don't you dare let her go."

THIRTY-TWO

SAHARA SAT ON THE BED, knees drawn up to her chin. She had watched the sky slowly brighten with dawn, and now the sound of cheerful conversation and laughter from the sitting room told her that Deor and Rafe were awake. She curled her toes on the coverlet and sighed.

Ergeron had promised them a meeting with his brothers today to discuss the terms of the contract with Halcyon, and she felt a knot of cold fear forming in her gut. It would be Deor's moment to shine, and she was terrified.

Her younger brother had proved himself capable of handling difficult situations already, and his whole life was a lesson in the power of the will to change fate. But if he didn't play this part convincingly, they were all dead.

And then there was the problem of Ergeron himself.

What if he drugs us all? What if Deor and Rafe have as much trouble resisting his influence as I do?

She shuddered. She felt only marginally safer around him when Rafe and Deor were with her.

I almost ruined everything, she thought, hugging her knees tightly. *What if I finish the job today?*

A sharp rap on the wooden door made her jump.

"Come in!" she called.

She expected to see Deor and was surprised when Rafe opened the door. Her face must have registered something of her shock, because Rafe stopped and knitted his brows.

"Can I...come in?" he asked.

Sahara smoothed her features and smiled at him. "Of course, Rafe. You just weren't the person I expected to see."

Rafe stepped inside the door and stood there, looking down at her. His quiet smile baffled her.

He really hasn't been himself these past few days, she reflected. *It's so unlike him to be subdued.*

"Are you...is everything all right?" she asked, lifting her eyebrows.

He seemed to shake himself. "Of course. We're figuring out our plan for this meeting...we hoped you would join us. They sent up some food. If you're hungry."

"I'll come."

He smiled at her again and then ducked back through the door.

As soon as he was gone, Sahara frowned. There was something decidedly strange about his behavior, but she had other things to worry about at the moment. She slipped off the bed and winced a little as her bare feet hit the cold flags of the floor. Her boots were slumped in the corner where she had flung them the night before, and she decided to leave them there. She ran her fingers through some of the more difficult tangles in her hair and stuffed her shirt into the top of her breeches. She wound her scarf around her waist once more to hold the pants in place and headed into the sitting room.

They had a cheerful fire going, and Deor was pouring steaming water into a cream-colored teapot. As she approached, he glanced up and smiled.

"There you are!"

"Why, Deor, how domestic of you," she teased, gesturing to the teapot. "I didn't know you could make tea."

"I can't."

Sahara laughed, and Rafe smiled at her.

"He does you good," he said. "I haven't heard you laugh like that since...." His voice trailed off, and he dropped his eyes to the plate he held in his hand.

Sahara and Deor exchanged glances.

"Rafe, something's eating at you," Deor remarked. "What's the trouble?"

Rafe shook his head brusquely, but his dark eyes flashed suddenly at Sahara. "It's nothing."

Deor studied him for a moment. "Fine."

They settled into seats with their steaming mugs, and Sahara sipped the spicy tea appreciatively in between bites of the warm sweet rolls that had been sent for their breakfast.

"For not knowing how to make tea," she said, "you did an excellent job!"

Deor smiled at her, then his gaze flicked back to Rafe.

"Deor should do all the talking today," Rafe said, ignoring Deor's persistent questioning stare. "After all, he's the one who knows Jaffa and knows this business."

"Do you think you can handle it, Deor?" Sahara asked, feeling that knot of anxiety in her gut again.

Deor glanced at her, starting to laugh until he noticed the look on her face. "You're not kidding."

"No, I'm not kidding."

"I'll be fine, sis. But I appreciate the concern."

"No, Deor, listen to me." She started an emphatic gesture and spilled some of her tea. Steadying her cup and her nerves, she tried again. "You can't take this lightly. What if he puts something in our drinks? What if he tries to manipulate you like he did me? What if they find out we're not who we say we are?"

"Sahara," Deor said, his voice calm and level, "I don't think they'll try that on all three of us. That was a special treat Ergeron saved just for you, I think. What do you think would happen to these idiots if we went back and reported to Halcyon that they drugged us to get a better deal?"

"But we don't work for Halcyon, Deor!"

"You miss the point, my dear. They think we work for Halcyon. They think we'll be reporting back with the details of our trip. And that's our best defense against any foul play. They're not ready to take on Halcyon yet. They haven't found that *zanthos* stuff they're looking for, and that huge stash of weapons is worthless without it. Halcyon would annihilate them without a second thought if they were double-crossed. And Ergeron and his brothers know it."

Sahara took a deep breath and blew it out again. "I just...he terrifies me, Deor."

Rafe regarded her quizzically. "You took down a Guardian with a knife," he said. "You infiltrated the prison on K'ilenfir I don't remember how many times. You defied the Drakkin...twice. I just don't understand how that sniveling wretch can frighten you."

"He makes me lose control," she snapped, her fear making her angry. "An honest dragon is one thing. But he's not honest. He's a snake."

There was a long silence. Sahara held Rafe's eyes with her own, trying to will him to understand. Deor finally cleared his throat, and Rafe looked away, leaving Sahara feeling strangely breathless and more than a little confused.

"Why do you give him so much power, sis?" Deor asked. "Don't let him have it."

"Do you think I let him influence me by choice?" she flared at him, her confusion now fueling her temper. "I'm not a fool, Deor!"

A knock at the door interrupted their argument. Sahara turned away from her brother and raised her cup to her lips, letting the fragrant steam soothe her rattled nerves. Before Deor could reach the door, it opened and one of Ergeron's servants shuffled into the room.

"My lords request your presence," he said.

"About time," Deor muttered. He glanced at Sahara. "You can't go downstairs like that. We'll wait for you outside."

Sahara was coming to hate the mazy halls of the Great House. They had been placed in a deserted wing of the house, as far removed as possible from the Triumvirate's own quarters. She usually had a good head for directions, but there was something about the layout of the house that always made her feel disoriented and lost.

When they finally reached the Great Hall, they found all three Triumvirate lords seated on the dais. The long wooden table was in its place in the center of the room, but it was bare save for a cut glass decanter filled with a rich red wine and six tumblers.

"Are these the emissaries?" one of the lords barked at Ergeron as they approached the dais.

"Yes, brother Azel, they are," he answered smoothly. His voice sounded even more languid next to the harshness of his brother's tone.

As they approached the dais, Sahara saw Ergeron wink at her, and she barely kept herself from shuddering. To avoid meeting his eyes, she studied Azel instead. He was a huge man, broad in the shoulders and well-muscled. His once-dark hair was now shot through with silver, but something about his face made Sahara think of a bird of prey—the hard line of his mouth, perhaps, or the cold fire in his piercing blue eyes. He wore a heavy ring almost identical to Ergeron's, but his was a deep blue sapphire.

"They don't look like the last bunch that came from Halcyon!" Azel snapped. "Did you check their credentials before you let them traipse all over Taur Isis?"

"We are here to negotiate for Jaffa," Deor said, stepping forward. "Perhaps we could discuss—"

"You'll speak when you're spoken to!" Azel shouted. "And I wasn't speaking to you!"

Sahara glanced sidelong at Deor and saw the muscle in his jaw tighten. But he never dropped his gaze, and Sahara noticed that it was Azel who looked away first.

"Brother," soothed Ergeron, "let's just get down to business, shall we? Of course I checked their credentials. Jaffa vouches for them, and he's an important supplier. We can't afford to lose his good will by mistreating his representatives."

The message was clear, and Azel finally subsided, grumbling. Even as he sat back in his chair, Baltek leaned forward, staring straight at Sahara. He was obviously a man who took great pleasure in the table, and though he had the same stunning blue eyes as his brothers, his were half-buried in folds of flesh.

"But why does Jaffa send a woman to bargain, eh?" he asked, rubbing his hands together. "And such a fine woman at that?"

"She's a favorite of his," Deor answered, shrugging. "And she has a good nose for the double-cross. Jaffa wanted her to come along, so she's here."

Sahara lifted her chin as Baltek continued to look her over like she were livestock at auction. His brazenness fired her anger and her disgust and she swallowed hard, desperately fighting to keep down all the things she wanted to say to this pig of a man.

"Well, he has good taste, I'll give him that," Baltek remarked at last. "He has no interest in the slave trade? You're sure?"

"We're here for the drug contract," Deor answered. "If he's interested in the slave trade, he didn't share it with me."

Baltek regarded him shrewdly and then shrugged. "Very well. Shall we to business?"

The three lords stepped down from the dais and Ergeron gestured for them to sit at the table. As they took their seats on one side of the table, Ergeron produced Jaffa's contract from the breast of his doublet. He and his brothers sat opposite them, and Sahara noticed that Ergeron made a point of sitting directly across from her.

He set the contract down in the center of the table and poured the wine, smiling easily at Sahara. She found herself staring at the decanter, and she couldn't help wondering if he'd drugged it again. In spite of Deor's assurances, she didn't trust him.

"You'll be pleased to hear, I'm sure, that we've agreed to all conditions in the contract," Baltek said. As he raised his glass and downed the contents in a single draught, Sahara noticed that he, too, wore a ring, this one set with an emerald.

I'll have to ask Aelred about these rings, she thought, unable to shake the sense that they were somehow important.

"That's wonderful," Deor said. "I'll have good news to bring back to Jaffa, then. And it seems that our business here is concluded."

He pushed back his chair, but Sahara laid a hand on his arm. Ergeron was smiling at them, and Sahara felt again that knot of cold building in her gut.

"Wait," she murmured to Deor. Then, addressing Ergeron, she said, "Was there something else?"

"We have accepted all conditions in the contract," Azel answered, "and we have added one of our own, at the request of our dear brother Ergeron."

Sahara's eyes snapped to Ergeron's face, and she knew, before he opened his mouth to speak, what he had requested.

"No."

It was Rafe who spoke, and Sahara knew that he had guessed as well. She grasped his hand under the table and squeezed it in thanks.

"She was never part of the negotiations," he continued, his voice trembling with the effort he was making to keep it level. "She's not part of the deal."

"Well, she is now," Ergeron said, and Sahara heard the threat under the rippling surface of his unctuous voice. "If you value your terms, then you must meet ours. And we have only one. Just one little stipulation. Tiny, really." His eyes hardened as he attempted to stare Rafe down. "She stays with us in Askalon."

Sahara felt Deor's body stiffen, and she wished desperately that she had the ability to communicate mind-to-mind with him. But since she had no way to give him fair warning, she'd just have to say what she had to say.

"You will give Jaffa the price he demands?" she asked. "You will sign to it?"

Ergeron shook out the parchment. Their signatures were already on the bottom of the page. "It has already been done," he said.

"Then we accept your condition."

She felt Rafe and Deor staring at her, and Rafe's hand tightened around hers. She pulled her hand out of his grasp and forced a smile onto her face. Then she rose, gesturing for Ergeron to hand her the paper. He held it out to her, his fingers brushing hers. She kept the smile plastered on her lips and willed herself not to shudder at his touch.

"Would that all negotiations could have such a lovely and desirable outcome!" he murmured.

"Good day to you, my lords," Sahara said, ignoring him.

Without another word, she turned and stalked out of the hall. She heard the scraping of wood on stone as Deor and Rafe rose to follow her, but she didn't look back and she didn't slow her pace.

It wasn't until they reached their own chambers that she finally turned to face them. Rafe slammed the door shut and ran his hands through his hair.

"What the hell are you thinking?" he ground out. "What has gotten into you, Sahara? You didn't touch your wine...you're not drugged again, are you?"

Sahara shook her head and smiled sadly at him. "You would have done the same for me, Rafe," she said softly. "If you knew it was the only way I'd get out alive."

Rafe stared at her, but as he opened his mouth to speak, Deor gripped his arm.

"She's right, Rafe," he said.

Rafe turned on him. "You said this couldn't happen!" he shouted. "You said they wouldn't lift a finger to hurt us because they wouldn't want to anger Halcyon! What's wrong with you, Deor? Why aren't you furious right now? This is your sister we're talking about, dammit!"

Deor studied Sahara for a long time. "I know," he said. "And I think she has a plan."

Sahara drew her knife from its scabbard and tested its edge with her thumb. Then she glanced up into Rafe's frantic eyes.

"I promise you," she said. "They will regret this."

Rafe's expression changed suddenly, a desperate pleading in their depths.

"Promise me that *I* won't regret this," he said softly.

She smiled at him. "I promise."

THIRTY-THREE

JARED HAD JUST JOINED the others at the table for their evening meal when the door to the barracks opened suddenly. They jumped to their feet, scrambling for weapons, until Jared recognized the two men standing in the doorway.

"It's all right!" he said. "It's just Deor and Rafe."

Rafe shut the door and they came forward into the room. As the others resumed their seats, Jared edged around the table to meet them, looking past them at the closed door.

"She's not coming, Jared," Rafe said heavily.

Jared's eyes swiveled to Rafe's face as a sudden chill of doubt and fear surged through his body. "What?"

"I thought she would have told you herself," he answered. "She's not coming home."

"What do you mean, she's not coming?" Jared's voice rose in spite of his efforts to control it. His hands clenched into fists. "What do you mean?"

"She stayed behind, Jared," Deor answered. "They weren't going to accept the contract unless she agreed to stay. And she made the call."

Jared stared at them for a moment, his chest heaving. Then he seized Rafe by the shirt and propelled him across the floor until he slammed into the wall.

"I trusted you!" he shouted. "I trusted you, Rafe! I trusted you to bring her back to me!"

"I'm sorry, Jared!" Rafe cried. "I couldn't..."

Jared shoved him hard against the wall. "How could you do this? How could you leave her there alone?"

"What do you want me to say?" Rafe snapped, pushing Jared away. "What the hell do you want me to say? That I wanted to leave her there? That I thought this was some kind of a good plan? That I didn't try to make her change her mind? What do you want me to say?"

Jared stared at him, saw the raw helplessness in his eyes. Then he remembered how he had been unable to reach Sahara, unable to break Ergeron's hold over her. She was beyond his aid. And it was all Rafe's fault.

"Jared," Rafe pleaded. "She knows what she's—"

"Don't. Just don't."

Jared left the barracks, letting the door slam shut behind him. The air outside was bracing, and he sank down on the stoop, staring up into the shroud of darkness that admitted no starlight. Then he closed his eyes, reaching out to Sahara with his mind, praying that she would answer him.

Sahara, why? Why did you do it? Why did you stay behind?

He waited. A tear coursed down his cheek from beneath his closed eyelids.

Sahara, please.

Please.

He felt a hand on his shoulder and slowly opened his eyes.

"What do you want, Rafe?" He suddenly felt so tired, so incredibly tired.

Rafe slid down to sit beside him and said nothing for a long time.

"She has a plan," he said finally. "But damn, Jared — it was hard to leave her there."

Jared studied him, wishing that he could see better in the darkness. The shadows of an old fear were beginning to creep into his mind again. "What plan?" he asked, swallowing the other question that burned in his throat.

"I think she's planning to assassinate them."

Jared stared at him for several seconds, then turned away, shaking his head and laughing softly. "That's her plan? She's going to do that? All alone? All three of them?"

"You don't think she can do it?"

"You think she can?" Jared turned back to him. "Come on, Rafe! Even for Sahara, that's asking a bit much."

Rafe shrugged, but Jared saw the flare of doubt in his eyes. "I don't know. I think she can handle it."

"Well, I'm not going to let her handle it alone. Assassinating the Triumvirate is part of our strategy, but there's no way I'm going to let her attempt that by herself. Too many things can go wrong." He swore softly. "It wasn't supposed to happen like this."

Rafe stared down at his hands. "Jared, I...." He stopped, seeming to reconsider his words. "I'm sorry."

Jared sighed. "I know. And I don't mean to blame you. I just..."

"You don't have to explain to me," Rafe interrupted. "You love her. You don't want to see her hurt. I get it. I understand."

Jared studied his friend again, the suspicion in his mind reinforced by something in Rafe's voice. He decided to put it to the test.

"Well, we'll have to leave her to fend for herself for a while," he sighed. "Brytnoth and I are taking a team to Perseon to find the *zanthos* mine. The ship leaves tomorrow. And I want you and Deor to come with us."

Rafe was silent for a long time, and Jared could tell that he was wrestling with something.

"I don't want to go off-world with her in that serpent's nest, either," Jared added. "But if we sacrifice the mission to Perseon to get her out of there, then we jeopardize everything. You said that she has a plan. We're just going to have to trust her judgment."

Rafe still said nothing. Jared frowned.

"I can't do it," Rafe said, raising his head and looking into Jared's eyes. "I can't. And if you love her as much as you say you do, I don't know how you can, either."

There it was.

Jared swore softly and stood. "Think about it," he said, swallowing everything else he wanted to say.

Rafe shuffled aside to let him back into the barracks, and Jared left him sitting there alone. The rest of the crew had already gone to bed, but Jared saw Deor sitting in front of the fire alone. He had changed back into his Triumvirate uniform and he was thoughtfully rotating a goblet between his capable hands. Jared joined him, slumping in the chair across from him.

Deor glanced up, a smile quirking the corner of his mouth. "Jealousy is hard as hell," he said.

"What?"

"I said, jealousy is hard as hell."

Jared met his gaze. "What are you talking about?"

Deor laughed softly. "You think I'm blind? Why did you go after Rafe and not me earlier, Jared?"

"Because...."

The question staggered him, and he realized he had no good answer. It was true. He had turned on Rafe immediately, completely forgetting that Deor was even in the room.

"You went after him because you think he's in love with Sahara. Am I right?" When Jared said nothing, he continued, "And that's why I said that jealousy's hard as hell. You would've been more justified blaming me for the fact that she's still up there. Rafe didn't want to leave her. But I told him we had to go. I was the one who left her there, Jared."

"She's your sister," Jared said weakly. "How could you do that to her?"

"She's capable of more than you fathom," Deor answered. "She's buried it, but I see it. It flashes through in glimpses sometimes. And maybe it's because I'm her brother, or maybe it's because my love for her is different than yours...or Rafe's. I want her to fight by my side." His eyes flashed at Jared. "You don't want her to fight at all."

Jared frowned at him. "I don't think that's exactly—"

"Of course it's true. If it wasn't true, you'd trust her to take care of herself. You'd believe in her like I do."

"No one believes in her more than I do!" Jared protested.

Deor arched an eyebrow at him, and Jared fell silent, confusion suddenly drowning his certainty. A hundred things that he might say to prove it rushed into his mind, and then suddenly all collapsed like a house of straw.

"Trust me," Deor said. "And trust her. It was her decision. She doesn't need you to ride up there and rescue her, Jared. She needs you to believe that she can save herself."

———

Jared thought about Deor's words as their transport ship hurtled toward Perseon. He sat alone at the square table in the midship gallery, frowning at the dull metal surface that almost, but not quite, reflected his face. He had tried again to contact Sahara before the ship left Askalon, but he was either unable to get through to her or she was blocking him.

It seemed that there was some kind of precarious balance that he hadn't quite discovered, some way to love her that left her standing on her own without leaving her to stand alone.

He shook his head. He didn't understand it, but he also knew that if he didn't figure it out, she would just continue to drift away from him.

Toward what...or whom? he wondered, knowing the answer even as the question materialized. *Toward whoever does have it figured out.*

He glanced up as Brytnoth came into the gallery.

"We'll reach Perseon in a few hours," he said. "It's an ice moon, so we're going to have to gear up for the cold."

"Fine."

Brytnoth peered at him. "Are you okay?" he asked. "You seem not okay to me."

"Very observant of you."

"What's going on between you and Rafe?" Brytnoth pressed, sitting down across the table from him. "I thought you were going to bloody him up last night when they got back."

Jared shook his head and leaned back in his chair. "No. Well...no, I didn't really want to hurt him...much." When Brytnoth frowned at him, he said, "Fine. Yes. I was trying to rough him up."

"You two have been friends since you were kids. And I've never seen you go after anyone like that. It's not...that wasn't like you, Jared."

Jared sighed. "I'm sorry it got ugly."

Brytnoth nodded and rose. As he was about to leave the room, he suddenly turned. "You're risking your lives to save my homeworld," he said. "I just want you to know, if none of us make it out alive, that it's been an honor." He hesitated, then added, "You're my brothers, you know. You and Rafe. So patch it up, all right?"

Jared smiled at him. "We already have."

"Good." Brytnoth ducked out of the room and headed down the corridor, and Jared could hear him muttering as he left, "We come halfway across the system to battle drug lords and tyrants, and they've got to fight over a girl."

THIRTY-FOUR

JARED HAD NEVER FELT such cold.

Having lived all his life on the sun-drenched desert planet of Silesia, he'd found Askalon's cloud-shrouded climate depressing at best. Now, as his boots crunched on ice and his breath clung to the fur of his hood in frozen crystals, he was miserable.

"Who the hell would ever dig for anything on this rock?" he muttered. "And why did I offer to come along?"

"He never told us it was ice," Rafe said, waving a mittened hand in Brytnoth's direction. "Evil. That's what it amounts to. If he ever offers to take us somewhere again, don't let him do it." He buried his hand in the pocket of his parka and shrugged against the cold, swearing as he did so. "I hate this place."

Brytnoth glanced back at them, grinned, and waved them onward. "Not far, ladies," he said. "It's just over that next ridge there."

Jared and Rafe lifted their heads to see the ridge he indicated, then they looked at each other.

"He has *got* to be kidding," Jared said.

The ridge was more of a small mountain, part of a long chain of much higher peaks. It looked as though the land had suddenly shivered, blistering in the cold. Jared could just make out what looked like a dark line swirling up its frozen side.

"Is that supposed to be a road? Tell me again why we didn't land on the other side of the mountains?"

Brytnoth stopped and waited for them to catch up. "We've been through this already. No one has been to these mines for years. Do you want to risk our only way home?"

"How much risk could there possibly be?" Rafe said.

Brytnoth raised his shoulders. "Prudence, dear fellow. And once we've made sure the area is secure, we'll radio the ship. We won't have to walk back. Now let's go. Frostbite spares no man."

"Love it," Rafe muttered. "Love this place. We're so glad you brought us here, Brytnoth."

They reached the foot of the ridge a short time later and paused, staring up at the ascent. The road leading up and over was barely passable, and even from their vantage point Jared could see several places where their way would be barred by huge chunks of ice-covered rock. Long stretches of the path reflected the watery sunlight that seeped through the thin membrane of clouds—he realized that these were sheets of ice that had formed over the blasted rock. He adjusted the pack on his shoulders and set his jaw.

As they trudged up the slope, the wind began to whip around them. Jared ducked his head, but it seemed to buffet him from all sides at once. He stared down at his boots, struggling to find purchase on the icy track. Ahead of him, he saw Brytnoth toiling against the wind and the ice. Once, he heard Rafe curse beside him as his foot slipped and his knee crashed down onto the rocky path. Jared tried to ask him if he was hurt, but his lips wouldn't frame the words properly, and his voice was lost on the wind.

Brytnoth called a halt at the second rockslide. They were more than two-thirds of the way up the slope, but they were utterly spent. Rafe's knee was badly bruised, and Jared had been helping him these last few hundred yards. Now, they sank wearily into the meager shelter provided by the tumbled stones, glad to be out of the howling wind.

"We can't stay long," Brytnoth panted. "If we sit here too long, our muscles will stiffen up and we'll never get over the summit."

Jared said nothing, but pulled his canteen from within his parka and moistened his parched throat. Then he passed it to the others. They sat for a few more minutes in silence, trying to restore some strength to their exhausted limbs. All too soon, Brytnoth stood, groaning, and motioned them up with a faint smile.

"Let's go. Not far now."

It took them nearly as long to reach the top of the crest as it had taken them to get all the way to the rockslide. When they finally stood at the summit, trying to catch their breath, Jared glanced at the sky. The sun seemed barely to have moved. Brytnoth followed his gaze.

"The sun won't set here for another twenty days, as measured on Askalon," he said. "And we're lucky. If it did, we'd freeze to death in seconds."

Jared shook his head and turned to face down the western side of the crest. To his surprise, the slope here was much shallower than the eastern side, and he could now see, far in the distance, that the mountain chain was actually a ring.

"What is this?" he breathed. "I've never seen a formation like this."

Brytnoth shifted his pack and started down the track. "It's a caldera," he called back.

"What's a caldera?" asked Rafe, looking at Jared. Jared shrugged.

"I don't know, but I see the mine." He gestured to where a sprawling complex of buildings squatted in the drifting snow, almost in the very center of the ring of mountains. He glanced again at the sky, and then shook his head. "Strange," he muttered. "I feel frozen in more ways than one."

Rafe stamped his boots. "Well, I'm literally frozen, so let's get moving. I hope there's heat down there or my toes are done for."

It was almost impossible to gauge how long it took them to cross the caldera. Jared felt like it would never end, but whenever he glanced at the sky, he felt that they had hardly begun. The strangeness of it grew on him until he thought it would drive him crazy.

When they finally staggered into the mine complex, Jared's legs would hardly carry him another foot. Rafe dropped to his knees in the snow, breathing hard, and Brytnoth was bent double, cupping his mittened hands in front of his mouth to try to keep the cold from searing his lungs.

Jared tilted his face to the sky, closing his eyes. He dropped his pack and stretched his aching back. When he bent to retrieve it, he caught sight of movement out of the corner of his eye.

"We're not alone," he murmured.

Brytnoth straightened and stared around them. "I don't see anything," he said, keeping his voice near a whisper.

"There," said Rafe, getting to his feet. "I saw something off to our right."

They stood completely still for what seemed like an eternity, waiting for whatever it was to show itself clearly. Finally, as they made no threatening movements, a small shape shuffled out of the shadowy shelter of the building to their right. It looked nearly as wide as it was tall, and only stood about four feet high. At first, Jared saw only a fuzzy bundle of furs, but then he saw the boots. Tiny, leather-thonged, fur-lined boots, miniatures of his own.

"It's a child!" said Rafe.

As if on cue, it pushed back its hood, and they saw disheveled blond curls and big blue eyes. Her little snub nose was slightly turned up at the end, and her cheeks were flushed.

"What are you doing here?" she asked, tilting her head to one side and regarding them quizzically.

Brytnoth dropped to one knee so that he could look her straight in the face. "Is your mother here?" he asked. "Or your father, perhaps?"

The little girl turned and beckoned. Three more figures

emerged from the shadows and joined her—a lanky boy who seemed to be about eight or nine, a woman, and a tall man who carried a staff with a strange metal cage fastened on the top. As they approached, the girl turned back to Brytnoth with a bright smile.

Fearless, thought Jared.

Brytnoth rose to his feet and held out a hand to the man. "We mean you no harm," he said. "But why did you send her to greet us? What if we had not come in peace?"

The man shrugged and smiled. "Mahiya would not mind. And if you had tried to harm her, you would all have died." He inclined the staff in their direction, and Jared could now see that the cage housed a small shard of some gold-hued stone.

"*Zanthos!*" Rafe exclaimed suddenly, pointing. "That's *zanthos*, isn't it?"

The man's face was instantly stern with suspicion. "Who asks?"

Brytnoth held up his hands. "Wait. Please, sir, we are nearly frozen to death. Do you have a place where we might warm ourselves and talk?"

The man's gaze snapped back to Brytnoth, and after a moment, he nodded brusquely. "Follow me."

The little family moved toward the buildings on their left, Mahiya skipping through the powdered snow. Jared, Brytnoth, and Rafe trailed along behind them, forcing their exhausted limbs to make one last effort.

The man pushed open the door to the largest of the buildings and stood aside for them to enter. Once inside, they stopped short. The door opened into what appeared to be a huge mess hall, and all of the twenty long tables in the room were occupied. Men, women, and children all stopped eating to stare at them. The man let the door swing shut once again, blocking out the cold.

"Welcome to Perseon," he said to Brytnoth. "My name is Alberic. And these are my people."

Jared swung his gaze from Alberic to the people in the hall. Many of them looked frightened, and Jared noticed that many of the mothers had gathered their children close.

"We're not here to threaten you or your people," he said, turning back to Alberic.

"I know that, or I wouldn't have brought you here," Alberic said with a warm smile. "Please, come and have something to eat."

They made their way to a smaller table set at the far end of the room. Jared and his friends sank gratefully onto the benches and took the steaming mugs of tea that a young woman brought to them.

"I think, just maybe, that my face is beginning to thaw," remarked Rafe as he sipped his drink.

Jared felt that he had never truly appreciated the calming and restorative properties of tea until that moment. Even the curls of steam rising from the mug were a luxury as they caressed his frozen cheeks.

"We cannot thank you enough for your hospitality," he said to Alberic as the young woman returned to the table once again with plates of hot food.

"Think nothing of it," replied Alberic with a wave of his hand. Then he smiled at the young woman. "Thank you, Gwyn."

Gwyn inclined her head to him and then moved away. Jared watched her as she slipped into the bench next to her three younger sisters. From the way she tended to them, and from the notable absence of an older woman at the table, Jared guessed that she was not only their sister, but their mother too.

"Where did you come from?" he asked, turning to Alberic. "Where have these people come from?"

"We are the Ellende Clan," Alberic said. "The Clan of Exiles."

"Exiled from Askalon?" Brytnoth asked.

"Yes." Alberic looked at him. "As were you."

Brytnoth set down his spoon. "But I was exiled by the Drakkin."

"I know." With a sad smile, Alberic gestured at the people in the hall. "We survived that first culling because the Triumvirate needed slaves. But then chance put a ship in our way, and we escaped here. The Triumvirate thinks that this moon is void of life. The secret of the *zanthos* mine, and of our survival, has been preserved. Until now." His eyes hardened suddenly and his hand closed into a fist. "So I will ask you, and I will ask you once only. Why are you here?"

Brytnoth raised a hand as if to ward off Alberic's anger. "We have come for *zanthos*," he said. "But not for the Triumvirate. For Lord Aelred, and for the revolution that will free our people and our homeworld."

Alberic's jaw tightened convulsively and his eyes bored into Brytnoth. "You mock me."

"No."

For a long while, Alberic measured them, clenching and unclenching his hand. They waited, silent, for him to speak.

"We thought Lord Aelred was dead," he said finally.

"And I thought no one else had survived the Drakkin," Brytnoth countered. "Obviously, I was wrong." He paused for a moment. "Will you help us? Will you come home?"

Alberic's gaze swung away from them and swept over the hall once more, pausing on the faces of the children. "We have fought so hard for so long," he murmured. "Fought for life, and for peace...for them. We have found ways to survive, finding it better to live a hard life in freedom than an easy one in chains."

Jared smiled. "You needn't explain that to us," he said. "And you don't have to risk yourselves, or your children. We don't ask you to fight."

Alberic fixed his eyes on Jared. "And what will you do with the *zanthos*?" he asked.

"The Triumvirate has amassed a store of weapons—" Rafe began, but Alberic slammed his fist down into the table so hard that they all jumped.

"Weapons." The word exploded from his lips.

"They're powered by *zanthos*," Rafe continued, his brow furrowed in puzzlement. "Even as we speak, Aelred's forces are infiltrating the weapons facility. We'll use the Triumvirate's own weapons against them."

But Alberic's frown was deepening as Rafe spoke. "I'm not sure you understand its power," he said. "The Triumvirate only knows how to bend things to evil purpose. But *zanthos* is a sacred trust. We have taken it upon ourselves to guard it—with our very lives if necessary—to keep it from those who would pervert its purpose."

"I don't understand," Brytnoth said. "You are exiles and fugitives, and yet when we promise you a way to take back your homeworld from those who are destroying it and killing and enslaving its people, you spit on it." His face was darkening with anger now. "I won't let you take this chance from us."

Alberic's smile now had no warmth left in it. "I'm afraid you have no choice."

Later that night, they sat huddled on the pallets that Alberic had laid out for them in the hall. It was empty and silent now, and it was lit only by a strip of golden stones that ran around the top of the wall and glowed softly. Jared studied them thoughtfully. They seemed to provide not only light, but also ambient warmth.

"More *zanthos*," Rafe said. "Seems as amazing as Aelred told us it was."

"It is."

Alberic stood near them, his arms folded across his chest. He stared down at them sternly for a few minutes, then dropped to sit cross-legged next to Jared.

"How can you refuse to help us?" Brytnoth said, his voice breaking. "Our victory is in your hands, Alberic. I hope you know that."

Alberic nodded. "I have been thinking...perhaps I judged in haste earlier. We've struggled so hard to live in peace and to guard the *zanthos* mine from the Triumvirate. It was never meant to destroy, you know. But the Triumvirate twists everything it touches."

"They've promised these weapons and the *zanthos* to Halcyon," Jared told him. "It isn't just the Triumvirate that you have to fear. Right now, we can win. We have a plan that can succeed. But if

Halcyon gets involved, then Askalon will never be free...and neither will you."

Alberic measured Jared for a long time. "You speak as one with experience and authority," he said. "But you are not from Askalon. Why should you care so much about our fate?"

"Brytnoth is like a brother to me. He fought by my side to free my own homeworld from the Drakkin. Isn't it just that I should do the same for him? But I also have a personal quarrel with the Triumvirate. They have killed some of my own people and enslaved many others."

"I suspected that they were taking slaves from other worlds," Alberic sighed. "There weren't enough of us left to serve their purposes." He looked down at his hands, deep in thought. Then, finally, he raised his head. "You must promise me that once this thing is done, you will destroy the weapons and return the *zanthos* to us for safekeeping once more."

Brytnoth's eyes lit up as a smile spread across his face. "You have my word."

THIRTY-FIVE

SAHARA STOOD ALONE on the balcony, her hands resting on the stone balustrade, and stared out over the roofs of the houses below. She could just make out the Village, and she wondered vaguely where Jared might be, and whether he was worried about her.

Jared. Jared.

It was the fourth time today that she had tried to reach him. And, as before, there was no answer.

She sighed, frustrated. And it was getting more and more difficult not to feel totally abandoned. And on the heels of abandonment, like a wolf on an iron chain, came fear.

The sunless chill was beginning to seep into her flesh.

"You didn't come for dinner," came a soft and supple voice behind her.

Sahara didn't turn. She didn't dare.

"I'm not hungry," she snapped. "Go away and leave me in peace."

The laugh. That hideous laugh. How she hated it.

"How can you not be hungry? You didn't eat breakfast either...or lunch. Truly, you must be famished."

And, as if on cue, her stomach began protesting her fast in earnest. She closed her eyes.

"Send something to my rooms, then. I'll eat alone."

Ergeron came to join her at the balustrade. She felt all her muscles tense, and she scarcely dared to breathe.

"Surely not alone," he said, turning his head to look at her.

"Yes, alone," she retorted. "And I thought I asked you to leave."

"But why did you agree to stay here with us?" Ergeron persisted. "It wasn't to closet yourself in your rooms, away from all company that might give you pleasure."

"I agreed to stay here for the sake of the contract and for my friends, so don't flatter yourself. I didn't stay for you."

Out of the corner of her eye, she could see Ergeron's mouth quirk up in a smile. "Never fear that, dear lady," he said.

"You're tiresome," she said frigidly. "Why won't you just go away?"

"But how I love provoking you!" he laughed. "You should see your face when you're angry...too exquisite for words, my dear."

Sahara took a deep breath, seeking desperately for that small store of calm she had been trying to collect for herself. It all seemed to have eked out of her.

Jared. Why won't you answer me? Why won't you answer?

It was becoming a desperate cry for help now, and the fact that Jared didn't answer her was beginning to make her frantic. All that time that she had resented him, resented his ability to reach into her mind, to read her emotions—she wished she could take it all back now. She would give anything to hear him speak to her. But there seemed to be a wall between them, as though she were shut out...or shut in.

Again she had that strange and almost overwhelming suspicion that it had something to do with the man standing beside her. But she couldn't understand how it would be possible for him to block her.

"Is there anything I can say to you to make you leave me alone?" she asked, hoping her voice didn't sound as unsure as she felt.

He seemed to consider her words for a moment. "Not really," he answered.

And now she felt the core of her fear of this man hardening into hate, a cold, calculated, patient hate, like the blade of a knife. And as the hate spread outward, the fear collapsed, and she finally turned to face him.

"I hope you're amusing yourself," she said.

He seemed surprised by the sudden shift in her attitude. For once, she had him fumbling for words.

"My...my brothers were disappointed that you didn't come for dinner," he remarked.

"Are we back to that again? You're so boring." As she spoke, she stared him straight in the eyes, and when his gaze wavered and dropped, she allowed herself a small smile. "You made a bad bargain, keeping me here," she told him.

He stood there, his mouth flapping wordlessly as he sought for something to say. Finally, he turned on his heel and stalked away.

"I guess now I know what to say to make you leave," she murmured, still smiling to herself.

When she went back inside the manor, she found that he had sent a tray of food up to her rooms as she had asked. A piece of cold fowl, warm, steaming rolls, and a tumble of fruits in a bowl. And the ubiquitous rich, red wine—a glass already poured, the rest in a cut glass decanter. She took up the glass and the decanter, went to the window, and dumped both out. The stain spread like blood on the crushed white stones of the drive below. Then she returned to the tray and settled herself comfortably in the settee to eat.

As she gnawed philosophically on the bone of the fowl, she considered her situation. She was alone. She had no way, apparently, to communicate with Jared. While she knew that assassinating the Triumvirate was part of their plan, the timing would have to be flawless. And now, isolated as she was, she had no way of knowing when to make her move against them.

What if I act too soon? Or, worse yet, what if I'm too late?

She looked at the window. Considered the angles. Distances. She tossed the bone onto the plate and selected a roll, tearing it into bite-sized pieces. Popping one into her mouth, she strolled back to the window, looking out now instead of down.

The drive is too conspicuous. If anyone happens to look out the window, I'll be spotted.

She looked to her right. The copse of trees that marched next to the drive could give her some shelter, and under cover of night she'd be almost invisible. She leaned against the window frame and chewed her lip.

She might have time. If no one came to disturb her for the rest of the evening. If no one came to fetch her too early in the morning. She might just have enough time.

She went to the wardrobe and flung open the doors. Ergeron had promised to send for some more appropriate clothes for her when the next trading ship left for Agora. In the meantime, he'd provided her with a few additional, serviceable garments. She quickly traded her white shirt for a black one and found a black handkerchief in one of the drawers. This she tied securely over her hair. She wound her green sash around her waist so that no ends hung loose, and then tucked her dagger securely inside, within easy reach if she should need it.

Satisfied, she went to the bed and pulled off the sheets. She returned to the sitting room and dumped them on the settee, and then, as quietly as she could, she shoved the heavy chair in front of the door, angling it under the handle to prevent anyone from entering. She knotted the sheets into a long rope and secured one end around the leg of the settee. Then she returned to the window to wait.

As soon as the gray sky had faded completely to black, Sahara flung her makeshift rope out the window. It wasn't quite long enough to reach the ground, but it got her close enough so that when she dropped she made no more noise than a large cat. She crouched there for a moment, waiting to be sure that she had not been seen or heard.

Then she moved, surely but silently, to the trees on her right. She stepped into their welcoming shadows and set off at a brisk trot, keeping the white stone drive always in sight so that she didn't lose her way. As soon as she came to the stone wall that marked the edge of the manor property, she edged from the cover of the trees, scuttled under the archway, and set off at a run down the road.

It was the darkest hour of the night when she finally stood, panting, in front of the barracks. Carefully, she pushed open the door and stepped inside.

She was immediately seized roughly from behind and her arms were pinned behind her back. The next moment, she fell heavily to the ground, grunting as her assailant planted his knee squarely in her back.

"What are you doing here?" a voice rasped in her ear.

She struggled to get a glimpse of his face. "Get off me, you colossal idiot!" she hissed. "Get off! I'm a friend to Aelred!"

The pressure on her back suddenly eased. "Sahara?"

"Of course it's me!" she snapped, coughing. "Let me go!"

Her captor released her arms and she pushed herself to her feet, gratefully sucking air back into her lungs. Then she turned to face the guard, squinting at his face in the uncertain light of the low-burning fire.

"Kirin! I should've known."

Kirin frowned at her. "Well, I had no idea it would be you. What are you doing here? Rafe said you had to stay at the Great House. Jared almost killed him."

Sahara started in surprise. "What?"

"We thought Jared was going to kill him," Kirin repeated. "He didn't, of course, but I've never seen him so angry."

Which is saying something, Sahara thought. Jared and Kirin had never been on the best terms.

"Where's Jared? I need to see him."

"He's gone. Rafe and Brytnoth, too. They went to Perseon."

"Perseon? Where's that?"

"It's one of Askalon's moons. It's where they mine for *zanthos*."

"When do you expect them back?"

"Hard to say," Kirin replied with a shrug. "Could be days...maybe a week, even."

"A week! I can't stay up there alone for that long, Kirin."

Her voice, which was suddenly loud in the quiet barracks, woke several of the others. Aelred sat up in bed, and then, seeing her standing near the door, he sprang up and hurried to join them.

"Sahara! You're back!"

"Not to stay," she said. "I had to find out what was going on. I can't communicate with Jared for some reason. Ergeron—he can block me somehow." Then she gripped Aelred's arm. "Wait. He has your ring."

"Ring? What ring?"

"The one with the ruby. And his brothers have ones just like it, but with different stones. An emerald, and a sapphire, I think."

Aelred's face suddenly paled. "Did he say where he got that ring?"

"He said it was a gift. By which I assume he meant he stole it."

"It was no gift." Aelred's face was grim. "He pulled it off my finger as he expelled me from my own chamber. Like so many of our precious artifacts, it has special...properties."

"Like what?"

"The ruby ring has mind-control properties. Hypnotic properties, of a sort. The wearer has to know how to use it. But that could be why you can't communicate with Jared. He may have figured out how to block your communication using the ring."

"How would he even know?"

Aelred frowned and rubbed his chin. "Perhaps he has the same ability," he suggested.

The thought made Sahara's stomach churn. *It's possible*, she thought. *It just means that I'll have to be even more careful around him.*

"What about the other rings?" she asked. "Do they have special properties, too? Ones that we should consider when planning our attack?"

"The blue ring channels anger. It's strength-enhancing. And the green ring has the power to conceal the bearer, at least for a short time."

"Fantastic," she muttered. "Super strength, mind-control, and invisibility. Damn. Do you have any good news for me?"

Aelred thought for a moment. "No. Not really."

Sahara frowned. "Not what I wanted to hear."

"I'm sorry, Sahara. Plan your attack carefully."

"I wasn't expecting to have to do this alone," she admitted. "Can I expect help or not?"

"I can't tell you that, I'm afraid. But Jared will be back in two days. We had word from them. They're recovering the *zanthos*, and it seems they found some kind of help on Perseon."

Sahara smiled. "Now, you see? You did have some good news for me. And when will you make your move against the Triumvirate?"

"We recruited Derrek on your suggestion, and he and Deor are working right now to infiltrate the weapons facility. Kalkas has a ready supply of the surrogate. As soon as Jared returns with the *zanthos*, we'll be ready."

"So three days, at most," she said.

"Three days."

"I should take care of things in two days' time, then."

Aelred nodded. "Just be careful, Sahara. We need you."

"I will. And send me some help if you can. Sunset on the second day." She clasped Aelred's hand, and then she ducked back out the door into the night.

THIRTY-SIX

"I NEVER THOUGHT I'd be so happy to see Askalon again," Jared confessed as their ship descended once more through the thick cloud cover that shrouded the planet. They had only been gone a few days, but it felt like years. Now, as he lost sight of the dawn in the bank of clouds, he felt strangely like he was coming home.

Brytnoth flashed him a smile. "I'm surprised at you, Jared," he said. "You were always the rough and ready type...but lower the temperature a bit and you're almost as bad as Kirin!"

"That's hardly fair. It wasn't just lowered a bit. I nearly lost toes out there." He grinned at Brytnoth, and then he turned to Rafe, who was silently staring out the window. "We got what we needed," he said, his smile fading. "You could be happier about it."

Rafe glanced at him. "Right."

Jared frowned. He opened his mouth to say something, but he felt the ship touch down. "Stay here," he said. "I'll make sure we're clear."

He lowered the ramp and stepped cautiously onto the platform. The area seemed deserted, but Jared didn't want to take any chances that Triumvirate troops might be prowling around. He edged toward the guard station. Then he froze as half a dozen men swarmed out of the hut, led by a huge man dressed all in Triumvirate black.

"Jared!" the man called, recognizing him.

Jared breathed a sigh of relief. It was Derrek.

He straightened and strode quickly across the platform. "What's going on?" he demanded as he approached. "Where are the guards?"

"You're looking at them," Derrek answered. "We took the platform last night. Figured it would be useful to have it secured before you returned. And we managed to secure the weapons facility without too much trouble. It's all been done quietly, just as you requested. Deor's in charge there now."

Jared beamed at him and gripped his hand in thanks. "I knew Sahara was right about you. I'm glad you decided to join us."

Derrek's eyes flicked to the cargo hold of the ship. "You got it?"

"Yes."

"I'll get my men to help unload it," Derrek said, turning away to bark some orders at the men standing behind him. Then he said to Jared, "Aelred wants to see you back at the command post. We'll get this delivered to the weapons facility tonight."

"Hey," Jared called as Derrek moved off toward the ship. Derrek looked back over his shoulder, one eyebrow cocked. "Be careful with that. It's on loan."

Derrek's brow furrowed in puzzlement, but he saluted and continued on his way.

Brytnoth and Rafe joined Jared on the platform, watching as Derrek's men unloaded the five crates they had brought back from Perseon.

"Brytnoth," Jared said. "Stay with the cargo. Make sure that everything runs smoothly."

Brytnoth nodded and jogged off to join Derrek and his crew. Jared watched for a few more moments as Brytnoth conversed with Derrek. Derrek looked in their direction and gave him a thumbs-up sign. Satisfied, Jared clapped Rafe on the shoulder.

"Let's go," he said.

When they reached the barracks, they found Aelred sitting at the long table, another man close beside him. Kirin, Emma, Althea, and Aliya were there too, watching the conversation between Aelred and the man with concerned faces.

"You're back!" Emma cried, running to Rafe.

Rafe allowed Emma to embrace him, but Jared noticed that he seemed strangely distant. He patted her back mechanically, and his smile was almost sad.

"Jared," Aliya called. "Come and greet your lord."

They came forward to the table, and the other man stood to meet them. It was Arnauld—haggard and pale, but still Arnauld. Jared dropped to one knee and kissed his hand.

"My lord," he said, his voice catching in his throat.

Arnauld laid a hand on his head. "Yes, and thank you, it seems. I can't see how you managed to find me...or Aliya. But I will always be in your debt. Always."

Jared got to his feet. "It was Sahara who found Lady Aliya," he said. "It was Sahara who saved her."

Arnauld glanced over Jared's shoulder at the door as if he expected Sahara to walk through it at that moment. "Where is she, Jared?" Jared said nothing, and Arnauld's eyes snapped back to his face. "She's not with you?"

"No, my lord."

"How long has he been conscious?" Rafe asked Aliya.

"Only just a few hours," she replied.

"I thought she would be with you," Arnauld said, bewilderment in his eyes. "Where is she?"

"She's on a different mission, my lord," Jared answered.

"She's up in the viper's nest." Rafe's voice cut over his own, and Jared knew that the venom was meant for him.

"She came back here, actually," Aelred interrupted. "Two nights ago."

Jared felt his heart surge within him and he spun to face Aelred. "What? She was here? She was all right?"

"Yes. She's planning to assassinate the Triumvirate, and she's planning to do it tonight, and alone. I was hoping that you'd be back in time."

"In time for what?" Rafe asked.

"In time to help her." Aelred sighed and gestured for them to join the others at the table. "She's going to need it," he said.

Jared's feeling of relief and hope drained out of him as he sank into his chair. Something in Aelred's face and tone made him uneasy, and he knew that Sahara was in greater danger than he had imagined.

"What is it?" he asked. "What's wrong?"

"Sahara is skilled, no question," Aelred began, "and if her targets were mere mortal men, the task would be hard enough."

"What's that supposed to mean?" Rafe asked quickly. "They aren't mortal?"

"Oh, no, they are. But those rings they wear give them more than mortal powers." Briefly, he explained the power of the three rings. "You see the problem, I'm sure."

Jared held Aelred's gaze, his hand clenched into a fist. "She needs help. I'll go." He hesitated, seeing the look that passed across Aelred's face. "I don't see why this is a problem."

"You can't go, Jared."

"Why not?" Jared spoke carefully, and his knuckles showed white as he tightened his fist. "Why can't I go?"

"I need you here, to help me coordinate the attacks."

Jared measured him for a long time, considering how he should respond. "When you approached us back at the inn on Agora," he said slowly, "it was because you needed assassins, not generals."

"Things change," Aelred said, with a shrug of his shoulders and the ghost of a smile on his lips. "This has become a much bigger operation than I'd ever imagined."

"That's your problem, not mine. I won't leave Sahara up there alone to die for your damn planet. I got you your power source. Now you have to let me go."

"I'll go instead, Jared," Rafe said quietly from beside him.

Jared swiveled his gaze to meet his friend's eyes. "No."

"No?" Rafe's expression darkened. "No? So you'd rather her fight alone—die alone—just because you can't be the one to save her?"

Jared's eyes narrowed. "This isn't a question," he flared. "I'm not staying here. If you want to come along for the ride, Rafe, then that's your call. But I'm not staying here, whether you go or not." He turned to Aelred. "You have to find someone else."

"What about Brytnoth?" Rafe asked.

Aelred pursed his lips, considering. "Do you trust him? Is he capable as a leader?"

"I trusted him," Arnauld said. "He served well and nobly for Silesia. I couldn't have asked for better."

Aelred nodded slowly. "Then so be it." Then he turned to Jared. "You have business elsewhere, I think."

Jared inclined his head. "Thank you, my lord."

"I'm coming with you, Jared," Rafe said.

"I can't let you do that."

Rafe gripped his forearm, his eyes earnest. "I'm your brother, remember? And I owe it to you—and to her—to see this thing through." Then he grinned and added, "And besides. It'll be just like old times."

Jared measured him for a moment, and Rafe's grip on his arm tightened.

"Fine," Jared said finally. "But if you come, you'd better not cause me any trouble."

Rafe feigned surprise. "It's me, remember?"

"Yes, exactly."

Rafe pushed back his chair and stood. Emma clung to his sleeve, tears welling in her eyes.

"Rafe," she choked, her voice breaking. "Don't go, please. Please don't go."

"I'm sorry, Emma," Rafe said softly. "I have to finish this."

He touched her tear-stained cheek with his thumb and smiled down at her. She clung to his hand for a moment, and then let him go.

———

They spent the rest of the day making last minute preparations. The women worked with Kalkas to make sure that the surrogate was ready for quick administration. Aelred had five teams of rebels stationed in and around Pentapolis—one at the Triumvirate soldiers' headquarters in the heart of the city, one in the warehouse district, one at the mine of Gil-Gareth, one in the Aymatis, and the last was with Deor and Brytnoth at the weapons facility. Some of the women would travel with the Gil-Gareth detachment, armed with enough of the surrogate to begin treating the slaves as soon as the area was secured. Kalkas and the rest of the women would stay in the Village and set up a triage center for the slaves from the city proper.

Jared jogged up the street toward the landing platform. He and Aelred were heading to Taur Isis to make a final inspection of the facility and to make sure that the *zanthos* installation was proceeding without a problem. As he passed Kalkas's workshop, he noticed that the door was wide open, so he stopped to peek inside.

The women they had rescued from the Aymatis were sitting on chairs and bunks, watching Kalkas as he demonstrated how to administer the surrogate. He noticed Aliya, Emma, and Althea sitting together in the front row, their faces solemn with intense resolve and concentration. Liana, the girl from Amaryl, stood just behind them, her arms crossed and her head thrown back. The steel in her eyes reminded him so much of Sahara.

She'd be proud of them, he reflected. *This is a dangerous mission. She'd be proud.*

His lingering presence in the doorway called Kalkas's attention, and the healer turned toward him with an inquisitive lift of his eyebrows. Jared waved at him to continue and ducked back into the street.

When he and Aelred arrived at the facility a short time later, Brytnoth and Deor were coordinating a massive production line. A hundred men fetched weapons from the racks and delivered them to the assembly tables, where another hundred were fitting them with the *zanthos* cartridges. Then another hundred packed the weapons into their transport cases, which were then loaded into the waiting shuttles.

"We're almost there," Brytnoth told Aelred. "In another four hours or so we should have enough weapons ready to arm the militia groups."

"Excellent," said Aelred. "You've done well."

"What about Sahara?" Deor asked, looking at Jared. "Is she ready?"

"She's ready. She'll strike the Triumvirate at sunset. Rafe and I are going to help her." He eyed the heavy rifles on the assembly table. "I'll take a couple of those," he added. "I can think of a perfect use for them."

"Pick some up on your way out," Deor said. "I'd offer to let you have the tank, but she's as slow as a hobbled ass. She's bound for Gil-Gareth."

Jared laughed. "I think the rifles will do just fine."

"Listen." Deor turned to Jared, his face suddenly serious. "You get my sister out of there, you understand? And put an extra hole in Ergeron for me."

Jared clasped his hand and smiled at him. "I will."

Aelred, who'd been speaking with Brytnoth in a low voice, now interrupted them. "Deor, I want you to continue working with Derrek to get these weapons battle-ready. Brytnoth is going to lead the Gil-Gareth division."

"Be careful," Jared told Brytnoth.

"You, too," he replied.

He threw his arms around Jared and slapped him on the back. Jared grinned at him and then he and Aelred turned to leave.

"And Jared!" Brytnoth called as they headed down the stairs to pick up their weapons.

Jared paused and looked up at him. "What?"

"Don't let Rafe do anything stupid."

THIRTY-SEVEN

THE LIGHT of half a dozen flickering candles danced among the silver and crystal on the table and made the dark wood gleam. The creamy china shone with an opalescent luster. Sweet and juicy fruits were piled in a bowl, enticing in their haphazard luxury. Succulent meats in rich sauces filled the air with a luscious and spicy aroma. Warm breads, golden and crusty and steaming, peeped from beneath a fine linen cloth.

Sahara sat, stiff-backed, heart pounding, and looked down the table at her nemesis, who was calmly cutting his meat. She had consented to dine with Ergeron tonight, hoping it would give her the opportunity she needed to kill him quietly.

Ever since her midnight escape from the manor and her conversation with Aelred about the rings, she had been pondering her approach to her mission. Taking on all three of them at once would be impossible. She would need to isolate and destroy if she was to have any success at all. So, when Ergeron had caught her on the balcony again that afternoon and asked her to dinner, she had consented. Much as his company revolted her, it meant they would be alone. And that meant she could dispatch him without too much trouble.

So here she was, staring at him down the length of the table and hating him. The ruby ring caught the light and glowed at her, calling her. And when he looked up, his blue eyes as stunning and deep as the Silesian sky, she felt her strength of will begin to ebb.

This was a bad idea, she thought.

She took a deep breath and forced herself to smile.

"Black suits you," Ergeron said, his deep voice soft and smooth. "Suits you very well, I must say."

She swallowed, kept the smile pasted on her face.

"You are too kind as always, my lord," she said. She hoped that the tremble she felt in her voice wouldn't carry the distance between them.

His smile, slow and intense, took her breath away.

This wasn't happening.

This couldn't happen.

She clung to her resolve and reached her hand behind her back, felt the welcoming familiarity of the leather grip of her knife where she had hidden it in her green girdle. It brought her back a little to herself, and she released it again, content to wait for the right moment. Gingerly, she tore a piece of bread and put it in her mouth.

"You know," Ergeron continued, "you weren't very nice to me the other afternoon. Absolutely rude, I think you were."

"I'm sorry," she apologized hurriedly. "I didn't mean..."

"I understand," he interrupted, waving his jewel-decked hand at her. "You are perhaps homesick. Or perhaps you are angry that you stayed behind with us."

"All of the above," she said, then bit her tongue before she said too much.

Ergeron fixed her with his steady gaze. "Yes, so I thought. So I thought." Then he smiled at her again. "I've been trying to think of some way to cheer you up, Calypso," he continued.

Inside, she started at the name, but she gritted her nerves and kept her expression smooth, never dropping her eyes from his.

"What might that be, my lord?" she asked. Those eyes, so blue, like the deep oceans of her homeworld.

This is a bad idea, she thought as her pulse began to race and she felt heat rising to her cheeks. Again that horrible, evil, seductive smile.

She hated him. And she loved him.

"I want to take you somewhere, away from all this," he said. "Pentapolis is so dirty and ugly, full of slaves. Not like Halcyon, from what I hear tell. Halcyon of the green fields and golden minarets." His voice was melodic, soothing, the rhythm of his speech rolling over her like waves. "So I want to show you somewhere beautiful. Askalon is beautiful. You are beautiful, like Askalon is beautiful."

It had to stop.

She felt her eyes closing, felt almost drowsy.

She had to make it stop.

She forced her eyes open. Met only the azure of his eyes, smiling in the flickering candlelight, smiling at her, loving her, desiring her.

"This beautiful place," he continued, almost murmuring, "is far to the south, by the cliffs and the sea. A great stone castle with high stone walls, gardens and flowers and honeybees drunk on sweet nectar."

Make it stop.

Make it stop.

"A little path leads to the village, where you can buy silks and ribbons for your hair. Soft silks, beautiful ribbons. And we can dance in the moonlight, just you and I." He smiled at her again. "Should you like that, do you think?"

"I...I don't...I don't dance," she managed to say. Her voice sounded far away, and she couldn't remember thinking of the response before it came out of her mouth.

"I'll teach you, then," he said. "Just you and I. We can go there tomorrow. Just say yes. Just say yes."

She stared at him, blinking slowly. She felt like she was just waking up, or just falling asleep. She couldn't focus, could hardly remember why she was here.

And then, like one drowning, she thrashed inside. Outside, she shivered. It brought a moment of clarity, and she slipped her hand behind her back again, feeling for the hilt of the dagger. Her fingers closed around it and her eyes closed in relief.

"No," she whispered.

"What did you say?" Ergeron asked, almost too quickly. "Did you say you'd come?"

She squeezed the dagger hilt, honing the steel of her hate once more. Then she opened her eyes. "No, I didn't," she said.

She slipped the dagger out of her sash. This had to end, and it had to end now. If he started to talk again, she didn't think she could resist him. Whatever awful power he had over her, it was stronger than she had ever felt it before, and she had nothing within her that could withstand it.

Suddenly, she was hauled out of her chair from behind and slammed face-down on the table. Her dagger clattered to the ground and skittered away toward the dais. She tried to rise, but the hand gripping her collar and pinning her to the table was like iron. She twisted her head to the side, gasping for breath. Then she kicked out viciously behind her, trying to catch whoever was behind her unawares.

She felt the pressure on her neck ease a bit as the man jumped back out of her reach. She bucked, trying to throw him off, but his grip on her was like a vise.

"What did I tell you, Ergeron?" the man said.

Baltek. The invisible one. Damn.

"I told you she was a treacherous—"

His words ended in a sudden strange gurgle, and his full weight crushed Sahara as his massive body suddenly crumpled on top of her.

She struggled for a moment and managed to squirm out from

under Baltek's corpse, rolling sideways and sending china plates smashing to the floor.

"Who…what…?" she heard Ergeron's inarticulate cries from the head of the table. "Baltek!"

She fell off the table and landed in a crouch facing Ergeron. He was on his feet, his face contorted with rage and his eyes fixed on the entrance of the hall. Sahara glanced over her shoulder. There was no one there. As she turned back to Ergeron, she caught sight of Baltek. Blood was dripping from his half-open mouth, and there was a blackened scorch mark on his back.

Something had blasted him.

"Azel!" Ergeron was shouting. "Treachery! Treachery!"

Even as he called for help, he started for her, one hand outstretched, the other gripping a cruel, curved knife that was almost as long as a short sword.

Sahara tumbled away from him, angling for the dais. Her dagger glinted on the stones and she scrambled for it, hearing Ergeron's footsteps quicken behind her.

She stretched out her hand.

Someone kicked the dagger away from her, sending it spinning once more across the floor. She swore and rolled sideways, acting purely on instinct. The blade of a sword sparked as it drove into the stone floor, missing her by inches.

"Azel! I want her alive! Alive!" Ergeron shouted.

But the huge hulk of a man seemed not to hear his brother. He was lumbering after her, a guttural growl deep in his throat. She crawled away from him as fast as she could, then rolled again as she heard the whistle of the sword. It slammed into the stones on her left, scraping as Azel drew it back again.

"Azel!" Ergeron shouted again. "Stop, you fool! Stop!"

And he did stop.

She rolled to the right again as his body toppled to the ground with a sickening crunch. He never made a sound, and she stared, horrified, into his blank, surprised eyes.

But she had no time to linger. She pushed herself to her feet and ran for her dagger. She could hear Ergeron close behind her.

"Calypso! Calypso!" he was calling.

She somersaulted, her hand closing around the hilt of her dagger as she tumbled. She came upright and spun to face him, separating the dagger's double blades as she did so. Twirling the two knives in her hands, she smiled at him.

At last.

They were on even footing now, and when Sahara saw the sudden panic flood into his face, she couldn't help feeling a surge of triumph.

"What?" he cried.

"You had to know it was going to end this way," she said.

"Calypso..." he began, his voice soft and pleading.

She let the first dagger fly so fast that he didn't have time to react.

"My name isn't Calypso," she said as her first dagger buried itself in his chest.

He staggered forward, clawing at it, choking on the words that bubbled out of him with his lifeblood. As his knees buckled and he fell into her, she caught him by the shoulder and drove the other dagger home.

"My name is Sahara."

She let him fall.

He moved feebly for a moment, then lay still. Sahara's breath came in ragged gasps, and she retreated until she felt the cold stones of the wall against her back. She slid down to the floor, her arms resting on her knees.

It was finished.

She closed her eyes, shaking as relief washed over her and through her.

For a moment there was silence, perfect silence, then the clatter of footsteps shattered the calm. Her eyes snapped open and she sprang to her feet.

I'm dreaming, she thought, staring wide-eyed.

No, you're not, came the answer.

And Jared was there, warm and real, smiling at her, speaking to her. She threw herself into his arms, feeling them wrap around her, strong and secure.

"I didn't think you'd come," she said, her voice muffled by his shoulder. "How did you know to come?" She pushed back from him, looking up into his dark eyes. Then her gaze shifted over his shoulder. Rafe was standing there, grinning.

"You came too!" she cried.

"Wouldn't miss it," he replied. Then he unhooked the com from his belt and turned away. She heard him say, "Aelred? We're all clear."

Sahara couldn't help the grin that swept across her face as she glanced up at Jared again. "I've never been so glad to see anyone in my life," she confessed. "Well…" The memory of the pillar and the dragon flashed into her mind. "Maybe this is a close second."

"I'm just glad we made it in time," Jared said, holding her close.

She nodded into his chest, then pushed away from him. As she stepped back, she noticed the strange weapon slung at Jared's hip. "What's that? I've never seen…" Suddenly, her eyes widened and snapped back to his face. "Taur Isis!" she gasped. "I saw guns like that at Taur Isis!"

"That's right," he said. "Your brother's managing things there now."

"Deor! How did that happen?"

Jared laughed. "Too much to tell standing here," he said. He turned to Rafe. "Did you call it in?" he asked.

"Already done," Rafe replied. "Let's go."

Sahara retrieved her daggers and found a cloth on the table to wipe them clean.

"Nice spread," Jared remarked, a smile quirking the corners of his mouth. "Too bad you squashed all the rolls."

THIRTY-EIGHT

SHE STARED at him for a moment, then she started laughing. And once she started, she couldn't stop. Tears rolled down her cheeks and her sides ached. She slid down to the floor, but the laughter kept bubbling up within her. Finally, Jared reached down and pulled her to her feet.

"Come on," he said. "We need to get this place cleaned up. This is no way to welcome the Lord of Askalon home again."

Sahara wiped her moist cheeks with her palms. "Will it be over that quickly, do you think?" she asked, heaving a deep breath.

"The Triumvirate didn't have many soldiers stationed here, remember," Jared said. "Aelred's positioned his forces to take them out with as little collateral damage as possible. If all goes to plan, it should be a quick fight."

He glanced up as Rafe approached, pushing two men in front of him.

"Look who I found dawdling in the hallway," he said, jerking them to a standstill. "One of them tried to knife me."

The two servants glared at him, murder in their eyes. Sahara noticed that one of them held his right arm tightly against his chest, as if it were injured.

"They look like they need something to do, don't you think?" Jared said.

"Why don't they clean up the mess?" Sahara suggested.

Rafe snapped his fingers and grinned. "That's the very thing for these fine fellows!" Then, giving the two servants a shove, he said, "Come along, gentlemen. Right this way!"

While Jared and Sahara sat on the edge of the dais and discussed all that had happened to them, Rafe monitored the two servants as they dragged the bodies of the Triumvirate lords out for disposal and then set about cleaning the hall. As soon as they were finished, Rafe tied their hands behind their backs.

"Aelred's going to have to decide what to do with them, but the cellar will be cozy for now," he said as he marched the servants out of the hall.

As soon as he was gone, Sahara turned to Jared. "Why didn't you just blast Ergeron like you did his brothers?"

Jared smiled. "I thought," he answered, "that you needed to fight that battle yourself."

Sahara nodded, but all she could manage to say was, "Thank you."

At that moment, the side door slammed open and Rafe burst into the room. He held the com link in his hand, and his face was grim. Sahara and Jared jumped off the dais and hurried to meet him, sensing that something was very wrong.

"We have a problem," Rafe said. "That was Deor. It seems that the slaves from Gil-Gareth are marching on Taur Isis."

"What?" Jared cried. "How? How did the Triumvirate have time to activate the slaves?"

"Azel must have done it," Sahara said, swearing. "And it doesn't matter how. Taur Isis has to stand...if the slaves take over the facility, we're finished."

"Ergeron has a ship," Rafe said. "Let's go."

They were halfway to Taur Isis when the call came.

"Jared? Rafe?" the voice, breathless, crackled over the com.

"It's Deor," Sahara said, starting forward. She leaned over Jared's seat, staring at the speaker.

"We hear you, Deor," Jared said. "Go ahead."

"Are you coming?"

"We're halfway to you."

There was a pause, and they heard shouting in the background. Then they heard Deor bark, "Secure that gate! Secure it right now!"

The cold hand of fear clutched at Sahara's gut. "They're being overrun," she murmured. "We're going to be too late."

"No, we're not," Rafe said, his jaw clenched. He maxed out the power on the ship, and Sahara felt the response as it surged ahead.

"Jared, do you read me?" came Deor's voice again. "Do you read?"

"We're still here," Jared answered.

"Jared, the women were at the mine."

Rafe's horror-stricken eyes were fixed on the comms. "Emma..."

"Aliya," Sahara whispered.

"Did you read me?" Deor's voice blared again. "And Brytnoth's troops must have been overrun. I've had no contact. I repeat, I've had no contact from the Gil-Gareth division."

Jared and Rafe exchanged glances, then Jared said, "Copy that, Deor." He turned to Sahara and Rafe. "What do we do?"

For the first time, Sahara saw panic in Jared's eyes. She balled her hands into fists and tried to hold herself together. Her brother's life was in danger. The women were trapped in the mine. She had no idea where Brytnoth was—or if any of them were still alive.

And there were only three of them. Three, against impossible odds.

Rafe swore under his breath, concentrating now on keeping the ship under control. Jared watched him for a moment, and then he turned to Sahara.

"What do we do?" he asked.

"I think…I don't know," she admitted. "There are three of us, Jared. What *can* we do?"

He measured her for a moment, and then seemed to come to a decision. "Deor, are you there?" There was a crackling silence, and Sahara's heart felt like it was beating somewhere in her temples. "Deor! Do you copy?"

After another long pause, Deor finally responded. "I'm here. Go."

"I'm contacting Aelred. It's his—"

"I already did, Jared!" Deor's infuriated voice cut him off. "He's pinned down in a firefight in the city, so we don't get reinforcements. He just told us to hold the facility. And he doesn't want slave casualties." A string of curses followed this, and then they heard him shout, "Hold your fire! Reinforce that gate!"

"You've got to be kidding me," Rafe said. "He doesn't want them to defend themselves? Does he know what will happen if those slaves…" His voice trailed off. "We're here."

Sahara rose and stared out the window. Her heart hammered in her chest and a cold sweat washed over her.

A seething mass of bodies was swarming around the facility. Men were clambering up the fence, and others had hold of the front gates, pulling on them so fiercely that they were rocking on their hinges. Sahara's gaze slid to the top of the facility, where the Triumvirate's guards had been posted. She saw Deor's men crouched on the roofline, weapons at the ready. Others stood just behind the gates, trying to block the entrance with a makeshift rampart.

"That's just useless," she muttered. "Once they tear that fence down, it's curtains."

"I see you!" came Deor's voice again. "Land her on the roof!"

Rafe made a pass, circling around the facility. More slaves were streaming up the valley from the south, and here and there in the mass they could see a banner bearing the Triumvirate symbol snapping in the breeze.

"They're driving them like maddened cattle," Jared said.

Rafe set the ship down on the northwest corner of the roof. Deor was there to meet them as they disembarked.

"We can't hold them much longer," Deor told them as he led them back to his position overlooking the main gates. "And once they're through, we're dead."

"And what about the women? And Brytnoth?" asked Sahara. "Any word from Gil-Gareth at all?"

Deor gripped her arm, his eyes intense. "Nothing. Nothing."

"We can't just leave them there," she said. "What are we going to do, Deor?"

His mouth twisted into a wry smile. "I was hoping you'd have some ideas for me," he answered.

"Aelred told you not to fire on the slaves?" Jared asked. "Even after you told him what's happening here?"

"Do I look completely stupid to you?" Deor snapped. "Of course I told him! The best we can do is push them off the top of the fence with poles." He gestured to the western fenceline, where a group of his soldiers were stabbing at a dozen or more slaves who had gained the top of the barricade. "It won't work forever. Sooner or later, they'll breach the line. And once they flood in here, we're done."

Jared took the com link from Rafe. "Aelred! Do you read me?"

"I hear you," came Aelred's voice.

"We're under assault at Taur Isis," Jared said. "I repeat, we are under assault. We need orders, sir!"

"Hold the facility and hold your fire."

"That's no good, sir!" shouted Jared. "We can't do that and survive. We need other options!"

There was a moment's silence. Then Aelred's voice, cold and hard, crackled over the com. "Do what you can to secure the facility. Do not fire on my people, Jared."

Sahara saw the furious working of Jared's jaw. Just as he raised the com to reply, a hoarse shout went up from the western side of the facility. They all spun to see what had caused the uproar.

Part of the fence was down and slaves were swarming through

the gap. Already a knot of them had surrounded Deor's soldiers. Sahara swallowed hard.

Deor sprang away from them, pelting toward the western edge of the roof. "Fall back! Fall back!" he screamed as he ran, waving his arms frantically.

Sahara watched, horror clutching at her, as one of Deor's men went down in the middle of the crowd. The others were scrambling, clawing, shrieking for help.

"Jared," she said, her eyes riveted on the scene below them. She seized his arm. "Jared."

"*Fire!*" The word exploded from Jared's lips.

Deor whirled around as men raced past her to fling themselves into position on the western roofline. Before Deor could countermand the order, the air pulsed as the men fired. Sahara watched as bodies of slaves fell, scorched and blasted. As soon as there was a breach in the circle, the surviving guards broke for the shelter of the facility.

The slaves continued to press forward into the withering barrage of fire from the roof, completely oblivious to their danger. They were falling by the dozens now. Falling without a sound, advancing without a sound.

"Stop!" Deor's voice thundered over the strange thrumming of the guns. "*Stop!* Hold your fire!"

Everything was still once more. Sahara tore her gaze away from the carnage below as Deor charged up to them, his eyes blazing.

"What the hell was that?" he demanded. He shoved Jared back and then followed him, planting his finger in Jared's chest. "How dare you usurp my command and order my troops to fire! We had an express directive to avoid slave casualties, Jared!"

"Your men are being massacred," Jared said. "Aelred's orders are nonsense, and you know it."

Deor's eyes narrowed to slits. "So you think it's fine to disobey orders in the middle of a battle just because you don't like them? Is that what they teach you on Silesia, Jared? Is it?"

Sahara swallowed hard and glanced at Rafe. He was tense, his eyes fixed on Jared. Jared was on dangerous ground, and they both knew it. Like it or not, Aelred was their commanding officer, and his orders couldn't have been clearer. Sahara's gaze swiveled to Jared's face, and she was surprised to see total calm there.

"Answer me!" Deor shouted. "This is on your hands, Jared! How are you going to explain this to Aelred?"

Jared, his eyes never leaving Deor's, flicked the com on. "Aelred, do you read?"

"Go ahead, Jared," came the commander's voice.

"Our men are being slaughtered, Aelred. I ordered the men to give them covering fire so they could escape."

Silence. Then Aelred said, "I thought I told you not to fire on my people, Jared."

"You did, sir," answered Jared. "But—"

"I should order Deor to shoot you in the head."

Sahara started violently and her eyes snapped to her brother's face. It was set like stone. Sahara's blood iced in her veins.

Deor raised his *zanthos* pistol and set the muzzle against Jared's forehead.

"Deor, don't!" Sahara screamed.

Deor squeezed the trigger.

THIRTY-NINE

SAHARA JUMPED AT DEOR, knocking his arm aside. The unexpected force of her assault sent the pistol flying from his hand and it skittered over the edge of the roof. Then Sahara stood in front of her brother, panting, everything in her body tensed.

It was only then that she realized that Jared hadn't even flinched.

"I should order you to shoot him, Deor," came Aelred's voice over the com again, "but I can't. We need him."

"You almost killed him!" Sahara shouted, shoving her brother so that he reeled back several paces. "What is wrong with you?"

"I wasn't going to shoot him, sis," Deor said, recovering himself. "Not this time. But he needs to know that if he ever mutinies again, I will kill him."

"I won't sit here and do nothing while we get torn apart," Jared said, making sure that Aelred could hear him. "Find a solution for this mob, or I will make sure they stay outside the perimeter. Whatever that takes, do you hear me?"

"Look!" Rafe cried, pointing. "They're through the fence!"

"They're at the facility doors, sir!" shouted one of the men positioned on the roofline.

Slaves were pouring through the gap now, flooding the inner yard and moving to surround the facility, a rising tide engulfing a boulder.

"You better think fast, Aelred," Jared added. "We can't abandon Taur Isis to them. If they get access to these weapons..."

With a gurgling shriek that died almost as soon as it began, one of Deor's men toppled from the roof.

"What the—" began Deor.

His men were scrambling wildly away from the edge of the roof, tripping over each other in their haste. As another man went down, they could see the scorched hole in his back.

"One of the slaves has Deor's pistol!" Sahara shouted.

Even as she spoke, another man dropped dead, this one without a sound. The rest of the men made it out of the slave's line of sight to the relative, temporary security of the center of the roof. They stood huddled together, their voices clamoring.

Deor started toward them, hands upraised to calm their chatter.

And then the world convulsed in a ball of flame and heat. The concussion slammed into Sahara's chest, flinging her like a rag across the roof. Her body crashed and skidded, grating the skin of her arms and hands. The building rocked beneath her. Acrid smoke plumed into the sky. Bits of blasted metal showered down on her, and she pulled herself into a ball, shielding her head and feeling the bite of the shrapnel through the shredded sleeves of her shirt.

As soon as the rain of metal stopped, Sahara uncurled herself, every muscle in her body aching. As she rolled to her hands and knees, she saw her arms oozing blood from a hundred tiny gashes. A moment later, the pain registered, and she bowed her head to the roof, gritting her teeth against the burning throb. She tried to lick her lips, tasted the metallic salt of blood in her mouth.

Get up, she told herself. *Get. Up.*

Forcing her body to obey, she pushed herself to her feet. She coughed as a wave of caustic smoke billowed over her and pain seared in her side. She clutched her ribs with one arm and staggered forward.

"Jared?" she croaked. "Deor? Rafe?"

Through the cloud of smoke, she saw two figures lying motionless a short distance away. She shook her head and coughed again, trying to clear her lungs and wincing at the burn in her ribs. Her ears were ringing, and she shook her head again, stumbling toward the bodies.

She fell heavily to her knees beside the first figure. He lay face-down, his back covered with shards of shrapnel. She reached out and grasped his shoulder, pulling him over.

It was Deor.

His face was cut in a dozen places, and at first Sahara thought he wasn't breathing. Her heart jumped into her throat, hammering as a surge of panic flooded through her.

"Deor!" she croaked, shaking him violently. "Deor, speak to me! Deor!"

He groaned and his eyelids fluttered. Tears streaked down her cheeks as she hugged her brother to her chest.

"You're alive," she mumbled. "You're alive!"

"Sis," he rasped, "can't breathe. Let go."

She smiled down at him and loosened her grip, letting his head rest on her lap. "Are you okay?" she asked.

"I'll live. Just got the crap pounded out of me. You?"

She nodded. "Just a bit bruised, I think."

He reached up a bloodied hand and pushed the hair out of her face. "You look like hell," he said, managing a brief smile. "Ow. Where are Jared and Rafe?"

Panic surged through her once again. In her relief at finding Deor alive, she had completely forgotten them. She helped Deor to sit up and then got back to her feet.

"Got to go find them," she said, coughing as another wave of smoke billowed over them. "Stay here."

She looked around, getting her bearings again in the hazy air, and spotted the other body still lying on the rooftop not far from her. She limped toward it. Fear closed her throat, and for a moment she forgot even the need to breathe.

She stopped, staring down at Jared, afraid to go any closer, and afraid not to.

Jared.

She reached out to him with her mind, a desperate prayer in her heart. She hugged her aching ribs with shaking hands and took a step nearer.

Jared.

He moaned softly, his arms and legs moving feebly.

It was all she needed. Relief turned her knees to water, and she sank down next to him, cupping his smoke-grimed and bloodied face in her hands. His eyes fluttered open, but he seemed unable to focus on her face.

"Sahara?" he mumbled, blinking rapidly. "Is that you?"

"Yes, it's me," she answered. "Can you move? Are you hurt badly?" The tears were flowing again, streaming down her cheeks and into her mouth, dripping off her jaw to splash onto his face.

Jared took a shuddering breath and pushed himself up on his elbows. He touched her cheek gently and managed a smile, then his eyes shifted past her to the chaos around them. "What...what the hell happened?"

Sahara sniffled, swiping at her running nose with the back of her hand. The smoke was slowly drifting away, and she could see bodies littering the roof in all directions. And there, at the far northwestern corner of the facility, was a gaping, blackened hole edged with jagged skewers of warped metal.

"The ship!" she cried. "The ship! It's gone, Jared."

"What?" Jared worked his way into a sitting position and followed her pointing finger.

"That slave must have fired at the ship," said a voice from behind Sahara.

"Rafe!" she cried, turning. "You're...you're...fine!"

Aside from one jagged and nasty looking cut on his left cheek, Rafe appeared to be unscathed.

"Why do you look so sprightly?" growled Jared. "How'd you manage that?"

Rafe grinned at him, crouching down beside them. "Just lucky, I guess."

"Glad to see you two are still in one piece," Deor said, hobbling toward them. He sank down next to Sahara, groaning with the effort.

"Well, they've blasted the ship to hell," Rafe said. "So now we're trapped."

They stared out over the rooftop at the sprawling forms of the dead and at the gaping maw of melted and twisted metal that marked where their ship had once been. Sahara shuddered.

"How many men did you have inside the facility?" Jared asked.

Deor swiveled his gaze back to the little group. "Ten. Maybe."

"Ten," Rafe repeated, running a hand through his hair.

"How could you hope to hold this facility with ten men inside?" Jared barked, his deep voice gravelly. "How many men did you bring with you?"

"Aelred sent me with fifty, and that was more than enough to take the facility," Deor said. "How was I supposed to know that I would have to hold it against a thousand mind-numbed slaves, Jared? This wasn't supposed to happen! None of this was supposed to happen."

Sahara laid a hand on her brother's arm. "I know, Deor. None of this is your fault. It's mine."

"How the hell is this your fault, sis?"

"I didn't do my job fast enough. Azel had too much time. My job was to make sure they were dispatched before they could call up the slaves, and I failed."

Jared took her bloodied hand and squeezed it gently. "Rafe and I take some of the responsibility for that," he said. "Don't blame your-self entirely."

She glanced at him. "I do blame myself. And now we're trapped here, and Aliya...and Brytnoth...." She shook her head, fighting back the tears that stung her eyes. "How are we supposed to get to Gil-Gareth without a ship?"

A sudden strange, metallic clanging brought them all to their feet.

"What's that?" Jared asked as the rhythmic noise intensified.

"They're beating the door down," Sahara murmured.

Rafe stooped suddenly and picked something out of the rubble at their feet. He turned it over in his hand, and then pitched it off the roof with a vicious curse.

"Well," he said, "the com's dead."

Another clanging stroke on the doors below shook them into motion.

"They can't breach those doors," Deor said, his face pale. "If they get hold of those weapons...."

Before he finished speaking, he was running for the hatch on the far side of the roof.

"What does he think we're going to do?" Jared said. "Aelred doesn't want us using those weapons on the slaves. So what are we supposed to do?"

Sahara started after her brother. "Come on! We can't do anything up here."

They followed Deor to the hatch and clattered down the ladder into the facility. He led them at a run toward the stairs that led down into the storage area. As they took the stairs two and three at a time, they heard shouts from below them.

"Find something else to brace the door! Now!" Deor yelled.

He jumped the last eight steps and landed in a crouch, using the momentum to push himself into a sprint toward the door.

"Captain!" cried the soldier as he approached. "We thought you were dead up there for sure!"

"No, Anton," Deor answered. "Not yet."

"Hoping you have orders for us, sir," Anton continued. "We're trapped like rats here!"

"I want five of your men to fire up the biggest guns we have left. Load them up and bring them here, is that clear?"

Anton saluted and hurried to relay the order to the men who were just returning with crates to try to secure the door. They saluted and dropped the crates, running for the storage area. The others scrambled to shove the crates against the door, which continued to shudder under the blows from outside.

"Deor!" Sahara called, her feet sliding as another crashing blow from outside jarred the barricade. "I thought Aelred ordered us not to fire on the slaves."

"My first priority is to secure these weapons," he replied. "And if that means we have to blow them all to hell, then that's what we'll have to do."

FORTY

JARED STRAIGHTENED, wiping the sweat from his forehead with the back of his hand, and caught sight of Deor's face. He felt a sudden rush of sympathy for the young man, and he pulled him out of earshot of the others.

"We're in this together, you hear?" he said. "Deor, look at me." Deor raised his eyes to Jared's and took a deep breath. Jared gripped his shoulder and continued, "I know I usurped your authority up there, and I'm sorry. Whatever decision you need to make here, make it. Aelred's not here. It's your call, and I'll support you, no matter what."

Deor swallowed hard and glanced around, as if to be sure that no one was paying attention to them. For a moment, he watched Rafe and Sahara, who were overseeing the defense of the door. Then he turned back to Jared.

"They have the tank," Deor murmured. "It's slow, so that's why it's not here yet. But it will be. And when it gets here, there'll be nothing left of us to bury."

Jared's grip on Deor's shoulder tightened convulsively. "What?"

"The tank." Deor's eyes flitted over the inside of the facility, and then returned to Jared's face. "We sent the tank with Brytnoth's division. If the slaves have overrun the mine, then that means Brytnoth couldn't hold them...and they must have taken the tank."

Jared swore and ran a hand through his hair. "Just when you think things can't get worse," he muttered.

"We can't hold this place with less than two dozen men," Deor continued, "and if we start firing on those crowds outside, we'll be guilty of genocide when it's all over. Aelred would never want that... and there's no way I want that much blood on my hands." Deor's face blanched. "Jared, what are we going to do?"

Jared clenched his jaw as the stark reality of their situation sank in. His thoughts were spinning, and he shut his eyes, trying to force his mind into some kind of order. The ceaseless, rhythmic pounding on the doors didn't help him to concentrate.

"Wait," he muttered. "Just wait."

He felt Deor shift his weight. "There has to be something we—"

Jared's eyes snapped open. "Wait! Back on Perseon, they used this *zanthos* stuff for lighting...a nice glow, like a candle or something." He paused, feeling the seed of an idea begin to erupt through the fog of his thoughts. "What did you do with the Triumvirate men who were working here, Deor?"

"There was hardly anyone inside the facility, actually. Just two men, and we locked them in the control room upstairs and set a man to guard the door."

Jared glanced around wildly and spied Anton returning with a crate full of *zanthos* guns. He snapped his fingers at him. "You! Go to the control room and bring me those men! Right now!"

Anton glanced at Deor for confirmation, and when the young man nodded, he set down the crate and bolted for the stairs.

"What are you thinking, Jared?" asked Deor.

"Look," Jared said, lifting one of the guns out of the crate. The chamber glowed faintly golden. "That's what I mean...you could use this thing to light a dinner party."

Deor's eyes flicked to his face, helplessness in their depths. "Jared, I don't understand."

Jared sighed, frustrated that he couldn't frame his thoughts into the right words. "If they use this for lighting on Perseon, then why can't we...dial it down a notch when it's in these guns? You understand?" When Deor's expression still registered bewilderment, Jared shook the gun, his voice rising. "Why do these have to obliterate people? Why can't we make them less lethal than that?"

Understanding finally dawned on Deor's face. "I see what you're saying. So what's the problem? Let's dial them down."

"I don't know how to manipulate this stuff," Jared continued. "I'm hoping those two you've got locked up might know something."

Out of the corner of his eye, he saw Sahara and Rafe start towards them.

"What's going on?" Sahara asked. "What's the matter?"

"The slaves from Gil-Gareth have the tank, sis," Deor explained. "We're trying to figure out a way to save the facility before we're overrun...or annihilated, whichever comes first."

Jared, intent on the weapon in his hands, heard Sahara's sharp gasp and glanced up at her. "We need to think fast."

At that moment, Anton returned, shoving two men in front of him. Their hands were bound in front of them, but neither looked dangerous in any respect. One was stodgy and shorter than average height, and the other was a skinny fellow with large round glasses. They pulled up short in front of Jared when they saw the weapon in his hands, and the taller man started blubbering.

"Please, we aren't...we don't...."

"Shut up," said Jared levelly. "I'm not going to kill you."

The man sank to his knees, wordlessly gabbling his thanks. Anton grabbed him roughly under the armpit and hauled him to his feet again.

"I need to know how these work," Jared continued. "And you're going to tell me."

"Well, you just pull that trigger there..." began the short man, pointing at the gun with his pudgy index finger.

"Do I look completely brainless to you?" thundered Jared.

"N-no...but you said—"

"Shut up!"

The man cowered into silence, pulling his head into the folds of his neck like an overgrown turtle.

Jared glowered at him for a moment. Then he tried again, deliberately keeping his voice low and calm. "What's your name?"

"Clovis. Sir."

"Clovis. Can you adjust these weapons at all? Can you make them less powerful?"

The man frowned. "Why would you want to—"

"Just answer the damn question!"

Clovis started violently and almost fell down, but Anton seized his arm and jerked him upright again. "O-of course," he stammered. "You can control the power levels if you want." He gestured for Jared to bring the gun closer, and Jared held it out to him. He indicated a small lever next to the safety. "See these hash-marks? This lets you select the power level. On the lowest setting, the gun issues a pulse blast that stuns but doesn't kill."

Jared beamed at him. "See? That wasn't so hard, was it? And that's exactly what I was hoping to hear!"

"We can't possibly shoot to stun every single one of those slaves out there, Jared," Deor said, guessing his line of thinking.

"No, I know that." He turned once again to Clovis. "Did you just build guns?" he asked. "Just guns and that tank that's about to blow us all to hell when it gets here?"

"No," said the other man, pushing his glasses up the bridge of his nose as best as he could with his cuffed and shaking hands.

"And who are you?"

"Nikolai, sir." The man cleared his throat several times, trying to expel the squeak in his voice. "We have other devices here too— grenades, bombs, missiles, cannons...."

"What about those?" Jared asked. "Can you control those too?"

Nikolai nodded. "We have two pulse cannons and a crate of concussion grenades. I'm afraid the rest are highly volatile...not suitable for non-lethal applications."

Jared couldn't keep from grinning, and he turned to the soldiers who were still trying to barricade the door. "Take these two and bring me those weapons!"

The soldiers saluted and scurried away, dragging the two scientists with them.

"What's your plan, Jared?" asked Rafe.

"We'll position the cannons on the roof. And when that tank shows up, we knock everyone out with a few massive pulse blasts."

"And that does...what, exactly?" Rafe pressed. "We still don't have a way out of this mess. We can't leave the facility. When they regain consciousness, they'll just go right back to doing what they're doing."

"Someone's giving these slaves orders. Remember the transport ship? When they're drugged, they don't do anything of their own will. Someone's pulling the strings. We saw those Triumvirate troops intermixed with the slaves—they have to be directing things. So we're going to take them out. All of them but one. We'll force him to order the slaves to stand down. Then we'll take the tank and the grenades and head for Gil-Gareth."

Rafe chuckled in admiration, and Deor's face, which had been creased with worry and tension just a few minutes before, was now alight with a huge grin.

"It's brilliant," he said. "Brilliant."

Another assault on the door jarred the barricade and sent the topmost crates tumbling to the floor with a crash. Rafe and Deor leaped toward the meager fortification and braced it, their feet sliding on the smooth floor.

Sahara glanced at Jared. "We may not be able to wait until the tank gets here, Jared," she murmured. "If they break through that door...." Her voice trailed off.

Jared's smile faded and he sighed. "I know."

As the door shuddered again, Deor glanced at them over his shoulder. "We have to rig these doors to blow if they get them open. And I want two soldiers posted here manning the most powerful mounted guns we have. Nothing gets through. Nothing."

"But Deor," Sahara said slowly. "I thought we were trying to avoid casualties."

"We are. But we have to do what we have to do to protect these weapons." Deor glanced at Jared, who nodded his approval. "Get it done."

They spent the next half-hour setting explosives and moving the heavy cannons to the roof through the freight lifts. As they positioned the cannons along the ridgeline, Jared gazed out over the tireless mass seething around the facility.

"Jared, look!" Sahara called suddenly.

His head snapped up and he recoiled. The tank was almost to the gates, creeping forward and raising a cloud of dust in its wake.

And then a massive explosion rocked the building to its foundation.

FORTY-ONE

AS SAHARA and Jared scrambled back to their feet, they heard Deor shouting.

"Breach! They've breached the main doors!"

Jared sprang for one of the cannons, waving Sahara, Rafe, and Deor to the others. As soon as they were in position, he gave the order.

"Fire!"

The cannons hummed and the golden light within grew suddenly brighter and then burst from the muzzle, sending up a cloud of dirt and showering those around the immediate impact zone with small stones. Everyone within a twenty-yard radius toppled to the ground.

"Again!" shouted Jared, taking aim at a point in the center of a large crowd of slaves swarming over the wall.

In a matter of minutes, nothing was left moving in the areas around the facility. Slaves lay in crumpled heaps, some draped over the fence, others face-down in the dirt.

"Hurry!" called Rafe from the other side of the roof.

He was running for the hatch, loosening his *zanthos* pistol in its holster as he went. Sahara, Jared, and Deor left their own cannons and followed him back inside.

There was nothing left of the main doors to the facility except a gaping hole with ragged edges where the metal had been vaporized. And there was nothing left of the slaves who had breached the entrance.

"I'm sorry, sir," said Anton as they approached. "But when the doors blew...."

Deor clapped him on the shoulder. "No apologies," he said. "You did the right thing. Now come with us."

They emerged into the eerily silent yard. Sahara bent and placed her fingers on the side of a slave's exposed neck.

"Still a pulse," she said, grinning at them. "Guess your crazy idea worked after all, Jared."

Jared pointed to a toppled flag a short distance away. "Look for the flags," he said. "And you know what to do."

They split up, hunting out the Triumvirate troops. Jared clambered up into the tank, which was hunkered just outside the fence line. He found a Triumvirate soldier slouched forward over the controls.

Perfect, he thought, popping his head out of the hatch to call for the others.

Sahara was already approaching the tank.

"It's done," she said, holstering her pistol. "Did you find something in there?"

"More like some*one*," answered Jared. "Our deactivation switch. Help me get him out of here."

They struggled for a few minutes to push and pull the man's deadweight out of the cramped confines of the tank. When they finally had his bulk stretched out on the ground, Jared crouched beside him, mopping his brow with his sleeve.

Sahara grinned at him, guessing his thoughts. "You can't expect a man of this much substance to walk all the way from Gil-Gareth, Jared!"

He laughed and rose, seeing Deor and Rafe jogging toward them.

"Get going to the mine," Deor said, gesturing to the tank. "I'll get this guy back to the facility and wake him up."

"Are you sure?" Sahara asked quickly. "He's no feather, Deor."

Deor grinned at her. "I can see that. But don't worry about me. We don't have time to waste—and we might already be too late."

"What if it doesn't work, Deor?" Sahara pressed.

Jared glanced at her, saw the fire of concern in her eyes. Deor seemed to notice it as well, and he reached out and gave her hand a squeeze.

"I can handle myself, sis," he said. "And if this doesn't work, we'll all be dead anyway. But don't worry. It'll work." His eyes snapped to Jared. "Right?"

"It'll work," Jared said, trying to sound more confident than he felt.

Deor's eyes flickered at him, and Jared knew that he hadn't been fooled.

"Go," he said again. Then he hooked his hands under the man's armpits and dragged him toward Taur Isis.

"Jared!" cried Sahara. "We can't let him do this alone!"

Jared turned to her and shrugged. "You want to stay? Then stay. Rafe and I are going after Brytnoth and the women."

He saw the struggle in Sahara's eyes as she glanced from him to Deor's retreating form and back again. Somehow, he knew what she would choose.

"I have to stay, Jared," she whispered. "I can't...I have to stay."

She turned and sprinted after her brother, calling his name.

"I know," Jared murmured. He watched her go, and then clapped a stunned Rafe on the shoulder. "Come on."

The ride south to Gil-Gareth dragged on, painfully slow. They met no resistance, no more slaves trickling from the mine to Taur Isis.

"Did they empty the place?" Rafe asked after an hour's ride showed nothing but a barren landscape.

"Maybe so. Let's hope they did."

They continued on in silence until they reached the final ridge before the descent into the mining colony. Jared slowed the tank to a stop and they opened the hatch, clambering out to stand on top of the tank.

"Damn," Rafe breathed. "How are we ever going to find them in there?"

From this vantage point, they could see what had been obscured from the air. The mouth of the mine was at least four stories high and twice as many wide, and it opened into blackness. A cold mist was seeping down from the north, dripping over the bluff and pooling in the hollows and depressions that pocked the road down into the mine. There wasn't a soul in sight.

Jared shivered a little as the breeze that swirled the mist bit through his jacket. "Let's hope they didn't get too far inside before all hell broke loose," he said.

A sudden sound made them snap to attention. Jared's eyes scanned the ridge. The sound came again. It was a rasping cough, and it seemed to be coming from a patch of gorse not far away.

"Stay here," Jared murmured, climbing down from the tank. "I'll check it out."

Cautiously, weapon at the ready, he edged toward the brush. As he approached, he could just make out two boots protruding beyond the cover of the scrub. His heart leaped into his mouth and he broke into a run.

"Jared? Is that you?"

Jared stared down in horror at Brytnoth. Blood oozed from a gash on his forehead, and he seemed barely conscious.

"Rafe!" Jared cried. "Rafe, quick!"

He dropped to one knee beside his friend and clasped his cold hand. "It's me, Brytnoth. I'm here." He tried to massage a little warmth back into his friend's hand, and Brytnoth managed a small smile.

"I was hoping you'd find me," he rasped, breaking into another fit of coughing.

Rafe bounded into view, and he skidded to a stop when he saw Brytnoth.

"Is he hurt badly?" he asked Jared, crouching beside him.

"I'll live, I think," Brytnoth managed. "But my ribs hurt like the devil...I think one's broken. And my head hurts."

Jared probed side gently and nodded. "Not broken...but bruised badly. And that gash will leave a nice scar when it's healed."

"Which all the ladies will love," Rafe put in with a grin.

Brytnoth glared at him from under half-closed lids. "Don't you dare make me laugh."

"Come on," Jared said. "Let's get you to the tank, and you can tell us what happened on the way."

They lifted Brytnoth between them and headed back to the tank.

"This...this is my tank," Brytnoth said as they eased him inside. "Where did you get it?"

"Took it from the Triumvirate scum who were trying to bring down Taur Isis," Jared said. Then, after a pause, he continued, "What happened here, Brytnoth?"

"It all happened so fast," Brytnoth answered slowly. "We thought we had taken out the Triumvirate guards. We sent Althea, Aliya, and Emma inside with a small squad of guards and the surrogate. Everything was going according to plan until...it all went sideways somehow."

He stopped for breath, and Rafe powered up the tank. They rumbled down the wide track into the mine.

"There must have been more Triumvirate troops inside," Brytnoth continued, "because, next thing we know, there's a stampede. The slaves came pouring out of the mine, looking like someone had set off a bomb behind them. We were overrun. And they killed everyone. Took the tank." His eyes were distant, reliving the horror of the attack.

"How did you escape?" Rafe asked.

"Someone hit me in the head," he said. "When I came to, I was under a heap of bodies. I guess they left me for dead. I crawled as far as that bush…and that's where you found me."

They said nothing for several minutes. The grinding of the tank's treads sounded loud in the empty mine, and the darkness deepened until Rafe finally stopped the tank and shut off the power.

"There's no way we can see them in this tin pot, Jared," said Rafe. "We're going to have to hunt for them on foot."

"And leave the tank unguarded?" Jared asked, bringing it to a stop. "What if the place isn't deserted?"

Rafe gestured to his pack and Jared's, which were stashed securely behind Jared's seat. "We can always use those grenades. But we're never going to find them this way. I'm just saying."

Jared sighed, staring out the window into the suffocating gloom. He knew Rafe was right, but the thought of leaving the tank made him profoundly uneasy. He swore softly and then shoved a gun into Brytnoth's hands.

"Don't let anyone in," he said.

"Except us," added Rafe. When Jared gave him a pained look, he chuckled. "Just wanted to make that clear," he said.

They set off down the tunnel, scanning the shadows to either side. A few minutes' jog brought them suddenly to the edge of a sharp descent into damp darkness. Far below them, Jared caught the sickly gleam of a solitary light, which reflected off rock walls slick with moisture and lichens. They hesitated, staring down into the guts of the mine.

Rafe pointed. "I count about five side passages between us and that light down there," he said, his voice as dull and heavy as the air around them. "And the girls could be down any one of them."

Jared shifted his pack and shouted, "Aliya!"

As his voice echoed in the cavern, Rafe recoiled. "What are you doing?" he hissed.

"No one else is here, Rafe," Jared answered. "And we can't follow all of these passages. We don't know the way, and we'll just lose ourselves."

"But what if they're hurt somewhere? They won't hear you calling, Jared."

Jared frowned, and the cold realization that his friend was right settled in the pit of his stomach. Without a word, he set off down the track again, his boots skidding a bit in the scree. After a few steps, he heard Rafe follow behind him.

As they came up to the first side passage, Jared paused and called again. "Emma! Aliya!" He waited a few moments. "Althea!"

Silence.

Jared's frown deepened. He stared into the black mouth of the passage until his eyes ached. Rafe drew his gun and headed inside. The *zanthos* in the chamber of the gun danced off the walls like a warm candle flame.

"Let me scout it out," Rafe called over his shoulder. "Stay there in case they come up the main tunnel. Give me five minutes."

Jared watched the light vanish around a curve in the passage and felt time come to a grinding standstill. The sound of his own breathing seemed to echo in the vastness around him, and he edged a bit closer to the entrance of the side tunnel.

He waited.

Loosened his pistol in its holster.

And waited.

He saw no approaching glow of light from the tunnel, heard nothing but the noise of his own breathing. Finally, unable to stand it any longer, he drew his own weapon and advanced into the tunnel.

"Rafe?" he called experimentally. But the passage swallowed his voice, and he edged a bit further inside, as far as the curve in the tunnel.

"Rafe?" he called again, peering around the bend.

At that moment, he saw a light approaching, bouncing rapidly toward him. The crunching of boots on the tunnel floor sounded suddenly loud in the dark stillness.

Then Rafe himself came into view. He was running.

"Jared!" Rafe shouted. "I found them! Quick! I found them...and Althea's hurt badly."

Jared was pelting toward him even before he finished speaking. "Show me!" he said.

Rafe took off down the tunnel once more, Jared on his heels. About a hundred yards down the tunnel, it suddenly opened out into a small cavern. Mining tools hung on steel pegs driven into the far wall, and a jumble of crates littered one corner under a sputtering light. As they came fully into the chamber, Jared could see three figures huddled behind the crates.

"Aliya!" Jared cried as she rose from her cover.

Her pale face was streaked with dirt and tears. "Althea is hurt, Jared," she said softly. "We've got to get her out of here."

Jared and Rafe shifted some of the crates and crouched over Althea's still form. She was breathing shallowly, and a large blood-stain had soaked through her shirt on her left side. A huge bruise discolored one cheek, and blood matted her dark hair.

"What happened?" Rafe asked, smoothing the hair from Althea's forehead.

"Kalkas told us to mix the surrogate in the water supply so that when the slaves came through the water line, they would get the dose without knowing it," Emma said. "But then something happened. We heard some shouting, and then there was a stampede. Angry... everyone was angry. And if anyone stumbled or got in the way..." She shuddered. "It was awful. The watering station is further down this tunnel, in another cavern like this one. We tried to get out. Althea got knocked down from behind. Aliya and I got separated from her. When we got into this room, we managed to hide behind these crates. We had to wait until everyone was out before we could go back for her. I think she was trampled...I don't know."

Jared eased the torn and bloody fabric away from the wound in her side. The ribs were bruised and scraped. "She may have broken a rib," he said, palpating the area around the wound gently. "But the scrape isn't deep. Looks like she may have grazed it on the wall as she fell."

"Let's get back to the tank and head for the Great House," Rafe said. "Contact Sahara and tell her to meet up with us there once they've handled things at Taur Isis."

"There were four or five shuttles on the landing platform when we got here," Aliya said. "They may be there still."

"Worth a try," said Jared.

Rafe lifted Althea gently and jerked his head toward the tunnel. "Let's get out of here."

As soon as they were back to the tank, they lowered Althea inside.

"Look," Rafe said to Brytnoth, "bring the tank up to the landing pad. I'll scout ahead. If there's a ship on the platform, I'll get her fired up and ready to go."

Jared nodded and Rafe jumped down again, heading up the tunnel at an easy jog. Jared helped Aliya and Emma into the tank and then slipped inside himself. Brytnoth engaged the controls and they headed back to the surface.

As they pulled up to the landing platform, Aliya pointed out the window.

"There. A ship."

FORTY-TWO

THREE DAYS LATER, Jared and Sahara stood on the balcony of the Great House, staring out over the city of Pentapolis. Parts of the city were still smoking where Aelred's troops and the Triumvirate had clashed in the streets. Deor and Sahara had arrived the night before, having secured Taur Isis at last and driven the slave population back to the shanty town of Gil-Gareth. Kalkas finished his work in the city proper and took Aliya and Emma with him to the mine to administer the surrogate to the slaves there.

And just this morning they received word that Aelred was on his way. He arrived with a hundred of his closest retainers just after the noon meal. Now they waited for him to summon them to the Great Hall.

"What are you thinking about?" asked Jared.

She glanced at him, surprised to find her eyes filling with tears. "I don't know," she confessed. "I guess I'm just wondering..." Her voice trailed off and she stared out over the city once more.

"Wondering what?"

"Where we go from here."

At that moment, a bell rang in the courtyard. Jared took her hand gently. "I think we head to the Great Hall," he said with a smile.

Sahara glanced up into his face, ready to protest that he hadn't understood her, but Jared winked at her. The gesture took her so completely by surprise that she forgot what she was going to say and smiled.

Aelred had already taken his seat on the dais when they entered the Great Hall. They slipped through the crowd and found Deor, Rafe, and Brytnoth standing in the second row. For a long time, Aelred said nothing. His hands gripped the carved wood of his chair, his eyes closed and tears on his cheeks. Then he came to himself with a deep sigh, opened his eyes, and smiled at the gathering in the hall.

"The Triumvirate is destroyed, their troops scattered or killed," he said, raising his voice so that those at the back of the hall could hear him clearly. "The mines of Gil-Gareth and the weapons facility of Taur Isis are secure. We have won the battle, my friends, but our work has only just begun."

He paused for a moment, and then beckoned for Brytnoth to come forward.

"Askalon has never been ruled by just one man. It is not my wish to rule alone." He paused until Brytnoth gained the dais, and then he continued, "Brytnoth, I ask you to serve with me. Stay in Askalon and join me on the high seat."

A roar of applause echoed in the vaults of the roof, and Sahara saw Brytnoth's mouth drop open in surprise. As the cheering died away, Brytnoth edged his way through the crowd to Arnauld, who was standing quietly with Aliya at the far side of the hall. He dropped to his knees before Arnauld, his head bowed.

"My lord," he said, "you took me in when I had nowhere else to go. You accepted my service and made me one of your own." He raised his eyes to Arnauld's. "Will you release me now, that I may return to serve my own homeworld?"

Arnauld laid his hand on Brytnoth's head. "You are an adopted son of Silesia," he said. "May the love I bear you become a bond between our worlds. You owe me no debt. Serve your own people now, and remember us fondly."

A huge smile spread across Brytnoth's face as he got to his feet. Amid the cheers that rang out once more, he ascended the steps to the dais and bowed before Aelred.

"I accept, my lord," he said simply.

Aelred gestured him to the second chair on the dais. "And now," he said, "we will take council together. For the council of the Lords of Askalon has always numbered ten, and I would have it so again. But these are dire times, and our people have not remembered themselves yet. So I would propose that we seat five Lords until such time as our people can appoint the rest."

Brytnoth nodded. "It seems wise to me."

"Then I submit Derrek, Kalkas, and Brogan as worthy candidates to join us. They have served well and nobly in this fight. What say you, my lord Brytnoth?"

"I agree."

Derrek, Brogan, and Kalkas all stepped out of the crowd to accept the high honor amidst thunderous applause.

"Let a meal be prepared," Aelred commanded. "We shall feast the victory tonight in our own hall!"

As preparations for the celebration got underway, Aelred summoned the Silesians and their company to the council room. Unlike the bright and soaring majesty of the Great Hall, the council room seemed designed for secrets. Dark wood beams supported the low ceiling, and faded tapestries dressed the stone walls, muting the echoes. The massive round table in the center of the room sat on an even larger rug, which seemed to drink in the sound of voices and swallow it.

As they settled in around the table, Aelred began. "We have need to settle some matters, and I ask for your advice." He paused for a moment. "Jared, you told me that you had made a promise to Alberic regarding the *zanthos*."

"We told him that we would return it, my lord," Jared answered. "We gave our word."

"These weapons that the Triumvirate created," added Derrek, "could destroy worlds if they ended up in the wrong hands. We only tapped a fraction of what lies in that warehouse. Some of those weapons are designed for only one purpose: mass casualties and total destruction."

"But weren't these weapons—and the *zanthos*—promised to Halcyon?" Sahara asked.

"The Triumvirate never intended to hand them over," Deor replied. "They never meant to yield to Halcyon—they meant to destroy them."

"But that doesn't change the fact that Halcyon still expects these weapons to be delivered in payment of the Triumvirate's debt," Sahara protested. "We need a plan for handling Halcyon. They won't discharge the debt just because the Triumvirate is no longer in power."

Aelred rubbed his chin thoughtfully. "It's true," he said. "But it's also clear that delivering these weapons as promised is out of the question. I won't be responsible for the damage Halcyon intends to do with them. And it's very likely that Askalon itself would be their first target." He sighed and shook his head. "No. Jared, we'll return the *zanthos* to Perseon as promised, and all of you are bound to secrecy as to its whereabouts. Long ago, the Lords of Askalon concealed its existence. It must be so again, for the safety of all our worlds."

A murmur of assent ran around the table.

"So, Jared," continued Aelred, "I would ask you to finish this task. Assemble your team and return the *zanthos* to Alberic with my deepest thanks. And I would ask him to stay on Perseon and continue as its guardian, under Askalon's protection and favor."

"I will do it gladly, my lord," Jared said.

"And now, there are other matters to settle," Aelred said. "We must consider the problem of Halcyon, but I'll set that aside for now."

He turned to Arnauld. "My lord," he said, "we will do everything we can to locate those of your people who are still here on Askalon."

Arnauld inclined his head in gratitude. "Thank you, my lord," he said. "And I would ask for a transport ship, that once my people are found, we may return home to Silesia. Like you, we have a world to rebuild."

"One will be provided for you," said Aelred. "And, as you return home, I ask you to consider Askalon a friend." As Arnauld inclined his head again, Aelred added, "There's so much work to be done now that the Triumvirate is gone. The trafficking in drugs and slaves must be stopped and those responsible for continuing the trade must be brought to justice."

"That will take years, my lord," Rafe cautioned. "Operations like these don't disappear overnight. Where there's a market, there will be trade."

"Of course," agreed Aelred. "But we can make a start. And, Lord Arnauld, I would ask Silesia's partnership in this."

"You have it," said Arnauld.

Aelred smiled and the two leaders clasped hands. "So," continued Aelred, "on to matters closer to home. Now that the Triumvirate is disbanded, our defenses are weak—too weak. Derrek, I ask you to take as your special task the rebuilding of our military forces."

"With pleasure, my lord," said Derrek, unable to hide the grin that swept across his face.

"My lord, I ask your leave to stay and help Derrek," Deor said suddenly.

Sahara turned to him in surprise. "You're staying here?"

Deor shrugged. "I have no other homeworld."

"Amaryl is our home!" Sahara protested. "Or Silesia—"

"They're not home to me, sister," he said bitterly. "What home have I ever known? We fight for what we love, and we love what we fight for. I fought for Askalon. If Aelred will allow it, I'll stay here."

"And I'll stay with you," said Althea softly.

Sahara's eyes flicked from Deor to the girl who had settled herself beside him. She felt a horrible grief building inside her and she swallowed hard.

Deor smiled at Althea and covered her hand with his. "I was hoping that you would," he said.

"Deor!" Sahara cried. "You can't stay here..." She felt the tears gathering just behind her eyes, burning so fiercely that she could hardly see.

Deor's face was serene, maddeningly serene. "And where will you go, now that you're free to choose?"

Sahara felt herself crumbling inside. His words unlocked that part of her where she had imprisoned her most desperate fear—the fear that, for her, there was no going home.

She had never known a life without war. She had never known a home without oppression. She had never lived without chains.

And now? What will become of me now?

"I...I don't know," she answered slowly, her voice sounding strangled. "But I thought we'd at least go there together."

Deor shook his head. A tear slid down her cheek, then another. She brushed at her eyes furiously. She would not cry. Not here. Not now.

I'll go with you, came Jared's voice in her head.

Her eyes snapped up and she found that he was watching her across the table. Wordlessly, she shook her head. It wasn't the same. She hoped he would understand. She saw the flash of pain in his eyes, but could think of nothing to say to him.

For the rest of the council, she sat next to Brytnoth, hearing only the vague swirl of voices around her. She felt stunned and empty, and she wanted desperately to get away somewhere where she could try to make sense of things. Then she felt Brytnoth stand up, and she realized that Aelred had dismissed the council.

She got to her feet and stumbled out of the room.

FORTY-THREE

THREE WEEKS LATER, the slave population on Askalon had been fully treated with the surrogate to the Demon's Breath drug and life was beginning to return to some semblance of normalcy. Arnauld had gathered what was left of his people, and they were preparing to depart for Silesia.

"I can't say I'm sorry," Kirin said, clasping Jared's hand. "I'm ready to go home."

"Take care of yourself, Kirin Hearth-Seeker," Jared said, grinning.

Kirin laughed good-naturedly and headed for the ship. "And you, Jared Desert-Stalker," he called over his shoulder.

"I wish you were coming with us, Jared," said a soft voice behind him. He turned in surprise and saw Aliya standing there, tears in her eyes. "It's hard for me to leave my son behind."

"If I can, I'll follow you," he said, taking her hands in his own. "But..." His eyes strayed from her face to where Sahara stood some feet away, watching them.

Aliya saw the glance and smiled. "I know. And I understand." She reached up and kissed his cheek. "Farewell, until you come to us again," she said. And with a last squeeze of his hands, she let him go and boarded the ship.

The engines roared into life, and the hatch closed slowly. Jared watched as everything he had fought so hard to save lifted out of his view and vanished into the bank of clouds overhead.

"I just hate good-byes, don't you? So sad."

Someone was standing next to him, and he started in surprise when he saw who it was.

"Rafe! I thought you were on board the ship...and had left without saying good-bye!" he cried, seizing his friend in a strong embrace. Then he let him go just as suddenly. "But, wait! What are you doing here? Aren't you supposed to be heading back to Silesia with Emma?"

Rafe coughed. "No. I'm not."

Jared stared at him, incredulous. "No? But I thought...I thought you were going home!"

"Not yet." He clapped Jared on the shoulder and grinned. "I'm staying here with you."

At that moment, Sahara ran up to join them. "Rafe? Didn't you go with Arnauld?"

"If I'm standing here with you, then manifestly I didn't go with Arnauld," he answered, winking at her. "I'm coming with you to Perseon. Figured you could use the help. And life back in Albadir would just be infinitely boring without the two of you."

Jared laughed. "Let's get these cartridges loaded and get this mission done."

Brytnoth had agreed to accompany them back to Perseon in order to convey formally the goodwill of the new Council of Lords to Alberic. When they landed at the outpost and disembarked, Alberic was there to greet them, beaming in genuine pleasure.

"You kept your word!" he cried, embracing them each in turn.

"As promised," Jared said, gesturing to the crates of cartridges. "All here and accounted for."

Alberic shouted to a couple of men standing near the main building. "Take these back to the mine for safe-keeping," he ordered as they approached. "And now, my friends, come and break bread with us once more!"

As they moved toward the mess hall, Sahara muttered, "You think it's cold enough here?" She pulled the hood of her parka further over her face and tried to huddle down into it.

"At least you just have to walk ten feet to the mess hall," Jared remarked. "No hike over the mountains for you."

Once inside, they were greeted with the same hospitality and generosity as before. The warmth of the place enveloped them, and it was impossible not to be merry among these contented people. As they ate, Jared saw Sahara staring fixedly at the small group of children gathered in one corner of the room. They were intent on some kind of game that seemed to involve a lot of noise and bartering for cherished items—bits of bone, queerly shaped stones, or scraps of cloth. Alberic noticed her interest and laughed.

"I don't know where they get those things or why they're so valuable," he said, shaking his head. "But there you are." He drew breath to order them out of the room, but Sahara laid hold of his arm.

"Don't," she said. "Let them stay. Please."

He looked at her in surprise and then shrugged. "As you wish. You're the guests."

"The Triumvirate is no more," Brytnoth told Alberic. "Aelred heads the Council of Lords once again, and he asks if you will serve with us as one of the Lords of Askalon."

Alberic considered the request for a moment. His eyes strayed to the group of children in the corner.

"Would I have to leave Perseon?"

"No. In fact, Aelred asks that, if you are willing, you remain here with your people to guard the *zanthos* mine as you have done until now."

Alberic's face broke into a wide grin. "Then I accept his offer," he said. "But now that the Triumvirate is gone, does the *zanthos* need to be guarded any longer?"

"Unfortunately, the danger hasn't passed," Jared said. "The Triumvirate promised the *zanthos* and the weapons to Halcyon, and we fear they'll come looking for it when it's not delivered."

"Then we'll be sure to keep careful watch." He smiled at them and rose. "Forgive me, but there are a few other things that I must attend to. Will you stay with us here tonight?"

"If we can impose on your hospitality, we will," Brytnoth said.

"I'll have rooms prepared for you. Someone will fetch you presently." With a slight bow, he left the hall.

A roar of laughter from the corner drew their attention. Jared saw a small boy holding up his prizes—two bone shards and a square of soft fabric—with a glow of triumph on his face. But he was not left alone to enjoy his spoils. Three other boys, all smaller than the victor but having strength in numbers, tackled him to the ground. For the rest of the children, the brawl was even more exciting than the game, and they widened the circle to give the boys room, cheering and laughing.

At the height of the uproar, a slim young woman entered the hall. She looked first at the group of strangers, and then her gaze snapped to the ruckus in the corner. She strode towards the children, her hands on her hips.

"And what?" she cried. "Get you gone, all of you!"

The crowd of children scattered like snowflakes in the north wind. The victor, battered but not defeated, collected what remained of his winnings and grinned sheepishly up at the girl.

"I won, Gwyn," he said.

"And you're the worst of the lot, Jace," she sighed. "Now get you home!"

As soon as the hall was quiet, she approached their table, smiling apologetically.

"You'll have to excuse my brother and his friends," she said. "They get carried away."

"No need," Sahara said. "You are blessed here. It's long since we saw such joy."

Gwyn shook her head, her eyes troubled. "Not all feel so," she muttered.

"Is there trouble here, lady?" asked Brytnoth.

She turned to him and then stared for a moment. "You are familiar to me," she said slowly. "You were here before."

"That's right."

Gwyn glanced at the door and hesitated. "No," she said finally. "There isn't trouble here."

Brytnoth and Jared exchanged glances, and Brytnoth frowned. The girl's tone clearly said otherwise, and then she mouthed the words, "Not here."

"I must go," she said, standing quickly. "I just came to fetch Jace home." She gazed at them each in turn, her eyes saying far more than she voiced. Then she turned and left the hall.

"What's going on?" Jared murmured, watching her vanish through the door into the frigid world outside.

They had no time to discuss it further, for two women entered to lead them away to their rooms for the night.

They didn't see one another again until they met in the mess hall again for the evening meal. Though there was no table of honor, Alberic invited them sit at his own table, and they were served before the others in the hall. Gwyn, as before, brought them their food and drink. Jared watched her face as she set down their plates. She was trying to catch Brytnoth's eye, so Jared nudged him under the table. Brytnoth glanced at him and Jared gave the barest nod in Gwyn's direction. When Brytnoth's eyes connected with hers, she immediately looked past him, staring at someone sitting behind them.

That man, Sahara said in Jared's mind.

From her position at the end of the table, she was able to see both Gwyn's subtle hint and where she was looking.

There's something about that man. Don't look. Not yet. Wait. After a few more seconds, she said, *Now.*

Slowly, so as not to attract undue attention, Jared turned and looked casually over the room. As his eyes wandered over the assembled people, he saw the man that Gwyn must have been indicating. He sat alone, unlike the others. He seemed to have neither friends nor family, and he wore a black scowl on his face.

"Who is that?" Jared asked in a low voice, turning back to Alberic. "The loner sitting behind us."

"That's Dirk," answered Alberic, not even bothering to look up. "My brother."

Jared glanced up at Gwyn, whose face now registered her uneasiness. She gave the tiniest shake of her head and then left them to their meal.

Something isn't right here, came Sahara's voice.

"Is there trouble here, Alberic?" asked Brytnoth. "Is there anything I should know?"

Now Alberic did look up, frowning at Brytnoth. "Why should there be trouble here?"

"I'm just asking. Now's the time for telling, if there's anything to tell."

"There's nothing to tell. There's no trouble here."

Brytnoth measured him for a moment and then shrugged. "As you say."

He let the matter drop, but as soon as Alberic's attention was back on his food, he met Jared's eyes and shook his head.

Later that night, Jared met Brytnoth in his quarters. The rooms were sparsely appointed, with a low bunk of warm furs, a small metal table and two chairs. Jared and Brytnoth sat in these, hunched over the small table illuminated by a single cube of *zanthos* in a glass.

"Sahara thinks there's something funny going on here," Jared said in a low voice.

"If there is, I think Alberic has no idea," Brytnoth said. "Or perhaps I should say that he *wants* to have no idea."

"It's something to do with—"

The door suddenly opened and Gwyn slipped inside. She closed the door softly behind her and leaned against it. Her cheeks were a hectic pink, her breathing shallow.

"I may have been followed," she whispered. "I cannot stay. But you have to know. Aelred has to know. Dirk can't be trusted. He's dangerous, and he has many friends on Askalon...and elsewhere. Tell Aelred not to take his eye off Perseon. Tell him."

And she was gone.

FORTY-FOUR

IN THE MONTH since the overthrow of the Triumvirate, Askalon had
slowly begun to recover herself. Aelred had ordered most of the
pumpjacks and derricks to be dismantled, and he was slowly
returning Askalon to the balance it had enjoyed before the Triumvirate came to power. The land was still scarred and would take years,
if not centuries, to heal fully. But the process had begun, and Aelred
was drunk on their success.

Jared, Rafe and Sahara spent their time helping Deor and
Derrek. They were rebuilding the military headquarters in the West
District. As word had spread throughout the system of the overthrow
of the Triumvirate, more and more people who had fled from
Askalon began to return. In addition to the troops which Aelred had
brought from Agora, there was now a healthy citizen militia. Deor
was in charge of the militia, while Derrek, as befitted his training,
took command of the standing military force.

They had already overseen the destruction of all of the *zanthos*-
powered weapons save one—a weapon of last resort, Derrek called it.
It was a world-destroyer, capable of enough destructive force to wipe
out a third of a planet's population. They stored it in pieces deep in

the mine of Gil-Gareth, and the control panel was hidden in the treasure room under the Great House.

Jared noticed that Sahara spent as much time as she could in her brother's company. But when Deor was working with the militia, he didn't have much time to talk to her, and when they retired to the Great House, Althea occupied his attention almost exclusively. Jared watched as Sahara seemed to slide into a constant state of quiet sadness. She followed Deor wherever he went, tried to help him, tried to be a part of his life. And while he slipped easily into the routine of his days on Askalon, loving his duties as militia commander and validating his importance to the Council, Sahara was cast further and further adrift.

As for Jared himself, she treated him with a hesitant shyness that he had never known in her before. It felt to him as though they had somehow circled back to the start of their relationship, but this time, they were on an equal footing. She knew that he respected her—that he was willing to let her stand on her own without standing in her way, and that had shifted their entire relationship. Jared was content to wait and watch, but as he saw her struggling with her detachment from Deor, he decided it was time to step forward.

He found his opportunity unexpectedly one morning. They had agreed to meet Deor at Brogan's tavern, which he had reopened and refurbished. It was now a bustling success, full of honest and cheerful folk once more. This morning, Jared and Sahara arrived at almost the same moment, but Brogan told them that Rafe and Deor had already gone.

"Five minutes late and they leave without us," grumbled Sahara, her shoulders slumping. She turned to leave, but Jared laid a hand on her arm.

"Wait, Sahara," he said. "We need to talk. Please."

She looked at him, her face tired and sad. The hollowness in her eyes pierced his heart and he swallowed hard. He gestured to a small table in the corner of the taproom, and she followed him wordlessly to it and sat down, hands folded in her lap.

He slid into a chair across from her and struggled for a way to begin. "Sahara," he said finally, "I know things are difficult for you..."

He stopped. She was staring at him, all fire of challenge or defiance gone. He fumbled for words again. How could this shell of a woman be the same woman he had known and loved all this time?

"Deor's building a life," he continued, finding his voice again. "He's happy here. But you're not happy. You're—"

"Why do you say I'm not happy?" she asked.

There it was. The tiniest spark of a challenge. But it was gone as quickly as it had come.

"Sahara, it's written all over your face."

"Can I help it if he doesn't want to see me? If he doesn't want me to bother him?" Her voice broke. "I thought he was dead, all those years. And now he might as well be dead for all the notice he pays me." She paused for a moment. "I thought we were going to be a family again. All I ever wanted..." But she couldn't continue. She just sat there, staring at him, the sadness welling to the brim in her eyes, but never spilling over.

"What? What is it that you want?"

It was a long time before she could speak. And when she did, her voice was nothing more than the barest whisper.

"A home."

"But Silesia is your home!" he protested. He stretched out a hand to her across the table, but she made no move to take it.

"No," she whispered. "Silesia is *your* home."

"Then Amaryl?"

She shook her head. "There is nothing for me there."

He frowned, growing more and more puzzled. "I don't understand."

"No. You wouldn't."

"Please explain to me so that I can understand," he pleaded.

"How can I explain to you what I don't understand myself?" she asked. "I feel...empty. Alone. And I have nothing to fight for now. I don't know where I belong, and I don't know what I'm supposed to do." The earnestness in her voice grew as she spoke, but then she stopped and sat silent once more.

Jared heaved a sigh and withdrew his hand. He had just opened his mouth to speak, when he heard a voice behind them, unmistakably Rafe's.

"*There* you are!" he called. He strode toward their table, edging around other patrons as carefully as he could. He glanced from Jared to Sahara and then back again. "Am I interrupting something?"

Jared managed a smile. "Always."

"Oh. Sorry."

Jared waved a hand dismissively. "What's going on?"

"Aelred's called an emergency gathering of the Council. He wants us there."

"Now?"

"Now."

————

They convened in the council room. Rafe, Jared and Sahara were the last to arrive, and they slipped quietly into the empty seats nearest the door. As hard as they tried not to attract attention, Aelred had apparently been waiting for them.

"There you are," he said, sounding genuinely relieved.

Jared looked around at the solemn faces. "What happened?"

"We've heard from Halcyon."

Rafe sat forward in his chair. "And?"

"Lord Azimir warns us that if we don't honor the contract they made with the Triumvirate, then they'll come here and take the weapons and the *zanthos* by force."

"We aren't ready for that," Deor said immediately.

"There's no way we can face Halcyon if they come here looking for a fight," Derrek agreed. "We have barely enough soldiers for keeping the peace, and even with Deor's militia, we could never stand up to an entire army."

"I know," said Aelred. "They will come here with their armada expecting to intimidate us into giving up the weapons and the power source, but when they discover that we have destroyed the weapons, they will annihilate us."

"Have you openly defied them?" Jared asked. "Have you refused to honor the contract?"

"No, not yet," Aelred answered. "All they know, it seems, is that power has changed hands. They want to be sure that their interests are respected. And they have no reason to suspect that we won't comply...not yet."

"So what do you want us to do about all this?" asked Sahara.

Jared could feel the surge in her energy. He glanced at her, saw her eyes bright. It was the Sahara he knew, and he couldn't help but smile.

She has a new battle to fight, he thought, and then a wave of sadness washed over him. *Why is it only war that brings her peace?*

Aelred studied her for a moment, seeming to consider whether she was challenging him or offering her help.

"I was hoping," he said slowly, "that you might be prevailed upon to negotiate with them. There's a window of opportunity here. Perhaps we can still preserve the peace."

Sahara snorted. "I think the price for peace with a bunch of drug kingpins is probably higher than most worlds can afford."

"Perhaps that is so," Aelred argued, "but we can still try. Askalon is a rich world—rich in many things. Perhaps we can pay the debt in some other way."

"We can try, my lord," said Jared, cutting off Sahara's next retort, which he knew would be even more cutting than the first. "If you wish it, we can try."

"If you succeed," said Aelred, "we will be forever in your debt."

"And what happens if we fail?" asked Rafe.

Aelred said nothing for a moment, and when he raised his eyes to Rafe's, they were hard and glittering. "Don't fail."

Sahara leaned forward, a half-smile on her lips. "I'm sorry, but was that some kind of a threat?"

Aelred seemed startled at her reaction, but then Jared saw the stubborn set to Aelred's jaw as his momentary surprise faded. He knew only too well how stubborn Aelred could be if pushed too hard.

Jared laid a hand on Sahara's arm. "Sahara," he murmured, a warning in his voice.

"I wasn't threatening—" Aelred began.

"I certainly hope not," Sahara cut him off, her voice like a razor. "After all, we're the ones who put you on that throne, and don't think for a second that we can't take you out of it again."

There was instant uproar in the room. Jared dropped his head into his hand. Deor was staring at his sister, horror written all over his face. But beside him, Jared could feel Rafe shaking with suppressed laughter.

Why did you have to say something like that? Jared wondered in Sahara's direction. Her eyes flashed at him, something like an impish sparkle in their depths.

"How *dare* you!" thundered Aelred from the other side of the table. "How dare you say such a thing?"

"We risked our lives for you," Sahara flared back. "We risked everything for you! And we almost lost everything. So if we choose to help you with this Halcyon matter, it's not because we owe you anything. And it's not because you have some kind of authority over us. Are we clear?"

Aelred frowned fiercely at her. "You're dangerous."

Sahara shrugged and grinned at him. "That's why you asked us to join you in the first place. You didn't enlist our help with your rebellion because we're a litter of kittens."

Aelred's eyes snapped to Jared. "Aren't you going to say anything?"

"What's there to say?" he replied. "Do you want us to negotiate with Halcyon or not? If you do, you want her kind of dangerous doing it."

Sahara glanced at him and smiled. A real, genuine smile. Jared felt its warmth in his soul and knew that, somehow, he'd finally given her what she needed. He had opened his hands to let her fly, and she'd chosen to stay. He returned the smile and nodded his head encouragingly at her.

Aelred was spluttering wordlessly, his hands gesturing as though they could convey what he couldn't find voice to speak.

"Do you want us to go or not?" Rafe pressed. "We're willing to do it, but you have to promise us one thing."

"Oh? And what's that?"

"We're going into the vestibule of hell for you," he said. "We're going to negotiate with the devil so that you can keep your damned planet. So if something goes wrong over there, promise that you won't abandon us to them. We're fighting for you. So promise that you'll fight for us. Whatever it takes."

Aelred's frown vanished and he nodded slowly. "I swear it," he said.

"When do we leave?" asked Jared.

"Tomorrow at dawn." Aelred laid a folded document on the table and slid it across to Jared. "Our conditions."

Jared barked a short laugh. "No. Those are your prayers."

FORTY-FIVE

SAHARA STARED out the window as the ship descended onto the landing platform in Aquila, Halcyon's capital city. After the gloomy gray of Askalon, this sun-drenched world lifted her soul and made her smile in spite of herself.

Aquila was an immense metropolis, and everything was dressed in coppers and golds, absorbing and reflecting the sunlight in all its shimmering glory. Far to the east, she could see a thin azure streak, and she guessed that it must be the ocean. Even from this height, she could see the bustle of people in the streets. It was as different from Askalon as Silesia was from K'ilenfir.

"What do you think?" Jared asked her, leaning over to glance out the window.

"I think...I don't know," she answered. "It's...it's just like he said it was."

"Who?"

"Ergeron. He must have been here before." She pointed to the huge temple that dominated the center of the city. Its dome was covered with gold, and tall minarets stood at each corner.

"It's beautiful...and cruel. Just like he described it."

The ship touched down and they disembarked, blinking in the bright sunlight. The platform was bustling with traders and travelers, reminding Sahara of the busy market world of Agora.

Before they could step into the crowd, a group of eight men in crisp, cream-colored suits approached them. The leader was tall, with dark hair and a neatly trimmed beard that accented the strong line of his jaw. His glasses, tinted against the brightness of the sun, concealed his eyes. His stride was powerful and uncompromising.

"Is this our welcoming committee?" Rafe murmured. "Because I'm not liking the looks of this at all."

The men halted in front of them. The leader studied them silently for a moment, and then made a short hand gesture. The entourage fanned out and encircled them, cutting off their avenue back to the ship.

"What is this?" Jared demanded.

"You are here from Askalon?" the leader asked. His voice was deep and resonant and the accent strangely foreign.

"Yes," Jared answered.

"You will come with us."

"What if we don't want to go with you?" Rafe asked, crossing his arms over his chest.

The man faced Rafe, his features completely blank.

"That would be unwise. Remember, you are on Halcyon now." He gestured to his men again and then turned on his heel, heading back down the platform.

They hesitated, and one of the men standing behind them gave Sahara a shove. "Ribbadi said move," he growled.

Sahara gritted her teeth, her hands clenching into fists. "Is this how you greet all your guests?" she asked.

The man grinned at her, his teeth flashing. "Who said you were guests?"

TEASER
SAHARA'S RANSOM

THE DOOR of the warehouse grated open. Gervais blinked rapidly in the sudden brightness that flooded the smelly, dank makeshift prison where he'd spent the better part of the last three months. A figure stood silhouetted against the daylight, and Gervais shaded his eyes for a moment, trying to see who it was in the glare.

"It's about time," he grunted, getting to his feet and dusting off his pants.

"I couldn't come any sooner," the man said. "I had to wait until they left. You're just lucky that they forgot about you...and that I remembered."

Gervais snorted. "We'll see how lucky I am, I guess."

"Your shuttle's waiting at the landing pad in Azdod," the man continued.

"That's a long walk. And that place is a ghost town. Don't I get a decent meal first?"

The man ignored him. "Dirk will meet you at the Ice Shelf and bring you in the rest of the way on foot." He paused, and then added, "I'd take your mittens. I hear it's cold on Perseon."

Gervais was at the door now, and he studied the man's face for a few seconds. "What's the plan?"

"No need for you to trouble about that," he answered with a short laugh. "Now get going, and don't make me regret this."

———

Continue the adventure in *Sahara's Ransom*.

WANT EVEN MORE ADVENTURE?

You already know that Sahara is an extraordinary and fearless warrior. But that's not how her story begins.

I can't wait for you to discover Sahara's origin story in *The Shift — A Silesia Story*...and best of all, it's yours for free!

Tap the cover or head to shannonblakebooks.com to pick up your copy today!

IN CASE YOU MISSED IT...

Don't miss the first installment in The Silesia Chronicles! Check out Sahara's Revenge today!

AUTHOR'S NOTE

Dear reader,

From the bottom of my heart, thank you. Thank you for coming along on this adventure with me, and for the gift of your attention and your time. It truly means the world to me.

I'd like to ask you for one more gift for me and for your fellow readers. You know how much a good review can help you decide which adventure to choose next, so please help other readers by sharing your rating and review on your favorite store and on Goodreads.

You can find all of my books on Amazon at amazon.com/author/shannonblakebooks.

See you on our next adventure!

Shannon

ALSO BY SHANNON BLAKE

ABOUT THE AUTHOR

Shannon has been dreaming up stories and writing them down for almost as long as she can remember. She's insatiably curious and loves science fiction for giving her the excuse to research the most random things — and for giving her the freedom to explore galaxies.

In addition to penning novels, Shannon is an award-winning screenwriter managed by Art/Work Entertainment in Hollywood. She loves giving back to the writing community through coaching and teaching, and she also works as a ghostwriter and creative entrepreneur.

When she's not writing, she loves running, dancing, obstacle course racing, and hanging out with her family and friends. And she has never been known to turn down chocolate or a chai latte.

You can find more about her upcoming projects and author appearances at shannonblakebooks.com or follow her on Instagram @shannonblakebooks.

You can follow all her latest projects on Facebook, Instagram, and on her blog over at skvalenzuela.com.